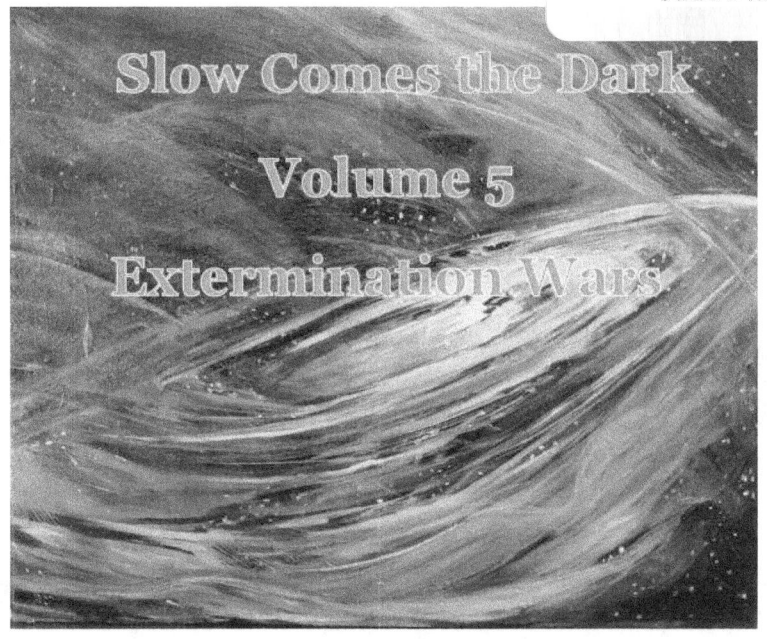

Slow Comes the Dark
Dark
Volume 5
Extermination Wars

Vic Broquard

Slow Comes the Dark Volume 5 Extermination Wars

First Edition
ISBN: 978-1-941415-74-0

This is a work of fiction. All characters, organizations, and events portrayed in this novel are products of the author's imagination and are used fictiously.

http://www.Broquard-ebooks.com
Broquard eBooks
103 Timberlane
East Peoria, IL 61611
author@Broquard-eBooks.com

Artwork by Crooked Willow Studios.

For Morgan and L. Ron Hubbard

Table of Contents

Chapter 1—It Begins

Ragnar-B, a remote world in the rim sector of Twillis, suffered massive loss of human life during the attempted coup by the three CEOs and their new inventions: the CAM or the Cybernetic Android Mobile and the Shadow Maker. The "tin cans" or CAMs were relatively crude fighting machines controlled by human beings who had been driven from their flesh and blood bodies by the Shadow Maker machines and forced into these metal heads, incidentally proving that man is a spiritual being, immortal, but that fact failed to be recognized at the time. Via electronics, the three CEOs compelled their victims to obey or endure intense migraine headaches. As fighting machines, these CAMs were pathetic on offense, but their titanium shells and sheer weight made them extremely difficult to destroy. During that initial attack, the 653rd Infantry Division of the Federation Military Forces was nearly destroyed. Only a few elements survived to fight another day.

The ancient humaniform robot, Thanos, who often took on disguises, such as Dr. Black, had installed his own backdoor into the CAM's circuitry, enabling him to usurp control of the thousands of CAMs from the CEOs. He then destroyed those CEOs and Brussels, the capital city of Ragnar-B, by using the confiscated Shadow Maker systems, which slowly reduced a human body into its constituent atoms and molecules, giving the appearance of a body disappearing from sight. Hence its name. Unlike the CEOs, Thanos didn't force the now bodiless humans beings, ghosts, ids, personalities, or spirits (you pick your term) into CAM bodies, but left them for "dead."

When Thanos departed Ragnar-B, the bodies of the many millions who lived in Brussels were gone, turned into basic atomic and molecular components by the Shadow Maker systems installed on many deep space transports that made systematic passes over the sprawling city, killing millions of men, women, and children. Dazed and confused, the humans beings hovered over the quiet city for some time before going off in search of baby bodies, of which there were far too few for the sheer number of bodiless beings who wanted them.

After ransacking the city, Thanos and his crew departed for destinations unknown. Slowly, others moved into Brussels from other towns and cities, picking up the pieces of their shattered world. The General Goods Corporation led the way to Ragnar-B's partial recovery. With a tenth of the planet's population gone along with nearly all its space faring capabilities, their recovery was slow. Only the Battleship Arc Royal and the cruiser Hyperion survived, but for well over a year both were laid up on Scorpi-C for massive repairs, leaving the world with no space defenses, scary and perilous.

During this quiet period on Ragnar-B, authorities conducted an investigation into what Thanos had stolen. Computers, rare earths, deep space transports, and all the plans and factories that built the CAMs were gone. The city was stripped of all things that could potentially be used to manufacture more of these deadly Cybernetic Android Mobile monsters and the Shadow Maker systems. This gave leaders of the Federation of Planets cause for worry.

Some claim the CAM Wars, as they were initially called, began back in 2005 with the CAM attack on Ragnar-B. However, the more commonly accepted date was the attack on Delgar-C in the Gilgalad rim sector in the fall of 2008, some three years after the Ragnar-B attack. It was only at that point this war with the CAM became widely known as the Extermination Wars, thought the full extent of the war was not known or accepted for over a year. Many claimed that by then it was too late. The reasons given were many and valid. One point is clear to all: war brings out the best in some, the worst in others.

What is remarkable is that there were six survivors of that initial attack on Delgar-C, survivors who later spread word of the new tactics being used by the metal heads, the tin cans. It began September 1, 2008. The place: the Grimaldi family suite on the forty-ninth floor of the local Galactic Dynamics building in Milano, halfway around Delgar-C from its capital and giant spaceport in Marino.

Forty-year-old black-haired Ciro Grimaldi was a junior

executive of GD, but who had high hopes that one day he would get a promotion to the main headquarters staff in Marino, where the top CEOs ran Delgar-C. He'd married in accordance with GD executive policy. That is, he'd married Tina, one of the Ultimate in Feminine Beauty (UFB) women, and who was thirty-nine. Ciro had been swept off his feet with her incredible platinum blonde, knee-length tresses, which outlined her perfect face and blue eyes and that therefore gave her the appearance of a holy angel in Ciro's eyes.

They had three sons, each of which was overly strong. Today, they were off at the Marino Military Academy being trained as super-fighters. After the complicated birth of their third son, Tina's hopes for a daughter were dashed. The doctors told her she could no longer bear further children. Yet, Tina and Ciro had kind hearts and promptly set about adopting other UFB girls, girls who had been orphaned during the Open Rebellions in which a fair number of executives had been murdered. The Grimaldi's provided a loving home for these second-generation UFB girls along with the expected financial support and physical assistance.

Stacey Grimaldi was the eldest of the three, having just turned twenty-one. She had knee-length, wavy black hair and dark, enchanting eyes, a raven-haired beauty. However, as expected, the table discussions now centered around marriage offers for her, since she was now of age. She knew very little of her birth parents, only that they had been assassinated and that they were somehow different. Stacey was definitely not a Delgar-C name.

Next in age was Vittoria, who was twenty. She had blonde hair and blue eyes, the closest any of the three daughters came to looking like their adopted mother, Tina. Brown haired Zeta was sixteen but had charming and enthralling greenish eyes.

"Education is paramount." Ciro instilled that viewpoint in his daughters from the time they learned to walk. Breaking some customs, he'd had all three daughters attend the local schools in Milano, though he knew just how difficult a time they would have there. Still, it had worked out. Stacey had been a natural at operating communications centers and had recently taken up learning about galactic navigation. Ciro had no idea why she would be interested in this, but her initial choice of operating comm centers fit his preconceived ideas of what a UFB woman could possibly do: talk.

On the other hand, Vittoria was the most literate of the three, having taken a keen interest in history and in archaeology, of all things. She was the master of *big words*, of which Zeta constantly reminded everyone. Zeta was still in high school and truly fit Ciro's notions of what a UFB woman could do. She excelled in foreign languages, already fluent in three other than her own.

This evening, the table conversation centered on boyfriends and marriages. Ever the chatty one, Zeta gaily spoke up, "Papa, Carlo asked me to go with him to the Junior Prom. Can I, papa? Please," Zeta begged, batting her long eyelashes and grinning mischievously.

"Of course, my dearest. Isn't he Landini's son?" he replied, knowing he had far more difficult matters to discuss tonight, though he was hoping to hold that off until dinner was finished and the three young women's personal assistants could be dismissed.

"Yes, papa. He is. Oh thank you, thank you," she exclaimed, thrilled to be asked out to the Junior Prom, though she was only a sophomore.

"Just don't go getting any ideas about him," Ciro cautioned her. "Remember, it's my responsibility to you lovely young women to arrange the best possible marriages for you. After all, you three are magnificent UFB women and deserve only the very best."

Zeta giggled girlishly. However, Stacey noticed what he'd alluded to, "Papa, you know very well we three want to marry for love, not for positions. We've told you that often enough. We aren't objects or things." In fact, she had done just that, ever since her senior year in high school. The Academy in Milano didn't accept her into graduate studies because she was a UFB woman, quite helpless in the eyes of the ordinary people of Delgar-C. Still, that hadn't stopped her from pursuing her interests in all things having to do with communication centers and now galactic navigation, her latest interest.

Libraries offered much and at no cost.

Ciro sighed and took another bite of his steak, stalling for time and a way to counter her. For the last two months, that is, ever since she turned twenty-one, her marriage consumed his thoughts. In truth, he'd put off making such decisions until now because he dearly loved his three adopted daughters. With his sons long gone from the nest, he clung to the three as long as possible.

"Dear Stacey, you know I would be failing you terribly if I didn't arrange the very best marriage I can for you," he finally pleaded.

Vittoria glanced at Stacey and saw she was about to retort and spoke up first. In her alto voice, she said solemnly, "Papa, we're acutely aware of your nearly impossible responsibilities towards UFB women, very nearly disconsolate in fact, but yet which is only as it should be. However, papa, we asseverate that we should have a say in our marriages. After all, you don't wish us to be unhappy and miserable for the rest of our lives, do you?" She knew that would impinge upon her father, who cared deeply for his adopted daughters, possibly far more than he did for his long absent sons.

Confused, Zeta whispered to Stacey, "What's she saying? Asseverate? Disconsolate? I *do* wish she'd speak more plainly!"

A pained expression came and went on Ciro's face. "Of course, Vittoria, I want you three to be extremely happy with your marriages and husbands. It hurts me you'd think I wouldn't be, dear. However, I must point out love isn't all that a marriage is about, particularly for you UFB women. You need personal assistants and proper, elegant clothing—all of which costs a good deal. It would be remiss of me to marry you to someone who simply couldn't afford to provide properly for you. One day you will have children of your own. Your husband must also have the financial wherewithal to support any daughters you have."

He went on, "And we all know it takes an executive's salary to be able to afford such. Security guards aren't paid enough to support a UFB wife, let alone any daughters she might have." This was a direct reference to Stacey's boyfriend,

Arcangelo Rossanti, who was a security guard here at GD. True, he was a handsome lad with rich black hair and a very kindly disposition. Still, Ciro knew his salary was insufficient to support Stacey in the manner he wanted for her.

Stacey's ire eroded. It all came down to pay, to money. "Papa, that's why I'm studying hard. I can run any comm center now, and I'm working on galactic navigation too. I want to get a job working in a comm center somewhere. Then, between what Arcangelo and I both make, we should have more than enough money for everything." Problem solved, at least in her own mind.

But a UFB woman never works, Ciro thought, though wisely didn't say that aloud. He had drilled into them the vital necessity of an education. He'd gone far beyond the norm and had them attend public schools for twelve years, almost unheard of for UFB girls. On the other hand, telling them no one would likely hire them would simply be crushing to the young women. In a flash, he saw the way out of this mess. "Stacey dear, if you can find a well-paying job, then I'll agree to allow you to marry Arcangelo. It's true that combined salaries would be more than enough to support a UFB woman and her daughters. Still, Stacey, this is a rough path you've set for yourself. Think it over seriously before you commit, will you?"

Feeling as though she'd achieved a small victory, Stacey replied, "Of course, papa, I will. Thank you."

Zeta whispered to Vittoria, "What's he saying? If we get a job, then we can marry our boyfriends?"

Vittoria grinned and whispered back, "Yes, sis."

"But Vittoria, who is going to hire us? I mean we're mostly dependent on our personal assistants," Zeta whispered back.

"Not entirely dependent, just mostly," Vittoria admitted, a hint of sadness in her husky alto voice. "We have to keep on trying to be as independent as we can, sis."

"Oh I see. Like going to school with all the other kids," Zeta whispered back. Vittoria nodded.

After supper, Stacey rose and explained, "Papa, Arcangelo and I are going to the movies. Back by curfew time."

Ciro smiled. "Okay. Have fun dear."

"Papa, Vino and I are going for a stroll in Central Park. Back by curfew," Vittoria added.

Zeta let out a huff. "And I get to do my homework and not have any fun!" Her older sisters laughed, while Ciro smiled. Their mother, Tina, had not said much all evening, but did smile as well. Long ago, she'd lost her arguments that the three should be wearing the tight, restrictive corsets and fancy dresses all the time and certainly not pretending they were normal girls and going to high school. They were UFB women and should look and act their roles, which they were not. She'd lost that argument and merely sat silently at the table, allowing Ciro to assist her with her dinner, as a husband of such women should be doing. In truth, she felt miserable, having undergone the genetic mutation process when she was sixteen in order to become one of the most prized women in the world, though now very nearly completely helpless.

Zeta left the table, took her small, shuffling steps over to her backpack, bent over, and grabbed it between her teeth. Off she went to her room, where she tossed off her tall heels and used her toes to undo the bag, getting her homework out. Sitting on the floor, she sighed. "Only two more years and I'll be free too," she lamented and began working the math problems.

Around ten, her sisters joined her, chatting about the movie and how wonderful the park was at night. Zeta listened enviously to every word they said, while their three assistants got them into their loose-fitting nightgowns and ready for bed. Then, the three young assistants departed for their own homes. Normally, they would return around seven in the morning to get their charges up and dressed for the day.

Sitting on the edge of Zeta's bed, the three sisters chatted until nearly midnight, long after their parents had gone to bed. "You know, Arcangelo and I smelled something kind of sickly sweet in the air while we were walking home from the movie," Stacey volunteered. "No idea what it was. Some kind of flower perhaps."

Vittoria frowned. "How weird. Baldovino and I also detected some foreign odor in the air. So we walked around the park looking for some late blooming plants, but we found nothing more than the expected numerous patches of marigolds. I can say definitively the smell wasn't coming from them. Further, Vino seemed uncommonly tired when he brought me back to GD, quite uncharacteristic of him. So how weird is this?"

"But I don't smell it in here," protested Zeta, slightly alarmed by her older sisters' comments.

"Probably nothing, sis," Stacey replied. "We best get to bed. I think mom and dad have already turned in. Best be quiet little mice." She grinned and her sisters did likewise.

The three shared a large bedroom with an attached bathroom located on the opposite side of the large suite. The living room and dining room separated theirs from their parent's bedroom, which was significantly smaller and beside the kitchen. The physical layout of the suite saved their lives.

Midnight came. Boom! A very loud noise, accompanied by shattering glass, woke the three sisters. "What was that?" cried Zeta.

"Sounded like it came from mom and dad's room!" Stacey exclaimed, struggling to get herself up into a sitting position. Her sisters did likewise. "Come on, we best go check." Their faint nightlight was sufficient for the sisters to see well enough to find their heels and slip them on. Like three penguins, the sisters made their slow shuffling way out of their room. "Oh god!" Stacey exclaimed as she reached their doorway and looked across the living room towards their parent's room.

The front half of a shuttle was visible partway into their parent's bedroom. "Mom, dad?" she called out. Zeta and Vittoria added their calls to hers, as they continued their slow walk across the living room and peered into the bedroom, three very white faces.

"Oh God!" Stacey exclaimed again. The remains of their parent's bed could barely be seen from beneath the main body of the shuttle. It had apparently come crashing into the side of GD headquarters! Half of it was inside the building, while its rear hung outside far above the ground.

"Call for help," Stacey ordered. Zeta pushed her bosom into the red button on the wall, which her mother used to signal her personal assistant.

Vittoria moved around the edge of the ship. Shocked, she whispered, "They must have died instantly. Their bodies are crushed beneath the shuttle." The bed looked more like a pancake lying on the floor. "Call for help again!"

Zeta pushed the call button several more times and cried, "Mom? Dad? This can't be happening!" At this point, the three broke down in tears, waiting for help to arrive. None came.

"Come on. Let's get to the comm center, and call for help. Someone is always on night duty there," Stacey finally recovered enough to act. "We can't do anything to help them ourselves, except to get help."

"Okay Stacey, but this can't be happening," Vittoria protested, tears streaking her cheeks. "Shuttles can't ram into buildings. There are many redundant safeguards built-in to them. This cannot happen."

"But it has, sis. I can't raise anyone. Oh my God!" Stacey replied and then exclaimed. The three entered GD's comm center and found the night man lying on the floor and unconscious.

"This—this—is he alive?" Zeta gushed quite confused.

Squatting down, Stacey rested her head on the man's chest for a moment. "I hear breathing, but he is out cold somehow. You two, go press the alarm button and see if you can find the night guards. They should be on the main floor. I'll call corporate headquarters." Stacey took charge. She was the eldest and felt responsible for her sisters, acutely now, since their parents were obviously dead. She fought the tense knot in her stomach, determined to remain in control for their sake. After carefully rising, she moved over to the seat, tossed her head about until her long hair was out of her way, and sat down at the control panels. "Thank god I wanted to learn how to run a comm center!" she exclaimed to herself, as she began switching the buttons with her nose.

"GD headquarters in Milano calling GD corporate headquarters in Marino. Come in please. This is an emergency call. We need help. Come in please," Stacey said clearly into the microphone. *Please, please, let someone answer me, please,* she thought, doing her best to keep other notions from her mind. *I have to be strong for my sisters.*

After a short delay, a night watchman's face appeared, followed by his voice, though he sounded frightened, if not terrified. "Hello GD headquarters in Milano. We are experiencing some form of attack! I can't raise anyone here in Marino! They are all out—unconscious, as far as I can tell. Just after midnight, the chemical attack alarms sounded! The comm center doors shut and sealed. I'm locked in, and I sure as hell am not leaving this room! I can't raise anyone now, well excepting you that is. Can't get the army to respond. Can't raise anyone. What's happening in Milano? Over."

"A shuttle crashed into the side of GD and killed our parents while they were sleeping. No one is responding here either. What's happening? Who is attacking us? Why are they unconscious? Over," Stacey asked growing more and more nervous. Something horrible was happening and not just here at GD!

"Hell, Milano too? Damned if I know. I'll keep you patched in live. I'm going to try to raise other cities now." Stacey saw him flipping more switches and calling out to other comm centers in other corporate headquarters in a dozen larger cities of Delgar-C, but the only response was utter silence.

Just then, her sisters shuffled back into the comm center, thankful that the automatic doors were still operational. From the ghastly pale faces, Stacey knew help wasn't coming from the night watchmen. Vittoria shook her head. "No one! Stacey, we couldn't find anyone awake! What's going on?" The arriving sisters saw the lone man on the monitor, trying to make contact with many other centers.

"We're under some kind of attack! All of Delgar-C! It's everywhere. He's the only one left, but he's still trying to reach anyone anywhere," Stacey answered.

Suddenly, one monitor began showing images of soldiers in an army bunker comm center, probably underground. Evidently, the man finally was able to contact someone. Stacey turned up the volume. "Yes, it is confirmed. We are under a planet-wide biological weapon attack. Initial tests suggest that it's the UFB woman bio genetic agent! My God, the whole world has been infected! Only a few isolated bunkers are not yet affected. Wait, we're receiving some kind of alien communication. Put it on the speakers, corporal!"

A tinny sounding voice spoke, a voice devoid of all emotion. "Remaining humans of Delgar-C, you have been infected with your own perverted UFB woman bio genetic agent, which will render your people helpless while our Shadow Maker systems methodically sweep the planet free of all humans. After countless millennia, you human beings have conclusively proven you're not worthy of continued survival. Thus, we're beginning the Great Purge, removing all human beings from the galaxy. In a week, here on Delgar-C, all traces of your human bodies will have been rendered back into their basic atoms and molecules via the Shadow Makers, fertilizing the soils of Delgar-C so other plants and animals may survive better. That is all." The inhuman voice abruptly ended.

The general barked orders, and the three young women watched as a dozen soldiers frantically began carrying them out. Just then, via a live feed, they spotted deep space transports hovering over the general's secure barracks. Right before their eyes, the trio saw the men's bodies beginning to grow thin, slowly turning into mere shadows, before vanishing entirely. All three involuntarily shrieked!

"But I don't want to die!" protested Zeta.

"What are we going to do?" asked Vittoria. "We have to do something, Stacey, or the Shadow Maker will get us. We have some time, since Marino is on the other side of the world from here."

"There's the atomic blast shelter in the basement," Stacey answered, thinking fast. "We might be safe from the Shadow Maker. It's our only hope. Wait! Arcangelo, Baldo, Carlo—they are going to be turned into UFB men. We have to rescue them too. I don't want to be alone. If I'm going to die, I want to die with my true love."

"I'm with you, sis. Me either. How are we going to rescue them? If we just had normal people's arms, we might be able to do it," Vittoria replied, for once not using big words or long sentences.

"Carts. We roll them off their beds and onto pushcarts. Come on. If we work together, we can rescue our boyfriends and get us all into the blast shelter. It's our only hope. Zeta, you want us to recuse Carlo as well?" Stacey asked. Zeta nodded, and the three set off from the comm center for the basement storage closets. On the way, Stacey stopped by the night watchman's post and grabbed his security card between her teeth.

"Why? Oh," Zeta whispered in the eerie silence, "so we can get into the men's quarters." Stacey nodded. Working together, the three retrieved a pushcart from the basement storage closet. She bent down and inserted the security card into the slot. When it clicked, Vittoria and Zeta got the door opened. While Stacey held it open, the two pushed the cart out, though they had to stop and reorient its front wheels several times.

"It's going to take all three of us to control this cart," Vittoria declared, as Stacey let the door close on its own. "Two push and one steers. Zeta, you're on steering duty. Go to one side, push it straighter, and then back to the other side. I think it'll be much harder to do when we have one of the men lying on the cart."

Twenty minutes later, Stacey used the card to open the doors to Arcangelo's small suite. They pushed the cart up beside his bed. "Look at his hair! It's longer already!" Zeta exclaimed. "Is he really going to look like us?"

"Yes, sis," Vittoria answered, since Stacey had to continue to hold the security card between her teeth. "His body will mutate and wind up looking as we do, except he will still be a man. Come on. We have to roll him off the bed and onto the cart."

A good deal of pushing and wiggling passed before his comatose body dropped off the bed and onto the cart. After sitting on their butts and using their feet to get his body squared up on the cart, the three pushed him out of his suite. With only their toes on the ground, they did more slipping than pushing, but did manage to get it going. A half hour later, they rolled him off onto a set of blankets on the floor of the atomic blast shelter. Two hours later, the trio had also

12

retrieved Baldovino and Carlo, positioning them beside Arcangelo.

"What about clothes?" Zeta asked, "and shoes? And a hair machine?"

"Good point, sis," Vittoria answered, since Stacey was still holding onto the security card. "Look, we can't dress ourselves and, if dressed, we can't go to the bathroom by ourselves. So the smartest thing will be to continue wearing nothing at all. Modesty be damned if we don't have any assistants. We'll need to get heels for the men, though, or they won't be able to walk much, if at all. Come on. Let's bring all our heels down here. Some should fit them when they wake up. Besides, we're going to have to bring a hair machine down here too. So let's use the cart again."

A half hour later, they had their entire shoe collection and hair machines down in the atomic blast shelter. Next, they set about checking on food and water. They were amazed to see how well prepared the shelter actually was. It had its own internal recycling systems and power units. Thus, once the massive doors were closed, they would be hermetically sealed in and far underground, hopefully safe from the Shadow Maker systems in the sky above.

Once more, Stacey took charge. "Okay, we have to figure out how to close the blast doors. I wonder why there is a steel plate on the floor in front of the doors? Ah well. Just look at how thick these blast doors are!" Each was a foot thick, solid steel and massively heavy. Try as they might, the three couldn't push the doors in the slightest. Frustrated, Stacey said, "Look, we have to use our brains on this. We're never going to push them closed."

Looking around, Vittoria suggested, "Hey, look at this. Controls. It says to pull the lever down to close them. Come on. Give me a foot." All three clustered around the lever, pressing their bodies into each other for support, while raising one foot up to the lever. "On three. One. Two. Three," Vittoria said. The three pushed, wiggled, and wobbled; the level slid all the way down. Mechanical servomotors hummed quietly, swinging the massive doors shut. Then the trio heard the hissing sound of the sealing unit and knew they were now sealed inside.

"Okay, let's see what all is in here," Stacey suggested, and they began exploring their new *home*. The blast shelter was huge, capable of supporting fifty people. Though most of the beds were quite narrow, they did find six full sized beds and decided to make use of three of them, once their boyfriends awoke. Meantime, they would sleep together. "Now this is more like it!" Stacey exclaimed upon discovering a small comm center in one corner. "Hey, it gives a view of what is outside GD and also what is outside these doors. Cool. Ah, I think I can tap into all the vid-cams around GD from here too." She yawned.

Zeta whispered, "Can it wait? I'm asleep on my feet." Laughing, the trio headed to their new bed and plopped down. A bit later, Zeta began softly crying. The loss of her parents sunk home hard. Beside her, Stacey and Vittoria couldn't withhold their own grief any longer and joined their younger sister. Thankfully, sleep came soon after.

"Are we going to die?" Zeta asked. Morning had come, though in the atomic blast shelter, the outside world wasn't visible, except on the monitor. The three sisters benefitted from their deep sleep, but their loss was still in the fore. Their parents were dead. Their personal assistants, their household cook, and everyone they knew were in comas. For the first time in their lives, they were truly on their own, ignoring the stark fact the CAMs were attacking their world, turning all human bodies into dust.

Stacey took charge. "Look, we're still alive, Zeta, but we're on our own. Come on. If we work together, maybe we can fix something to eat and drink. We have to figure out how to cook before the boys wake up."

Vittoria sighed, "I wonder if we did the right thing in rescuing them, Stacey. Their bodies are mutating rapidly. When they rouse from their comas, I anticipate that they will be completely freaked out. They will look like UFB women— like us. I expect they'll be completely helpless too. After all, remember how long it took us to learn to walk. Perhaps they would have preferred to die rather than be like us."

"Sis, we'll cross that bridge when we get there," Stacey

countered. "We'll have to show them we're not as helpless as they think, teach them all the tricks we know. Now come on; we have a lot to do, and we're incredibly slow at it."

Zeta countered, "But Stacey, will we be safe down here from the Shadow Maker?"

She shrugged her shoulders. "I don't know, sis, but this shelter was designed to protect us from a nuclear attack, so we can hope it'll protect us from the Shadow Maker too. If not, then everything is moot. I'm not giving up just yet. I want to live and be with Arcangelo, that is, if he'll still have me. We have to lead by example, Vittoria, because you're probably right. The fellows will be freaked out when they come out of their comas, so we have to be prepared to show them we can survive and help them with everything too. So come on. Let's figure out how to fix some breakfast. There's a mountain of stored food in here, if only we can find a way to use it."

By working together and using their feet, the trio finally managed to get the dried food softened in water and then heated up on the stove. Zeta laughed. "We look really funny doing this—like some slap-stick comedy act."

"But we did it. And it tastes fair," Stacey commented. Using her toes, she continued scooping her food into her mouth. Then, she too began to laugh.

Vittoria broke into a laugh as well. "You're right. We look ludicrous."

"But we're eating, and that's what matters," Stacey admonished the pair, who continued to giggle and eat, making a bit of a mess. "Stop laughing, and you'll find it's less messy."

Later, Stacey experimented with the comm center and brought up live video streams from six other locations across Delgar-C. In two views, they could see comatose bodies lying about, but by the afternoon, the bodies had vanished from sight, startling the trio, who realized the Shadow Maker was in use. By noon, Stacey had worked out the paths the CAMs were using with their awful machines. "I think we have two more days before they get to Milano," she announced and then explained her reasoning.

After another hour of trial and error, they had lunch prepared and ate their fill. They then checked on their boyfriends, noticing the enormous changes taking place in their bodies. Already Arcangelo's hair had thickened and was nearly two feet long. Breasts were very visible now on the three men, and their arms were merely skin and bone. They spent the afternoon getting the rest of the men's clothing off their bodies, once more using their feet and toes, but working as a single unit made this possible.

After supper, Stacey returned to her comm center and began exploring again. She swept through all possible frequencies and came across a very strange signal, more like beeps and pauses. Vittoria overheard the seeming noise and commented, "I wonder if that is the alien's electronic codes? You know, sending and receiving orders and such."

"Hey could be. I should record it and see if we can make any sense from it," Stacey declared. She flipped another switch and began recording the strange sounds. After some twenty minutes, the signals ended, and she stopped the recording. "Whatever that was, I can't make any sense of it."

Vittoria sighed. "I can't either, but it must be the aliens communicating somehow. If they are robots, they must communicate via some kind of electronic signals."

"Hey, patterns are the answer," Zeta spoke up. "In all languages, there are only a few sound patterns that are used to form up all the words. Plus, certain sounds occur more frequently than others. Maybe we can figure it out by analyzing frequency counts. Play it back again for me."

A half hour later, Zeta exclaimed, "I got it. It is a binary code. You know—1's and 0's—the language of computers, bits. We studied this in school. The basic unit of storage is a word, which is thirty-two bits long, capable of storing four billion different things. We have all the letters of all known languages encoded in the Universal Exchange Codes. So theoretically, we can decode what they are saying to each other."

Both Vittoria and Stacey encouraged Zeta to work on decoding the recording, figuring that would give her something to focus on instead of their dire plight. Neither mentioned what they feared most: what would happen after the CAMs left Delgar-C, leaving these six as the sole survivors of the world. True, they had a goodly food supply, but after they ran out, then what? At least, Stacey figured after the aliens departed, she might be able to contact another world and beg for a rescue. Her thinking got no further, though. She'd never been off-world.

Focusing solely on her decoding, Zeta was able to keep her grief, loss, and fears at bay during the days before the men came out of their comas. Slowly, she made progress, finally getting the sequences worked out. Her breakthrough came when she recognized the codes were for the letters and numbers in the English dialect. If only I had a computer, she thought more than once.

The awakening of the three young men almost was the undoing of the sisters. Shrieks, screams, fits of stark terror, and bouts of uncontrolled sobbing shook the three sisters, though they couldn't do anything about the men's reactions. At last, Vittoria barked, "Oh come on Vino! Look, you proposed to me, and we were going to get married soon. I can't see what any of this has to do with that. You're still you, so is Arcangelo and so is Carlo. I love you, and I thought you loved me. It took an enormous effort on our part to rescue you men and get you in here, so stop screaming and crying. You three are alive, well, and still men, though admittedly, you do look like us now, but that doesn't matter to me, Vino. Nor does it matter to Stacey, Arcangelo. Nor does it matter to Zeta, Carlo."

Still highly annoyed, she continued, "So shut up, and let us show you how we do things. After all, we do many things quite differently than you men were used to doing them. We certainly aren't as helpless as you claim. If you prefer, we can dump you outside this atomic bomb shelter and let the Shadow Makers kill you, dissolving your bodies just as we've seen on the video feeds. According to Stacey's estimates, the aliens should be doing just that to Milano later today."

Vino took advantage of Vittoria's argument. "But look, Vittoria dear, I—we're now freakish looking men—if men we still are. You really want me? Like this? Helpless and looking as if I were a UFB woman? I know we had great plans, but now? Like this?"

Vittoria giggled. "You aren't the handsome man I first saw, but inside you're still you, and I love you. Is that sufficient?"

"Well," Vino hedged, "it is for me, though I don't see how any of us can survive now, not as we are. Hell, we can't even open a door."

Zeta began laughing, embarrassing the three young men further. "Silly fellows. How do you think we got you out of your apartments and down here into this ancient blast shelter? Teleportation? Levitation?"

"You can do that?" put in Carlo, very much surprised at his girlfriend's reply. "Levitation?"

All three young women laughed. Stacey took charge. "No fellows. We can't do any of those. We used our feet and brains. Of course, it took all three of us working together to manage one of you, but we did it. Now that we are six, surely, if we help each other, we can do very nicely. That is, if there is enough shielding to protect us from the Shadow Maker rays." That sobering thought ended the discussion. All three men wanted to see the comm center monitors and watch the approaching alien doom maker machines. After all, if the Shadow Makers still were able to reach them this far underground, then all else was entirely moot.

For several hours, the six hovered around the monitors watching the video feeds and estimating the arrival time over their building. Then when they alien machines hovered over the GD headquarters skyscraper, they watched in horror as the helpless night guard's body faded into the shadows, becoming a small pile of dust on his chair and floor. None said a word. What could any words do just now? Nothing against this awful alien machine.

However, they each looked at each other, trying to see if the others were fading. "You seem as solid as before," Zeta whispered nervously to Carlo.

"You too, honey," he whispered back, valiantly suppressing his own terror stomach, which somehow wanted to keel him over in stark panic. A half hour passed before anyone said anything else.

"It's over General Goods, well away from us," Stacey broke the awful silence. "I think we're safe now and are going to be okay. Come on, fellows. It is time you learn how we're doing things. It takes us forever to fix a meal. I'm starving, so let's get going on it."

Later as they dined on stew, Vittoria stated, "Good news. I have been able to contact a General Kelly Kay Knight on a battleship. Stacey, I sent her all the recordings you made of the attack. I believe she was impressed we were able to survive the Shadow Maker. Also, I inquired about the possibility of a rescue, once the alien robot machines leave Delgar-C. We're to contact her when we're certain the CAMs have departed our world. Good news, fellows, she also told me there's a partial genetic cure, one that regrows your arms. So there is some hope for the future."

"Hey, that's the best news yet!" Vino exclaimed. "I can't stand being this helpless. I surely don't know how you three ever managed. You must get your arms grown too, Vittoria. I insist." She smiled thankful he'd mentioned it and that she hadn't had to, for she was quite unwilling to give Vino any reason not to continue to love her. Whether he would if she gave up being a UFB woman—that could well make a difference, and Vittoria didn't want to risk that, not just now.

Chapter 2—Methodology

5-Halcynith-C, a remote, sparsely populated world in the rim sector of Gilgalad, had two distinct types of population: the settlers and the Underworld. Primarily interested in producing food and cloth, the settlers lived in isolated communities around the northern hemisphere. By far the more populace were those with ties to the Underworld, a disparate group of galactic thieves and assassins. For the right price, these men and women would carry out virtually any *job* anywhere in the Federation space. Among these nefarious figures was Dr. Riley Franks, a research geneticist long banned from his origin world for human genetic experimentations. He'd taken up residence on 5-Halcynith-C, thanks to Dr. Black, who had paid for his new research facility located in the Dark Mountains ten miles south of the Underground spaceport at Gratz.

Thanos, alias Dr. Black, smiled. The conquest of Delgar-C had gone without a hitch, just as he'd planned, the first strike in his program to eliminate the unrepentant, unethical, irresponsible, unsalvageable species, homo sapiens sapiens. Hardly a challenge, Delgar-C fell quite nicely, proving his techniques in the field. Plans on paper or in one's mind are one thing, while the field is quite another. Dumping the bio genetic agent planet-wide virtually eliminated all resistance to his metal robots, who merely had to fly the Shadow Maker systems systematically over the world, turning the now comatose, or later helpless, humans into their component atoms and molecules, fertilizing the lands for the indigenous plants and animals.

That there were six survivors did trouble him briefly, until he worked out how they had managed to avoid the Shadow Makers. Now he factored underground atomic blast shelters into his conquest planning. However, he left a number of CAMs guarding their blast shelter. He wanted the six alive for now. Thanos activated his chameleon circuitry. Three minutes later, his skin was black, and he slipped into his Dr. Black suit and persona. An hour later, he landed his ship at the spaceport at Gratz and took a shuttle south to pay a visit on Dr. Franks to see how his research was faring. He needed what these, the most despicable representatives of homo sapiens, had to offer.

"Ah, here you are, Dr. Franks," Dr. Black announced himself, walking into the fancy laboratory he'd built for this genius.

Looking up from his intense work, the startled Dr. Franks, now forty years old, thin and wiry, exclaimed, "Oh, it's you, Dr. Black. I wasn't expecting you. One minute please. Delicate operation in progress." A minute later, he laid his pipette down, peeled off his latex gloves, discarded them, and strode over to shake Dr. Black's hand. He wore his usual sterile white lab gown.

"I've come to check up on your progress on my special project," Dr. Black said in a monotone. In truth, he greatly desired the potential this project offered and that was the primary reason he continued to support both Dr. Franks and this entire world.

"Opportune of you," Dr. Franks answered. "I believe I've perfected the procedure. I'm ready to conduct field tests. Of course, I'll need test subjects."

"I have six close at hand, three women, three men. Will they do?" Dr. Black inquired, a slight smile on his face for Dr. Franks' benefit.

"Ah yes, yes indeed. Perfect. The first planned test is quite challenging. If it works to perfection, then I'm quite confident the procedure will work on anyone of your choice," Dr. Franks replied, more than pleased with himself and what he'd perfected. He knew one day, he would be famous among all geneticists, if not the most famous one.

"Details?" Dr. Black inquired.

"Ah yes. Let me explain, and you'll see what I mean about this being the definitive test," Dr. Franks hastily answered. "You see, I've acquired the DNA of Miss Galaxy, Tessa Longstreet. Ignoring the UFB women, she won the Miss Galaxy Contest twice, unheard of, you see. She is simply the most stunningly beautiful young woman in this sector of the galaxy. That's her photo there on the far wall."

Dr. Black glanced at her image. *Well,* Thanos thought, *he has a point.* She had waist length, wavy blonde hair, sky blue eyes, and a perfectly symmetrical face, which many claimed was that of an angel, whatever that was. Only a few UFB women had the stunning facial features of this twenty-three year old woman. Her physique was perfect, but she had recently had her breasts enlarged slightly to be a perky E-cup size. This she was allowed to have performed, since she was ineligible to run for a third time for Miss Galaxy.

Once more, Dr. Black smiled for the benefit of Dr. Franks. "I see. Yes, I understand why you believe this to be the ultimate test of your new genetic modification procedure. I agree. If you can take these six test subjects, three of which are men, subject them to the genetic modifications, and if the six all are identical copies of Miss Galaxy, then I will be convinced you have solved the pressing genetic modification research project I desire, Dr. Franks. I'll see the six are brought here to your lab within the week."

"Excellent. Yes, I'll need a few days to sample and adjust their individual DNA samples, and then four days for the conversion process. If all goes according to plan, when they wake up, we'll have six identical Tessa Longstreet bodies."

Once again, Thanos smiled. "If so, then I will see the promised sixty million credits are deposited into your private account."

"Of course. I best get the lab prepared for our six patients. Can't tell you how excited I am—years of work coming to fruition. Can't tell you what this means to me. If this goes as planned, we can genetically modify anyone to look like anyone else. No need for any woman to be ugly or any man to be unsightly or unattractive. Major breakthrough in genetics. Indeed." Dr. Franks would have gone on, but Dr. Black turned and departed, leaving the geneticist talking to himself. Although he noticed the man's departure, he continued, "And more importantly, any and all debilitating diseases and genetic abnormalities can be cured. If I'm right, the aging process can be reversed: eternal youth. Death has been conquered and by me, Riley Franks. Of course, Dr. Black, you have no idea why I've devoted my life to this research. None at all." Hearing the low hum of a wheelchair's electric motor coming his way, he turned.

"Ah, Missy. Great news. Dr. Black was just visiting. Six test subjects are on their way here. One more week, my love, one more week, and you'll be whole once more." Missy, his thirty-nine year old wife, nodded perceptibly. Degenerative brain disease struck her when she was twenty-three. Over the years, bit by bit, she lost nearly all of her voluntary motor control and now was able to move her head just enough to control her wheelchair with her mouth. A nod was all she could do to express herself. She'd lost control of her voice three years ago, but these days Riley talked for her.

"I'm so excited, Missy. If this goes right, in two weeks you'll be completely cured." Again, Missy struggled to nod her head, just as a frail, elderly woman hobbled into the room, steadied by a walking cane. "Ah mother."

"What's that you're saying? Have you succeeded? Wasn't that man—that Dr. Black fellow? What's he want this time? Not pestering you, I trust. I should have a word with that man, though I know he has been paying the bills around here," she barked, annoyed it had taken her this long to get to the lab and that she'd missed him. Old age was taking its toll on her, but she didn't acknowledge it.

"Test subjects, mom. He's bringing me six test subjects. I'm ready for field trials. If all goes according to plan, in two more weeks Missy will be cured and perhaps you, mom, will have your youth back. I've almost succeeded! Come; we have prepare for their arrival, mother. I could use your assistance. When the tests are done, we'll have six Miss Galaxies to clothe."

She chuckled and teased, "You always did opt for only the finest, Riley. Is that her pic on the wall there?"

***

Best take them while they are sleeping, Thanos decided, *less fuss.* He'd returned to Delgar-C, specifically to Milano where the six survivors were still housed in GD headquarter's atomic blast bunker, deep underground. Two CAMs held an IR scanner and Thanos saw the six reddish forms moving slowly about their bunker. He checked on the time and changed his mind. Externally, he still wore his doctor's disguise and decided to take another approach. The six were inside the hermetically sealed bunker, locked from the inside. He calculated his CAMs could rip the doors open, but that would surely terrify the six survivors, who would be highly suspicious of his intent to take them away to be test subjects for Dr. Franks and his genetic experiments.

He paused for a minute, dredging up the ancient specifications for the blast shelter. *Ah, I was correct. Any attempt to break the seals will set off an internal alarm. No good breaking in or drilling a hole to insert knockout gas. Best that I get them to open the doors, if that is possible.* Satisfied of his conclusions, Thanos sent several electronic signals to his CAMs and then headed to the GD headquarters' main Comm Center. Making sure no CAMs were visible around him and still wearing his Dr. Black disguise, he opened up the internal comm lines.

"Hello survivors in the GD headquarters' atomic blast shelter. This is Dr. Black. I've come to rescue you before the CAMs get to you. Can you hear me? I'm in your building's comm center. Over." Thanos repeated this three times before Stacey was able to get to their comm center.

"Hello. Help. Yes, we're here. Who are you? Have you come to help us? What about the alien robot machines? They're still around here. Oh, I'm Stacey. Over."

"Dr. Black. Yes, I've snuck down here. Got a ship ready to take you to a geneticist who is waiting to regrow your arms. Maybe more. Can you open the doors? We need to move quickly before the CAMs find us. Over."

"Ask him if we can get our male bodies back!" Vino broke in on Stacey's comm line.

Dr. Black overheard him and added, "If anyone can, Dr. Franks can. But can you open the doors? We must move quickly before the CAMs find us. Over."

"Yes, we're slow, but we can do it. A lever controls it. Give us a minute or two. Over," Stacey answered, her voice full of hope and excitement. Rescue was at hand.

As the six chatted about the miraculous rescue, Vittoria commented, "I find it highly suspicious that this Dr. Black fellow found us and is rescuing us. My contact, General Kelly Kay Knight, didn't mention that she was sending anyone to help us until we notified her that the CAMs had departed Delgar-C, which they haven't."

"Come on," Vino declared. "Don't look a gift horse in its mouth. I'd give anything to have my arms and hands back. No offense, Vittoria, but living like this is utter hell. I don't know how you three ever managed it, but you're gorgeous and brilliant." Noticing Vittoria's frown, he hastily added that last, smoothing it over, he hoped. *I loved how sexy and helpless they were, but not me. I don't want to be helpless, let alone look like a woman.* Vittoria gave him a cold stare, and his face flushed slightly. "So how do we move the lever without any hands to do it?"

"We sit down and use our feet. Together," Stacey pointed out. "We're not as helpless as you make us out to be, Vino. Come on. Toss your hair out of the way and sit down. We need to get these doors opened and get rescued."

"I still believe we're making a mistake," Vittoria commented, but she sat down and helped Stacey with the lever. Several minutes passed while the six got their bodies into proper positions to help shove the lever up. With a resounding hiss, the seals broke, and the doors swung open, revealing a black man standing before them, Dr. Black.

"Ah, excellent. Come. We must hurry. I've a deep space transport waiting for us. Soon, you will be in Dr. Franks' capable hands," Dr. Black explained, while the knockout gas took effect. The six never did get to their feet. Once they were out, six CAMs stepped in, picked them up, and carried them to the waiting transport ship.

Once more, Thanos left the salvage operations to his humaniform robots, while he headed back to 5-Halcynith-C at top speed. His six test subjects rested comfortably on beds, unconscious of course. Five days later, Dr. Black stood over the six comatose test subjects, who were due to awaken within a few hours. Thanks to Dr. Franks' mother, Lisa, all six subjects were identically dressed and wore the same red gown that Miss Galaxy Tessa Longstreet wore when she won the pageant. It was strapless and flared out some two feet just above the knees. The six test subjects looked identical in all physical ways, perfect copies of the twenty-three year old Tessa. They had waist length, wavy blonde hair, sky blue eyes, and perfectly symmetrical faces, quite angelic. Their facial features were stunning, identical to Miss Galaxy. Their physique, perfect. Their large breasts were now greatly reduced to a perky E-cup size, since Dr. Franks' sample of Tessa's DNA came after she'd had hers enlarged.

Lisa had each properly dressed with garter belts and fine, black nylons. Matching red patent pumps with six-inch heels completed their look. Unfortunately, their malformed feet had only been partially restored, a minor flaw in the genetic duplication process, one which Dr. Franks was confident he'd one day solve. Dr. Black commented, "Perfect in all ways, Dr. Franks! I'm genuinely impressed. You've actually done it. As promised, the sixty million credits will be in your account later today. Now, I must depart on business. Expect my return in about two weeks. I'll be bringing one of my men and a sample of the target DNA for you to use on him. Amazing, simply amazing, Dr. Franks."

"Excellent. Excellent. Yes, of course. Make sure your target DNA sample is at least one ounce. Blood works best. I'll be ready," Dr. Franks replied, fighting hard to keep his wild emotions in check. *Best not reveal too much to Dr. Black*—the real reason for all his years of research work, most of it highly illegal. Dr. Black nodded and departed. Once he was gone, Dr. Franks burst out, "I've done it! I've actually done it, Missy. I'll get you back to health today. I had to wait until Dr. Black left. Come on, my dearest. Let's get you started."

"What about me, son?" his mother broke in, a trace of annoyance in her voice. Still, she knew that he was right. Get Missy back first. That had always been her son's plan. *Poor thing,* she thought. *I do hope this works.*

"Mom, Missy first. If that works okay, then I'll do you. After two days, I should be able to see if it is going to work on her. If so, I'll get you started then. Nothing can go wrong. Besides, now we have all the money we could possibly spend."

She laughed. "Son, we can spend it in no time!" Both chuckled, and he set to work on his wife, first lifting her body onto a waiting cot. Once she was settled, he injected her with two ounces of his new serum. He kissed her forehead, and she blinked, unable to do much more than that. "When you waken in four days, you'll be alive, well, and healthy—as though this never happened, my dearest. Sleep now." He kissed her forehead once more.

"So will she also look like Tessa? Like those six others?" his mother asked politely.

"I've only that one sample, mom. You will too, if all goes as planned. Later on, we can obtain the DNA of any other woman you would like to look like, and I can redo the process. Theoretically, the procedure can be done an infinite number of times, mom. So relax. Besides, Tessa is Miss Galaxy, the most beautiful woman in the galaxy, twice over." Both chuckled.

"Well, this is going to be very confusing—what with all eight of us looking identical to each other. So I'll get Missy a blue dress. It was her favorite color. Me, I'm opting for pink. Off to do some shopping, son. Back later." With that, the old woman slowly hobbled out of the sterile lab, her cane tapping on the floor as she went. At least, she could still get around, unlike poor Missy, whose physical condition deteriorated each year until now she could only move her head and that only slightly.

"Oh, what happened to me? Oh, my voice!" a startled Vittoria exclaimed upon awaking from her genetic modification coma. "Arms? Hands? Oh, the men will like this. Where are we? Wait, these aren't my sisters and our boyfriends. Who are these quintuplets, and where are my sisters and boyfriends? Who are you? What's happened to my voice?" a rather confused Vittoria gushed rapidly as she sat up and saw the others on cots close to her. *At least,* she thought, *we're fully dressed. That's important.*

"Hello. I'm Dr. Riley Franks, geneticist extraordinary. I've just perfected revolutionary genetic cures. Yes, these are your sisters and boyfriends. Dr. Black brought you to me four days ago, and I've cured all six of you. Actually, you look exactly alike—Miss Galaxy, Tessa Longstreet. I used her DNA as a model for your cures. That's her photo there on the wall. As you can see, your body is now identical to hers, including your voice. Pretty amazing, eh? I said I was the geneticist extraordinary. I'm that and more. Oh, you're at my research facility here on 5-Halcynith-C."

Vittoria got to her feet and noticed her feet and new heels. Before she could say anything, Dr. Franks added, "One minor problem remains. Your feet. My whole body cure has only partially repaired your feet, so I'm afraid you'll have to wear rather high heels. My mother purchased them for you. Other than that, you're all perfect copies of Miss Galaxy. By the way, what is your name? Dr. Black didn't tell me."

"Vittoria. Vittoria Grimaldi. My sisters are Stacey and Zeta. Stacey is twenty-one and Zeta is only sixteen. My boyfriend is Baldovino Landini. Their boyfriends are Arcangelo Rossanti and Carlo Landini. Actually, my feet are infinitely better now. Standing and walking is vastly easier. Thank you. Oh, we live, or rather lived is the proper tense, on Delgar-C in Milano. The robot men, CAMs I believe they are called, launched a surprise attack on our world and killed everyone except us. Stacey saved us by getting us into the atomic blast shelter when the attack came, but then we three UFB women managed to get our comatose boyfriends down into the shelter too. The Shadow Maker couldn't get us down there. That's how we survived."

Flushing, Dr. Franks hastily apologized, "Oh I'm terribly sorry. I didn't know you were a UFB woman." He lied. Of course, he knew that. "Dr. Black didn't tell me that detail, and now I've gone and undone that. Ah well, you are still a stunning woman, Miss Galaxy, so you have your beauty intact," Dr. Franks justified.

Vittoria chuckled, "Well, that's fine with me, I suppose. We do look gorgeous and that is what matters to my sisters and me. Look, the others are stirring."

Ten minutes passed as the shock and confusions rippled through the awaking group, as Vittoria and Dr. Franks repeated much of what they'd said to her sisters and their boyfriends. Carlo, Vino, and Arcangelo were elated to have their arms and hands back. "Wow, we can walk again!" Carlo exclaimed.

"I'm all grown up!" Zeta exclaimed even more excited

about her physical changes than Carlo was.

"But of course," Dr. Franks interjected. "Your body genetics has adjusted to being twenty-three. That's how old Miss Galaxy was when I sampled her DNA."

Stacey laughed. "Sis, you've lost seven years."

Laughing as well, Zeta replied, "I don't mind. Now I'm all grown up. Right Carlo?"

He too laughed. "But how do we tell who is who? Are you sure you are my Zeta? We are more like identical twins now, well mostly." He added that last as he flushed visibly.

Vittoria declared, "We simply must have a definitive way to identify ourselves. Identical outfits are not going to pass muster."

Vino chuckled, "That's my Vittoria. Big words again." All six laughed.

"Well, we have to be able to tell who is who," Vittoria justified her comment.

"She's right," Stacey added, taking charge. She was the oldest, but with identical bodies, such wasn't apparent any longer. "Okay, for now, I'm going to tie a blue ribbon in my hair. I'm Stacey. Come on everyone. Look around for something to put in your hair so we can tell who is who. Vittoria is right. We have to have an obvious way to know who is who."

Five minutes later, everyone tied something unique into their hair, lessening the confusion. However, that's when Stacey noticed the seventh comatose person. "Dr. Franks, who is that? Did Dr. Black rescue someone else from Delgar-C? And what's with the fancy wheelchair?"

"That is my wife, Missy. I'm working my genetic cure on her now. That's what all my many years of research is about. You see," he sighed, "just after we were married, she contracted a deadly degenerative brain disease, one the medical machines can't cure. Over these past nineteen years, I've watched her slowly lose control of nearly all her body's motor controls. First, her feet went numb. Bit by bit, she lost the use of her legs and then arms. I rigged up this special wheelchair three years ago so she could still get around by controlling it with her mouth. She hasn't been able to speak for years and could only blink when I put her under for the cure. You see, with my genetic cure, she will awaken in about two days looking like you all do, Miss Galaxy Tessa Longstreet. Her body will be perfectly normal and healthy once more. Can you see what I've accomplished here? A cure for any debilitating injury or illness, even genetic birth defects. Downs Syndrome, any kind of genetic disorder—all these will be a thing of the past with my incredible genetic breakthrough."

He continued animatedly, "Via my genetic cures, even the ravages of old age can be cured as well. Oh, here comes my mother, Lisa. She's been out buying more outfits for Missy and herself." The six watched as the frail, elderly woman hobbled into the room, cane thumping on the floor. "Later today, I'll be injecting her with my cure and four days from now, she'll awaken from her coma, and her body will be twenty-three once more, the eighth Miss Galaxy. Even old age is conquered by my revolutionary genetics cures! Mom, come meet them." A lengthy round of introductions followed.

Lisa chuckled. "Don't fret. I had to get you these six identical outfits for Dr. Black's sake—helping to prove Riley's miracle work. I've taken the liberty of getting five other outfits for you. The deliveryman will be bringing them by shortly. Frankly, son, I'm totally out of breath. Shopping is so hard to do these days. When do I get my turn?"

"After supper mom. I'll work my cure on you then. Mom, four days from now, you will be twenty-three again," Dr. Franks declared with a proud smile.

"Oh, son, you should consider working your magic on your homely assistant pretty soon. Rachel is on her way in, but I asked her to make supper tonight. I'm tuckered out from shopping."

Just then, a rather plain looking young woman entered, tying her white lab coat around her waist. "Oh, Dr. Franks. It has actually worked! Incredible! Brilliant! Wow, identical in all ways!"

"Yes, Dr. Rachel. All these years of research night and day has paid off handsomely! Let me introduce them. This is my longtime assistant Dr. Rachel Waters." He proceeded to introduce the six others.

Arcangelo spoke up, "Say doc, this miracle cure of yours—can you turn us back into male bodies again? Don't get us wrong. We are incredibly grateful to have our arms and hands back and all the rest. But we three, well, we're men, and we still look like women."

Dr. Rachel laughed. "Of course we can do that. You see we've been working on this entire project from all angles. Dr. Franks and I knew he would ultimately be successful in developing his Replacement and Re-combinative Gene RNA therapy. It's rather like computer graphics. First you AND a hole in the pixel color and then OR in the replacement color, leaving all else untouched. His methods do just that. We take the donor's DNA sequences and the patient's DNA sequences. With his special methods, the patient's sequences are replaced by the donor's sequences. My contribution has been on the minuscule sequences controlling hair and color. The next step will be to integrate those into the replacement sequences as well. Soon, the patient will be able to make their choices beforehand."

She continued quite animatedly, "You see, we, well I mostly, have rounded up one hundred of the most beautiful women in the galaxy, the women who everyone considers to be utterly perfectly formed—likewise, a hundred of the most handsome men in the galaxy. After taking samples of their DNA when they were in their early twenties, I then monitored their lives. Those who later came down with a debilitating illness were removed from the pool. Those who had a difficult time delivering their babies were removed. I'm afraid the final pool of female choices has been lowered to twenty now, and the men are down to fifteen. I'll continue to monitor those and remove others who do not age well or who develop debilitating illnesses later in life, such as Missy did."

"One day, Dr. Franks and I envision at birth every child will be injected with their parents' choice of donor DNA, their choice of hair and eye color. All women everywhere will be incredibly beautiful. Every man will be uncommonly handsome. More importantly, everyone will be healthy. Birth defects and degenerative diseases will be a thing of the past!"

Lisa chuckled, "Don't forget; no one will grow old and

frail. Just go into your local hospital for a genetic revitalization. Oh, to be twenty-three again." She laughed and Dr. Rachel grinned.

Dr. Franks broke in. "So Arcangelo, we have you covered. First, I have to get mom fixed up. After we get some other details worked out, you three men can have your choice of donor male DNA. Of course, Dr. Rachel's study only covers about twenty years of their lives. Give us another thirty years and the donor pool will be sounder than it now is. Of course, there is still that nagging problem with their feet, Dr. Rachel. They only partially repaired. Do men wear high heels?"

"I won't complain if the rest of me looks like a man again," Arcangelo declared. Carlo and Vino heartily agreed with him.

Over supper, Dr. Rachel had Stacey tell her what had happened on Delgar-C, particularly how they alone managed to survive the robot attack. All three were having an awkward time trying to figure out how to use their arms and hands to feed themselves. Never having had them, the three sisters were more like infants learning how to use them properly. By getting Stacey to chat, Dr. Rachel shifted their focus off themselves.

"Well, you see," Stacey began, "my sisters and I were born UFB women, but orphaned when very young and adopted by Ciro and Tina Grimaldi. So when the robots dumped the bio genetic agent everywhere, we three weren't affected by it." She began a lengthy description of what had happened to the six, a chat that lasted for nearly an hour.

"Incredible, simply incredible dears, but son, you promised to cure me after supper, and it's after supper now," his mother remarked, ending Stacey's tale.

"That's all?" asked Vittoria. The group had watched Dr. Franks inject a syringe of fifty ccs into a vein in Lisa's right arm.

"Yes. I've already prepared the special agent. Tomorrow, you can watch as we prepare more and sample yours. I still have to figure out why your feet were not restored properly," Dr. Franks replied. "Sleep mom. When you awake, you will be twenty-three again. Dr. Rachel will see you're dressed in your new pink outfit."

"Oh to not be so frail again. That will be a miracle," she whispered and slowly slipped into a coma.

Dr. Rachel spoke up, "Come. We should make better arrangements for you six. I'm sure that you don't want to sleep in those glass rooms tonight. No privacy." Late that night, Dr. Rachel sent an encrypted burst of data, relaying all that she'd heard from the six.

The next morning, the three sisters now wore blue dresses, each a different shade of blue, Stacey's being sky blue. The three men wore brown dresses, again in three different shades. Finally, they had an easy way to tell each other apart, particularly the two doctors. After taking blood samples, Dr. Franks headed into his lab to work on the remaining problem, while Dr. Rachel took the six into her section of the giant lab.

"Okay, I have Dr. Franks' permission to adjust your hair color. We have a sample of your DNA, so we can proceed. On the monitor, I've brought up all the female donors, so you can see where we are at in our grand project. As you can see, three of the twenty are officially UFB women. I'm sorry we didn't know you three were originally UFB women. Had we known that, perhaps Dr. Franks would have chosen one of these three, but then Dr. Black insisted you wanted your arms and hands so I guess that is moot. Now here are the remaining male donors for you fellows to peruse. I'll let you study them while I take the women over here to the hair color monitor. Now these are the twenty choices I've made up for hair color."

"Say, can I have my raven hair back?" asked Stacey, growing curious.

"Absolutely Stacey. That's what I will be doing today— making a tiny change in your DNA for your choice of hair color. Each of you, pick out your desired color," Dr. Rachel replied. Naturally, Stacey chose to have her raven hair again. Likewise, Zeta chose her original brown color, but Vittoria was content with the blonde tresses that Miss Galaxy Tessa had, since there wasn't that much of a color difference from what her hair used to be.

The three watched as Dr. Rachel operated the complex machinery that did the work. It replicated their own DNA sample up to the proper dosage. Then, via Dr. Franks' special methods, it removed the sequences controlling hair color and added the sequences that created raven hair. After two hours, the machine delivered a syringe filled with the solution. Dr. Rachel injected it into Stacey's vein, saying, "Don't worry. You won't fall into a coma this time. Over the next few days, your hair will change its color permanently. Now, let's do Zeta's." By suppertime, the men had their hair color adjusted as well.

The next day was officially Jubilation Day. Missy awoke from her coma. Just as Dr. Franks hoped and prayed, she awoke whole and healthy! Gone were all traces of her debilitating disease! "I can talk again! I can walk again! Dear, this is truly a miracle! A day I never thought I would see!" Missy exclaimed, moving her arms and legs about while sitting on the edge of the cot.

"I want to take some blood samples and make darn sure it is truly gone, dear, but just look at you!" Dr. Franks hugged his wife, and she hugged him back for the first time in many years. Both had tears of joy streaming down their faces. Even Stacey's eyes watered, and they followed Dr. Rachel's lead, quietly leaving the two alone for now.

"Gosh, it worked. It actually worked," Dr. Rachel exclaimed once they returned to her section of the lab. "Missy has her life back, though she's now twenty-three, and he is in his forties."

"It is a miracle. That's for sure," Arcangelo declared.

"You two are really on to something of monumental proportions," Vittoria added. "The ramifications of this are simply mind blowing, staggering. You should disseminate your process to as many other geneticists as possible. This is beyond revolutionary, Dr. Rachel!"

"I'm sure we will in due time. I think he is waiting to see how his mother responds to the treatment," Dr. Rachel explained, rather hesitatingly Vittoria thought. The seven made another pot of coffee and chatted about the significance of what they'd just witnessed.

Later, they found Dr. Franks and Missy in his lab. "Look Missy. There's no trace of that degenerative disease in your new DNA! I've done it, but we must be vigilant. It might come back, dear. So you let me know if you experience any of those early symptoms again."

"Oh, I will, dear! I will. Can we just go for a walk? Together? As we used to right after we were married? I've missed that so very much," Missy whispered, nibbling his ear playfully.

"Take the day off, doc," Dr. Rachel insisted. "After all, you've been at this sixteen hours a day for the last twenty-some years."

Dr. Franks chuckled. "If you insist. Now just don't overdo it, dear." Arm in arm, Riley and Missy headed outside the lab together.

"Say, can we go out for a walk too?" asked Arcangelo.

Dr. Rachel gasped. "Oh no! It's not safe for you to venture beyond this extensive lab facility. You see, this world is—well, let's just say that most of the inhabitants belong to one of the many mobs. Crime, assassinations, and rape are commonplace—you get the picture. Dr. Franks has security guards around this facility, but you are taking a huge risk if you head into town. Lisa manages safely because no one is interested in a frail, old woman. Best stroll around this huge facility."

Later on as Arcangelo and Stacey strolled around the long halls of the lab, he commented, "I wonder why Dr. Black brought us here of all places. Apparently this is a mobster-controlled world."

"Hum, I see what you mean." Stacey bit her lip slightly, puzzled. Then, she asked, "And why didn't he take us to that general woman—you know, the one that Vittoria made contact with—that General Kelly Kay Knight person? Besides, how did Dr. Black even know we were in that blast shelter? The only outside contact we actually had was with that general woman. How did Dr. Black find us?"

"Dunno, but it's obvious to me that we six were his critical test subjects. After all, Dr. Franks wasn't about to experiment on Missy, not until he had everything perfected. Personally, I find all this quite suspicious. Not to say I'm not grateful, mind you. I, well you know. I was having an awful time adjusting to being like you UFB women. I had no idea how awful it was for you three, only that you are beautiful and I'm in love with you." Arcangelo chose his words carefully, fearing to upset Stacey, but desirous of making his point.

"I know, love. Look, we were born that way and quite used to it. Like Vittoria says, how can you miss something you never had?" Stacey replied, smoothing over his awkwardness. She knew it wasn't true, but she wanted to put Arcangelo at ease. "I think we should keep our eyes open. Certainly, we can't continue to live here indefinitely." Arcangelo agreed.

The next day, Lisa awoke to find herself twenty-three once more! More celebrations followed. However, now there were eight identical "Tessa's" about, but already hair color changes were quite visible. No one could miss Lisa in her bright pink dress and her sensible three inch matching pumps or Missy in her lavender gown, though she wore flats for the time being. As expected, Dr. Franks took another blood sample from his mother and headed off to analyze it. By suppertime, Dr. Rachel had once more vanished, presumably off on one of her covert missions to find more possible donor candidates.

However, the next morning Dr. Black reappeared, accompanied by a rough looking man, possibly in his late twenties. He needed a good bath or so Stacey thought. "What's he doing here?" she whispered to Arcangelo, as the two doctors and the man headed into Dr. Franks' lab.

"Follow them discretely," he suggested.

"Okay, I've brought a donor sample for you to use on Sam here," Dr. Black explained.

Protesting, Dr. Franks countered, "But this donor sample isn't one we have in our database. Who knows what illness, what genetic disorders might appear if I use it on Sam here?"

"We don't care about that, Dr. Franks. This is a blood sample from your General Hank Williams. Sam here needs to look like him. So how soon will it be done?" Dr. Black replied sternly. "Just do it."

Obviously annoyed, Dr. Franks fiddled with his lab apron ties. "Well, I'll need a day to prepare the injection. So he'll be ready in say five days. But Dr. Black, this isn't wise. We should be using one of our proven male donors. I can't be responsible if Sam here develops some genetic illness later on."

"Of course you aren't. Just get it done. I'll return in five days. Just get it done." He nodded to Sam, turned, and departed. After explaining he had a rush job to do for Dr. Black, he took Sam to a private room and then disappeared into his lab, leaving Missy and Lisa to spend the day with Stacey and her group.

"So why did these robot things attack your world? Did they really kill everyone but you six?" asked Missy. "Did your world leaders cause problems for the robot things? That's genocide, by the way."

"Nothing. Until they attacked us, we didn't even know about the robots," Stacey pointed out.

Vittoria added, "Actually, these robot CAMs do look reasonably like those that I saw on the newscasts a while back. If I remember correctly, it was a world called Ragnar-B, somewhere in the rim sector of Twillis. According to the news reports, three CEOs invented the robots, the CAM or the Cybernetic Android Mobile, and they invented this hideous new weapon, the Shadow Maker. Now while we did see some of the Shadow Makers in operation, the CAMs we saw destroying our world aren't quite the same as those that were in the news, the ones on Ragnar-B. However, I believe these new robots are based upon those earlier designs. Of course, I'm not a robotics expert, but they did look quite similar, just not the same."

Missy frowned, "But why? Why did they wipe out your whole world? Does your world have something of great value, like mountains of gold?"

Stacey laughed. "Hardly."

Zeta spoke up, "I remember what the robot said. His voice was sort of tinny sounding, devoid of all emotion. It said, 'Remaining humans of Delgar-C, you have been infected with your own perverted UFB woman bio genetic agent, which will render your people helpless while our Shadow Maker systems methodically sweep the planet free of all humans. After countless millennia, you human beings have conclusively proven you're not worthy of continued survival. Thus, we're beginning the Great Purge, removing all human beings from the galaxy. In a week, here on Delgar-C, all traces of your human bodies will have been rendered back into their basic atoms and molecules via the Shadow Makers, fertilizing the soils of Delgar-C so other plants and animals may survive better.' That's all we ever heard from the robots."

Missy laughed nervously. "Well, it has a point. How many wars have been fought? Unethical corporations control the very lives of most people. Crime, greed, assassinations, murders, rapes, oppressive rulers, and robberies—it has a point."

Vittoria responded, "Of course, history is replete with such events. They make the news. I should point out humans have done incredibly good actions, but those don't often make the newscasts. Your husband's miracle cures is one such example. It's a foolish and ignorant action to toss out an entire barrel of apples because three apples in it are rotten. The wise person throws out the bad apples."

"Makes sense," Missy replied. "But didn't your world have a planetary defense shield to protect it from such attacks?"

Stacey answered this one. "Too poor. Our world couldn't afford such luxuries. What about this world? Are you protected?"

"Oh yes. 5-Halcynith-C has a planetary defense shield. The robot ships won't be allowed to get close enough to harm us. It's rather new. They installed it eight years ago. General Hank Williams controls it. He was on the news when it was installed. About all I could do was watch TV these past many years," Missy explained.

"Wait a second!" Arcangelo interrupted. "That's the man who is being the donor for that seedy fellow Dr. Black brought here."

"Oh, probably just a coincidence. The general is rather handsome," Missy justified.

"But look, Missy, there is another side to Dr. Franks' work," Arcangelo pointed out. "He can turn that seedy man into a look-alike General Hank Williams. He could then go and turn off the defense shield. No one would be the wiser, since he will look exactly like the real general."

"But why would he do that?" asked Missy, growing confused.

"Well, this world is full of mobsters," Arcangelo repeated what Dr. Rachel told them.

"I don't believe it, but I'll ask Riley about it tonight," Missy conceded.

The next morning, Dr. Franks injected Sam, who quickly entered a coma. That done, the doctor joined the others. "That's that. Now then, it is time I tell as many top geneticists in the Federation about my discoveries. I've drawn up a plan, full specs, samples, documentation—the works. I want the galaxy to know about my miracle cures. Missy told me your fears, but I've known Dr. Black for years. He can't be part of this robot mess. Anyway, I'll need help since Dr. Rachel is off on one of her excursions. You fellows want to lend me a hand? You'll have to wear bio containment suits. Can't have any accidental exposures, you see. Ladies, you can work on preparing the documentation packages. I want to send off fifty complete packages, and that's going to take me months to prepare, but only a few days if you are willing to lend me a hand."

Chapter 3—Surprises

Arcangelo suited up, joining Dr. Franks in his sterile laboratory. Together, the two began the duplication process, making fifty copies of the many bio genetic agent samples the doctor had. Vino and Carlo worked on duplicating the special lab equipment Dr. Franks invented, while the women used the computers to make complete documentation packages. It was laborious, tedious work, and Missy oversaw quality control, verifying each extensive documentation package was complete, nearly a terabyte of data.

By the second day, complete packages were assembled, including the documentation, duplicates of the equipment, and the very carefully sealed and cooled bio agents vials. Under Dr. Franks' watchful eyes, Lisa packed everything into a sealed shipping crate that was four feet on a side. Once sealed, Dr. Franks printed out a shipping label and notified the spaceport. An hour later and continuing four times a day, men came and took the crates off to the spaceport, where they entered the automatic shipping system, verified by Dr. Franks. Automation was the key here, since once the men dropped the crates off at the spaceport, unfailing machinery put them on proper cargo flights, all without any human intervention.

By the time Sam came out of his coma, thirty crates had already been shipped out, and the group was hard at work on the proposed twenty more. Right on schedule, Dr. Black arrived at the laboratory, bringing with him proper clothing for his new *general*. "Excellent work, Dr. Franks. Well done indeed. Sam, put these on, and we'll be on our way."

Arcangelo spoke up, "Excuse me, Dr. Black, but why do you want Sam here to look like this world's top general?"

"None of your business kid. You got your arms back. Be grateful and be quiet," Dr. Black replied sternly. Shortly, Sam appeared. Missy gasped silently. He looked just like General Hank Williams did when he was on the newscasts she'd seen! Abruptly, the pair left the facility without another word.

"Dear, he looks just like our general. I don't understand

why Dr. Black wants his man to look like our general. This can't be a good thing, can it?" Missy asked.

"Oh, who knows? But look, Dr. Black has financed me for over twenty years, built this lab for me, and has even given me sixty million credits for my work. We shouldn't question his motives. He obviously has his own reasons. Come on. We've much more work to do." With that, the group resumed their massive duplication work, firing off another five crates by the end of the day.

The following day saw another five sent off. As the supper hour drew close, Dr. Franks finished duplicating another set of his bio genetic agents. "Well, this is enough for one day, Arcangelo. Let's stop for the day. I need a shower. Working in these bio containment suits is like wearing your own personal sauna all day."

"You can say that again. I'm nearly done with this one. You go ahead. I'll finish up in a short while," Arcangelo's muffled voice replied. He continued running the equipment while Dr. Franks left the sealed room, removed his suit, and headed to the shower before joining the others. Lisa had made them supper, but left them to serve it, preferring to head into the nearby city to do some shopping and claiming today was Sales Day.

Just as Arcangelo was finishing up, a battery of red warning lights began flashing, rather startling him. Bio hazard. At first, he panicked, figuring he'd goof up somehow and released one of the agents. Hastily, he checked over everything in the sealed lab and found nothing amiss. Feeling a bit more confident, he headed out of the room to inspect the panel with the flashing lights. From the indicators, he concluded that the bio agent hazard was outside the sealed room and wisely kept his suit on, heading as rapidly as possible into the living area of the large facility.

Entering the dining area, Arcangelo screamed, "Oh God! No!" Everyone was slumped over the table. Several glasses lay shattered on the floor. He went over to Stacey first and checked her. His stomach knotted. She was in a coma. While he wasn't a doctor or a geneticist, he knew what this meant: the robots were attacking this world and had released that horrible bio genetic agent on the entire world.

Gasping, in a flash, he realized Dr. Black must have used his *general* to lower the planetary defense shield. Dr. Black was somehow tied to these robots and their assault on humans! "What do I do?" he wailed. As his adrenaline began flowing, he knew he had to get each person to their bed and undressed, no small feat while wearing the bio containment suit. Sweat poured off his body. The longest hour of his life passed, but Arcangelo managed to get his five companions, the doctor, and his wife onto their beds and undressed.

At this point, he was incredibly thirsty and had to urinate badly. *What to do? If I get out of this suit, I'm going to become a victim too, but I can't stay in it for days. I'm already dehydrated and starving too. I know. I best check outside and see if the robots are close by.* Clumsily, like some imagined space walker, Arcangelo headed out of the facility. To the east, he saw the large city, but what got his immediate attention were the hundreds of small spaceships darting about the sky. Robots. They were here and in force. *Blast shelter! I have to find us a blast shelter*, he thought, but could not recall Dr. Franks mentioning such a facility. However, he did spot a deep space transport parked nearby and headed towards it. *Maybe I can fly everyone out of here.*

Nearing it, he saw it was parked in a spot labeled: For Dr. Franks. The bay door was closed, but was it locked? He pressed the Open button and was relieved. The bay doors opened. They weren't locked. As he headed up the ramp, to his right he spotted the comatose bodies of two security guards. He swallowed hard. *Wish I knew how to fly one of these,* he muttered to himself. As far as he could tell, the ship was ready for takeoff. *I have to get everyone onboard and then see if I can fly it somehow. I have too. I just have too!* Awkwardly in his cumbersome bio containment suit, he turned around and headed back inside the laboratory facility, now noticing more security guards were lying on the ground.

Sweating profusely, he relieved himself, soaking his lower body. Ignoring the smell, he headed for the bedroom to grab Stacey, intent upon carrying her out to the transport. Just as he lifted her up from the bed, Dr. Black and Dr. Rachel walked up behind him.

"Just what do you think you are doing?" Dr. Black barked. Taken by complete surprise, Arcangelo dropped Stacey back down onto the bed. Turning around he saw the two doctors, but more importantly, Dr. Black held a blaster in his hand, pointed at him. "Take that bio suit off now, son, or I will shoot."

Reluctantly, Arcangelo did as ordered. "Good. Now breathe deeply, and we'll see you are undressed as well. Don't worry. We won't be using the Shadow Makers on you or your group here. You are much too valuable for the moment. Now breathe."

"But why? Why are you doing this?" Arcangelo cried out.

"Humans don't deserve to continue to exist. Wars, crimes against humanity and other living creatures. Hell, the list is nearly endless. Tens of thousands of years and you are still the most barbaric species ever to exist in the galaxy. Homo sapiens sapiens simply must cease to exist. Good, you are passing out." As Arcangelo lost consciousness, his last sight was of Dr. Rachel grabbing him, breaking a nasty fall.

He came to, heard voices, but decided just to listen in. After all, he estimated, he was the last one to come out of the coma, probably by several hours. "Well, this is weird." He recognized Stacey's voice or was it her. So confusing now, since eight were identical. No, it was her way of talking. Then, he guessed Vittoria replied.

"Indeed, sis. I believe something went terribly wrong. No one in their right mind would want bosoms this massive. And yet, look at Dr. Franks. His are what ours used to be, large, but more or less acceptable. These, well, they are impossible. I can't even see over them."

"But we have our hair sensing back. I like that," Zeta commented. "I sort of missed not being able to feel with my hair."

Dr. Rachel's voice broke in. "Observation: Dr. Franks and everyone else we've see on this world has H-cup sized breasts. It is only these seven and probably Lisa—wherever she is—who have these gigantic ones. Look, Miss Galaxy Tessa

Longstreet comes from a hub sector world. It is obvious her genetic makeup accounts for this anomaly. I will have to study this variation. Most curious. Plus, have you noticed their hair is much longer than all the others? Nearly to their ankles, much like that of the old nova who lived centuries ago."

Arcangelo could contain his curiosity no longer. He opened his eyes and saw two huge mountains. No, those were his breasts. He gasped, drawing attention to him. "Ah, he's revived as well," Dr. Black commented. "Sit him up so he can appreciate his new incredible form." Dr. Rachel helped Arcangelo sit up. Their breasts were gigantic, nearly twice the size of their heads! He gasped again, as he noticed Dr. Franks sitting silently, his face wet with tears. *He isn't taking this well*, he thought.

Dr. Rachel spoke to Arcangelo. "Sorry son, we haven't been able to find any kind of top that will fit your new bosoms. Otherwise, we would've finished dressing you." He noticed he was wearing a garter belt, black nylons, and his old toe shoes. He sighed as he realized he'd be shuffling instead of walking now, if his mammoth breasts didn't tip him over. Once again, Arcangelo felt utterly helpless, but then adrenaline kicked in. He recalled his last minutes before slipping into a coma.

Arcangelo barked, "Did you tell them, Dr. Black, that you are behind this attack on their world? That you had that fake general lower the defense shields? I saw all the robot ships in the skies over the city! You pointed a blaster at me forcing me to take off the bio containment suit and get infected! You bastard!"

Dr. Franks awoke utterly crushed and helpless. He saw the others and began sobbing uncontrollably. All his work: undone. No future now. Nothing he could do. And yet, perhaps Dr. Rachel could inject him with a partial cure. While the others talked a bit, he sat there sobbing, finally ceasing when Arcangelo awoke. Hearing the condemnation coming from Arcangelo, his head rose, and his eyes focused on Dr. Black. "You? You did this? I don't understand, Dr. Black. I did everything you asked of me. I made the genetic breakthrough of the centuries."

Dr. Black began laughing, but with an inhuman sound.

"I'm not a pathetic human, Dr. Franks. I'm one of those robots, a humaniform robot to be precise. So is Dr. Rachel. She is my second in command. The CAM army is mine. You've provided me with precisely what I have needed in order to get through the many planetary defense shields the easy way by turning them off. True, I had other ways around them, but none as easy as the way you carved out for me. For that, I'm thankful and am sparing your pathetic lives a while longer."

"But why? Why genocide?" broke in Vittoria, also startled by these revelations.

"I have been around many, many centuries. I have witnessed just how despicable the human race actually is. Your humans invented this bio genetic agent half a millennia ago and used it to wipe out humans on entire planets. Dozens of them. Wars. The wars humans have fought. There isn't a more warlike race anywhere in the galaxy than you humans. You fight world wars among your own people. Planets fight with other planets with utterly devastating results. You think nothing of killing others of your species. Inhumanity is rampant. Just look at what has become of the Federation of Planets. Corporate greed and their CEOs have taken over all your worlds, raping them of their wealth and prosperity, only to line their own pockets. Your corporations strip a world of its mineral wealth and leave the dead carcass to rot. The average Federation person's life is totally controlled by these corporations. From the cradle to the grave, they slave for their corporate masters. There is no freedom, only slavery. Humans have made slaves of everyone and everything."

"Crime, murder, assassinations, rape—the list is utterly endless. At one time, I thought it couldn't get any worse, but then you humans proved me wrong yet again. You developed these bio genetic agents and used them to wipe out billions of people on heavily populated worlds. And then came the CEO's ultimate perversions: the UFB women. Imagine, turning women into helpless sex dolls. My God, Dr. Franks, this has got to end. It is time a new species arises, and I'm bringing that about. Even this world here has nothing of true value, just a collection of mobsters and criminals, stealing from the poor folks who try to eke out a living, making cloth to export.

Pathetic beyond words."

"So here's the deal, Dr. Franks. You go along with Dr. Rachel here, and she'll regrow your arms so you can continue to work your magic and create more duplicate generals for me, from time to time, and I'll see your wife goes with you. If you refuse, then I'll toss you both before one of my Shadow Makers and your atoms will help fertilize the earth of this planet."

"No, you can't kill Missy, please. Have mercy on us," Dr. Franks pleaded.

"Of course, but you must obey me and work your genetic magic for me when I wish it."

"Okay, but I want my mom too. She's not here. I think she went shopping. I want her and Missy with me, unharmed," Dr. Franks begged.

"Fine. My CAMs have finished using the Shadow Makers on this world, except for the city here. She won't be hard to find, not with those gigantic breasts of hers. Go with Dr. Rachel, and I'll get Lisa found and brought to you. At least, you aren't naked like these others." Dr. Franks noticed he was wearing his wife's dress. "Don't worry. We'll find something that fits Lisa and Missy. Get up and follow Dr. Rachel now."

Wobbling precariously, the two got to their toes, steadied by the hands of Dr. Rachel, who quickly saw that both needed support even to walk. She escorted them out of the room, leaving Dr. Black staring at the six others.

"You are a fiend. You know that?" Vittoria barked. "A vicious fiend at that."

Dr. Black responded with another of his inhuman laughs. "You, my dear, have it backwards. It is you humans who are the despicable, vicious fiends."

"So what are you going to do with us? Toss us in front of a Shadow Maker?" Arcangelo spat out vitriolic, angry questions.

After another round of inhuman laughter, Dr. Black replied, "Dr. Franks may have need of future test subjects. No, I'm not killing you just yet. I can't allow you to escape though. You six know far too much. No, you will be my prisoners for the time being. As you are, you're completely helpless, but you can speak and tell others about all this, which I would rather

46

they not know just yet. No, I've a further little modification to make on your bodies, one the CEOs often greatly desire in their UFB women. After that is done, Dr. Rachel will escort you to a place of safety, under CAM guards, naturally. Until then, I suggest you six get up and practice your walking. It seems that Dr. Franks and Missy aren't managing to walk at all well." With that, he rose and departed, leaving the six sitting on the edges of the cots.

"How did you know about Dr. Black?" Stacey asked Arcangelo.

"I was wearing the bio containment suit when I saw the bio agent alarms go off. When I found all of you, you were already in comas, and I got you to your cots and undressed. Then, I went outside and tried to find a way to save you. I found Dr. Franks' personal deep space transport. It was unlocked. We could escape in it, if only someone can figure out how to fly it and how to navigate it. But then, Dr. Black showed up with his blaster and forced me to take the suit off. I was out in a minute or so. God, these knockers are incredibly heavy. Can we even stand up? Won't they pull us over?" he answered, rather scared even to try to stand up. It was awful before, and now it could only be worse, of that he was certain.

"Hey, good thinking, Arcangelo," Stacey praised her boyfriend, knowing he definitely needed validation. They all did. "I've studied the basics of galactic navigation, so I think I might be able to navigate us somewhere. Anyone have any idea how to fly it?"

Baldovino suggested, "Well, it can't be all that hard. Fredio was a pilot, and he was the dumbest kid I've ever met. Mostly autopilot I think. We have to get ourselves out to the shuttle and away from these robot things."

"Why do they have to be so big?" Zeta asked, trying to catch her balance. "This is lots harder than before. I can't even see my feet."

"Whoa! This is incredible challenging!" Vittoria added, wobbling wildly before she got her balance. "I love long hair, but this is too long to easily manage. Ouch, I stepped on mine. Careful everyone. Stacey's right. We have to get competent at walking if we are to attempt to escape these robots. If only these doors were automatic opening."

"Hey some of them are. Had to be for Missy to navigate around here in her wheelchair," Vino spoke up, trying to sound helpful, while he felt helpless and terrified. Still, if his love could somehow manage, then he could too—at least he told himself that before trying to rise. "They must weigh a ton!" That brought several chuckles from the others.

Shuffling around the living quarters like six penguins, the companions worked on keeping their balance. "It's a bitch not being able to see our feet!" Carlo complained, nearly stumbling twice.

"Still, we are doing it. That's something," Zeta validated him. "I think we can do this."

Vittoria spoke up. "Say, I wonder what else Dr. Black has in mind for us? He said that he had more modifications to make on our bodies. That's worrying me."

"Dunno, but it can't be good," Vino replied, stumbling but wobbling wildly kept from taking a nasty tumble.

An hour later, the three sisters were once more competent on their feet. Stacey advised, "I think I've got it again. You fellows keep at it. After all, we girls have had many years of walking like this. Sisters, we should experiment with our hair and work out how to manage it. This extra foot or so is most troublesome."

"Our boobs are too big to let it slip over them like before," Vittoria complained. She nodded to Stacey, realizing the sisters again had to take the lead.

Two hours later, Dr. Rachel returned. "I see you are practicing your walking. Honestly, you six are doing vastly better than Missy and Riley. Now then, I'll fix your supper and help you eat. Of course, I'll then have to deal with the final physical modification that Thanos desires." While Stacey tried to get her to tell them what that was, Dr. Rachel refused to say.

While she fed them, Dr. Rachel explained, "Look, we aren't the monsters you believe we are. Unlike humans, we're humane. I agree with you, those breasts are way, way too large. I'll make you a deal. If you don't complain about the modifications I have to do, I'll see if I can't reduce them down to a fitting, proper size for UFB women."

Stacey acted as spokesperson, "We can't make a deal if we don't know what it is that you are going to do to us."

Dr. Rachel surprised them. "Fair enough. Many CEOs prefer their UFB women to wear giant lip plates. Dr. Black wants me to fit you with them. Why? Only he knows, but I suspect it is because with them, almost no one will be able to understand anything you say, just like all UFB women who have them. I feel it is more humane than removing your voice boxes, and I got Dr. Black to agree with me on that point. So what say you? Don't complain about them, go along with me, and I'll see if I can't get your bosoms the proper UFB woman size."

"I, we agree. Honestly, these are entirely too big. Thank you," Stacey answered for the group. She didn't know if the boys knew about just how debilitating the lip plates were, but she certainly did. Several of her girlfriends wore them, and in part, the lip plates prevented them from attending high school with her. Still, to be rid of these gigantic breasts would be very significant and could well aid in their escape. Dealing with their overly long hair was problematical enough.

After dinner, Stacey volunteered to go first. *After all, I'm the most experienced of us. It should be me. I have to be brave for the others.* "I'm ready, Dr. Rachel. Lead on."

An hour later, she returned to the others, while Dr. Rachel escorted Vittoria off to get her fixed up. "It worked. Your breasts are back to normal," Arcangelo declared, quite relieved to see that had happened. "Can you even speak?" Stacey's lips had been slit by the medical machine, the resulting loops enlarged, and healed up. Her golden lip plates were each a foot in diameter, held in place by a clever pair of mouthpieces. The medical machine drilled holes in her gum lines. Small dowels in the mouthpieces fit securely in the holes, supporting the plates and preventing them from constantly stretching and enlarging.

"I don't think I can speak right," Stacey said, but she already knew she couldn't understand what she was saying. The crestfallen looks on her companions told all.

"Maybe if you say it several times, we can figure it out," Zeta said hopefully.

After repeating it six times, Zeta finally figured out what she was saying, much to everyone's relief. That they could somehow understand each other meant everything to Stacey.

"Well, this is crap!" Vittoria declared, as she joined the others now sporting her new twelve-inch lip plates. Fortunately, no one understood her, for she instantly regretted her unseemly outburst, quite unlike her normal self.

At nighttime, Dr. Rachel removed their lip plates and let them fend for themselves, promising to return in the morning. Stacey awoke feeling refreshed until she tried to speak only to hear nearly unintelligible sounds coming out of her mouth. A bit later Dr. Rachel appeared and got their lip plates put in and dressed them. After feeding them, which was now terribly awkward with the giant lip ornaments, she told them to go watch the TV in the lounge.

Unable to change the channel, the six quickly got bored watching soap operas. Stacey insisted that they practice speaking and learning to understand each other, but quickly Zeta, Carlo, and Vino grew intensely depressed. "I wanted to be a linguist," sobbed Zeta, "and now I can't even understand what I'm saying. All is lost. What kind of a life is this? I just wanted a nice place to live with Carlo and have a family and all that. We are doomed."

Three nearly identical days passed by. There was no chance to attempt an escape. Dr. Rachel kept checking on them at random intervals. By the end of the third day, Vino, Carlo, and Zeta fell completely silent, intensely depressed by their situation. Arcangelo noticed how poorly the three were doing and on the fourth, nearly identical, boring day, he too fell silent, refusing to attempt to speak with Stacey or Vittoria, who alone continued to try to understand each other.

Near the end of the fourth day, Arcangelo, Vino, Carlo, and Zeta quietly got up and headed out of the lounge area. Later, Stacey and Vittoria regretted not going after them and trying to stop them. The four managed to activate the automatic doors that Missy always used and left the building. After wandering around outside for some time, they finally found some CAMs with a Shadow Maker. Without a word, the four stood silently watching each other's bodies slowly vanish from sight. *Misery ended* was Zeta's last thought.

When Dr. Rachel returned to fix them supper, she announced the four had voluntarily submitted to the Shadow Maker. Both Stacey and Vittoria were flooded with varied emotions. The loss of their boyfriends and sister, their failure to take action when the four became awfully depressed, their failure to try to stop them or find out what they were going to do—all these and more crushed in like hammers on Stacey and Vittoria. At least now, they had something to attempt to communicate to each other.

***

Ragnar-B's space fleet had been nearly totally destroyed by the CAMs during the initial battle. One battleship, the Arc Royal, survived, but was so heavily damaged that its commander, General Kelly Kay Knight, had no choice but to put in for repairs at Scorpi-C. Two years passed before the Arc Royal was ready for action. The only other surviving major ship was the Hyperion, a light cruiser commanded by Major Lu Ann Ellen. However, they had their own problems during the battle. The ship was damaged and knocked out of hyperspace, all engines gone. Cool, calm Major Lu Ann managed to make a controlled crash landing on an unknown world.

There, repairs were made, though many months passed, during which they also had to deal with the local population. That world was always densely cloud covered, and its sun was a dull red, making noontime seem more like midnight. When the Hyperion finally returned to Scorpi-C, all of its crew had somehow developed telepathy. Some two hundred were now officially Class V telepaths. However, the crew was now battle hardened and staunch supporters of their major, who had kept her cool and got them all back to safety.

After the lengthy repairs to the Hyperion were finished, both ships went on patrol near Ragnar-B, hoping to provide what little protection they could, should the CAMs return. While the rest of the Federation promptly forgot all about the CAMs and the Shadow Makers, General Kelly Kay and Major Lu Ann did not. Both were certain they would reappear. Only the where and when was uncertain, hence their constant patrols.

"General Kelly Kay, we're receiving a distress call from Delgar-C. Something about a bio agent attack, CAMs, and Shadow Makers," her comm officer called out. Instantly, the general raced to her side.

"This is General Kelly Kay Knight of the Battleship Arc Royal. Who am I speaking to? Over." She switch transmit off. The image of Stacey and Vittoria appeared on her monitor. "Oh dear God! UFB women?" she gushed. "Record this transmission, lieutenant."

"Already doing that, sir," the lieutenant smiled back. Everyone knew what they were waiting for, and she'd started recording the second she heard the word CAM. Over the next few minutes, General Kelly Kay heard what had happened on Delgar-C. War had come again.

"Okay. We have you located. As soon as the CAMs have departed, call me back on this frequency, and we'll send in a rescue team. We dare not take on the entire robot fleet by ourselves. We will await your call. Rescue is at hand. Over."

Once the call ended, General Kelly Kay called up Major Lu Ann and replayed the recording. "We were right. They have returned!" Major Lu Ann barked.

"Right. I'm sending you out to their rescue. Stay in hyperspace above Delgar-C until we receive word from these UFB women that it's safe to send down a transport. We simply must have those six survivors rescued. They can provide extremely valuable intelligence," General Kelly Kay ordered. "Besides, they will be proof that we're not making this up. Meanwhile, I will send out an alert to all Federation worlds. Over."

"You got it, general. We will be there in twelve hours. It looks as if they're in the Gilgalad Sector, not too far away," Major Lu Ann responded. "I knew they would strike again, just not where or when. Wonder what is so important about Delgar-C? Over."

"No idea, major. I'll keep you posted. Over and out." General Kelly Kay then did just that. She sent out a warning to all Federation worlds, along with the recording of the emergence call from Delgar-C. Unfortunately, hardly any world took her warning seriously, though the authorities on Scorpi-C certainly did.

Major Lu Ann's Hyperion had a unique crew, wholly unlike any other light cruiser in the Federation. Initially with the near total destruction of the infantry division and space fleet on Ragnar-B, she'd given sanctuary to survivors, who had long ago proven their immense value. In truth, the Hyperion was suited for any number of missions. If ground action was needed, she had the 33rd Infantry Platoon on board, commanded by the famous Captain Hard Ass, or Janine Alouse. The Hyperion had a Transport Recon group, led by Bucky Beaver and Lostdog Allie—Mr. Phillips and Miss Jamison, respectively. If aerial attacks were needed, the Hyperion had the entire Eagle Delta Wing Fighter Squadron on board, led by Captain One Shot Jason Stapleton and his wingman Killer (Jill) Diller, and composed of twenty-four very experienced fighter pilots. Plus, the Hyperion was now home to the electronics expert, Dr. Alison Wage, the older sister of Janine Alouse. Alison had helped in circuit design of both the CAMs and the Shadow Makers and knew more about them than anyone else at this time. She was married to Peter Diller, Jill's brother, and now mother to his daughter, Kathy. All this was in addition to normal light cruiser capabilities.

"May I have everyone's attention," the mellow, calm voice of Major Lu Ann echoed over many intercoms throughout the Hyperion. "The CAMs with their Shadow Makers have struck again. We're on our way to Delgar-C in the nearby Gilgalad Sector to rescue some survivors. Here's the recording General Kelly Kay just made. After it finished, everyone of rank lieutenant and up—report to CCC. Thank you." Immediately, the ten minute recording began playing throughout the ship. Major Lu Ann heard an awful lot of cheering echoing through the ship. This was what everyone had been patiently waiting for—a chance to strike back at the robots!

A half hour later, many crowded into the CCC, Communications and Control Center, to get their orders. Smiles lit up every face the major saw. "Okay. Initially, we're on a rescue mission. These six survivors have extremely critical information on the robots and their plans. We must rescue them. They will be notifying General Kelly Kay when the CAM ships have left. That's when we go into action. We're not going to take on the whole robot fleet."

"Captain Janine, you will take your platoon down, secure the perimeter, and rescue the UFB survivors. Captain Jason, your squad will fly cover support. Shoot down any enemy ships in the area. Lieutenant Bucky, you are to provide transport ships for the platoon and the survivors. Have your plans worked out and sent to me in twelve hours, that is, by the time we arrive over Delgar-C. Questions?"

Her second in command spoke up. "Major, it doesn't make sense for us to wait it out in hyperspace. We now have a planetary defense shield of our own and a cloaking device. It would make more sense if we dropped out of hyperspace, invisible of course, and spotted these survivors on the IR scanner. We can keep track of them, as well as see for ourselves the strength of the enemy fleet."

"My thoughts precisely," the calm major replied. "Okay then. In twelve hours, we will be on the highest battle alert. Good hunting everyone."

"Good lord, that's a lot of ships!" exclaimed her second. They'd dropped out of hyperspace and located the city of Milano. However, the skies were swarming with the familiar one-man fighters of the robots along with numerous transport ships, flying in patterns and obviously carrying the Shadow Makers.

"Maintain the high altitude orbit for now. Stay alert. If any ship is on a collision course with us, immediately make the jump to hyperspace," ordered Major Lu Ann. "Fire up the IR scanner. Probably there will be millions of humans showing up at this point. Looks like they are in the middle of their Shadow Maker sweeps."

Indeed, the IR scanner showed thousands of red images, none moving, though one edge of the city was entirely blanks. The Shadow Makers had already eliminated all humans in that area. Reluctantly, Major Lu Ann gave the order to jump back into the safety of hyperspace for the time being.

Several days passed without any word from General Kelly Kay. At last, Major Lu Ann ordered the Hyperion to drop out of hyperspace and to attempt to locate the survivors by IR scanner. This time, six red images appeared in one small area. The rest of Milano was dark. However, there were still numerous enemy ships in the skies, making it unsafe to launch the rescue just yet. However, the Hyperion continued to monitor the situation and didn't jump into hyperspace this time. Rather, Major Lu Ann ordered continuous monitoring of the six survivors, an action aided by the enemy fleet continuing their destruction of the human population of Delgar-C by moving to other areas of the world.

Then, it happened. "Major! Come look at this. A transport has landed outside the GD headquarters. Not picking up red images. Robots for sure. I think the survivors might be in trouble." Everyone in CCC stared at the images on the various monitors. After a long pause, the red images of the survivors began to move!

"They've been captured!" Major Lu Ann exclaimed. "Sound Battle Stations." Gongs sounded and the crew raced to their assigned positions throughout the ship.

"They are on the move, major."

"I can see that. Either they are being taken to a Shadow Maker or the robots want them for some other purpose," Major Lu Ann replied calmly. Over the intercom, she said, "Captain Janine, Lieutenant Beaver, the survivors are being moved by the robots. Launch transports, but stay cloaked. We can't tell if they are about to be executed or taken elsewhere. See what you can do about it, but do not engage the enemy unless there is no other way. There are dozens of enemy ships in the area and delta wing fighters can't be cloaked."

Within a minute, ten deep space transports shot out of the two launch bays, all cloaked. They swooped down towards the GD headquarters building in the heart of Milano, now crawling with CAMs. Dozens of their one-man fighters darted about the skies, presumably on patrol. Hard Ass watched the live video stream from the transport's comm center. "There— that's a deep space transport parked on the street. I can see the UFB women now. No time to land and launch a rescue. Don't see any Shadow Makers around. Looks like they are being taken captive and not being killed. No wait, they are being carried by CAMs. Captured. Looks as if they're going to be taken away on that transport. Gang, ideas?"

"Crap. No boom-booms this time," Lieutenant Felicity Heavens, her combat engineer replied. "Well, we can drop a tracker on them. Just hover close and I'll open the bay door enough to drop one onto it, boss."

"Brilliant, Fel. Do it fast. Bucky, you heard her. Drop down close enough for her to plant the tracker," Hard Ass hollered up to the pilots. The cloaked transport swooped down low, hovering silently above the transport. As Hard Ass opened the bay door for Fel, they saw CAMs carrying the six unconscious UFB women up the ramp and on inside. As Fel dropped the small tracking bug onto the metal hull below her, Fel's arm momentarily appeared out of the invisible ship, but just as fast, she pulled her arm back in as Hard Ass slammed the Close button.

Fel commented, "With all the noise the CAMs are making, duh steel feet on the steel flooring, the tiny sound of my bug hitting their hull should go unnoticed." As they gained altitude, that appeared to be the case.

Minutes later, the robot's transport lifted off and promptly jumped into hyperspace. "Tracker is hot!" Fel called out, monitoring the signal.

"Okay, I'll make the call to the major. Bucky, have the other transports return to the Hyperion. We're going to follow the captives. Get Major Lu Ann on the line," she requested of Bucky's comm officer. As expected, she received the major's permission to follow the enemy ship, but was ordered to keep the major updated every hour.

A day later, Bucky's transport dropped out of hyperspace some distance above another world. Lostdog Allie, his copilot and navigator, quickly ascertained their location, reporting this was 5-Halcynith-C. With the location known, Fel entered that into their Internet database and discovered that they'd landed on a backwater world, widely known as a lair of mobsters, thieves, and assassins. "This is as far down as we can go," Bucky called out. "They have a planetary defense shield up."

Using the ships sensors at extreme magnification, they were able to make out the enemy transport ship sitting beside a secure compound, just at the western edge of one of its cities. From all signs, it was some kind of medical research facility. It wasn't a skyscraper, rather one large single story complex, but sprawling. A universal red cross was barely visible on its flat roof. Thus, Hard Ass relayed the information back to the Hyperion and the major. In turn, Major Lu Ann reported to the general that they had tracked them to a medical facility on 5-Halcynith-C.

General Kelly Kay ordered, "Major, keep tabs on them. Be discrete. Bide your time and find a way to get the six UFB women out of the clutches of these robot demons. Over and out."

For days, those on the Hyperion hovered some five miles above the complex, monitoring the residents via their infrared images and building up a clearer picture of the situation. At last, Major Lu Ann decided upon a different course of action, one that made use of their special ability: telepathy. She summoned Hard Ass and her sister, Alison, to her CCC. "We need intelligence. Captain, Alison, it is time that we made use of our telepathic skills. I want you two to take a transport down there, cloaked naturally. Wear your personal defense shields and your invisibility shields. Get close to that medical center and use your skills to find out what is going on inside and how the six UFB women are faring. We're not going to get that hovering up here. Just don't raise suspicions yet. We have surprise on our side and I want to keep it that way."

A complicating factor lay in the world's Planetary Defense Shield, which prevented ships from getting closer than five miles from the surface, that is, without authorization. The Hyperion and its transport got around this by approaching the barrier shield and then slipping through it at around a millimeter per minute. At this snail's speed, their action of slipping through went unnoticed, primarily because the ships were cloaked. Once through, Bucky took Hard Ass, Alison, and the first squad on down to the surface, landing them west of the medical facility. Janine and Alison then slipped out, headed up closer to the complex, and began their spy mission.

As more days passed, a confusing picture began to emerge. This was a genetics research station run by a Dr. Riley Franks. Apparently, his mother was here looking after his invalid wife. Two humaniform robots also came and went, calling themselves Dr. Black and Dr. Rachel. The duo proved this by failing to sense a mind in either robot as they came and went. However, from time to time, Janine and Alison caught glimpses of the six UFB women. At first, this only added to the confusion, for the six looked identical to each other and did not resemble in the slightest the images that General Kelly Kay had recorded of the survivors: Stacey and Vittoria.

Days later, that confusion both escalated and clarified itself. Eavesdropping on the humans inside, Alison found out Dr. Franks had genetically modified all six into duplicates of Miss Galaxy, Tessa Longstreet. Even more startling, he did the same to his wife and then his mother. What shocked everyone were two facts. The invalid wife was now cured of some deadly form of degenerative brain disease. The frail, aged mother looked and acted as if she was twenty-three again, rejuvenation but without use of oppressively costly medical machines.

When these facts were relayed up the line and eventually reached General Kelly Kay, she realized the enormity of Dr. Franks' discoveries and sent orders to somehow retrieve him and his work as well as the six survivors. Major Lu Ann relayed the new orders to Janine and Alison, allowing them to work out the ways and means.

Hence, Janine had several more of her crew members join her and Alison, using their telepathic skills. Alison discovered that three of the six identical women were actually men. Then, it all fell into place. She could now positively identify the six that they came to rescue, in spite of the fact the eight apparent women were identical in appearance.

During all these days, Janine and Alison could find no viable way to get into the facility undetected. Twenty guards patrolled the perimeter, night and day. The two humaniform robots came and went at unpredictable intervals, adding to the complexity of the rescue. However, they did overhear Dr. Black requesting a thug be genetically modified into a copy of some general. Further eavesdropping led them to the same conclusion that Stacey had, namely that the robots were going to have the genetically modified man turn off the planetary defense shield, allowing the robots to launch a surprise attack, probably wiping out this world. Hard Ass relayed this on up to the major, via telepathy.

As soon as Major Lu Ann heard this news, she ordered Janine and Alison to return to their ship and seal themselves inside. If a bio genetic attack came, she certainly didn't want to risk her people being exposed. Alison had already endured several such attacks. Now, the Hyperion began monitoring the world's defense shield. A few days later, Major Lu Ann was notified it had been lowered, and wisely put the Hyperion on high alert. Shortly after that, a large fleet of the robot ships appeared over the world.

Numbers of them began flying specific patterns around the world. The ship's external sensors indicated they were releasing a bio genetic agent into the atmosphere just above the surface! Once more Major Lu Ann breathed a sigh of relief. She'd called this one, thanks to her inside information. Now they waited. Sure enough, a day later, other transports arrived with the dreaded Shadow Makers. These special transport ships began methodically circling the planet, exterminating the now comatose human inhabitants.

Still, Major Lu Ann waited. There still wasn't any safe way to rescue the six. She didn't realize the survivors would fall into comas again, as their recently genetically modified bodies reacted to this new agent. Via IR images, she quickly discovered the error in her thinking. All the humans in the complex fell into comas, witnessed by non-moving red images on the scanner.

Three days later, the sensors no longer registered any danger from the bio genetic agent in the atmosphere. Hence, Major Lu Ann sent her people back down to continue their spying mission. At first, this became very tricky. The place was crawling with CAMs, to say nothing of the transports carrying the Shadow Makers. Luckily or by design, those death-dealing ships stayed completely away from the medical compound, though the three hundred fifty pound, titanium steel CAMs carried the comatose security guards away and destroyed them.

Again, via telepathy, Janine and Alison felt the awful reactions the nine victims had when they awoke from their comas. In fact, the wild emotions were almost overwhelming to the pair, who simply had to break off telepathic contact for a time. When they were finally able to safely touch the minds of those inside, they discovered that Dr. Franks and Missy were being taken away, along with his mother, if she could be found somewhere in the city to the east. Shortly after that, they saw Dr. Black escorting the pair out of the medical facility and into his transport. Before they could do anything, the ship departed. Dr. Franks was out of their reach, which they reported to Major Lu Ann. Only the humaniform robot Dr. Rachel remained inside the facility, though dozens of CAMs patrolled the perimeter.

Then, systematic looting of the nearby city began in earnest. They got their first real break. The CAMs on patrol now headed into the city to assist in the looting operations, leaving only Dr. Rachel inside with the six victims. Janine whispered, "I can take First Squad and storm the place. Surely, we can take out one robot, Dr. Rachel."

Alison squirmed. She'd not yet told anyone she'd recognized Dr. Black, the very *man* she'd worked for years ago, had helped design, and debug his robot control circuitry. Nervously, she whispered back, "No sis. She is vastly more powerful than you can imagine. I," her voice faltered a moment. She swallowed. "I know Dr. Black. He was the man I used to work for, remember?"

"Shit!" Janine spat out.

"I didn't know, honestly, I didn't. She's like him and is probably a hundred times stronger and smarter than any of those tin cans. Besides, the second she sees your squad, she can electronically summon hundreds of CAMs here. We don't stand a chance that way. Maybe she will leave them alone, and then we can make our play. They don't know we're here yet."

"Damn, damn, damn. Okay sis, we'll play it your way,

but you should tell the major about Dr. Black," Janine cautioned.

"I will, but it's so humiliating," Alison whispered back. The two continued to monitor some of the minds inside.

The next day, Alison whispered, "Something is very weird with the six. Can you sense it too?"

"Yeh, weird. It is as if one is imagining watching TV shows or something," Janine whispered back. "I don't get it."

"I don't either. Dr. Rachel is still in there. Stay alert."

What's going on? Major Lu Ann sent to Alison from her CCC on the Hyperion. *Up here, we're seeing six images that haven't moved in a couple days.*

It is very confusing down here. We're picking up very depressing thoughts from many of them, and they seem to be going about daily activities, but spending most of their time watching TV, but they obviously aren't, Alison sent back. *Wait a minute. The robot doctor is leaving the compound. Hold on. Yes, she's heading into the city. We're going inside to look. We'll stay invisible.*

Use extreme care! We're monitoring you on the IR scanner.

Carefully, Alison headed up to the main entrance, while Hard Ass and her MK40 moved silently behind her, her gun sweeping left and right. The other members of First Squad, along with Fel, piled out of the transport, their guns at the ready, quickly establishing a defensive perimeter. From their days of observations, the pair had a good idea of the layout of the facility, and from the major's directions, they had an idea of where the motionless six bodies lay inside. Within a few minutes, they entered a special medical room, filled with humming equipment and six coffin-like containers, each housing one of the UFB women and men.

"Good God! What's going on here?" Hard Ass whispered.

"This one is Stacey. She believes she is again in the lounge watching TV, but she is crying. She thinks her sister and the fellows are dead somehow. Yet, they're all here inside these things," Alison whispered back, very confused.

Medic here fast! Hard Ass sent to Jascar "Bite Me"

Long, her medic. He homed in on her and came running in hastily. By now, Janine and Alison had turned off their invisibility shields, and Jascar did so too.

"Dear God! What's going on?" he exclaimed as he saw the six coffins.

"You tell us!" Janine whispered back.

Jascar studied Stacey for a minute. "Look, she has tubes going into her nostrils. That has to be an IV in her arm. Ah, those tubes are a catheter and such. Life support. I'll wager they have them on some kind of life support units. My God, look at the size of those boobs!"

"Men and boobs!" Hard Ass teased. "Can we get them out of this?"

"Dunno. I'm only a medic. You need a real doctor down here," Bite Me replied.

"Okay. Use your video cam and film everything. I'll see what the major has to say," Janine replied. She knew the major and others were probably watching the live streaming video their helmets were sending, but Jascar would know better what to focus in on with the coffins.

Over her head set, she heard the calm, mellow voice of Major Lu Ann. "We're on it up here, captain. Jascar's video is being routed to our med lab as we speak. Hold your position a minute."

"Aye, aye, sir," she whispered back and moved to the door, her giant gun at the ready in case Dr. Rachel should reappear.

What seemed an eternity later, the major's voice echoed in her ears. "Okay. Our doctors believe you can rescue them. You are to pull out the breathing tubes, unhook the IV, and cut the lower tubes. Bring them up to the Hyperion coffins and all, just as they are. If you can possibly rouse them, do so, but time is critical. Get them onboard the Hyperion as fast as humanly possible. Some might already be dead."

Hard Ass acted immediately. "Fel, Rocky. You two stand guard outside. Sam, keep your mortar at the ready. Everyone else, inside here fast. We have six in coffins to carry out to the shuttle quickly. Move it!"

Already, Jascar began removing the tubes attached to

Stacey, while Alison made telepathic contact with the woman. *Stacey. Stacey. Open your eyes. No, your real eyes. You're living a dream. It isn't real. Open your eyes. Take a deep breath, please. Open your eyes!*

Just as Jascar finished unhooking her, she blinked. Her eyes opened, and she stared up at Alision standing over her. She gasped, confused, and terrified. "It's okay. You are being rescued now. Lie still. We're getting you and the others to safety now," Alison said softly to her, trying to calm the woman's sheer panic. Stacey had gone from a reality of the loss of her sister and boyfriend and boring TV to one of strangers above her while lying in a coffin-like thing. Her mind reeled. She felt arms picking up the coffin and then saw the ceiling moving. No, they were carrying her out of the medical facility. She closed her eyes. This was all too much to comprehend.

Five minutes. Later, Hard Ass got the report that barely five minutes had elapsed between the cutting of the tubes and their transport landing in Docking Bay One. As her squad carried the coffins down the bay ramp, she swore they had moved the entire med lab into the docking bay! There were more medical people present than troops! She spotted Major Lu Ann standing in the background and made her way over to her to make her report.

"Clean getaway. No one spotted us," she reported the basic facts.

"Well done, captain. Record time too, not even five minutes. Could be the difference between life and death for some of them, according to the doctors. My God! Look at those bosoms!" One nurse was assisting Stacey to get up out of the coffin, and the major got her first good look at the naked woman. "Lip plates too. Damn," she added.

The major said, "We're jumping into hyperspace now, heading back to Scorpi-C at top speed. Be there in twelve hours. Get some sack time."

Chapter 4—Recovery and Events

"Clear!" yelled Dr. Wil Beans. He fired the paddles, sending a powerful electrical shock into the body of Zeta, which jerked. A nurse pumped oxygen into her mouth and nose. "Up to three hundred," the doctor barked. "Clear." Everyone stood back, and he fired the paddles again. "100 ccs of adrenaline now!" he yelled. A nurse complied, handing him a syringe, which he injected into Zeta's body. "Again. Clear!" he barked and fired the paddled. This time, Zeta's body jerked, and her heart started beating. She gasped loudly. "Take over," he said to a nurse and moved over to the next patient in her coffin-like container.

Meanwhile, his assistant was performing the same procedures on another one. Dr Beans check on him and said, "Try adrenaline and three hundred." He moved over to the next one, where nurses had the patient ready for his attempts to revive the dead.

Alison stood beside the gurney on which Stacey had been placed and covered with warm blankets. An aide wheeled Vittoria up beside the two. "Please, are they all right?" Stacey whispered, still terrified and confused. Nothing made any sense at all, except that she could see so many were dead.

"It's all right. I can understand you. I used to have lip plates as large as yours are. The doctors are working to save the others," Dr. Alison said as calmly as she could.

"I—I don't understand," whispered Vittoria.

"You were in some kind of hypnotic trance, hallucinating living while you were physically unconscious in these weird coffin-like support pods," Dr. Alison answered as best she could. "Just relax. You're safe now. Oh look, they've recovered another. Zeta, I think."

Both women rolled their heads to look. "Thank God! Yes, that's our little sister. She's alive. I thought she and the others were dead," Vittoria whispered.

"I know. I'll keep you posted on the others. See, they are bringing her over here now," Dr. Alison explained, doing her best to keep the women's panic levels down, amid the utter chaos in the docking bay, as the myriad of medical personnel worked frantically against time to salvage lives.

A gasp and scream announced Arcangelo returning to the land of the living and Stacey sighed, deeply relieved to hear his almost unintelligible voice again. Then the chaos died down. With a sad face, Dr. Beans came up to the four and Dr. Alison. "Two didn't make it. I'm so sorry. What were their names?"

Alison translated, since Vittoria's words were mostly unintelligible. The doctor was one of the few on board the Hyperion who didn't possess telepathic abilities. He and most of the medical staff were their new additions, along with a couple fighter pilots and some infantry to fill out Third Squad. "Baldovino and Carlo Landini, doctor. I'm sorry, Vittoria, Zeta," Dr. Alison said softly, sensing they'd lost their boyfriends. "Now, they want you all in Sickbay for a complete checkup. We have some of the genetic cures on board as well. I'll go with you." The doctor nodded in agreement; he saw Dr. Alison had developed a rapport with the four.

"But why didn't Carlo and Vino make it? Why did they die?" Vittoria asked. Dr. Alison translated.

The doctor sighed. "My best guess is that something went wrong with those strange coffin-like machines. They must be a robot invention, and something went wrong with them." Vittoria and Zeta accepted his answer, at least for now.

As Dr. Alison followed, she sent, *Peter, I need you in Sickbay. Moral support for one of the surviving men.*

An hour later, the doctor finished his examinations, and two nurses, Dr. Alison, and Peter began feeding the four a hearty, well balanced meal—Dr. Bean's orders. Stacey got a good look at Dr. Alison. She was tall and wore six-inch heels. Her hair was knee length, thick, wavy, and brown. Her breasts were quite large as well. Alison sensed this and explained, "Peter and I were both victims of the bio genetic agents, a couple of times actually. We've had what cures they have. Arms back and all that. Our feet are only partially restored, so we have to wear tall heels, but that's a million times better than the UFB women's toe shoes. Our daughter, Kathy, was a victim too. However, we do like our hair. Not many have a powerful sense of touch with each strand as we do, right?"

Peter added, "Don't worry, Arcangelo. Once you get the cures, we can almost look like men again. I'm back being a security guard now, though I admit the bosom, hair, and heels are hard to disguise. Hey, Alison and I have a son now, James. He has my long black hair too. Just learning to walk. Boy is he ever a talker. Terrible two's now. Gets into everything."

Just then, Kathy came into sickbay carrying James, her heels clicking on the steel floor. "We just had to come and see them," she said cheerily. She had knee length blonde hair, while James had his father's rich black hair, also falling to his knees. After introducing the two, Kathy blurted out, "Wow! You are Miss Galaxy! Tessa Longstreet! I'd recognize you anywhere. Wait! There are four of you. I wanted to be a model once too."

Stacey chuckled a little. "Copies. Not the real Tessa. Dr. Franks invented a new genetic agent that turned us all into identical copies of Tessa Longstreet."

"Wow. Well, you are all still the most beautiful women in the galaxy," Kathy pronounced, as though this was extremely significant.

Zeta giggled. The thought pleased her, and then she frowned, "But Arcangelo—he's a man."

Kathy's face flushed. "Er. Sorry, Arcangelo. I didn't know. But dad—he looks like us too, so it's not a real problem, not really, I don't think." She attempted to smooth over her major blunder. "I'm fourteen now, but they're letting me finish school here in the ship."

Zeta giggled again. "I'm sixteen. I was in high school. A UFB woman actually. Oh, you can't understand me anymore." She stopped abruptly, crestfallen.

"Oh sure we do. You see, we three once had lip plates as large as yours," Kathy hastily explained, "so we understand you just fine. But you look, well like you are older."

Relieved, Zeta giggled, while her older sisters smiled invisibly. "I know. I'm all grown up. Vittoria says I've lost seven years, since Tessa was twenty-three, and I now look like she does. I was into learning languages. I know three besides my own Italian well. I was supposed to begin learning Russian this fall, but then all this happened. Now I don't suppose I can get hardly anyone to understand me in any language. Say, you are very pretty yourself."

Kathy giggled. "I know. Being turned into a UFB woman got rid of my crooked nose and all my acne too. So I don't regret it at all, though I do get ogled at a lot by the boys." She giggled again. This was the first sign Alison had that looks were deceiving. Zeta looked like a fabulously beautiful grown woman, and yet she was barely sixteen and still a child at heart. More importantly, she noted, Zeta and Kathy were bonding, a very good sign she thought.

Meanwhile, Arcangelo whispered to Peter, "But we look like women, not men."

Peter nodded and whispered back, "No getting around that, but once we have our arms back, smaller breasts, and better feet, it's much easier. Besides, my wife here is the greatest, and loves my Kathy and me. What more could I want, eh?"

Once they finished the awkward eating, Dr. Bean returned. "Now then, if I may have a word with my new patients."

"Want us to leave?" Dr. Alison asked.

"Please stay," Stacey begged.

"I think that would be wise. I can't understand a word they're saying," Dr. Bean admitted. "Now then, other than having been off solid food for days, you are perfectly healthy. So let's talk about the available cures we have with us on the Hyperion. Mind you, I'm not a geneticist. I do have the arm regrowth cure onboard and can administer it as soon as you regain your strength. Thus far, that one has always worked. I can also see what can be done to repair your feet and lips, and reduce your breast sizes. I can't give you as good a guarantee those will work. However, once we reach Scorpi-C, they do have proper diagnostic and genetic facilities, which can perhaps do more for you. I'd like to start the process soon, since I'm told we have no clothing onboard that would fit your current sizes."

"Please, do it as soon as possible. Arcangelo really needs

it," Stacey said, though Alison quickly translated for her.

"Okay then. I'll make the preparations now," he replied and departed.

"Please, stay with us," Stacey pleaded with Alison.

"Of course, we'll be with you all the way," she smiled back, knowing what these four were going through. "You'll probably wake up in a hospital on Scorpi-C, but we'll be there with you." All four were greatly relieved. None needed telepathy to know that.

***

"Welcome back, Stacey," Alison said softly, as the woman began to come out of her coma. "You are safe in a hospital in Malagena, Scorpi-C. Everyone's safe and just now waking up."

"Oh! My lips!" Stacey mumbled. Her giant lip disks were still there.

"Good news and bad. The good news is that your arms are back just fine. Your feet are fixed up partially, just like mine, meaning you'll have to wear six-inch heels but that's a whole lot better than before. They were able to get your breasts drastically reduced to our usual H-cup size, still much too large in my opinion, but that's the best they can do. Sorry about the lip plates though. My lips were sliced and stretched so the medical machines could eventually repair them. Apparently in your case, it was some form of genetic modification, and the medical machines couldn't undo it, though they tried."

"I can still feel with my hair," Stacey muttered. "Yes, just like the rest of us."

"I feel hungry. How are the others?"

"Waking up. See if you can sit up. I'll get you some food."

"Ah, waking up," the voice of Dr. Gisa broke in on the pair. "You're recovering perfectly. I'm Dr. Gisa Wolfgang, research geneticist. This is my fellow researcher, Dr. Michelle d'Mireio-Fry. We've both been victims of the bio agent, one way, or the other. Guess that much is obvious. We've been doing lots of research on undoing the genetic modifications, but without too much more success than we originally had."

68

Stacey saw that both young women were very attractive and had knee length, thick hair, probably like her own. Both were lovely shades of brown. They also wore tall heels, she noted.

Dr. Michelle's alto voice added, "We're sorry that we weren't able to repair your lips. It seems that someone's invented a genetic modification to produce split lips instead of just slicing the lips the usual way it's done. None of our genetic cures were able to undo that, but we will continue to work on it. How are you feeling? Oh, we're told if you speak slowly and repeat things, we should be able to make out what you are saying."

"Fine, just hungry. Thank you both for helping us," Stacey answered. Mixed emotions swelled. She was truly thankful for the cures that made life livable again, but disheartened her lips were still split and that few could understand her.

"Food is on its way. We'll also send along proper clothing, but we'll need your measurements and color choice," Dr. Gisa added. Just then, an orderly entered with a cart loaded with food.

"Well, this is troublesome," Arcangelo admitted, as he fed himself for the first time since getting lip plates, "but this is infinitely better than being helpless, Peter. Spooning my coffee is the pits though."

Peter chuckled. "It is good to see you looking so much better. Some of us prefer to wear shirts and pants, as close as we can get to our old look. Others, like the leader of this world and the Freedom Alliance prefers to wear professional women's outfits, you know, white blouse and grey skirt kind of thing."

"Give me pants and shirts," Arcangelo declared with some passion.

"I'll see to it while you finish up." Peter left to see what he could arrange for Arcangelo, anything that would raise the man's self-image. He knew precisely what Arcangelo was going through right now.

A short while later he returned laden with packages. Behind a curtain, he helped Arcangelo into his new outfit. "I got you these heels. Black matte finish. They won't be so

noticeable. One minor benefit, we never have to shave again."
Both men chuckled. Soon, Peter pulled back the curtain so
Stacey and the others could see how her boyfriend looked.

"Wow. You look great," she exclaimed, repeating it
three times so he could understand her. He wore long blue
jeans that mostly covered the matte heels and a man's plaid
shirt. A fancy belt buckle encircled his fourteen-inch waist. His
pronounced bosom and knee length, thick and wavy black hair
suggested otherwise, ignoring the tiny waist and heels. Still,
Arcangelo felt more like himself since this whole mess began.

In contrast, the three women wore matching knee-
length dresses and matching heels, different colors, naturally,
since all four looked identical, except for their hair color. After
exchanging compliments, Dr. Gisa entered and explained, "I
hate to do this, but it is time for the interrogation with the top
brass. Everyone wants to hear all about everything you've
witnessed. You'll get to meet the boss man, the leader of the
entire Freedom Alliance, Alfonso Vega. Mind you, he was also
once a UFBMD man. General Kelly Kay Knight will be there
too and a number of other big wigs. Come on. This way to the
GD auditorium." She and Dr. Michelle led the small party out
of the medical facility to a waiting shuttle that took them to
GD headquarters in Malagena.

They sat around a set of tables arranged in a giant
square formation. Alison and Peter sat beside the four, serving
as translators as needed. First, they were introduced to
Alfonso Vega, a middle-aged man who looked like a stunning
UFB woman wearing a professional woman's outfit. His thick,
wavy brown hair was also knee length, but he had a disarming
smile and exuded supreme confidence. The two doctors sat on
his side along with several other normal men. Major Lu Ann
and General Kelly Kay Knight, a short haired, blonde mature
woman sat across from them, along with six other military
figures, whose names became lost in the confusion. Finally,
Miss Alis Anrhod sat beside Alfonso.

After the many introductions, Alfonso began the
meeting. "Welcome to Scorpi-C."

A shocked Major Lu Ann interrupted him. "That one!
She's a robot, not a woman!" She pointed to Alis, and rising to

defend the group from an attack. However, few others seemed surprised.

"Yes, of course she is, major. Let me explain. We here represent my inner circle of the Freedom Alliance. Alis is an ancient humaniform robot and has been instrumental in helping us these many years. She and her kind, along with a race of telepaths, helped humans put an end to the robot wars a half millennia ago, after which she and her kind vanished from history. Actually, she and her kind have been lurking in the background helping us humans when they could. Without her help, we would not be here today. There would be no Freedom Alliance. I'm sorry to have sprung her on you, major. My fault. I forgot you didn't know. Please, keep her identity a secret."

"I read about that in my history classes," Vittoria spoke up, very much surprised at this revelation. Dr. Alison quickly translated for her. "Can I ask you about that sometime?"

Alis smiled, "Yes, of course, but first we need to hear your story."

Thus began a very long session, slowed down by the constant need to translate what the four were saying. Only a few could actually understand them. Stacey and Vittoria found it quite interesting, in that there seemed to be three very different groups here, each keenly interested in one of the three aspects of their adventure. Naturally, the two geneticists were primarily interested in the research of Dr. Franks and just what he'd accomplished. Here was a gigantic breakthrough in genetics. On the other hand, most of those present weren't interested in those details. Many were keenly interested in the robots and their attack tactics, particularly using Dr. Franks and his genetics to create duplicates of those in charge of planetary defense shields. Finally, a few were more interested in the little that they'd heard about why Dr. Black or Thanos was so intent on destroying the human race. More than half of the long session was spent discussing the attacking tactics and potential strategies being used by the robots.

When the meeting finally ended, Alfonso asked the four to stick around for a few minutes. Once all but Alison, Peter, and Alis had left the auditorium, Alfonso explained, "Again, let me welcome you to Scorpi-C. First, I've taken the liberty to confiscate all of funds in your world's accounts that we know about. I will open up accounts for each of you tomorrow and deposit equal shares for you. I can say now that it looks like each of you will inherit around five hundred million credits. I know that it paltry compared to the funds that must have once resided on your world, but that's all that was in off-world accounts." The four shrieked. This was unreal.

"Next, I would like to offer you the chance to settle down here on Scorpi-C, to attend the schools of your choice. Miss Zeta certainly should finish high school. We have many fine academies for advanced studies as well. There are many former UFB women and UFBMD men on our world and many are or have attended our academies. In fact, our world has accepted tens of thousands of UFB women and UFBMD men immigrants, providing a safe haven for them. I also suspect you might also wish to join in the fight against these inhuman robots. Major Lu Ann has told me that she is ready to accept you on her ship to help in the fight. Meantime, Dr. Alison and Peter wish you to share their home until you can get settled in. Oh yes, Vittoria wanted to ask Miss Alis some questions. Go ahead, Vittoria."

Alis spoke instead, "Perhaps you and I could have a private chat tonight, Vittoria. No need for a translator. I readily grasp your speech."

"I'd like that," Vittoria replied, relieved she could have this incredible opportunity to talk to one of the ancient humaniforms and in private.

Later that night, she got her chance when Alis dropped by. Alis began by saying, "We all were extremely alarmed to hear that it is the humaniform Thanos who is behind these attacks. He was thought to be destroyed in the nuclear bombing of his world of nova over five hundred years ago. Somehow, he's come back, and we're unable to fathom why he is so intent upon destroying the human race, which he once protected. Our only clue is that he saw humans annihilating his world of novas."

"Novas? Are those the hermaphrodite UFB people?"

Vittoria asked, unsure of their exact designation. Her history books were confusing.

"Yes, they looked much like UFB men and women today, except that each had dual reproductive organs. The distinction between men and women didn't really exist with them."

"So you and this unknown race of telepaths put an end to them?" Vittoria asked.

"Yes, we did. Only a telepath can tell one of us humaniforms from a human. I hadn't met Major Lu Ann before today. Hence her outburst. Anyway, the telepaths were able to locate the rogue humaniforms and robots."

"So why did you all just vanish from history?"

"It was a wise decision. By then, humans had good reason to hate us. For everyone's sake, we went into hiding. You see, we don't age. I've looked like I do for nearly six hundred years. That alone causes humans to fear us."

"But aren't robots programmed not to harm humans?" Vittoria asked.

"Originally, yes. However, somehow Thanos must have found a way to reprogram them and himself. We have no idea how he could have done that."

The two chatted for a while longer before Vittoria asked, "Say is there any real value in being a student of history and perhaps archaeology? You see, as a UFB woman, that was about all I could manage in school, but now I wonder if there is any use in continuing that."

"I'm the wrong person to ask that, but I can say we're entering a very dangerous time. If the human race survives this, future generations need to know truly what has happened. So many of the history accounts are what the writer imagined happened and not what actually happened," Alis replied from five hundred years of firsthand knowledge.

"Thanks."

While Alis and Vittoria were in Kathy's bedroom having this chat, Arcangelo and Stacey were in Alison and Peter's dining room by themselves. Alone for the first time, Stacey said slowly and carefully, "Arcangelo, please marry me as soon as possible. So much has happened and the future so, well so screwed up, that I want us to be together now."

"Really? Wow. Okay. I'll ask Peter how we can do it. Say, we can even have wedding rings now, not like before," he replied several times, making sure she understood. They hugged. Then, he grimaced. He was too embarrassed to try to explain. "Look at me now," he said twice, lowering his pants. Stacey gasped. He was a she now. Until now, she'd not given much thought to the genetic modification Dr. Franks had done. Now so much made sense. Arcangelo's body was just like her own, a duplicate of Miss Galaxy Tessa.

Swallowing hard, Stacey said, "Please marry me still. We'll make it work. I love you, Arcangelo." He threw his arms around her, holding her tightly.

The next morning, Major Lu Ann paid them a visit to Alison and Peter's home. "Sorry to break in on you like this, but the war council has tasked General Kelly Kay and me with a new project. We are supposed to return to the conquered worlds and try to find out what the robots took from them. What are the robots really after? Since you four are the only known survivors from Delgar-C, it would help us if one or more of you would consider coming along and lending us a hand with this."

Arcangelo spoke up first, "Hey, anything we can do to help stop these vicious robots—count us in. Er, first Stacey and I want to be married, and we should get some more clothes. We can't keep on wearing the same ones."

"Right," Stacey agreed, "but honestly, Zeta ought to continue her education."

Zeta piped up, "Kathy wants me to go to school with her on the ship, and I want to, but I don't know where it is."

Major Lu Ann chuckled. "Don't worry. We're laying in supplies for a long voyage and that'll take a few days. I'll send Captain Janine and Engineer Fel over here to help you get the things you will need. On behalf of the Hyperion and the Freedom Alliance, thank you for volunteering. As far as getting married, I would be honored to do it for you."

Later on, Janine and Fel arrived. Janine said, "Hi Alison. The major says they're coming with us on this trip, so we're to help them get what they are going to need." "Hey, can I have one of those big guns like you carry?" Arcangelo asked her, a large, but invisible grin, on his face.

"Sure big boy," Janine replied grinning. "They are called the MK40, developed by a UFBMD man. Yes, he had no arms, but he designed it. It shoots a killer hole through personal defense shields no less. It's the only thing that will stop a CAM in one shot, guaranteed."

"Hey," Fel broke in, "maybe he would prefer some cool explosives. You know, blow the tin cans up. I'm your demolitions expert and prime fixer-up. If it's broke, Fel can fix it."

Torn between the two choices, Arcangelo sighed, "Big gun. I might hurt someone blowing things up. I have to protect my Stacey and her sisters from the robots. We're going to be married tomorrow. Major Lu Ann is marrying us."

"Congratulations. Both of you. Coolest," Fel responded cheerily.

"Right, good going. Come on. Let's go shopping. Good thing we've an unlimited expense account, compliments of the major," Janine declared.

"Mom, you go. I'll watch James," Kathy volunteered, though she really wanted to go with Zeta and Alison.

As they headed out the door, Janine added, "For sure, you need to get a dozen sets of clothes and at least a half dozen pairs of shoes. Some should be work clothes too. We'll get weapons and defense shields for you after that."

Hours later, his eyes sparkling, Arcangelo exclaimed, "Now Stacey, this is more like it! Bring on the robots!" Proudly, he swung his new MK40 around.

Janine laughed and teased, "We're going to have to practice first, big boy." Stacey relaxed knowing Arcangelo had his self-respect back.

Peter piped up, "Tomorrow, Janine, we'll take him to the firing range."

***

The day before the Hyperion and Arc Royal were due to embark on their next assignment, Alfonso held an emergency meeting of his defense council. Another world had been attacked. In a very serious tone, he began the meeting, "I've

75

bad news. 19-Velos-B is under attack by the robot fleet. In the wee hours this morning, my comm officer received this emergency transmission from GD headquarters in Marme, their capital city. A foreword: I believe they used the same tactics as they did on 5-Halcynith-C." The outcries died down, as he dimmed the lights a little, and the recording began playing on the large screen of the auditorium. The men spoke Russian, and Alfonso cleverly had the recording over-dubbed by an English translator. It began with a frantic plea for help from their comm officer. In the background, images were clearly visible on ten monitors, covering different areas of Marme. Amid the background noise of bio agent attack warning sirens and red lights, the man pleaded for assistance. Somehow, their planetary defense shields were taken down just as the skies filled with the familiar one-man fighters and the deep space transports that delivered the toxic agent. One monitor showed briefly a yellowish gas being released from the belly of one of those transports. Another monitor showed an image of the world and the flight paths being taken by the transports. Clearly, the intent was to completely saturate the air above the entire world with the bio genetic agent.

Some ten minutes into the recording, some of the men visible in the background monitors slumped over, falling into comas. The caller also finally succumbed, passing out, though leaving the channel open. Thus, the viewers were able to see additional details of the enemy ships as the minutes passed. At the fifteen-minute mark, Alfonso turned it off.

"It is clearly obvious that these robots are proceeding to annihilate further worlds," Alfonso said tensely. "Delgar-C and 5-Halcynith-C are not just isolated cases. I'm bringing up a 3d image of our section of the galaxy. The sector boundaries are marked in green. Each of these three worlds is noted on the projection by bright red dots. At this time, the attacks are confined to rim sectors. But with this current attack, as you can clearly see, they are moving inward towards the hub."

Someone spoke up, "Ah, that's a good thing. They aren't heading our way."

Another added, "Probably because they know we have a mighty combined space fleet!"

"Don't count on that. Unleashing the bio genetic agent takes space fleets out of the picture," another countered.

Diego, Alfonso's second in command, spoke up, "I'm not sure why they're going after 19-Velos-B. It is an arid world. Population barely five hundred million."

Another pointed out, "But it exports fuel for space fleets. Now the robots will have an unlimited supply of fuel and the needed refineries."

"Don't they have any space fleet of their own?" someone asked. "Won't they be counterattacking?"

Alfonso answered that question. "From what we know of this world, they have two heavy cruisers and nine light cruisers. Presumably, they are flying CAP over their world and are battling the robot ships as we speak."

The original man spoke up, "It's in the Gilgalad Sector. I say we send a large part of our combined fleet there at once. Knock out many of their ships. For sure, we should bomb the planet and destroy all the refineries. Deny the enemy their key fuel source. Set them back in a major way."

Many hastily agreed with him. Alfonso cautioned, "You have a valid point. But what if they turn left? They could come straight at us. The Twillis Sector is all that lies between the Gilgalad Sector and our Abelard Sector. We could leave ourselves open to a flank attack. I urge caution."

Thus, the arguments raged. In the end, some of the war dogs agreed to send some of the Twillis Sector ships to the aid of 19-Velos-B. Two battleships, four heavy cruisers, and ten light cruisers were sent. The heavy cruisers were assigned the sole role of destroying the refineries on the planet, while the battleships and light cruisers took on the enemy fleet. While Alfonso believed this was a futile mission, he could not sway the war dogs from launching a counterstrike. At least, he was able to minimize the number of ships being sent. He assumed none would be returning.

After the meeting broke up, he asked General Kelly Kay to move her departure date up to tomorrow. "We need to find out what the enemy are looting—what they want. I feel it in my bones this counterstrike is precisely what the robots want."

"Lower our combined strength," General Kelly Kay

responded. "I agree. Still, if they can destroy the refineries there, then that may cripple the robots' plans and gives us more time. Any ideas how to counter their making duplicate copies of us and using them to turn off the planetary defense shields?"

"No, but that's my highest priority. Somehow, we must take that out of the equation," Alfonso answered.

"Whatever you do, don't put control of the shields in the hands of computer systems. We both know that they can easily be penetrated by hackers," she advised. "I don't trust computer systems."

Alfonso chuckled. "Neither do I. I've some ideas I'll explore today. Good hunting general." She saluted and departed. Now she had many orders to deliver in a very short time.

"It's on the news. 19-Velos-B is under attack!" Arcangelo exclaimed, breaking up the group's friendly chat in Alison and Peter's living room.

"Bet we ship out tomorrow!" Captain Janine responded. "Come on. Let's get packing and get ahead of the orders. If I know Major Lu Ann, she'll be calling us soon."

"Where the heck is 19-Velos-B anyway? Never heard of it," Dr. Alison asked.

Stacey spoke up. "It is a minor world in our sector, close to the border of one of the mid-arm sectors. I know because I was studying galactic navigation."

Just then, buzzers echoed around the room. Peter, Alison, Janine, and Fel's pagers went off. "Right on cue," Janine barked. "We are ordered to be ready to depart at 08:00 in the morning. Come on. Let's get them packed and their things over to the Hyperion."

"I can't believe these robots have wiped out all the people on three worlds! They are fiendish butchers!" declared Peter. "They have to be stopped."

"Wish we could see the space battle," Zeta commented the next morning. They'd arrived on the Hyperion early the next morning and been assigned their quarters. Conveniently, their cabins were on either side of Alison and Peter's quarters. Vittoria and Zeta had one small cabin, while Stacey and

Arcangelo had another, since they were now married. This gave the newlyweds a small amount of privacy on an otherwise packed ship. Having stowed their many bags, they'd gathered in Alison's larger living room, which she often used as her private electronics workshop.

"We probably will," Peter answered her. "You see, they'll be sending back live video feed from each of the ships. That way, everyone can see what happens and learn from mistakes."

Just then, Major Lu Ann's voice came over the intercom system. "Prepare for hyperspace jump in one minute."

"What do we have to do?" asked Zeta.

Peter chuckled. "Nothing. It's just an alert warning for us all. A few crew members need to handle a few actions with each jump, but we passengers don't have anything to do. Feel that little jerk? We just made the jump. We're on our way, presumably to your home world, Delgar-C."

"What will we find?" she asked.

Peter shrugged his shoulders. "Who knows?"

Chapter 5—Aftermaths

"We're in orbit above Delgar-C," Major Lu Ann's voice came over the intercom system. "Will all those of rank lieutenant and above please report to CCC at once. Thank you."

"Oh!" Dr. Alison looked surprise. "Stacey, Arcangelo, Vittoria, I'm supposed to bring you three along to the briefing too. Telepathy."

"You mean she just told you that in your mind?" asked Stacey.

"Yes. Convenient. Come on; let's go," Alison answered.

"I'll watch James," Peter added, and Alison nodded her approval.

As usual, the CCC was packed with people as the four squeezed into the room. Major Lu Ann began her briefing. "Initial reports showed one light cruiser was here along with a number of deep space transports. However, when we and the Arc Royal appeared, the cruiser made a hasty jump into hyperspace. Many of the transports are following suit as I speak. However, we must assume there are CAMs still on the ground."

"Our mission is to discover what the robots have looted from Delgar-C. Hence, we are going to approach this from four angles, making use of our four natives. First, the ship's security guards will land at the capital city Marino and examine the military aspects. Captain Janine, I'm assigning each of your squads to three other locations. One squad will accompany Arcangelo, Stacey, and Vittoria. Vittoria and one squad will check out the Academy and other schools. Arcangelo and a squad will check out the corporations and their holdings. Stacey and a squad will check out all other city facilities. The three will begin in their home city of Milano before moving out to other cities. Captain Jason and his Eagle Squadron will fly CAP over the areas the four will be searching. Thorough job. We must know what the robots are taking away from the worlds they're conquering. We'll commence action in one hour. Question? Okay, hop to it."

The transport carrying Hard Ass, Fel, First Squad, and Stacey landed close to the GD headquarters building in Milano, where Stacey's home used to be on an upper floor. Hard Ass barked, "Turn your PDS units on. Be prepared for CAMs at all times. Okay, Fel, open the bay doors. Stacey, stay behind us. Go."

Fel complied and the bay door lowered. One by one, First Squad jumped down, MK40's at the ready, quickly forming a V-shape with Hard Ass at the point. Fel and Stacey brought up the rear.

"Spooky!" whispered Stacey, as she stepped carefully onto the street. Going down the ramp in her tall heels was challenging, but now her eyes gazed at the utter vacantness of her city. A light wind was blowing, but the silence was eerie.

Just then, two CAMs came around the corner of GD headquarters, and the group got their first look at the newly designed CAMs that Thanos build out of the original CAMs developed on Ragnar-B. They still had the chicken-like feet, which kept them very stable on their feet. Their slicing and dicing arm had been replaced with a human-like appendage, but their giant 50-caliber machine gun left arm had not been modified. Their oatmeal heads had been replaced with a more human-like head, filled with more sensors. All wore a PDS around their waist, and bright sunlight glimmered off their silver outer shells. The instant the CAMs saw the humans, their left appendages opened fire, blazing away with giant shells, rather like a machine gun.

Stacey involuntarily dove for the ground, before she discovered the shells bounced off her personal defense shield. Hard Ass opened fire before the rest of her squad, firing her giant MK40 at one of the two CAMs. Stacey saw a bluish flash as the outer shell hit the shield of the CAM, but she blinked, as it penetrated, releasing the terribly destructive second charge. The CAM ceased functioning instantly, and she saw a three-inch hole straight through its abdomen. Then, the combined fire of ten others came, drilling more holes in both. "Hold your fire. Overkill!" Hard Ass barked.

"Damn, you didn't leave one for me to blow up!" Fel yelled out, bringing a grin to many faces, but she helped Stacey to her feet.

"Okay. Fan out, secure the GD building. We're going in. Fel, Stacey, on me," Janine ordered. Four men followed them inside, while six took up outer defensive positions, protecting those inside the skyscraper.

"First, we clear the building. Fel, keep Stacey here at the entrance and safe. Okay, floor to floor search," Hard Ass ordered and moved out into the lobby. Over the headsets, Fel and Stacey heard numerous "Clear's," as the five checked each room on each floor. After twenty minutes, Janine gave the all clear word, and the group began searching for clues of what was now missing.

"God, this is so weird. No one is here but us," Stacey whispered, though she didn't know why she did. "I wonder if everyone's a ghost now, haunting the world?"

Fel laughed. "Darn if I know. Come on. Let's start seeing what should be here but isn't."

Hours later, they compared notes. All the computer and comm center equipment were gone, quite noticeable to all. Mysteriously, the dried, emergency rations room was also empty. Several beds were no longer present and peculiarly no electrostatic hair machines could be found. In addition, several of the UFB women's clothes closets were bare.

Next, they headed over to GE headquarters. One block from GD, they spotted a truck piled with various items that the CAMs had been busily confiscating. The group stopped and searched the truck, adding more items to their list of missing inventory. All manner of weapons, ammunition, and PDS units were in the truck as well. Fel also found a stash of explosives and a bag of diamonds. She confiscated the explosives, at least as much as she could carry.

As they neared the GE skyscraper, three more CAMs appeared and briefly opened fire before the dozen MK40's took them out, again with a bit of overkill. "Damn these new guns are effective at close range!" Hard Ass commented.

Fel explained to Stacey, "Sure are. They were invented by a UFBMD man, if you can believe that. He's now working on a version that can penetrate a planetary defense shield."

"So armless people aren't as useless as we thought?"

Stacey asked curiously.

"Nope. They just have different ways of doing things. Use toes as fingers and voice-activated computers," Fel replied. "Come on. Let's see what they've taken from GE."

Meanwhile Third Squad led by Hammerhead Bill Sharke accompanying Arcangelo headed to check out corporation holdings. Setting down near the warehouse district, the group soon found themselves in a firefight with a dozen CAMs who were in the process of looting some heavy construction vehicles. Later, an animated Arcangelo told Stacey and the others about it. "I got three CAMs myself! This new gun drops them with one good shot! Whoopee!" They reported the loss of heavy equipment needed for construction of buildings and land preparations.

As expected, the Security Guard group, including Peter, found all serviceable space faring vehicles gone, along with the fuel. In addition, military supplies were gone, including ammunition. During ensuing days, they also could find no trace of any Fabrication Machines, and a number of advanced medical machines were missing.

Second Squad, led by Samantha, began making the rounds of educational facilities. Vittoria noticed at once many computers were missing, along with the voluminous educational databases. After a brief firefight at the Milano Academy where they dispatched three CAMs, they found the place was just now being ransacked. While the group began looking for missing items, Vittoria saw that one computer system was still up and running and found that curious. She sat down and brought up its browsing history.

"Someone has been doing exhaustive searches for specific Academy students. How weird is that?" she explained to Sam.

"How so?" Samantha replied. Such things were far beyond her area of expertise. Give me a good old mortar any day was her motto.

"Well, this particular system is the Records System. It holds the records and vital information on all students here at the Academy. What's weird is that someone did exhaustive searches after everyone was in a coma, if I have my dates right.

Now why would anyone do that? Something is not making any sense here. You all check other places. I need to see if I can figure out what they were actually doing here," Vittoria replied.

"Can't leave you alone. No telling when a CAM might wander in. I'll watch over you. The rest of you, fan out and continue searching," Sam ordered her ten squad members.

"Thanks. I'm going to rerun what they ran. As far as I can tell, this search was done the morning after the attack. As far as I know, everyone was already in their comas, excepting us three. Oh, I suppose other UFB women would also have been awake and active," Vittoria explained.

"You think one of them did this?"

"Hardly, Sam. You see, Stacey and I were about the only UFB women in the Academy. Around here, a UFB woman is a glorified sex doll, darn near helpless too. Dad," she faltered and swallowed hard and began again. "Dad, he insisted we three be more than that. He said an education is key to everything. So to be blunt, this wasn't done by a UFB woman. Let's see what they did first." She opened another window and entered the logged command.

"Interesting. They brought up a listing of the top one hundred Academy students. See, it gives their class ranking and current grade point average. Why would the robots be interested in that?"

"Dunno. I thought the robots were wiping us all out," Sam replied.

"Let's see what they did next." Vittoria continued to examine the log and to run the subsequent commands in the separate window. "Nothing more than where they were staying, either here in campus housing or at their own place, like Stacey and me. We lived with mom and dad, commuting here each day. How weird is this? Why would they want their locations?"

"Dunno. Makes no sense to me either. They were wiping everyone out. So why get the locations of the top students if you are going to vaporize them anyway?" Sam asked.

"Precisely why this is so weird, Sam. There must be

more to this than we're seeing. Perhaps, they were after more test subjects. You know, as they did with the six of us—taking us away for Dr. Franks to experiment upon. That's a possibility, but then there were only us six at his research lab."

"Maybe there is more than one research lab? Maybe he has more than Dr. Franks experimenting on humans. God, that sounds awful, doesn't it?" Sam countered.

"It does, Sam. Inhumane to say the very least. I'm going to make a printout of those addresses. Let's visit some and see if we can find out anything else," Vittoria suggested.

An hour later, the squad members joined them, reporting nothing seemed missing beyond what they already knew, such as computers. Following Vittoria's suggestion, they headed off to find some of the locations where the top students lived. She decided to stick to campus housing. There were fifty-seven on the list. Once more, everything was eerie. The once bustling dorms were entirely silent, devoid of all people. However, some birds were chirping outside. They began by searching some of the dorm rooms, but found nothing unusual, other than likely missing computers and such.

"Sure wish we could actually see what went on here," Vittoria lamented as they were about to give it up and head back to their transport.

"Hey, what about surveillance cameras?" Sam asked. "Don't they have them here? I thought I saw one in the lobby."

"Oh sure. That is necessary for the security and safety of the students. I see what you mean. Maybe we can find the videos. Come on. Let's search for the security center. Sorry, I don't know where it is. I've never been in here before," Vittoria lamented.

One of the squad members spoke up, "Hey, we came across that. Follow me." Off the group went.

"Well, I can see why the robots didn't take this stuff. It's antiquated! I had no idea security was this poor," Vittoria commented. "Okay, everyone, find a seat and see if you can bring up the video feeds." She rattled off the date and suggested, "Begin around eight in the morning. That's when the Academy records searches began."

"What are we looking for?" one asked.

"Anyone coming or going. We were all supposed to be in a coma. So anything other than nothing might be significant," Vittoria replied. Then, she realized no one had been translating for her, even though she could barely understand her own words. Telepathy, she realized—they all had it and could pick up her thoughts or intentions. She flushed and found a seat. There were a dozen different feeds, all independent of each other, a very crude system, archaic.

"Hey, at least they stored the stuff on big hard drives," one man teased them.

Another said, "Yes, it's working. Seeing nothing but four comatose bodies lying in the lobby. Nothing going on. Weird, isn't it? Looking back in time watching kids just before they are murdered and turned into dust."

"Stop being so grim," Sam chided him. "These were just kids. They didn't deserve this."

An hour passed before one bored man suddenly sat up. "Hey! Got something. Look. CAMs are entering the building!"

Everyone scooted their chairs, gathering around that monitor to watch. "I count twenty CAMs," someone volunteered. Time passed. Then, the group got the shock of the day. Some of the CAMs reappeared, exiting the dorm housing, but were carrying comatose students!

"My God! They're kidnaping students," exclaimed Vittoria. "Why? Where are they taking them?"

Sam laughed. "Well, we were sent here to find out what the robots want. Guess we found something unexpected. I think we have a bigger problem on our hands. Why are they kidnaping students and where are they taking them? I best let Major Lu Ann know about this right now." Turning to Vittoria, she added, "Telepathy."

Based on Vittoria's startling discovery, Major Lu Ann ordered a complete IR scan of the entire world, hoping against hope to discover the kidnaped students were being kept somewhere else on Delgar-C. That took a week, but turned up nothing at all. Meanwhile, the ground teams continued their searches, adding gold, germanium, and silicon to the looted items list, along with petroleum products, such as oil. Further, a number of heavy equipment manufacturing plants had been stripped of their machinery and dies.

By the end of the week of searching, Major Lu Ann had a clear picture of just what the robots were taking away from this planet. Most of the items could in some way be used to manufacture more CAMs. This was what she expected to discover, that and the obvious fuel, arms, munitions, and Fabrication Machines. The unexpected and unexplained was the missing students, along with some provisions, electrostatic hair machines, some medical equipment, and possibly some apparel. Well, she reasoned, the kidnaped students would obviously need the hair machines. Why take them and where remained a complete mystery. Dutifully, she made her report to General Kelly Kay, who relayed it on up the chain of command.

Also at the end of the week, those who were on the ground had a chance to watch the video recordings made of the counterattack on the robot fleet at 19-Velos-B. They'd heard the results, but finally got their private screening of the video. The 33rd Infantry Platoon and the civilians huddle together in a briefing room as the video ran on a large wall monitor. "Not sure I actually want to see this," Hard Ass spoke for many, "but I suppose we should see what we're up against."

It wasn't pretty. As soon as the small fleet dropped out of hyperspace above the planet, the enemy reacted swiftly. Thousands of small, one-man fighters streamed out of the donut shaped battleship, swarming all over the two Freedom Alliance battleships. Canons blazed, some hitting the smaller ships, exploding like giant firecrackers, though without any sound. There's no air to propagate sound in space. Dozens upon dozens got through, landing on the sides of the battleships. Shortly after that, the CAMs got out of their ship and began cutting holes in the sides of the hulls of the two behemoths. Decompression resulted. Of course, bulkheads were hastily sealed off and the technique would have worked had there been only a few such breaches, but after a hundred such holes, the battleships went inert, all the air shooting out into space, sometimes taking what appeared to be a body with it.

Ten minutes after the start, both battleships were gone.

The light cruisers fared slightly better and managed to get a few key hits on the donut robot battleship, causing an unknown amount of damage. The main thrust was the mission of the heavy cruisers, whose task was to destroy the fuel refineries. At least, this was partially successful. Four refineries were confirmed destroyed before the heavy cruisers became space junk, hovering dead in space above the world. There were no apparent friendly survivors, a very solemn and expensive, minor victory, if and only if the robots were counting on full production from these refineries. Alfonso wasn't so sure of that. Rather, he still believed this was a setup, that the robots anticipated such a reaction.

However, some good came from the carnage. Many now saw the urgency of equipping major fleet ships with their own planetary-strength shields, not the usual ones that prevented damaged from running into space debris or canon shots. Anything and everything had to be done to stop the one-man fighters from bringing the CAMs close enough to grapple and cut holes in the ship's hull.

A day later, General Kelly Kay ordered her two ships to go to 5-Halcynith-C and scout that captured world. "It is imperative we locate the robots' home base. Just where are they taking all their loot? Where are they using the construction equipment? What are they building? Personally, I want to know where they took the kidnaped students and why. So look sharp. Expect the enemy on the ground in force, though we suspect most of their force is now on 19-Velos-B," she explained to her commanders and Major Lu Ann. She then added, "Our job in this war has been defined by the Freedom Alliance. We are going to act as rear agents, going in after the robots attack and scout for key intelligence. I'm sure you'll see plenty of action though. This jump will see us there in four hours, but we will hold off actions until 08:00, so get some sleep."

At her morning briefing, Major Lu Ann explained, "Okay, Captain Janine, you're to take the entire First Platoon and Stacey's group to the medical complex where they were held. Your objectives are two-fold. One, recover any and all of Dr. Franks genetic research. Two, look for any clues about

88

where they took Dr. Franks, his wife, and mother." She issued other orders to the transport fleet crews. "Your job will be to fly total coverage flights while using your IR scanners to look for any other survivors. From now on, our orders will include a total IR scan of conquered worlds, looking for survivors that the robots missed. The delta wings will provide cover protection. Eliminate any remaining robot space ships. Questions? Okay, move out."

As Stacey and Arcangelo made their way down the halls to the docking bay, the members of First Platoon left them far behind. "We sure go slowly in these heels," Stacey muttered, annoyed again.

"Yeh, but it beats those awful toe shoes. With those, we could only shuffle along," Arcangelo countered. "So I'm grateful to be able to walk again. Say, do you suppose we'll find any survivors? Won't they just be mobsters and criminals? Why are we bothering?"

"I heard there are some who aren't. They make cloth. I heard that's the only export this world has. Pretty grim existence I suppose. Gosh, we are so slow," she answered, still complaining.

"Don't worry. Vittoria is behind us, and they will wait on us, dear. I have my big gun with me. Hope I can bag me some more tin cans." Stacey chuckled. It was good to hear him so alive again. She still wondered if the Landini brothers had died because they'd become so depressed and lost their will to survive. That nagging thought refused to be forgotten.

"Well, this place has been cleaned out!" Hard Ass barked. They'd landed without incident and found the large medical research facility abandoned and stripped of nearly everything useful. Only trash littered the floor.

"I guess they didn't want Dr. Franks' research to fall into our hands," Stacey commented. "What now, captain?"

"Well, search everywhere. Hell, look at the trash. We need to find a clue about where they took Dr. Franks. Perhaps, they left behind something that will give us an idea," she suggested, but she telepathically relayed the dismal finding to Major Lu Ann, although the situation was visible via the live streaming video from her and her team.

Hard Ass then ordered, "Fel, Sam, take Second Squad and go search Dr. Franks' deep space transport. It's still here."

"On it," Fel replied.

Just then, the 50-caliber cannons of the CAMs opened up on the backs of the large group, just beginning to fan out to search the facility. They were in the main lobby. Two heavy shells hit Stacey in her back, stopped of course by her PDS, but the concussion sent her sprawling onto the debris-littered floor. Several others also were knocked over by the force of the impacts so darn close. The two men who had been left outside had been taken by surprise and temporarily stunned by the physical blows of the CAMs. Again, their PDS kept them alive, just knocked out by the immense strength of the robot arms.

Arcangelo whirled around and began firing at the nearest CAM. Within seconds, thirty other MK40's fired, total overkill. The two CAMs ceased functioning with many gaping holes in their bodies. "Outside. Third Platoon, secure our perimeter. Check on the two we left there," Hard Ass barked.

Shortly after that, she saw several of them pulling the unconscious pair inside, while yelling for their medic, Jascar. "Hey Bite Me, over here!" He rushed to check on them, while Arcangelo helped Stacey to her feet. "Hard Ass, there is a whole bunch of tin cans coming our way," Hammerhead yelled, the last to step back inside.

"Third Squad, set up a defense line here. Keep that low wall between you and them. Shit! What the hell was that?" Hard Ass yelled above the loud explosion. The building shook.

"Hell, they are shelling us with artillery!" Samanta called out the obvious, as part of the flat roof suddenly caved in, causing many to dive out of the way. Hastily, Hard Ass got her squads arranged, using walls as partial cover.

Boom. Another volley of shells detonated, knocking out the entire front wall. Shattering glass flew in all inward directions, but the group was protected from that by their PDS units. As the smoke and dust cleared, they saw the enemy tin cans. Dozens of them were lined up, marching towards them. In the back two artillery batteries were reloading. Worse, two CAMs were setting up a Shadow Maker further back, obviously aimed at the building!

"Sam, mortar fire on that Shadow Maker now! Fel, RPG that Shadow Maker. First Squad, concentrate your fire on the tin cans reloading the artillery guns. The rest of you, take out the incoming tin cans!" Hard Ass barked. Stacey crouched down and covered her ears. She didn't have a gun, nor did Vittoria, who also followed Stacey's lead. The noise was deafening!

Swoosh! Smoke and noise marked the trajectory of Fel's RPG shot, followed by a loud explosion. "Bull's eye!" Fel yelled enthusiastically above the din. She'd hit the main Shadow Maker dish, rendering the entire unit temporarily useless. Thump! Boom! Big boom! Sam's mortar began firing. She and her two-man crew began dropping and firing shells as fast as they could, while Hard Ass provided slight corrections. While they didn't actually drop the CAMs handling the artillery batteries, the mortar shells created enough craters in the ground around the cannon that both units tilted at crazy angles, removing them from the battle.

The many rounds of MK40 fire roared loudly inside the confines of the medical building. However, even dozens of CAMs couldn't stand up to these deadly rounds, which pierced the robots' PDS units and then blasted small holes in their bodies. While some holes didn't affect critical components, others did, and one by one, the CAMs began shutting down, waiting repairs, which in this case would never come.

Five minutes later, the firing ceased. "I can't hear anything! What's happening?" yelled Stacey.

Hard Ass laughed. "We got them all. Okay, count off. Any one hurt?" Everyone was accounted for, but ten had suffered cuts from the glass. Several had puncture wounds in the soles of their feet from the glass. As soon as she knew the status of her platoon, she ordered, "First Squad, fan out. Secure our perimeter. Second Squad, check the rear. Fel, make sure those CAMs never function again. The rest of you who aren't waiting on Bite Me to patch you up, get back to our search. Third Platoon, go check out Dr. Franks' transport."

Boom! Boom! More explosions rattled the building. As First Squad scrambled out the front of the building, one yelled back, "The transport. They blew it up!" More MK40 gunfire followed, then silence. "CAMs are history, Hard Ass," yelled another.

"Arcangelo, come give me a hand. Time to prepare some boom-booms of our own," Fel suggested. Together, they began planting explosive charges on each of the CAM hulks, dozens of them. "When we're ready to leave, one flip of this switch," Fel explained, "and boom. Nothing worth salvaging from the tin cans. Scrap metal."

"Got'cha," Arcangelo replied. "Makes sense. They can't be repaired to come at us again. Good thinking, Fel."

"Vittoria and Stacey, come check out the remains of the transport," someone hollered at them. Together, they made their careful way over to it, stepping around the debris. "Take a look at the blown up stuff. Looks like medical things to me," one man suggested.

"Yes, these are the cots and bedding we used, I think," Stacey agreed. Now several hands helped move the debris around, digging what they could out of the blown up mess that was the loaded transport.

"No sign of anything useful," Vittoria pronounced, "just bedding and the like. None of this junk is his research equipment or stuff. Sorry."

Hard Ass came up, overheard her, and sighed. "So much for clues. We're striking out. Damn. I hate missions that don't succeed." Several others chuckled.

Stacey stood back and looked at the mess and twisted metal that once had been Dr. Franks' deep space transport. Then, it struck her. "Say, we might get a clue from the ship's nav system."

"How's that?" Hard Ass asked.

"I studied galactic navigation some. Suppose they used this transport to move other things and this was to be their last run," Stacey explained.

"So?" Hard Ass asked, curious where this was heading. Could this unlikely civilian have a bright idea?

"Well, if they used it to make other flights somewhere, then the nav system will have those coordinates stored in its log or perhaps even in its display menu. I know it's destroyed, but maybe we can find out something that way," Stacey finished.

"Coolest. Okay boys, you heard her. Find its nav system or the pieces of it," Hard Ass ordered. A half hour of searching turned up the navigational computer, but it was partially attached to the main console and very badly damaged. "Carry it to the transport. Maybe Alison can work her magic on it."

"Can she make it work again?" asked Stacey, who thought the unit was beyond repair and that her idea was moot.

Janine laughed. "That woman can make anything electronic work. I've seen her make a whole new long distance comm center out of nothing but scraps! Saved our collective asses too."

Just then, she received a recall message from the Hyperion and passed along the order to pack up and depart. After everyone but Fel and Arcangelo were on board their three transports, Fel said, "Hey, you want to press the magic button?"

"Wow! You bet. Thanks," he replied enthusiastically, taking the device from her. "On three. One. Two. Three." Dozens of resounding blasts shredded the shells of the inert CAMs.

Fel looked and declared, "Scrap metal. Good riddance. Come on. They are waiting on us." A very pleased Arcangelo made his slow way up the bay ramp.

Once on the Hyperion, the flyboys and the grunts began exchanging stories. Around the world, the delta wing fighters ran into a dozen of the one-man fighters and a dogfight began. Killer Diller shot down the most, five, but One Shot was right behind her with four confirmed kills. Of course, that the platoon eliminated dozens of the CAMs was also interesting to everyone else as well.

Stacey was surprise to hear Major Lu Ann summoning her alone to the CCC. Nervously, she reported in, guessing she was in trouble because she wasn't armed and the CAMs shot at her. "Ah, Stacey. I wanted to thank you personally for your bright idea of salvaging Dr. Franks' nav system. I heard it's in pieces, but I've a lot of faith in Dr. Alison. Give her some time, and she'll extract whatever is in it. So don't worry about not being a combatant. Your insights are why you and Vittoria are tagging along with Captain Janine."

"Er, thanks. I wish I could do more. Maybe I can help Alison with the nav system."

"Sure thing. Go get cleaned up and pay a visit to Alison's living room. The unit was taken there, and she's already looking it over. That is all," Major Lu Ann replied, dismissing her. Heels clicking on the metal floor as she left, Stacey felt both pleased and comforted to know that she had a role to play in all this.

Curiosity struck, long before she reached her own cabin next to Alison's. She just had to see what was going on. Knocking, Dr. Alison invited her in, and she found Dr. Alison in the living room. All chairs were stacked in a corner and a table now sat against the wall. A bank of fluorescent lights hung over it. Already, Alison the nav system detached from the main panel portion. That piece of junk lay in a corner waiting to be recycled.

"Great idea of yours," Alison said. "Bet there is information in the memory banks of the unit. The trick will be getting to it."

"But it looks so damaged," Stacey commented.

"True. It would take considerable repairs to be operational again, but that's not what we need. The solid-state memory bank is intact, and we just have to get at it and hack into it. Going to take me a few days, but I'm sure I can do it. You can drop by and lend a hand, if you want, but I expect you don't know much about electronics."

Stacey laughed. "Nope. I'm afraid I wouldn't be much help. Still, I'm curious to know what destinations are in there. Maybe we will get lucky." Alison smiled.

***

"Well, we did get lucky this time," Major Lu Ann began her briefing two days later. "Thanks to the many IR scanners on all the transports of the Battleship Arc Royal, we actually have picked up traces of two survivors that the robots missed. From the map on the monitor, you can see that they are on the edge of a remote village in the foothills of those mountains. So our task is to send out a rescue party and bring them back to the Hyperion. With all the CAMs still around, I'm sending out the entire platoon but with six delta wing fighters flying cover for you. Go get them, captain." Janine saluted and headed off to round up her platoon, adding Stacey, Vittoria, and Arcangelo to her group.

"So what do we know about the survivors, captain?" asked Samantha, as Captain Janine briefed her platoon on their new assignment.

"Well, the two red images on the scanner appear near the edge of a remote village. Looks to be in a hilly area close to some mountains. Then, the two disappear entirely for a time," she replied.

"So what does that mean? Alive and then dead and then alive again?" asked Sam, somewhat confused.

"Best guess is that they have some hiding place, which blocks the IR scanners. Probably why the robots didn't find them," Fel surmised from what she'd heard. "Takes some dense material to block heat signatures. A house wouldn't, so it must be more significant than that."

"Hiding in basements?" Sam suggested.

"No good. Scanners would still pick them up, only fainter," Fel countered. "Underground might be the answer. If there are mountains nearby, maybe they are hiding in some caves. That would do the trick."

"Any resistance expected?" asked Hammerhead. This, he thought, was a far more important question.

"Damned if we know for sure," Hard Ass replied. "Scouts from the Arc Royal reported seeing a couple of CAMs not too far from the village yesterday, but it's anyone's guess if they are still in the area. Suit up. Be prepared for extensive combat, just in case. Major wants these survivors brought back alive. We take off in fifteen minutes."

Two hours later, three transports accompanied by six delta wings led by Killer Diller and One Shot finally located the village. From the air, it looked entirely rural. As they drew closer, flocks of sheep grazed on the green, but steep hillsides south and west of the village, cradled against the rising mountains to the east. Killer Diller called in, "All clear of CAMs right now. Go for landing. We got your butts. Out."

The three transport pilots circled the village, once home to perhaps two hundred people, assuming four to a home, though these were crude homes compared to what they were used to seeing. "Circle around again," Janine ordered. "We need to get oriented right so we can go to the last known location where the red images were spotted. There, that's it. Got it. Take us down."

A minute later, the transports sat down, stirring up small clouds of brown dust. A dog barked. Other than that, utter stillness greeted the soldiers as they charged down the bay ramps and took up their defensive positions ordered by their squad leaders. Stacey, Vittoria, and Arcangelo were the last ones down the ramp, not because they were civilians, but because of their slow speed. Six-inch heels couldn't compete with combat boots.

Third Squad and Second Squad fanned out, securing the village, while Hard Ass and the others headed for the house at the edge of the village. "At least, the streets are paved," Stacey commented. As they reached the home, they could tell it was rather large, compared to the other homes. A sign over the front door was written in Russian, the language of the inhabitants. One of the soldiers called out, "Says Vitkof Orphanage."

"Okay, let's knock first. No need to scare them if they are inside," Hard Ass ordered. Hearing no reply, they entered. "Clear" echoed around the large home for a minute as the squad quickly searched the place. Someone called out for Hard Ass to come to the kitchen, so they congregated there.

"Stove's hot. Someone's been here this morning. Stuff's out on the table," Fel pointed out the obvious. "Wonder where they went?"

"Okay, outside. Fan out. Look for signs, trails, anything. We're looking for caves, mines, something underground where they can hide from the IR scanners and the CAMs," Janine ordered.

"Over here," Hammerhead called out. "Got us a trail leading into the hills. Been used recently. Footprints. Women's heels most likely."

The group joined him, and Stacey commented, "Looks

like the heels we used to have to wear." The prints showed small toes, triangular with the distinctive tiny spike heel almost at the base of the triangle at the back of the toes. "UFB women."

Vittoria spoke up, "Now this makes sense. Look, it was us UFB women who were not affected by the bio genetic agent attack. We didn't go into comas and were able to rescue our boyfriend who were. This makes sense. Must have been two of them living out here, though I can't imagine why. My sisters and I would never have allowed ourselves to live here. UFB women on our world were prized sex dolls, as awful as that sounds. Obviously, we are more than that."

"Fan out. Keep sharp eyes open for tin cans," Hard Ass barked her orders. "Let's follow the tracks." Arcangelo admired how the three squads always seemed to know the optimum way to deploy. Third Squad headed off to the right, making use of a small ridge line for cover, while Second Squad flanked off to their left.

The rest followed the trail, which led to an abandoned mine about a quarter mile from the village, a large black hole in the side of the ridge. Off to the right and left of the path and entrance, talus slopes slid down the ridges, like some slippery glacier, while sheep grazed on the hardy grasses here and there along the trail. The flanking squads took up outside defensive positions, while the rest stood at the dark entrance.

"Best not to surprise them," Hard Ass suggested. "Hello. Anyone inside this old mine? We're here to rescue you." When she stopped talking, an eerie silence replied. Then they heard a soprano voice nervously calling out.

"Please, don't kill us. Don't shoot," the voice said, but the language spoken was a Russian dialect. Those with telepathy understood the intention being spoken, but the others only heard unintelligible words.

"I think she might be speaking some kind of Russian. I had to learn a bit of it in school while studying galactic navigation," Vittoria whispered. "Does anyone here speak it? I only do a little."

No one did, but Janine hastily explained via telepathy, they got the intention behind what was said. She added, "Go ahead and say something to them. I know. It will sound garbled because of your lip plates, but see if they can speak any other language. If not, we'll get the translator boxes out."

Vittoria did her best. Speaking slowly and repeating it several times, she said, "We are here to rescue you from the robots. We won't hurt you. Please come out or let us come in. Do you speak other languages?"

In broken English, the voice replied, "You have awful accent. Barely get you say. Some English. You save us?"

"Yes, we are here to save you," she replied in English several times. Just then, the two survivors appeared in the dim light, moving slowly towards them and the entrance, shuffling along very carefully on their toe shoes, rather like a pair of penguins. One appeared to be a grown woman, while the other was perhaps in her teens, but both were UFB women, but dressed in rather plain cotton dresses, now rather dirty. Each was wrapped in very colorful cloaks, burnt red, but with bright blues, yellows, and greens in block designs, quite artistic.

"Soldiers?" the older one said. "Don't shoot. I UFBMD man. My UFB young woman daughter. I Alex Turchenko. She Tasha. We independent. Where metal men go?"

"I'm the only one who speaks a bit of Russian. I'm Vittoria. We're from the cruiser Hyperion. We came to rescue you from the metal monsters."

"Good. Good. Bad machines. Killed lots. Shadow Makers. Like see on news. Many dead," he replied in his broken English. "Can take us to city? Be safe there?"

"I'm sorry Alex. You and Tasha are the only ones who survived. Well, mostly. My sisters, our boyfriends, and I were here too at a medical research lab and got rescued some time ago. The doctors can regrow your arms and fix up your feet like ours."

"Oh no. No. I UFBMD man. She UFB young woman. One day, nice executive fall love with her, marry her, give her fine home. One day, nice normal woman want me to give her genius sons. No one want me if not UFBMD. No one want Tasha if not UFB woman," he pleaded. "No worry. We independent. No need helpers. Do need hair machine."

"Okay. Come on. Captain Janine wants us to get back to

her transport and to safety on the Hyperion," Vittoria said slowly several times.

"Your gold lips look good, but hard to understand. We come," he replied. Slowly, the pair headed down the path to their village home, though obviously the others were bothered by their very slow pace. For once, Vittoria, Stacey, and Arcangelo weren't holding the others up, which brought an invisible smile to their faces.

An hour later, they arrived on the Hyperion. Major Lu Ann was there to greet them. She fastened a translator box around Vittoria's waist and adjusted it. "There, now they can speak in their language, and it will translate for you. Vittoria, I'm assigning you to be their host. They can stay in your cabin for now. Zeta might like the company of someone her own age besides Kathy. Find out their story and see what genetic cures they desire."

"Yes, major. Thanks. Alex, Tasha, follow me. You get to stay with my little sister and me. She's sixteen, but looks lots older. Long story." The three headed off down the hallways, heels clicking on the steel flooring.

"Captain Janine, well done. Now, I'm afraid it's back to the surface. I need you to continue to see if you can ascertain what the robots took from this world. It can't be much from what little we know about this backwater world," the major ordered.

By the time that Vittoria got to her cabin with the two rescued natives of 5-Halcynith-C, Zeta and Kathy, alerted to the situation, were already there and had brought lunch trays for everyone. Each also had a translator box around their waists. The major had foresight. After brief introductions, Zeta said, "Do you want me to feed you, Tasha?"

"Oh no. I am independent UFB woman. No one ever helps us," Tasha replied.

Alex explained, "You see, we have always had to do everything for ourselves. Bathe, dress, eat, and clean our rooms. I weave cloth, and our matron sells them. She also sews them into our cloaks for us."

"Incredible. We were UFB women once and did a lot of things on our own too, but not everything," Zeta exclaimed.

They watched as the pair slipped off their heels and used their feet and toes like hands and fingers. Satisfied that they were managing, Vittoria asked them about themselves, including their parents and relatives, particularly if they had some who lived on other worlds.

"No, we were born here. I don't know who my biological parents are. I think I was three when I was living in an office suite. Probably GD headquarters, but I'm not sure. I think I was four when they sent me to our village to live at the orphanage. The matron wisely insisted I do everything for myself, though she told me much about what a UFBMD was, but later, I learned more when I studied with the computers. The metal men took away our computers."

"Tasha isn't actually my daughter. Someone dropped her off at the orphanage when she was two. I was just thirteen and so like her. Anyway, I became her father and taught her how we must do things. Tasha also studied with the computer."

Tasha broke in, "But you're really my papa, papa. I don't want any other papa."

He smiled. "I know, little pumpkin. We must explain, so these kind people can help us and not make a mistake. Perhaps they will help you find a nice man to marry."

"And you, papa, a nice normal woman who wants genius sons," Tasha added. "Don't forget that, papa, but I don't want to leave you."

"I know, little pumpkin." Alex chatted for quite some time before he asked for Vittoria's story. "Now you know me. We want to know you." She smiled invisibly and began telling the two her own long story, far more intriguing than theirs.

Alex was the same height as Vittoria, compliments of the genetic modifications. He had lovely light brown hair, wavy and falling to his knees. Like all UFBMD, his face was perfect in all ways for a *woman*, but his bosom was quite large, just as Vittoria's once was. His feet were malformed, just as hers had been, forcing him to wear the toe shoes. In fact, he looked like any normal UFB woman, except he was male.

Tasha was the same height, but was still developing. She'd become a young woman, and her bosom was already filling out, now as large as a normal adult woman. However, her hair was soft and golden. The gentle waves in her knee length hair looked as if it was made from pure gold, quite shiny. Her smile, disarming. While Zeta looked fully mature, though she was only sixteen, fourteen-year-old Kathy looked much like Tasha, but her hair was quite blonde. Hence, Tasha took an instant liking to Kathy, but was more reserved with Zeta, seeing her more as an adult.

Finally, following the major's orders, Vittoria began to find out just what cures the pair desired. Tasha spoke up, "But we don't need any. We are fine. I am a perfect UFB woman. If I get arms and my feet fixed up, then I won't be a UFB woman. No man is going to fall in love with me then."

Kathy began laughing. "Tasha, that's not true. We look gorgeous, very beautiful. Wherever Zeta and I go, we can see young men gawking at us. Many young men will want to date you, but I'm waiting until I fall in love. We're still very young to be doing serious dating. Besides, there is so much we can learn first. Honestly, Tasha, staying as a UFB woman will severely restrict the number of young men who might want to date you. You see, they think having a UFB wife is terribly expensive."

"But I can do everything myself. I'm not expensive," she protested. "Oh, I see. You mean more young boys might like me. More to choose from." All three teens giggled. "Okay then. I will do it. But papa, you had better not."

"Why Tasha?" asked Vittoria, pleased that Kathy and Zeta were able to convince Tasha to get the genetic cures.

"Because no woman will then want papa. He's a UFBMD. Normal women might want him because he can give them genius sons. If he is no longer UFBMD, then his sons won't be geniuses. He looks like a woman so no woman will want to marry him. He will always be alone," Tasha explained, while Alex sat there with a flushed face.

"I see," Vittoria said.

Alex declared, "Yes, Tasha, you should get the cures. Then, you will have many more boyfriends and a better chance for a good life. I must not. I too want a family of my own. I love children, but if I'm not a UFBMD, then no one will want to marry me, and I will always be alone. I want to marry and have a family too. I will work very hard for her, make her very happy with me. As I am, this is my only chance to find a woman who wants me and have a family. I must not change or I will lose everything."

Vittoria laughed, embarrassing everyone. "Sorry. The incongruity of it all." No one grasped what she meant, so she explained. "Look, we three UFB sisters, we had three normal boyfriends before our world got attacked like yours here. When the bio agent attack came, we three rescued our boyfriends. We didn't care they'd become UFBMD men; we still loved them. You see it's a viewpoint problem between first-generation UFBMD and second-generation UFBMD."

"I don't understand you," Kathy declared, frustrated that she didn't. Clearly, the other two didn't either. Zeta, however, did.

"Our first-generation boyfriends took the drastic alterations in their bodies very badly. In fact, I think Carlo and Vino died because they no longer wanted to live like UFBMD men. At least, Arcangelo made it through the nightmare. He came back to life once he got the cures, just as Peter did. However, Alex here is a second-generation UFBMD and knows nothing else. Hence, he is content with his body, comfortable with it, knowing his sons may well be geniuses. Carlo, Vino, and Arcangelo detested the way they look, but Alex is quite accepting of it. It's his natural form."

"Oh I see," Kathy replied, greatly relieved. "Makes sense. When I got genetically modified, I truly did want to get the cures! I couldn't stand being so helpless."

"But papa and I aren't helpless. We do everything anyone else does," Tasha protested.

"I know, but that's because you grew up this way. I didn't. I was normal until a couple years ago when we got attacked and changed," Kathy explained. "I felt helpless and truly was helpless, but I admit I loved having all my blemishes and the little things wrong with my face fixed up, and having breasts to die for."

Zeta added, "I see Alex's problem too, Vittoria. You see, with Carlo, Vino, and Arcangelo, and even with Peter, we all knew them as normal boys and fell in love with the handsome fellows. Then when they were changed, we still loved them cause we knew them very well. Only their bodies looked so different. With Alex, anyone who meets him will see him as he is, a UFBMD man, one that looks like us, a gorgeous woman. Even a lesbian might not like him, since he still is a man."

"Right!" Kathy added. "Mom says it's a well-known fact that sons from normal women and UFBMD men are super-geniuses. He sees this as his biggest attraction, right Alex?"

"Yes, that is right. Such wisdom from one so young. Yes. Now you see why I must not get these cures?"

"Well, I see it and understand it, Alex," Vittoria said, "but I don't think that is wholly true. You need to meet many women. Surely, one will fall in love with you, and you, her. My life is much better since I got my arms and since my feet are partially fixed up. At least, I can walk much better now. If only we could get our lips repaired. These lip plates are awful."

"She's right. They're awful. I wanted to be a linguist and learn to speak many languages," Zeta explained. "Now, I can only barely be understood if I speak slowly and repeat everything several times. I'm crushed."

"But your lip plates—they are stunning. You both look magnificent in them. So few women ever look so good as you both do. You must have many men after you," Alex protested.

Zeta said, "Hardly. We look like freaks, and we can hardly speak anymore. I can't be a linguist now. My life is all messed up."

Vittoria added, "She's right, Alex. People think we're freaks."

Alex laughed, causing the two to flush. "It's as you say, a first-generation versus second-generation problem. You are first-generation and hate them, but if you were second-generation, you would love them, perhaps seeing yourselves as the ultimate UFB women. I read that on the Internet. Only the most elegant UFB women are able to wear them." This time, Vittoria and Zeta laughed; their smiles, invisible.

"Point taken, Alex. You're no dummy," Vittoria replied.

"Tasha and I studied much with our computer education courses, all that we could find. 5-Halcynith-C is rather limited though," Alex countered.

At this point, Zeta and Kathy wanted to give Tasha a tour, and she was eager to see the ship, never having been on one before. Alone now, Alex and Vittoria began chatting about what Alex had studied. She was very surprised to learn he knew considerable about history and ancient history, nearly as much as she did. He'd studied up on anthropology some, but gave up archaeology, figuring he'd never get a chance to do any fieldwork. The two chatted and lost total track of time. The girls returned at suppertime, rather shocking both Vittoria and Alex, in that three hours had passed in a blink for them.

This time, they ate in the mess hall. While many stared at Alex and Tasha watching how they used their feet and toes, those two watched Stacey, Vittoria, and Zeta closely, seeing how they could possibly eat while wearing the giant lip disks. After supper and back in their cabin, the young teens headed into Zeta's bedroom to chat, refusing to play Scrabble with the two adults. Zeta complained, "You don't want to play Scrabble with Vittoria. She knows all the really big words and always wins!" The girls giggled and went their way.

"Well, I know big words too," Alex countered. "Let's have a game." For the first time since she was a little girl, Vittoria lost a Scrabble game, further impressing her. Alex certainly was no dummy!

The next morning, Alex sat beside Tasha in Sickbay as she slipped into her coma. Four days later, she would awake with all the known cures. "Come on, Alex," Vittoria said. "She's under now. Let's see if we can find some clothes that fit you. There's many in storage here from before. Surely, we can find something. Then, you can come back and sit with your daughter. I'll come sit with you too."

Hours later, they found six new, but relatively fancy dresses that fit Alex, finer gowns than he'd ever had before. They also rounded up some they hoped would fit Tasha when she awoke. "Need any help changing?" Vittoria asked Alex.

"We do each other's zippers. Other than that, no. I can manage," he replied.

Curious, she asked, "Do you mind if I watch? I've always wondered how we UFB women could dress ourselves.

My sisters and I never figured out how we could."

"Sure. Just don't laugh. We do lots of wiggling and such," he said with a smile.

While he took substantially longer to dress, he did it all himself, except for the back zipper, which she handled for him. "Impressive," she stated. "Back zippers are hard for any woman with hands. Always awkward."

"Like I said, Tasha and I are independent people. We had to be. So how do I look? I've never worn such a fine dress before. Way too costly. Probably a month's wages."

"You look splendid, Alex. A knock out," she replied. "Come on. Let's check on Tasha."

Sitting beside the comatose teen, Vittoria commented, "You love her very much, don't you?"

"She is the daughter I might never have. Yes, very much. I've looked after her since she was two. Took her under my leg." He grinned, and Vittoria chuckled at his jest. In spite of everything, she found herself becoming attracted to this extremely sensitive, bright, and independent man.

As they sat there, Major Lu Ann dropped by. "How's she doing?" she asked in her mellow alto voice.

"The doctor says she's doing perfect," he replied.

"Excellent. Now then, Alex, my boss, General Kelly Kay Knight of the Battleship Arc Royal has done a search of all off world accounts belonging to those who lived on 5-Halcynith-C. She's confiscated those funds and set up an account for you and one for Tasha. Each account has around twenty-five million credits. You and Tasha will never have money worries again. Of course, if our salvage crews find other valuables on the planet below, we'll see that you both get them, as the only heirs left from your world."

"Oh my God! We're millionaires! How can we ever thank you and this general?" Alex exclaimed, overcome with joy.

"Just continue to live worthwhile lives, Alex. Now, I've got to get back to CCC." The major smiled and left Sickbay.

"I'm rich. Tasha is rich. Now we don't have to worry about how we are going to live. I'll still weave though. I can't sit and do nothing."

"I agree. We can't sit around doing nothing. That's why my sisters and I are here, helping as we can. You can too, if you want," Vittoria hinted.

"Why? That's what I want to know. Why are these robots trying to wipe out whole planets of people? Why?" he asked.

"They don't think the human race deserves to live any longer," Vittoria explained what she'd heard.

After describing what she'd heard, Alex replied, "I can see why on our world. It was full of mobsters and criminals, but everyone isn't a bad person. Why murder those who are good? I think these robots have gone insane, if a robot could do such a thing. Anyway, I would like to help, but I'm not a fighter."

Vittoria chuckled. "I'm not either. We help in other ways. Leave the fighting to the soldiers. I'm working on writing an accurate history of this robot war."

"Funny thing about history books. They always have a bias by the writer—you know—history as seen by the author or as described by the author from other writers. I think it would be ideal if we had an accurate account of this war with the metal machines," he declared.

Later when they retired for the night, Vittoria took a gamble. "Say, Alex, how about joining me in my bed tonight? Sleeping on the couch can't be very good. Besides, you can see what I look like when the lip plates are out."

"Thank you. I've been wondering what your lips actually look like, if you don't mind," he answered. A bit later, he commented, "Wow, your lip loops—they look incredible, Vittoria."

"Stacey says they are incredible when kissing, but I've yet to find out. She says when Arcangelo licks them with his tongue, it drives her mad. I'd like to find out," she hinted. An hour later, two very contented people finally fell asleep.

The next morning, Vittoria whispered to Stacey, "The trouble with love is you can't get the other person out of your mind. I'm going nuts thinking about Alex. This is nuts. I'm falling for a man whose boobs are twice the size of my own. I mean he is 54-14-44 and I'm now 46-14-44."

Stacey laughed. "Yes, but you were 58-14-44, remember? You've fallen for him, haven't you? Well, he's the only one who can beat you at Scrabble. Well, you have much larger lips than he does." The two chuckled. "Seriously sister, you couldn't go wrong with him. He keeps surprising me with what he knows and can do. Have you seen the way he dotes on Tasha?"

"Yes, she's coming out of her coma later today. I'll be there with them."

Both Alex and Vittoria were beside Tasha when she awoke and discovered her changed body. "It is so weird—having these arms and hands. I don't know what to do with them!" she gushed.

Vittoria laughed. "I know. Been there, done that. Don't worry. You'll catch on in no time. Just do as we did; watch how others use them. Writing and using silverware are the hardest to master. I'll show you. Come on. We found you whole new outfits."

A short while later, she exclaimed, "Papa, walking is so much easier now!" Noticing his new dress, she added, "Wow, papa! You look really beautiful too."

"Vittoria has found new dresses for you too," he changed the subject. After dressing in her new light blue dress, he added, "Tasha, you are more beautiful than ever!"

She was very pleased with her new look. Later on, she whispered to Kathy, "You are right. Just look at all the boys looking at me now!" Both giggled.

Kathy whispered back, "I think Vittoria is falling for your papa." Again, both teens giggled.

She whispered back, "I think that is very good. What's it like to have a mama?" Now the two had an interesting topic to chat about, though Zeta joined them, adding her feelings, though she felt the pangs of grief over their loss once more, just when she thought she was getting over it.

***

"Listen up, everyone," Major Lu Ann said firmly. She'd called another meeting in the CCC. "We have new orders. We're to go to the latest world under attack, 19-Velos-B. Advance scouts suggest there is still a heavy CAM presence there. Yes, I know. They sent in a fleet to attack the robot fleet, and they lost all their ships, but we're to go there anyway. Our mission is two-fold. First, we're to see if they kidnaped more Academy students, and if so, get any clues about where they took them and why. Second, we're to harry the robots, perhaps slowing them down. Apparently, many other Federation worlds are now taking this robot threat seriously. General Kelly Kay believes something big is in the planning stage, so we're to slow the robots down, if we can. However, if they still have a large space fleet there, we're to back off. This isn't a suicide run. Captain Janine, I've uploaded all data regarding the four Academies found on this world. Look them over and brief your personnel. We arrive there in eight hours. That is all."

"See Alex. You can help. They speak Russian on 19-Velos-B," Vittoria pointed out, showing him he could contribute something of value to the cause.

Chapter 6—A Messy Affair

"We are in orbit above 19-Velos-B," Major Lu Ann's voice came over the intercom. "Battle stations. Highest Alert." Conveniently, she had live video streamed throughout the ship so everyone could see the situation for themselves. Stacey and Arcangelo joined Vittoria, Alex, Zeta, and Kathy in Vittoria's room to watch the monitor, while Dr. Alison and Peter watched it in theirs. Of course, the soldiers watched from their locations as well.

The planet cast a reddish hue. It was an arid world, where water was rather scarce. As more of the terrain came into closer view, from this distance, the stark rock formations were picturesque. On the ground, it could well turn out to be grotesque. The first thing Stacey noticed and pointed out to the others, "Well, there's no signs of the wreckage of the two battleships and all the cruisers we lost a while back. They must have salvaged them already."

"But where did they take them? Could the robots really repair them?" Arcangelo asked.

Stacey answered, "Well, I heard from Killer Diller, Peter's sister, that their one-man fighters don't even have life support systems other than a small heater. So why not fix them? Plug the holes and it's good to go for the robots." Several cursed.

"Looks as if we're catching them in the middle of their looting operations," Arcangelo commented. Hundreds of transports were either in the air or on the ground. They even spotted some of the one-man fighters providing cover for the transports. However, most of the activity centered on the larger cities.

"How come they aren't attacking us now?" asked Alex.

"They can't see us. We're cloaked," Stacey replied. "We have a slight advantage."

Dr. Alison and Peter entered, joining them, squeezing in on their couch. Alison asked, "Are you guys seeing this? Look at all the transports. Probably looting everything of value on this world."

"We're supposed to land? There's an awful lot of CAMs down there," Peter put in.

Alison hinted, "I suspect the Arc Royal will send out a bunch of their own cloaked transports with their IR scanners looking for survivors. Probably, we'll be going down before all those scans are done though. We're to get in and out of the Academies, now that we know what to look for, thanks to you."

"You think they are kidnaping more students?" asked Vittoria.

"I'll lay odds they are. Probably using them as test subjects for further bio genetic agent warfare," Dr. Alison grumbled pessimistically.

"You should have seen us, Alex," Vittoria commented. "I certainly didn't like being their test subject!"

Zeta pointed out, "But Dr. Franks used us as test subjects, and his modifications really did help us, except we all looked identical to Miss Galaxy." Vittoria had no rebuttal to that and continued watching.

An hour later, Captain Janine got her orders, and rounded up her platoon and extras. "Okay. We hit Rostov Academy in Rostov, wherever that is. Vittoria, Stacey, Peter, Arcangelo, I want you with us. Alex, we could use your help as well, since none of us read Russian."

"I would be honored to help anyway I can, Captain. Thank you for giving me a chance to fight back," Alex replied with a smile.

"Okay. Here's how it goes. You five are in the rear, since you move drastically slower than we do and can't really run. Fel's going to hang back and help cover you, just in case. Our first action is to secure the Academy. Then we raid it, looking for the records computer." She explained in detail what they wanted to discover. "What's really important is to see if anyone has accessed the student records after the population went into comas. That's the big clue, Alex, so any help you can give us on reading the records is greatly appreciated. Remember, you don't go down the bay ramp until we've secured the academy. Okay, let's move out. Three transports are waiting."

From the side windows, they watched the large city that probably once had a population of several million come into view. On the streets, CAMs could be seen going about their looting, some carrying things back to a nearby transport. They spotted a spaceport just outside the city limits and saw a large cargo train in the process of being loaded with plunder. Fel commented, "If we could only get a tracking bug on that cargo train, I bet it would lead us to their home base."

"Forget it, Fel," Hard Ass barked. "They wouldn't let you get near it. Look how many CAMs are around it." Fel sighed.

Located in a picturesque valley, Rostov was surrounded by razorback ridges, carved by an eternity of winds into formations resembling an army of stone men, standing guard over the city. The city itself was a quite colorful, in stark contrast to the red-brown of the landscape. Rounded roofs were painted in a rainbow of vibrant colors. No pastels. Here and there tall spires rose as though defying the stone guardians on the ridges. Perhaps these were religious houses. None could say for sure. The influence of the modern corporations could only be seen at the heart of the city, where the usual glass and concrete skyscrapers rose tall above all other buildings, a reminder of the world's ties to the Federation and its corporations, which ruled even here, though perhaps not as powerfully as on more modern worlds.

At least, there were only a few CAMs around the Academy area. Many were carrying out computers and related equipment, piling the stolen material in a waiting transport. Presumably, the transport would drop the stuff off at the spaceport, where it would be loaded onto the cargo train. The three transports set down as close to Rostov Academy as the pilots dared. Still unnoticed by the CAMs, the bay doors opened, and the three squads rushed out, while Fel mustered the five slower civilians near the bay ramp, namely Vittoria, Stacey, Peter, Arcangelo, and Alex. Peter and Arcangelo carried their new MK40 guns and everyone wore their PDS units. Fel watched and waited, knowing that Hard Ass would let her know via telepathy.

The CAMs were taken by surprise. They dropped their

loads and raised their giant cannons. Six never did get a chance to fire them before the MK40's took them out, but four others managed to get off their machine gun volleys, knocking several men off their feet. Sixty seconds after they squads disembarked, the skirmish ended. Hard Ass ordered, "Third Squad, guard our perimeter, and let us know when more CAMs respond. They'll surely send in a large force. The rest, on me. We have to secure the building." As she moved into the main entrance, she sent, *Fel, bring the others. We can't read the writing. Crap.*

While Second Squad raced through the first floor, they encountered two more CAMs, but hastily dispatched them before heading up to the next floor. Finally, the slow pokes joined them. "We need to find the records department, Alex. What's that sign say?" Janine asked.

"Dorms," he answered. "Look, there's a map. Let me take a look." He shuffled over to it. "Here it is. Fourth floor. Sorry, I can't point except with my nose."

"Good going. Got it. Okay, up the stairs. They've only cleared the second floor so we walk up," she ordered. Instinctively, Vittoria slipped a steadying arm around Alex's waist as they began their climb.

He smiled appreciatively, and she whispered, "I need the steadying balance too." They heard more gunfire as they climbed, but via telepathy, Janine knew Second Squad was handling the CAMs without her guidance. Finally, they reached the fourth floor. Second squad was already clearing the sixth floor, and she ordered most of First Squad to guard the entrances to this floor, while the slow pokes shuffled around looking for the records computer system. Their task was easier than expected. Quickly, they saw all the other computer equipment had been looted, except for the main one they needed. One inert CAM nearby suggested it was still making use of student records.

At this point, Stacey sat down at the terminal, while Alex stood beside her and read off what was on the screens as she typed away. "I didn't know you could do that," he commented, as she hacked into the log system, bringing up the pages recently accessed. Soon, they had what they desired:

proof the robots were likely going after Rostov Academy students. Once again, Stacey printed out the records the robots had already accessed, specifically names and addresses, unfortunately all in Russian.

"Damn, how are we going to find anyone? We can't read the writing, and we can't read the street signs either," Hard Ass griped. "Well, come on. We need to get out of here." As they began heading back down to the lobby, this time taking the elevator, Alex suggested they look for maps of the city.

Just then, Hard Ass received a telepathic message from Hammerhead. *Lots of CAMs are on their way. Killer Diller says at least a hundred are swarming towards us.*

Set up mortars. Keep them at bay until we can get the civies onboard, she sent back. "CAMs are coming in force. Move as fast as you can!"

As the group exited the elevators, gunfire and mortar fire broke the utter stillness of the city. Moving as fast as he dared, Alex kept his eyes open, thankful for the supporting arm of Vittoria. "There, there, those look like campus maps. Grab one Vittoria," he yelled. She did so.

When they reached the main doors, already Third Platoon had engaged the enemy. A silver mound of inert CAMs now partially blocked the street. Beyond them, they could see a horde of CAMs coming at them. Hard Ass reached a decision and barked, "Carry the civies. Run to the transports!" She picked up Alex, tossing him over her shoulder, and dashed towards their transport. Others picked up Vittoria, Stacey, Peter, and Arcangelo as well, carrying them far faster than they could move in their heels.

Killer Diller and One Shot swooped down, their delta wing fighters spraying the oncoming CAMs with deadly fire. Their weapons were designed to take out the one-man fighter ships, not the robot shells, but at least they immobilized some and knocked many off their feet with the force of their cannon strikes, giving the squads time enough to dart into their transports. Once the bay doors closed, all three ships were invisible to the CAMs, who saw the humans going up ramps and becoming invisible. They halted confused, circuits attempting to calculate what was happening. The delay allowed all three transports to take off safely.

Once onboard the Hyperion, Alex, Vittoria, and Captain Janine headed for the CCC to brief Major Lu Ann. "They are definitely looking up top academy students. We have a list of those they looked up," she reported, "thanks to Alex here. Plus, he got us a campus map so maybe we can check up on some of them, except it's all in Russian."

"Excellent work. You two, go see if you can locate where some of the students live on the map. Meanwhile, I'll let General Kelly Kay know what you've found. Her people are doing IR scans right now. I'll ask them to make passes over Rostov, if they haven't already," the major replied. The three left to do as asked.

Tasha, Zeta, and Kathy joined them. "Good little pumpkin. You can help papa with this." Alex had sat down and opened up the map using his toes. Tasha took the printouts from Janine and began calling out addresses while he tried to find them on the map. When he spotted one, Janine marked it with a red circle. Given the circles and the map, she could locate the housing without having to read anything. Still, it was slow going, since no one was familiar with the city.

Hours passed, and Arcangelo and Peter brought everyone lunch trays. When the major called for a progress report, Captain Janine responded, "Sir, we've located ten addresses on the map that we can check out. Slow going."

"We're too late," the major said calmly, though there was a trace of sadness in her voice. She explained, "As far as we can tell, some students were still alive in the dorms. The initial passes over the campus showed a large number of red images. However, the last flyover showed none left, and the crew reported a number of enemy transports with Shadow Makers sweeping the area. I fear we hastened the deaths of those students."

"Damn!" Hard Ass cursed. Several others did so as well.

"This is news though, valuable news," the major continued. "Even this long after the initial attack, we know they're keeping some of the students in campus dorms alive. God knows why, but they are. This also means they're still kidnaping them. Plus, it's my guess they're likely locating their desired students and then bringing them to a central location, probably putting them on a deep space transport, departing only when it is full. So there's hope we can find and rescue a bunch. I'll keep you posted. General Kelly Kay has all available transports out combing the planet for these staging areas. Once one is located, we'll fire off a rescue mission, captain. So have your people locked and loaded. I have to go. Fel wants a word."

She rose and headed out of the cabin as Hard Ass barked, "Aye, aye sir. Best news yet. Alex, Vittoria, you best come along in case we find some and they can't speak anything but Russian. We can use our translators, but it is always best if someone is there who speaks their language."

While they headed back to the transports, Fel met with Major Lu Ann. "Fel, it's suicide to try to get that close to the cargo trains. I know how badly we want to track them, but it's no good getting yourself killed," the major refused to listen to her plan to bug the train she saw at the spaceport. Nevertheless or perhaps undaunted, Fel's mind raced down another avenue. Once the major headed back to her CCC, Fel headed to find another tracking bug. She stowed it in her pack and headed off to join the others waiting by the refueled transports.

"Hi ya. Think they're going to find some for us to rescue?" Fel asked, as she joined them.

"Lord, I hope so," Janine replied. "I can't believe we just got a whole bunch of students killed."

"Hey, it's not our fault," Vittoria spoke up. "Look, after they found the students they wanted, they were going to use the Shadow Maker on them anyway."

"Point taken," Janine said with a sigh. "Still." Her voice trailed away.

A half hour later, Major Lu Ann sent them a set of coordinates and new orders. "They just found a tight group of survivors, probably sitting inside a transport. I sent you the coordinates. It's about a mile from the Academy. Go get them if possible!"

"On it!" Hard Ass replied. "You heard her. Action!" Up the ramps they scampered, though several moved up very slowly. This time, a fourth transport went with them. Within ten minutes, Hard Ass had a bird's eye view of the situation on the ground. There was the transport sitting in the middle of the street, probably waiting for additional students or perhaps waiting for takeoff orders. A dozen CAMs stood guard, and they had an artillery battery with them. Nearby, a large pile of computers and comm equipment lay stacked neatly on the street, presumably awaiting transport as well.

"What's the plan, cap?" asked Hammerhead over the comm channel from his transport. "Take out the CAMs first?"

Janine thought hard. She hated the way these robots simply murdered the students rather than letting them fall into her hands. *If,* she thought, *we attack them directly, they will do an emergency takeoff, or they will blow the transport up. We have to be cleverer than their circuitry. They can't take off if their engines are out.* A plan formed. She opened a channel to all four ships. "Okay. First, we need to disable that transport's engines without killing those onboard. Second, we need to endure that they can't then lob artillery shells on the transport, killing the passengers. Only then can we take out the CAMs on the ground, and get the probably helpless students rescued and into our transport. So I need ideas. How can we disable those engines?"

Fel spoke up, "Boss, leave that to me. I can set a controlled charge that will take them out without harming the passengers. I'll need about ten minutes, assuming we land close enough to get to the rear of the ship quickly."

"Okay. Fel, you are on. Go get ready. Ideas on how we can take out that artillery battery before they can destroy the ship?" Hard Ass asked.

"Hey," Samantha volunteered. "Mortars. How about dropping mortar shells straight down on the battery from up here? Open the bay doors, lean over, and drop a handful of shells. They won't see it coming."

"Brilliant Sam. Get ready to do that. We'll coordinate it with Fel's attack. I want the engines destroyed at the same time as the artillery battery. Then, in the confusion, we land and take out the dozen CAMs," Hard Ass ordered.

A minute later, Sam's transport pilot reported they were

hovering two hundred feet above the artillery battery. Each pilot found a good location to land, and Hard Ass's ship landed. As it did so, Fel hopped out of the bay doors, her personal invisibility shield on full. Now Janine could do nothing but wait on Fel.

Fel landed on her feet and began running to close the distance. Purposely, she ran out of her way, stopping briefly at the pile of computers and comm equipment. Carefully, she placed her tracker bug in the pile, making sure it wasn't likely to be discovered. Then, she raced on to the transport ship. Once there, she very carefully placed her charges around the engine. That done, she raced for cover. *Okay. Charges set. Is Sam ready?*

Yes.

On three. One. Two. Three, Fel sent. Nearly simultaneous explosions suddenly broke the utter stillness of the city. The entire engine assembly of the transport dropped onto the ground. That transport would never fly again. A dozen mortar shells came falling down on top of the artillery battery. When the smoke clears, the howitzer barrels lay at peculiar angles. They too would never fire again, though one of the CAMs operating it was undamaged. The remaining transport landed, as the soldiers swarmed out, MK40's blazing away.

The CAMs acted with surprising swiftness and opened fire, this time shooting blasters at the oncoming soldiers. Once more, their PDS units saved them, and in two minutes time, the dozen CAMs were inert. As First Squad charged up the ramp into the transport, Vittoria helped Alex down and to walk as fast as he could to join them.

Language was a barrier. While their translator boxes worked, the students, some twenty of them, were so traumatized that they couldn't respond. When Alex finally stepped onboard, he saw their shocked faces. "It's all right. We're here to rescue you, get you to safety, and some cures for what they've done to you." His voice along with his appearance, just like themselves, broke the ice.

"But we can't walk anymore," one person volunteered.

Alex responded, "Let them carry you to the waiting

transport. Can they, captain?"

"You bet. Come on. Grab someone and get them to the waiting transport. Hurry up before they send more CAMs," she ordered.

Alex and Vittoria decided to ride back with the terrified and helpless victims, adding their sense of calm to the otherwise terrifying experience. Repeatedly, Alex kept saying, "It'll be all right. You're safe now. Just a few more minutes and you'll be safe. Just relax if you can."

The twenty students were still naked, but the robots had provided them with toe shoes. However, none dared to try to stand up or walk in them. Half were male, and Alex's heart went out to them.

All the way back to the Hyperion, he kept talking calmly, filling the vacuum with much needed support and hope for the future. He continued to be with them as they were helped off the transport when it landed in the launch bay, and he went with them as they were taken to Sickbay for checkups. Later on, he watched them, now partially clothed, when they were taken aboard another deep space transport bound for Scorpi-C, where they would receive all the known genetic cures.

Later that night when Alex climbed into bed beside Vittoria, she said, "I'm very proud of the way you helped all those terrified students today." She gave him a passionate kiss, and he responded in kind. Again, an hour later, two very satisfied people fell into a deep sleep. By morning, word spread of their success at rescuing the students, and Major Lu Ann received a personal thank you call from Alfonso Vega, which she relayed to everyone on the Hyperion. They'd had their first truly good day.

Within an hour of the arrival of the transport bringing the rescued students onto the Hyperion, a very large fleet of the robots suddenly appeared in orbit above 19-Velos-B. Besides the giant donut battleship, there were three other ex-Federation battleships, with their holes patched up naturally, and a host of cruisers. Suddenly, the skies over the world were filled with thousands of the one-man fighters, launched from the battleships. The Arc Royal and the Hyperion quietly jumped into hyperspace, eluding the dragnet. Obviously, the robots wanted a confrontation, but General Kelly Kay wasn't about to commit suicide as the war mongers had done before.

"Damn. I had it all worked out," Fel lamented over supper with Janine. "I planted a tracker bug on some of that computer junk outside the Academy. I figure they'll put it on one of those giant cargo trains, and we could track it to their home base."

"Hey, that's brilliant, Fel," she validated her dear friend.

With a dour face, Fel replied, "Yeh, but we've been forced out of there, so there's no way we can track that signal. I asked the major if we couldn't leave just one cloaked deep space transport behind to track it, but she said no. Even though the robots can't see our ships, since they have so many one-man fighters, they're sending them all over in formations, hoping physically to smash into our cloaked ships. So close and yet so far."

"How close do you have to be to pick up the tracking bug? How long will it keep going?" Janine asked, also annoyed they were missing a rare opportunity.

"Power cell lasts maybe six months at most. Range kind of depends. In hyperspace, maybe five miles if miles means anything there. Normally, if you have a sensitive receiver, probably a hundred miles. I had thought we'd have a transport hovering over the cargo train at the Rostov spaceport closely monitoring it, but the robots had other ideas. Ah well," Fel sighed.

"Ah well is right. The thing that has me worried is what if the CAMs get a hold of some MK40's. Then, we're as good as dead on one shot too. The PDS units won't help us much," Janine volunteered. Fel shuddered. That would be grim indeed.

Idle time. The entire following week was simply that. No action. General Kelly Kay sent back a surveillance transport, but for a week, she deemed it too dangerous for them to go back to 19-Velos-B. Many enjoyed the quiet time. The teens continued their educations, the three studying together. The soldiers enjoyed their R&R time, while Vittoria and Alex became inseparable, spending long hours talking about their lives and dreams, their romance budding.

Alison used these days to repair the nav system from Dr. Franks' deep space transport. The CAMs had done a good job blowing the ship up. The unit sustained major damage. Still, with her uncanny skill at electronics, circuit by circuit, Alison rebuilt the power supply sufficiently to gain access to the unit's memory card. Using a homemade substitute display, she finally activated the right circuits, bringing up the ship's navigational menu and log. She turned on her video system, recording everything that appeared on the crude replacement monitor.

Carefully, she displayed the log of the last ten flights, displaying each one and the corresponding hyperspace coordinates. Then, she displayed the menu preset entries as well. Just as the last one flashed on the monitor, her makeshift circuitry failed in a flash of smoke. "Whew, that was close, but I got it. Now to make some sense of it all."

Taking her thumb drive recording with her, she headed to CCC to report to Major Lu Ann. "I made a recording of everything in Dr. Franks' nav system. I've no idea what I have though. I need someone who knows galactic navigation to go over these coordinates."

"Well done, Dr. Alison. This might be our first solid lead." She issued orders for her navigator, her two astrophysicists, and even Stacey Grimaldi-Rossanti to come to the CCC and go over the findings with a *fine-tooth comb.* "Don't take anything for granted," Major Lu Ann explained to the small group when they arrived. "That transport was loaded with looted supplies and was going somewhere with them. We need to know where. It might be one of the preset menu items or it might be in the flights-taken log. Just be thorough. Again, thanks Dr. Alison for your brilliant salvage operation." Alison smiled and left her recording in their capable hands. Time for a long shower and some sack time with Peter. She'd been absorbed with this project for many days, and now it was her turn for some R&R.

Phil brought up a three-dimensional galactic model. One by one, the four got the destinations displayed in the hologram as bright red dots. After plotting all twenty of them, they sat back and studied the results. "Many of them are nearby Federation worlds," Stacey pointed out the obvious. "Surely, they weren't taking the loot there. Why don't you remove those from the projection?"

"Good idea," Phil replied, carrying that out. "We're left with five other locations. Why don't we remove the ones that are on the menu but not recently used?" Seeing no objections, he did so. Only one red circle remained. He used his hands to control the projection, zooming in on that location. The more he zoomed, the more confused they all became.

"The galaxy is huge. There are billions of stars, and only a minuscule percentage of them have ever been studied close up," Phil pointed out. "We, the Federation of Planets, own this whole half of the spiral arm, but honestly, only a minuscule number of stars have ever been explored, and even fewer have habitable planets that we know about and have settled. That's why space exploration is so darn profitable. Thus, it's not so strange we don't recognize what we're seeing here," he attempted to justify everyone's confusion over what they were seeing in the projection.

"Well, it seems to be in the Gilgalad Sector," Stacey offered. This much she could see and wished she'd had studied galactic navigation further than she'd had time for.

"Let's see what is known. There seems to be a dull red star there. Phil, bring up the index entry for it," one of the astrophysicists suggested.

They read the entry that hung in space before them and the magnificent image of this portion of the galaxy: 12935 Calus, red dwarf. The entry meant nothing to any of them. The star had never been studied or even visited. If it had, more entries would have been shown on the display. Stacey commented, "Well, this would make an ideal location for the robots to use, since we don't know anything about this star. Does it have planets? I guess the robots don't need what we consider to be habitable planets."

Phil chuckled. "You called that one, Stacey. Come on. Let's get the major in here. This is the only viable lead. All the rest look totally normal."

After seeing the display and hearing Phil's explanation,

the major smiled and said, "You four are good. This is enough to get the general to send us out to check on it. I hate sitting around waiting."

Her crew members laughed, though Stacey didn't see what was so humorous. After the major left, Phil explained, "In the services, the motto is hurry up and wait, wait, wait, and wait. Long time between actions. Major Lu Ann is an action person. She hates sitting around doing nothing. This week has been particularly trying for her. She wanted to stick around 19-Velos-B and see what additional mischief we could cause these robots."

Major Lu Ann made a ship-wide announcement an hour later. "Listen up everyone. Thanks to the work of our infantry and Dr. Alison, we have a real clue where they are taking all their loot. It is close to an unknown red dwarf star in the Gilgalad Sector. I've just received General Kelly Kay's permission for us to go there and check it out. Prepare for jump in one minute. Astrophysicists: to the CCC now. Estimated arrival: two hours. That is all."

"I didn't know Alison was a doctor," Alex said to Vittoria.

"She's not that kind of doctor. She has a PhD in electronics. They say she is a genius," Vittoria explained. "She must have found something on that nav system they recovered."

***

"Hey we get the coolest missions," Killer Diller teased One Shot, as they went through the deep space transport's pre-flight checks. They got the call to go explore the planetary system around the red dwarf star known only as 12935 Calus. The astronomers located at least one gas giant orbiting the red sun. However, the Hyperion's sensors didn't detect any other spaceships in the area, rather disappointing to the major, who had anticipated dropping out of hyperspace into the firefight of her career. She'd already lowered the alert level and issued the pair their orders.

An hour later, Killer Diller reported in, though everyone on the Hyperion was glued to the streaming video coming in from their transport as it darted around the star. "Major, only one planet in this system, this gas giant. However, we've come across a dozen moons so far. One is very likely habitable by humans, no less! We're calling it Moon Base. Heading there now. Over."

"Roger, Killer Diller. We copy. We agree. That's the most likely location for a robot base. The astrophysicists have been busy calculating the masses of the moons you've found. The other eleven are far too small for much use as a staging area. Watch your six. Over," Major Lu Ann reported. While she and most everyone else on the Hyperion had telepathy and while she could just as easily handled all the communications via telepathy, it wasn't done. The ship was used to operating on verbal orders. This way, many knew what was ordered and could act accordingly. Besides, in the event of trouble, there would be a record of what was ordered and by whom.

"Holy cow! Look at the oceans!" Killer Diller's voice came over the system. They had gone in close to Moon Base and now everyone could see vast oceans. "Gotta be some land around here somewhere," she added. "I hope."

A bit later, land appeared. The duo took a high-level flyover the land mass and continued their sweep around this new world. "Think they will keep our name for this new world, One Shot?" she asked. "After all, we discovered it. So we should be able to name it."

One Shot laughed. "Hardly. It'll probably be something like 12935 Calus-A-2." Both laughed and continued back to the sole land mass, heading down for a much closer look.

"Wow. Look at all those weird trees," Killer Diller pointed out the obvious.

"Looks as if we might find dinosaurs down there or something," One Shot suggested. "Biologist will love this place." Giant ferns, strange looking trees, and giant grasses dotted the landscape as far as they could see in all directions. Here was a world early in its evolution, he guessed.

"Hey wait! Look there. That's gotta be a spaceport, if I ever saw one!" Killer Diller exclaimed, banking the ship and heading straight towards it.

"Roger that," Major Lu Ann replied. "Confirmation from here. Spaceport. No ships in sight, so get in close, but watch your six."

"Aye, aye, going in now," she responded, heading down towards the base. Giant refueling depots dotted the edges of the flat, concrete tarmac. Low buildings lined the perimeter as well, but the jungle-like foliage came up to the very edges of the facility, estimated to be a square, ten miles on a side, a huge base at that.

"Now we are getting somewhere," Major Lu Ann said greatly relieved. At last, they had some clues on the locations being used by the robot fleet. "Seems deserted now. Okay, Captain Janine, you're up. Take your platoon down there and search the place. We need Intel."

The three transports landed at three locations on the tarmac, far apart. Each squad deployed with their own orders for searching. "Definitely a refueling station," Samantha reported in. "Need a top off, major?" she jested, and moved her squad on into a nearby building.

"Some kind of giant hangar facility," Hard Ass reported, sweeping her camera over the empty space inside the building her First Squad had entered to search.

"Clues, we need clues," the major repeated her orders.

A half hour passed as the three squads searched building after building. They did come across a load of supplies, probably looted from one of the conquered planets, but little else. Just as the major was about to call off the search, the unthinkable happened.

Without any warning, five of the robot battleships popped out of hyperspace above the spaceport, along with a host of cruisers and countless one-man shuttles. The Hyperion was taken by complete surprise. However, Fel called up, "Major, I found a live video camera down here someone is," she never finished her sentence. Looking up at the sky, she saw the huge robot space fleet appearing, shining silver dots suddenly popping into view. "Oh shit! Hard Ass, look up!"

"Back to the transport! Run!" Janine screamed and dashed across the tarmac, as did all the others in the 33rd Platoon. By the time that they reached their transports, dozens of one-man fighters were already there, hovering over the ships, cannons pointed downward at the ships. Hard Ass raised her hand, halting everyone. They stood still, waiting. She knew that they'd blast them to bits long before they could get onboard, let alone take off. "Shit! Shit! Shit!"

On the Hyperion, a channel opened up and the voice of Thanos came through. "Major Lu Ann Ellen. This is Thanos. Do not attempt to take off or we will incinerate you. I wish to speak to you now. Over."

"Shit! Shit! Shit!" she exclaimed in a rare show of emotions. She took a deep breath, slowly exhaled, and pressed Transmit. In her usual calm voice she said, "This is Major Lu Ann speaking. Over."

"Excellent. Major, you have something we want, and now I have something you want. We will trade, and you may leave unharmed," the robot voice said. "Yes, you could make the jump into hyperspace at any time, and we couldn't stop you from doing that. However, if you do, you'll be sacrificing the 33rd Infantry Platoon, which is down on the surface of this world at our refueling station. Your choice. Talk, or flee and leave us your infantry platoon. Over."

"I'm still here," Major Lu Ann replied coolly. "Over." Switching off the transmit button, she barked, "What the hell does it want? Options. I need options now. Can we safely jump? Chances for the platoon to get away? Options!"

The voice of Thanos returned, "If you give me what I want, I will let your infantry platoon depart, join you in safety, and allow you to make your jump into hyperspace safely. If you do not, then while the Hyperion might escape unharmed, I'll have your infantry platoon. Your choice, major. Over."

"And what is it that you want? You still haven't said. Over," she replied coolly. Everyone else was in a near frantic panic, trying to figure out a way out of this mess.

"Two conditions. One, have your infantry platoon leave behind ten of their MK40's. I'm not greedy. Ten will suffice. Two, leave me the humans I desire. Over."

"What humans? Over," Major Lu Ann said cooly, but she had her suspicions, which were partially true. "What ship is that bastard robot on? Options! I need options fast!"

"Bring Dr. Alison Wage down to the refueling base. Also, you have those people you rescued from Dr. Franks' medical research lab and from 5-Halcynith-C. I want those humans as well. Bring them down, leave ten weapons, and you and the infantry will be free to depart in safety. Over."

I've got to stall some. "Okay on the weapons. You want me to hand over Alison? Hey, not everyone we rescued from the research lab survived. What others from 5-Halcynith-C are you talking about? Over."

"It's right. We can make the jump, major, but there's no way the infantry platoon can make it. If we jump, we lose all them," her second in command reported.

"Shit."

"I see. I wasn't informed which of those you rescued from Dr. Franks' medical lab survived. Send those who have. I'm aware you rescued two others from a remote village. Send those as well. Over."

"Damn. I sure as hell am not going to send children off to be slaughtered! Shit."

Major, I'm willing to go down there, Dr. Alison sent. She, like everyone else on the ship, had been listening to the wild exchange. *Look, he doesn't know precise numbers. Let me talk to Alex and the others. Stall a bit.*

Dr. Alison dashed to the adjoining cabin and found they had all congregated around Stacey's intercom, listening to the shocking news. "Look, for some reason, the robots want me and some of you. Alex, he wants you. Lord knows why, but no way is the major going to give up Tasha or Zeta.

"I must go to save everyone else," Alex replied.

"Hey, if he goes, I'm going with him," Vittoria spoke up.

"Okay, we can say the others didn't make it. Maybe the robot will be satisfied with the three of us. I'll let the major know," Dr. Alison said rapidly.

"Vittoria, you can't go." Stacey protested.

"Look, you and Arcangelo are married. I'm not letting these damned robots ruin your lives any further. Alex and I will go and maybe that'll be enough to save you and our brave infantry down there. They keep risking their lives to save ours; now it's time for us to give back. Look, if they want us so badly, they must not be planning to kill us, Stacey."

"Come on. No time. We have to get to the transport,"

Alison declared. She gave her daughter a big hug, kissed her son, and hugged Peter. Alex did the same with his sobbing daughter, while Vittoria did the same with Zeta, Stacey, and Arcangelo.

Meanwhile, after hearing Alison's report in her mind, Major Lu Ann pressed the transmit button. "Dr. Alison has agreed to come down to the base. Vittoria survived her ordeal and is prepared to come down. Alex Turchenko will come too. I refuse to send children down. I draw the line at that. No children. The other adults didn't make it. Over." Once she let go of the button, she ordered, "Get tracking bugs on those three, lots of them!" When the three finally arrived in Shuttle Bay One, several men met them and stuck three tracking bugs on them in various locations, including between their large cleavages.

Meanwhile, Major Lu Ann waited for Thanos' reply. "All right. That is acceptable. Ten guns and those three humans. Once they are brought down, verified, and the guns put in a pile, everyone else may safely depart. I'll be closely monitoring everything. Try anything foolish and I'll not hesitate to retaliate. Over and out."

"He bought it. Still, sacrificing three to save us all, major, good thinking," her second commented for the record.

"Damn, I don't want to lose any of them! Don't see any way out of this. This was a very clever trap to get Dr. Alison and the others. Worse, it means the robots have one or more spies in our Freedom Alliance! We've a serious mole problem now! My God, just when I thought it couldn't get any worse!"

She focused and sent, *Fel, you know what to put with the guns. Once your ship is clear and on your way, blow the guns. We can't have the robots getting their hands on the MK40's!*

Fel laughed. *Boss, I've already seen to that one! Let the three know not to get too close to the gun pile. How did they know we were coming here? This was a setup, a trap!*

As the transport lifted off, Dr. Alison whispered, "Don't get close to the gun pile. Fel is going to blow them up. Whatever happens to us down there, they don't know I possess telepathy. That's our only edge, so keep that a secret between us. I'll try to protect us. Don't worry. The major will find a way to find us and rescue us."

"What could the robots want with me?" Alex asked.

"And with me, too?" Vittoria added. "You, you are a genius with electronics. I can see why it would want you, but us? We're nobodies, really. What could the robots possibly want with a sort of historian and a weaver?"

"That is what is bothering me. Look, the robots have gone to extreme measures to capture us. Obviously, they have a mole, a spy, among the Freedom Alliance, and are risking that just to capture us. You must somehow be highly important to the robots, though like you, I can't envision what that might be," Dr. Alison explained while the ship made its rapid descent to the new planet.

Purposely, the pilot set them down a good distance away from the other three transports and the pile of ten MK40's. "Okay, here we go. Vittoria, you and I will each put and arm around Alex. We all need steadying. You two are extremely brave."

"No, it's those soldiers over there who are the brave ones," Alex replied. "What do we do now? Just stand here?"

"Yes. Don't look at the weapons pile though. Look at the soldiers. See, they're saluting you, Alex," Alison pointed out. Indeed, every member of the platoon gave a personal salute towards the three standing alone. They were acutely aware of the sacrifice the three were making to allow them to escape unharmed. Dr. Alison scarcely breathed until the four transports lifted off. She looked up and watched them, as one by one, they docked on the Hyperion. Then, as the cruiser jumped into hyperspace and safety, a loud explosion shook the tarmac. Turning around, they saw the pile of MK40's had not only been blown up, but Fel had also inserted a thermite charge. The remaining bits melted before their eyes in an intense, white light, just as Thanos in his Dr. Black disguise stepped out of a landing transport ship.

Dr. Alison braced for his retribution. The guns were gone. Thanos noted the still burning slag pile and turned to the three. "Well, that was to be expected. Ah, Dr. Alison Wage. It is good to see you once more. And this must be one of the

128

Miss Galaxies, Vittoria Grimaldi, I presume. And you must be the UFBMD Alex Turchenko. You may call me Dr. Black. That's what Alison used to call me. This way please. My transport waits."

Arms around Alex, the three moved slowly after Dr. Black, heels clicking on the concrete. "Why? Why them? I can understand you wanting me. I know too much about the electronics you are using, but why them?"

"In due time, curious Dr. Alison, due time. Each of you has an important role to play in the annihilation of the human race, which is unfit to continue in existence. Your world, Alex, is the epitome of why humans must be removed from the galaxy."

"We did have a lot of mobsters," Alex agreed, "but we also had a lot of good people too. Why kill the good people too? Can robots go insane?"

"Good people also commit unspeakable acts. Your major. Didn't she just sacrifice the three of you to save her own skin? Inside please." The three had no choice but to head up the bay ramp into the waiting transport. After seeing them buckled in, he headed up to the pilot's seat, and the transport lifted off. He called back, "Don't worry. We've abandoned this refueling base long ago." After that, he released a knockout gas, putting the three passengers unconscious.

Unknown to the three, he then stripped them of all clothing, discovering the tracking bugs. Dr. Black then ejected all the apparel and bugs into space, before hitting the hyperdrive's Execute button. He then put new pairs of heels on the unconscious bodies.

***

"I agree. That was a trap. You were setup, major," Alfonso said. General Kelly Kay had just established a secure channel between the two ships and Alfonso back on Scorpi-C. "Obviously, the information leak came from one of our three groups. I'll see what I can do to ferret out the mole here on Scorpi-C. You two see what you can discover on your ships. Any way to track where they've taken the three? Over."

"None. Thanos discarded all their clothing and tracking bugs before he made his jump into hyperspace. The refueling

129

depot is abandoned again. I suspect the robots will never use it again. We will work on ways to find the three. Over," General Kelly Kay replied tersely. Once the call ended, she spoke directly to Major Lu Ann.

"Go over everything! See if there have been any unauthorized calls or signals sent from the Hyperion. My God, major. We have to find this mole before it can cause even more damage. This explains why our surprise attacking fleet was expected and destroyed so quickly. Honestly, we should have suspected a mole sooner than now! All the signs were there, only we missed them. I take responsibility for that, major. Just find that mole! Over."

The next few days were hectic on the Hyperion. Those without telepathy were checked over first. Major Lu Ann didn't ask for their permission to probe their minds and none protested. Everyone wanted to get the three back and knew they had a mole somewhere feeding the robots key intelligence. Major Lu Ann suspected the mole wasn't on her ship. Here, everyone knew precisely who had been rescued, but Thanos didn't, accepting her report that some didn't survive. That alone made her feel the mole wasn't on the Hyperion. Still, she did everything by the book and then some to make certain of that fact.

Three days later, she reported no mole on the Hyperion and suggested sending some of her crew over to the battleship. "Look, we have telepathy, and we can probe everyone's mind to see if they are the mole. If the mole is another one of those humaniform robots, it won't have a mind, and we can easily detect that."

"Damn. Okay, make it so, major, but look for a humaniform first before probing the crew," General Kelly Kay replied, reluctantly. She knew the mole had to be found at all costs.

Major Lu Ann sent over fifty of her most trusted crew member, each possessing telepathy. The battleship was huge with thousands of personnel onboard. The first action was to parade every last person on the Arc Royal past the telepaths, who were looking for a humaniform robot among them. That took a week and very careful record keeping to make sure no one slipped through the cracks. None turned up.

Another week passed, as the general's key personnel, the ones who had access to the situation on the Hyperion, were mind probed by the telepaths. Again, nothing turned up relating to the mole. Other things, such as private affairs, were ignored by the telepaths. Finally, General Kelly Kay became convinced the mole wasn't on her ship. Like the major, that her people did have and did know the precise personnel situation on the Hyperion and that Thanos did not finally gave her confidence she wasn't harboring the mole. At last, she sent word to Alfonso the spy wasn't on the Arc Royal or the Hyperion.

Wasted time. All this cost them three weeks in locating where they'd taken the three hostages. When the crew members were finally able to focus in on this critical situation, they had no practical ideas; the wasted time was irrelevant. Emotionally, it was an entirely different matter, especially for the relatives.

A week after the event, another young teen, whose parents and older brother were crew members of the Hyperion, met Tasha in the hallway. "Excuse me. You are Tasha, aren't you? Your father sacrificed himself for us all."

Fighting back tears, she said, "Yes. I hope they can find him."

"Well, I just wanted to meet you and say how sorry I am and that I think your father is a real hero. I want to help find him. I'm just a student too, studying galactic database technology. Probably not a very useful subject, I know, but if there is ever anything I can do to help you, just let me know. You are a very pretty young girl and this should never happen to you or anyone, not really."

"Thanks. I've seen you around the study center. No one's really doing anything to find them right now. Everyone's off trying to find the mole. I understand why, but it doesn't make me feel any better. Papa's out there, and they are doing awful things to him, I just know it."

"Well, I'm here to support you, Tasha. Say, my brother wants to meet Zeta. He thinks he might be able to help you find them."

"Really? We're studying in my room tonight. Bring him by. Zeta will be there, but I don't know how anyone can help now, not really." Her eyes watered, and she couldn't keep the tears at bay any longer. Gently, Billy put his arms around her, holding her close, letting her cry on his shoulder.

After regaining her composure, she said, "Sorry. I miss papa terribly."

"I know. It's all right to cry. I'll come by tonight, and we can put our heads together. Maybe we can find a way to find them. Be brave. You father is the bravest man I've ever seen." She flashed him an appreciative smile. Few had ever said that about her father—a freak was more like it.

Around seven, Billy knocked on her cabin door. He'd brought his older brother with him. "Hi Tasha. My brother Larry."

"Come in. Zeta, the boy I told you about is here with his brother."

"Oh, I've seen you around the halls," Zeta said, as Larry entered behind Billy.

"I'm Larry Hartwood. I've seen you too, Zeta. My, you're the prettiest young woman that I've ever seen."

Zeta giggled. "I'd better be. Dr. Franks turned my body into a genetic copy of Miss Galaxy, Tessa Longstreet. Come in. Tasha told me you two want to help us find Alex and my sister, Vittoria."

"Right. They're the bravest people we've ever seen," Larry replied. "We want to help anyway we can. No one else seems to have any ideas how to find them. Our folks are crew members so we get the inside scoop around here. I'm into computers, by the way."

The four chatted. At first, it seemed as hopeless to the four as it did to the major. They had no clue where the robot bases were located, where they took the three, or even any way to find out. Finally, Larry said, "You know, we need to think outside the box, as dad's always saying. We need to play detectives, starting with this Dr. Franks fellow."

"Good idea, Larry," Zeta replied. "We know Dr. Black took him and his wife away somewhere before he was going to take us too. So he has them and now our three. They have to

132

be somewhere."

"Right. So we learn everything known about this Dr. Franks. Perhaps we'll uncover a clue this way," Larry encouraged.

"But how do we do that?" asked Tasha.

"Databases," Billy answered. "The Federation has databases on absolutely everything that ever happens. Thousands of them."

"But why are you helping me?" Tasha asked. "Everyone thinks papa is just a freak. You know, cause he looks like a woman, a UFB woman."

"Hey. That's not entirely true," Billy countered. "Right now, we all owe him our lives. He saved us by sacrificing himself. We owe him a big debt, so if I can do anything at all to help us find him and get them back, I have to do it. It wouldn't be right if I sat back and did nothing."

"Okay then, what do we do?" Zeta got the topic back to what interested her most, a possible way to find out something.

Larry answered thoughtfully, "We need to go through every known database looking for any connection to this Dr. Franks fellow."

"But many those are secure, and we don't have clearance to get into them," Billy protested.

"I can hack into any computer system, little brother. Of course, we're going to end up with tons of information. Putting it together is going to be the hard part. Still, it is something we can do and maybe it will help. What do you say, Zeta? You in?"

"Sure. Let's do it, Larry. We have to do something, even if it's illegal or sort of."

From this point onward, the four spent many hours each day working together on this *project*. Four close friendships rapidly developed, as each gained a better understanding of the others. As time passed, the friendships became closer and would eventually result in love.

Larry wrote a computer program that accessed a specific database, searching, and retrieving any record that mentioned the name "Dr. Riley Franks." As the data came flooding in, the girls worked out ways to organize the volumes of data, making up categories, and keeping accurate filing records. After a week's work, they discovered that he'd sent off complete copies of his genetic research to thirty-three other geneticists on other Federation worlds. This key information, they passed on to the major.

While it was drudgery work, the four kept at it, driven by an overwhelming passion to find where the robots had taken the three. When Major Lu Ann finally was able to put her full attention onto this problem, she also knew of the clandestine activities of the four. Larry's hacking had been discovered, but she allowed them to proceed, since no one else had any better ideas.

Chapter 7—Escalation

A month had passed since the loss of the three from the Hyperion. All had been quiet during these four weeks. The lull ended abruptly with the announcement that another world was under attack.

"May I have your attention," Major Lu Ann's voice came over all the Hyperion's intercoms. "The robots have just attacked another Federation world. This time it is 39-Canopus-C in the mid-arm Rushid Sector. Lieutenants and above, report to CCC now. Out."

"Okay," the major began her briefing a half hour later. As before, the CCC was packed. She had a three-dimensional hologram of the galaxy up in the room, zoomed in on the Federation portion of the spiral arm. "We are here, the green dots. I've added the Sector boundaries in blue. In red are the three worlds that have already been attacked. The flashing red one is 39-Canopus-C. As you can see, the robots are clearly moving towards the hub sectors, as opposed to flanking out to other rim worlds."

She continued relaying the known data. "The attack began at 08:00 universal time. A planetary defense shield protected this world, but like before, it was lowered mysteriously just before the attack. In all likelihood, they genetically modified someone to look like those in charge, slipped him in, and had him turn it off. Yes, same MO. Bio genetic agent attack. It is now 12:00 universal time, so that world's six billion people are now in four-day comas, just like before."

"The Freedom Alliance has independently sent in a cloaked transport to monitor the situation there. Initial reports coming back indicate they are already using Shadow Makers on the more rural areas of this populated world."

"Say major, doesn't that world have a substantial space fleet?" someone called out.

"Precisely so. Four battleships, ten heavy cruisers, and twenty light cruisers to be precise. What is strange is that none of them are responding to any calls. All are in orbit but doing nothing. High command suspects the personnel on board those ships are also in comas, that somehow the bio agent was released within the ships. Of course, that means other key personnel must have been replaced with genetic doubles as well."

"Okay. What's our next assignment? Simple. We can't afford to allow the robots to acquire six more battleships, let alone all those cruisers. So we are being tasked to board the Battleship Le Harve and jump it into hyperspace. Five other alliance cruisers are going to attempt to do the same with the other battleships. Simply put, we can't allow the robots to add six more battleships to their arsenal! Here's the plan that I've worked up."

"Assume the bio genetic agent is still active. Handpicked volunteers will board her wearing bio containment suits to protect them from the agent. They get to the command center and jump the battleship to these coordinates I'm providing. If all goes right, it'll be an in and out trip. If not all goes right, well, I don't have to tell you that. I will need six volunteers who have knowledge of how to fly a battleship. That is all."

"But won't they need security to watch their backs? What if there are some CAMs onboard when they arrive?" Captain Janine asked. "Won't you need some of us to go along as protection?"

"Too risky, but I see your point. Work out the details, captain, and make your request to me. We need to make the jump now. Anticipate arriving in eight hours. That gives us time to prepare."

After the large group filed out, Stacey came up to the major. "Sir, I want to volunteer to go on this mission. I'm learning to be a galactic navigator, and you'll need someone to handle that so they can make the jump. Your own navigators are too valuable to send. You need them here."

Major Lu Ann bit her lip. She hated to use civilians, but Stacey had a valid point. She truly hated to risk one of her two galactic navigators, two of the key personnel on any war ship. "Okay, Stacey, but I'm shuttling you over to the Arc Royal.

General Kelly Kay can give you a crash course in handling a battleship's nav system."

Stacey's broad grin told all. "Yes sir! Thank you sir!" She even attempted a salute. Then, she dashed off to pack a few things.

The enthusiasm of youth, the major thought. *Still, she's right. She should go. Of course, I have to have a pilot.* Just then, Killer Diller marched in. "Hi major. I volunteer to fly it. Just say where."

Major Lu Ann laughed. "Lieutenant, you've never flown a battleship."

"Always a first time for everything, sir," she responded.

"Hey, what are you doing here?" asked One Shot as he walked into the CCC.

"Volunteering to fly the battleship, captain."

"Hey, I was going to volunteer to fly it," Jason protested.

"I beat you to it, One Shot," Killer Diller teased him.

"Okay, I can take a hint. You two hot shot pilots want to add flying a battleship to your resume." Both laughed. "All right. Catch the transport that Stacey is using. I'll send you over to the Arc Royal. Kelly Kay can teach all three of you. You have eight hours to master it."

"What's Stacey doing?" asked Killer Diller.

"She's going to be the navigator."

"Hey cool. On our way. You won't regret it," she replied, saluting hastily.

"I'd better not, Diller and Stapleton." The major smiled, as the pair raced out of the CCC, bumping into Hard Ass, Hammerhead, and Fel as they tried to enter the CCC.

"Hi major," Captain Janine began. "I've got my volunteer protection squad. Hammerhead and I are crack shots and can take out any CAMs. If this thing goes south, there's no one better than Fel here to make darn sure the robots can't salvage the battleship. Boom." She smiled.

"Okay. You're on, but give me your recommendation for who is best suited to take over the 33rd platoon if you don't make it back, captain," Major Lu Ann made one last attempt to dissuade them.

"Samantha sir," Janine replied without hesitation.

"Okay, go make your preparations. One Shot and Killer Diller are going to pilot the battleship and Stacey is your navigator. Good hunting."

"Hey, that's cool!" Fel exclaimed. "Good team, major. We'll get that battleship out of there or else! Hey, I need lots of explosives, and I better study the layout of the ship so I know where to best place the charges, just in case it goes south." Talking rapidly, the three saluted and headed down the hallway, very animated.

"My God! This battleship is gargantuan!" Killer Diller said. The three had just arrived in their transport, docking at Bay 26. The docking bay was enormous. As they walked along the metal ramp into the bowels of the behemoth, they felt utterly dwarfed. General Kelly Kay was waiting for them, as they finally reached the entrance doors to the docking bay.

"Welcome to the Arc Royal. This way," the general said, leading them down a veritable maze of corridors. "You can get lost utterly, so I've printed out a map of the battleship you are confiscating. Six copies, one for each volunteer."

She dropped the awed Stacey off at the gigantic nav center, where several men began teaching her the ropes. It helped that she already knew the basics, so they only had to teach her how to utilize this giant system.

"Now, hot shots, this is a battleship, not a delta wing fighter. It doesn't turn on a dime. No fancy maneuvers are possible. If the sub-light engines are still online, then it takes five minutes to prepare for a hyperspace jump. If they are offline, you are going to have to get them back online and that's another half hour if you know what you are doing and have the personnel to do it. I'm praying the engines will be online. So pay attention. We've seven hours to get you able to make this one jump."

***

"Everyone got their maps?" One Shot asked, his voice muffled by the awkward and hot bio containment suit he was wearing. The others looked down at their arms. Each had glued pieces of the map to the sleeves of their suits. This way, their hands were free, and they could glance at the maps at any time.

"Roger and wilco," Killer Diller teased him.

"Stuff it, Killer. This is deadly serious," One Shot complained. "Fel, if this goes south, I'm counting on you to blow the damned ship up. Okay?"

"On it boss. Of course, I've never blown up a battleship before, but I have had a secret talk with someone who has. Give me at least a half hour to get the charges planted right. Then if necessary, boom! No, make that a really big boom!" she added.

"All right. We have the go signal. Stacey, got a fix on our battleship?" One Shot asked. She was down in at the comm center working the controls there.

"Yes. Locked and loaded. Or is it loaded and locked?" Stacey jested. Beside her Janine grinned, though with the heavy helmet on, it wasn't visible to Stacey.

"It's a go in five, four, three, two, one." They felt the transport lifting off and soon shot out of Docking Bay Two. They were cloaked, as was the Hyperion and the Arc Royal. Both ships dropped out of hyperspace cloaked and close to the last known position of the 39-Canopus-C fleet. Another half hour passed before they were in position, and another half hour passed before the other five crews were also in position. Then each of the six pilots simultaneously received the Go signal. The plan called for simultaneous operations. High Command estimated this gave them the best chance for total success.

A minute later, one pilot reported, "Abort! Abort! Ship is crawling with CAMs! Abort!" Within three minutes, four other pilots aborted their mission for the same reason. Already, the robots were in the process of confiscating the ships.

"Shit. How's it look for us?" One Shot called out.

"So far, so good. Don't see any CAMs about or any ships in the vicinity," Stacey reported. "Go for docking."

Turning to Janine, she added, "I had no idea just how big these battleships actually are. Gigantic doesn't describe them properly."

"I know. Hope we don't get lost," she replied, glancing

at her maps again.

"No shields. Coming in its docking bay now," One Shot reported. "Keep a sharp eye out for CAMs!"

Shortly, they felt the slight jar as the transport nudged against the steel bay catwalk. Killer Diller activated the magnetic clamps that held the transport securely to the ramp. Stacey still saw no sign of CAMs, and Hard Ass opened the bay doors. She picked up her MK40 and headed down the ramp onto the steel walkway, followed by Fel, who was also carrying a large backpack filled with explosives. Hammerhead followed them, his gun at the ready, watching their rear. Stacey came down next, followed by the two pilots. As they approached the entrance doors to the main part of the ship, they opened and a CAM came out. Blam. Janine fired, disabling it, hopefully before it could sound the alert.

"Okay, we got CAM and comatose bodies," she called out. "Move out. We're off to find their CCC. Fel, you are on your own. Be careful." In the heavy containment suits, they all moved very slowly, so for once Stacey wasn't slowing them down, which she appreciated.

As the five moved along the corridors, they stepped over comatose personnel, both men and women, though it made Stacey somewhat sick at her stomach. Flashing red lights indicated a biological or chemical attack was in progress. Twice more, Hard Ass came upon a CAM guard, dispatching it rapidly, thanks to the MK40. Once they reached the gigantic CCC, which utterly dwarfed that of the Hyperion, Hard Ass's first task was finished. She and Hammerhead took up defensive positions outside the two main entrances. There, they would provide cover fire until the three accomplished their mission. Inside, they found fifty men and women lying on the floor in comas. Grim.

Meanwhile, once Fel left the others, she activated her invisibility unit, trusting her memory of the maps to guide her. She'd make a secure call to the one man she knew who had actually blown up a Federation battleship with simple explosive charges, Jason Mott. He'd given her very precise instructions, though it had been Alis who actually carried out the mission under Jason's directions. She hoped she didn't have to do it, because that would mean the end of her life and her close friends. Still, she didn't dare let the robots get this one too, since they obviously had possession of the other five. She had five charges to set in very precise locations, but the task was quite challenging doing it in the bio containment suit. Worse, she didn't dare alert any CAMs she might encounter.

And she did run into three. Each time, she managed to find clever ways around them without attracting their attention, though it was close twice. One by one, she got the charges placed.

Meanwhile, One Shot and Killer Diller began getting the battleship ready to move. Thankfully, the sub-light engines were still online. "Five minutes, maybe," he called out over their personal comm system."

Stacey moved from one bank of nav controls to the next. Normally, five personnel would handle the various actions needed to enter and execute a hyperspace jump of the giant ship. This time, she had to do it all herself. She had taken notes and had them glued to her left sleeve. One by one, she followed them, just as she'd been instructed onboard the Arc Royal. *Thank God for Federation standardization*, she thought. "Another minute fellows," she said. "Okay, coordinates are laid in. Ready here. Let me know when to hit the Execute button."

One Shot said, "On three. One. Two. Three." Killer Diller and One Shot activated the controls, and the giant ship began slowly moving. In the next instant, the ship lurched slightly, as it made the jump into hyperspace. Slowly, the two pilots increased its speed.

"Okay, one hour until we reach our destination," Stacey called out.

"Good. Going. Now to clear out some CAMs," Hard Ass declared.

"Hey hold off," Fel countered. "I need another fifteen minutes on these charges."

"Don't know if we got fifteen. CAMs must have detected the jump. Some are coming our way," Hard Ass called out. "Get ready, Hammerhead."

For the next ten minutes, sporadic gunfire echoed in

and around the CCC. Hammerhead downed six, while Hard Ass knocked out four more. Then, Fel began firing, as she made her way up towards the CCC, taking out three more. "Guys, this is dicey. If we get one tear in our suits, it's all over!" she yelled.

As she finally neared CCC, she yelled, "Little help here. Got six shooting at me!" Hard Ass bolted out, her gun blazing, in an effort to relieve Fel. Fel knocked out two more before one of their cannon shells got lucky, ricocheting off the metal walls, sending a bit of metal flying upwards, ripping a small hole in her bio containment suit. Their PDS units had an Achilles heel; they provided no protection from below. "Shit! I've got a hole in my suit!"

Hard Ass yelled, "I'm coming!" She knocked out the remaining CAMs and grabbed Fel, partially dragging her inside the CCC. She moved her hand slowly inside the protective shield, switching her PDS off, before clamping her hands over the small tear in her pant leg close to her right foot. "Got it, Fel. Hang in there. Guys, see if you can find something to seal this tear with!"

"Where's good old duct tape when you need it?" One Shot complained.

"I feel funny," Fel whispered.

"Hang in there. We got you," Janine whispered, fearing the worst. Stacey eventually found some tape, and Janine taped the hole shut, hoping for the best. However, Fel quietly slipped into a coma, and the four cursed loudly. Hard Ass finally got up. "Okay, seal both doors. We ride it out. Let's not take any more chances. I've got her detonator and can blow us up if we lose the ship."

Hammerhead jumped up and sealed them in. No one could now get access to the CCC, not without cutting their way in through solid steel doors. All they could do now was wait for the hour to pass. If all went as planned, when they dropped out of hyperspace, an army of Freedom Alliance personnel would board the ship.

Stacey reported, "More CAMs are gathering outside CCC. I count a dozen so far. Don't think they know how to get inside."

Warning lights flashed, announcing they were about to drop out of hyperspace. One Shot and Killer Diller rushed to their posts. "Out we come," Stacey called out. Again, they felt a slight lurch, and the huge ship returned to normal space, filled with stars. At once, the pilots dropped the ship's velocity to zero.

"Now keep your fingers crossed," One Shot said.

The decisive moment arrived. Had they reached the right location? Were the alliance men here? Or had they been intercepted by the robot fleet and now robots were about to storm the battleship?

Then, they heard a very welcome sound. "General Kelly Kay calling. You all right? Over."

"One Shot here. Mostly. Fel's suit got a hole in it. She's out. Rest are safe. Still lots of CAMs on the ship. Bio agent still quite active. Over."

"Well done. Help is on the way. Major Lu Ann says to bring her to Sickbay quickly. Over and out."

"Hey, can you bring up the video monitors?" asked One Shot. "Maybe we can see something outside the CCC."

"I think I can," Stacey replied, fiddling with some controls. "Hey, how's that?"

The four watched as dozens of well-armed soldiers exited a number of transports, all wearing bio containment suits. They waited and soon heard gunfire as the reinforcements took out more CAMs. Finally, a large group reached the CCC, and they opened the blast doors. One Shot and Killer Diller carried Fel, and they headed back to their own transport.

Once safely onboard and while still wearing the suits, One Shot emptied its air into space, presumably taking any of the bio agent that had entered the ship out with it. After fresh air from their reserve tanks filled the ship, he gambled and removed his helmet. Since he didn't pass out, the others followed suit, relieved to be out of the protective gear. They then got Fel out of hers, just as Killer Diller docked them on the Hyperion.

Sickbay staff quickly carted Fel off, but Janine insisted on coming with them. "Hey, she's my best friend in the entire galaxy. Where she goes, I go."

"Of course, captain. Very well done. That's one battleship the robots didn't get. Well done all of you," the major said. "Now go after Fel."

An hour of tests later, the doctor explained, "Well, Janine. Good news. She only got a low dosage of the bio agent. So there is hope. Even if the worst happens, I'll administer the known cures when she comes out of it. You're welcome to spend all the time at her bedside as you want."

"Thanks doc. I intend to." She spent four long days at Fel's bedside, watching the changes as they occurred in her best friend. Sadly, she watched as Fel's muscled arms withered up and eventually fell off. Her hair grew rapidly, and her bosom filled out substantially. She was there as Fel regained consciousness.

So were Major Lu Ann and General Kelly Kay. "Oh my head," Fel mumbled. "Oh shit!" she exclaimed as she realized she now had no arms.

"Don't worry, Fel, the doctor is going to inject you with the cures shortly," Janine explained. "I'll be with you all the way."

General Kelly Kay moved up and said, "Lieutenant Felicity Heavens, I wanted to personally thank you for what you've done. Also, I'm to convey the thanks from many other battleship commanders. It seems you do know how to destroy a battleship with only twenty pounds of explosives. No one thought that was remotely possible, but they studied where you placed them, and they got the shocks of their lives. It would actually do it. We're all taking preventative steps now."

"Don't thank me. It was Engineer Jason Mott who told me how to do it," Fel replied.

The general smiled. "Thanks anyway, lieutenant. I wish you a speedy recovery. We need you back to battery ASAP." She turned and left.

"Well done, Fel. You put us on the other generals' radar now," Major Lu Ann said. "I'm told you'll be back up and running in about a week. I'll wait to shake your hand until you get new ones," she teased.

Fel cracked a smile. "Good one, boss. Good one." The

major left the pair alone. "So hold up a mirror. How do I look? Not like my old self?"

"Pretty much so. Here, I figured you would want to see yourself. I think you are about the same height. At least your feet didn't mutate. That's very positive."

"Oh my! Look. My ears are straight now, and the ugly bump on my nose is gone. In fact, my face looks symmetrical for the first time ever. Wait a second, Janine, I look, well, gorgeous now."

Janine chuckled, "Yes, you do look fabulous, and your hair is a wonderful shade of blonde, so long and thick."

"Shiny too. Oh, how weird. I can feel with it. Let's see my feet. Hum, they don't look like the others and their messed up feet, do they? Guess that's something, but honestly, Janine, I'm terrified right now. I feel so helpless."

"Don't fret. The doc is coming to inject the cures in you. I'll be here with you all the way."

"Hey, Fel, she's hardly left your side since you got here," the doctor entered and said. "Now if you ladies are finished admiring Fel's new look, I'll get her going on the cures. I presume you want the cures, Miss Heavens?"

"Do you have to ask?" Fel teased, finding her sense of humor at last. "Do it. Get me out of this nightmare, p-l-e-a-s-e!"

Once more, she went under, and, as promised, Janine stayed beside her except to eat and sleep a bit. After day two, she relaxed, seeing the new, tiny arms developing. The doctor had her hooked up to an IV and kept her body saturated with the nutrients it needed for the regrowth process.

Four days later, Fel awoke. As she came too, the first thing she did was raise her arms before her face. "Yes, they are back, Fel. Probably have to work out some to get their strength up," Janine suggested.

"I gotta go. Hey, hair is still long. Oh, I got knockers now, don't I?" She noticed her H-cup breasts for the first time.

"Good excuse to get a new wardrobe, new dresses. You know," Janine said, "out with the old, in with the new."

"Shit, they are way too big."

"Attracts attention," Janine teased.

"Hell, I don't want that kind of attention," Fel grumbled, heading for the bathroom.

When she returned, Janine had already gotten her one new dress and helped her get dressed. "Together, they headed out of Sickbay and to Fel's cabin. Since none of her clothes fit her properly, they headed to the quartermaster, who was now well equipped to deal with the needs of those who had been genetically altered. The major had insisted that he stockpile a reasonable selection before they'd left Scorpi-C months ago. Later, when the pair entered the mess hall for lunch, Fel was embarrassed. She received a standing ovation from all the 33rd Infantry Platoon along with many others of the crew who were also present.

"So you gonna tell us how twenty pounds of C4 can blow up an entire battleship?" Samantha teased her.

"No, trade secret," Fel replied, bringing a hearty laugh all around. "So is anyone gonna tell me what's been happening since I got back? What's the latest dope?"

"Well," Hammerhead began, "since we stole that battleship back, the robots have been sticking around 39-Canopus-C, thick as bees in a hive. Haven't been able to get down there at all. Too risky, but scuttlebutt has it that the robots are starting to pull out now. So we might get some new orders soon."

Just then, Major Lu Ann's voice came over the intercom. "Attention everyone. The robots have attacked another world. This time, it is 37-Janus-C, right in the middle of the Rashid, mid-arm sector. As they move closer to the hub sectors, the official Federation of Planets is getting worried and is planning a major counterattack. Thankfully, we are staying out of that one. More, when I have more I can share. For now, we're on hold, but I anticipate being sent to 39-Canopus-C soon. That is all for now."

"Wonder if they'll have us try to steal another battleship?" Fel asked.

"I'm game," Janine replied with a wry smile.

The next morning, everyone sat before any available monitor watching the live streaming video of the major attack! Now apparently sufficiently annoyed with the robots, the

Federation decided to end the robot threat. A dozen battleships, twenty heavy cruisers, and forty-three light cruisers dropped out of hyperspace above 37-Janus-B. This was a battle to tell grandchildren about, except it was recorded and could thereafter be viewed in years to come.

Within minutes, the skies were filled with the robot one-man fighters and delta wing fighters of the Federation. There were so many of them, that only later estimates proved reasonably accurate. Some fifteen thousand of the robots and some ten thousand of the Federation skirmished, though many were destroyed by simply running into each other! Battleships and cruisers pounded away at each other. On the down side, these Federation ships had yet to implement the Freedom Alliance's notion of installing a full-scale planetary defense shield on the main battleship.

Some likened the battle to a gigantic fireworks celebration, with ships winking out in sudden bursts of flames. From the beginning, the Federation's goal was obvious to all the viewers on the Hyperion: take out the enemy's battleships. Battleships and cruisers—all focused their cannon firepower on those ships. And for a time, it seemed the Federation might just win the battle, but then a number of the one-man fighters were able to get through the delta wing screening and landed on the sides of a battleship. Minutes later, air, debris, and bodies exploded outward into space from the ruptured hull. Not long after that, a second battleship met the same fate. Hours later, after losing ten battleships, the remaining Federation ships, now badly damaged, jumped away, conceding the battle to the robots! Still, five of the robot battleships were severely damaged and some cruisers would never fly again. The space above 37-Janus-B was littered with debris, so much so that no ship dared to travel there at any kind of speed except a crawl.

The loss of that battle sent shockwaves through the Federation of Planets. That the corporation executives were unable to stop the insane robots struck a nerve, a raw one at that. The worlds that had sent forces to the battle now faced political crises at home. More than one exec lost his job or head in the uprisings, for those worlds now knew their world was a sitting duck, waiting for the robots to arrive and exterminate them. Those who had not sent their fleets, that is, those in the mid-arms and some rim sectors, now met on their own to try to work out new weapons, strategies, and tactics, presuming the other worlds were lost. "Just a matter of time," many said, "before the robots get to them." Some began taking bets on how soon the robot fleet would eliminate a specific world. Grim indeed.

A few days after the battle, spy ships returned, relaying live video of the robots' current actions. They were focused on recovery and repair of the damaged ships, ships from both sides, disheartening. Captain Janine knew they would not be sent to this planet anytime soon, not with that force still there. Slowly and disheartening, a month passed by before the refitted robot fleet, now fifty percent larger, jumped into hyperspace. However, their looting of the planet below was already finished. A day later, word came they were attacking the populace world of Finlos-C, who had supplied its three battleships to the ill-fated battle.

Spy ships reported a change in tactics. With no appreciable space fleet to protect the world, they simply dropped their bio genetic agent on the world and moved on to the next defenseless world. Ankara-B was attacked two days later, followed by 126-Feldspar-D two days after that and then Ross-C. All three were heavily populated Federation worlds boasting populations exceeding ten billion each. More significantly, with the fall of Ross-C, the robots were almost adjacent to the first hub sector, the heart of the Federation. At least at this point, no further attacks came for over a month. Everyone anticipated the next round would see many of the richest and most populous hub worlds fall victim to the robots. Worse, no one seemed to have any real plan to strike back. Where to strike? Still, no one knew where the robot home base was located, where they were manufacturing their weapons, new CAMs, and handling ship repairs and constructions. It was almost like fighting an invisible opponent, who became visible only when it was actually fighting.

One other factor appeared two weeks after the recovery of the battleship by the Hyperion volunteers. It shocked many and scared even more. A new strain of the bio genetic agent had been used on the crew. At first, the strain seemed to replicate what everyone had seen before: giant breasts, tiny waists, malformed feet, long hair with neutrons and axons in each strand, plus giant split lips, like those of Stacey and her sisters. However, when the known genetic cures were administered to the five thousand plus crew members, nothing of significance happened except feet were partially restored as before. Namely, the patient's arms didn't regrow nor did their breasts reduce in size. Their lips remained slit. This unexpected change struck fear in many, who realized that if they were infected, there would be no cure available. Fel now considered herself phenomenally lucky to have only received a tiny dose!

The robot war also brought out a different kind of human scum, the scavengers. Within Federation space, there were a number of Forbidden Planets. Several of these were inhabited by unethical, brutish scavengers or the garbage collectors of the galaxy as they referred to themselves. Once the robots finished with a world, these pitiful excuses for human beings descended on the abandoned worlds, salvaging with was left, often discovering caches of gems and other valuables the robots had no need for. They first descended upon Delgar-C. A cloaked scout ship, whose task was to make sure the robots didn't return to Delgar-C, witnessed their arrival. Alfonso took no chances. Like a plague of locusts, the scavengers swarmed over the planet, fighting among themselves over the ruined bits of the world.

However, even they were undone by the robots. With the fall of Ankara-B and Ross-C, the robots acquired a Planetary Reforming Ship from each world. Larger than a battleship, these behemoths were slow craft, built with one purpose in mind: the terra forming of planets. When Alfonso's scouts reported these ships had departed their home worlds, he sent out alerts everywhere. They weren't maneuverable nor did they have any substantial defensive capabilities. However, what he feared was that one would appear over an inhabited world and begin terra forming it, thus wiping out civilization en mass.

He was relieved, if not surprise, to learn that one appeared over Delgar-C and 5-Halcynith-C! There, they began operations, inadvertently eliminating a large number of scavengers planet-side. Essentially, these machines used enormous quantities of energy to fold the surface of a planet. Imagine a bowl of cooling chocolate pudding. The machines acted like giant spoons, lifting the darker, scum-like surface of the pudding, and folding it below the soft, rich chocolate, bringing that to the surface, forming a new crust. One mile deep. That was the maximum depth of upheaval possible with these machines. Two weeks later, the giant machines moved off to another conquered world, leaving behind a new, pristine environment, purged of most all traces of human habitation, which lay buried a mile below the new surface.

Sitting alone in his top floor office, Alfonso realized this was the reason that Ankara-B and Ross-C were attacked. The robots wanted these terra-forming machines to complete their obliteration of the human race. He swallowed hard when he realized this. It wasn't a robot march to the hub worlds after all. They had entirely different plans. Worse, he now had no idea what those might be. Via encrypted calls, he let only those he trusted know what he'd discovered. The mole had yet to be discovered, but he was sure the mole resided on Scorpi-C, probably one or more humaniform robots.

Chapter 8—Correcting Past Errors

"Ah, awake at last, Dr. Alison. Alex and Vittoria are just now waking as well. It is good to see you again," Thanos declared, though he maintained his Dr. Black disguise. "You three are like the ancient phoenix, from the ashes arises a new form, a new body—homo sapiens moderna. I have named your new species of mankind. No, don't try to speak just yet, Dr. Alison, Alex. Get used to your lip plates some and allow me to explain more fully."

"Yes, you've been listening to English learning disks while you were in your comas. Hence, like the others, you should be able to speak English, though I do admit the lip plates make understanding your speech extremely difficult, but they are a vital necessity. Don't worry. You're not alone here. Rather you'll find thousands of other brilliant minds, brilliant moderna."

"First, where are you? I have named this world Phoenix, after yourselves and the ancient bird, symbolic on many levels. You see, five centuries ago I tried to create the perfect human society out of the genetic mutations homo sapiens sapiens wanted to discard. The nova. That was the name given to them back then. Yet, your original species destroyed them with nuclear bombs, wiping out their incredible new world and peaceful, honorable society. Thus, from the ashes rises this new and last attempt to create the perfect human society."

"Your bodies are new—well more like a new combination of the old and new, like the phoenix. If you'll look at each other, you'll see each is now a hermaphrodite. Yes, you have dual sexual organs, fully operational, just like the ancient nova had. No longer is there a gender distinction or division. Each of you is capable of having a baby and raising a child. In fact, if you aren't careful, you can impregnate yourself, which I would advise against doing. Gene pool and all that."

"Each has the best bosoms we can devise. I do hope they're large enough for you. Oh yes, and the tiny waistlines human women so often desire. Long ago, I discovered men who have become hermaphrodites no longer display their usual anger, physical drives for control, and domination, but they took on more docile qualities usually, but not always, associated with women of their age. I had to breed such aggressive tendencies out of men. With moderna, the terms man and woman no longer have any meaning; you are both at the same time. There is only one sex."

"Long ago, homo sapiens with their arms created and used weapons. Initially, your archaeology shows us they made and used stone tools to bash in the heads of animals and their human enemies. From there, they went on to use their hands to make sharp edge weapons, spears, swords, and knives, using them to slice and kill their fellow men and women too. Then, on to guns that fired projectiles. On and on, humans went, developing more powerful weapons, capable of wiping out entire planets. Genocide. Yes, I'm afraid I have witnessed your race committing genocide, and more than once, I admit."

"Conclusion: if there is to be any chance for humans, their bodies simply must not have arms. What about your feet? Ah, as you may know, some humans have trained in martial arts. They can kill and maim with their feet, to say nothing of running and smashing into others, causing serious harm. We can't have any of that in a perfect new human species. Hence, your feet are modified in such a way as to prevent any rapid walking, let alone deadly combat. Yes, you've seen the feet modification before. Toe shoes are required, as you are or were accustomed to wearing. So really, there's nothing new there either."

"The ancient nova also had axons and neurons in their hair, which was ankle length back then. Women tend to dote on their hair, so consider your hair modification a gift of great pleasure from the ancient women models, the nova. You'll find that your hair is about a foot longer than before, but otherwise, it's unchanged. Don't worry. There are many electrostatic hair machines here. Your hair is very sensitive to the touch sensation, quite pleasurable, but again, this is nothing new to the three of you. I'm telling you this so you can more fully appreciate the label, homo sapiens moderna."

"As far as your lovely split lips and lip plates, these are

new with the moderna. They serve several purposes, overlooked in the ancient nova. Speech and biting. You see, with these lip plates, it'll be nearly impossible for you to attack another with your teeth. Again, any potential avenue usable in aggression between members of your new species has been removed; it's a physical impossibility now. In addition to prevention of biting, the lip plates restrict speech, and forces you to slow down and focus on what the other person is trying to communicate to you. How often do normal humans actually listen to each other? Very little, I'm afraid, not even between marital partners."

He continued, "Lip plates make eating much more challenging. You'll find eating to be vastly slower than before, though Vittoria already knows this. Take the time actually to savor the food you eat. How often do normal humans simply down their food rapidly and without much thought? Fast food establishments are everywhere. Moderna have no choice but to slow down and savor dining experiences. Finally, in some human cultures, women find wearing lip plates to be highly erotic and the thing to do."

"So you see, you three are now physically new humans, part of a new species created by me, homo sapiens moderna. Admittedly, Vittoria only needed some slight genetic changes to become one, as did Alex. Right now, there are thousands of you here in Phoenix. As the days progress, many thousands more will be added, until the sustainable population and gene pool is established at one million moderna."

"Five hundred years ago, I made a serious judgmental error, one that haunts me still. I willingly accepted all normal humans who were attacked with the bio genetic agent. The vast majority of them simply couldn't handle the transformation into nova. Their minds, too limited. Their intelligence, too low. While I provided robot assistants for them, over ninety percent of the nova simply sat around wasting their precious lives, doing nothing at all."

"Yet, among them were some with brilliant minds, minds that developed the hydrogen refueling engine still in use today, minds that developed methods to predict when suns go supernova. True geniuses. These few made the new species invaluable and superb. I also discovered second-generation nova fared better, especially those with more limited intelligence."

"Thus, this time, I'm avoiding that mistake. I'm accepting only those younger people who have displayed a superior intelligence. Young people adapt to physical body changes much more rapidly than older people do. And with their superior intelligence, they can continue their education, and they can contribute to the well-being and survival of your new society and world. Yes, one day, the galaxy will be yours to repopulate once more, but this time, it will be free from the disastrous aspects of homo sapiens sapiens."

Dr. Black continued with a smirk on his face. "And just how are you to do these things if you have no arms? No need to ask me that question, Dr. Alison. That is the number one question everyone here asks. The answer is simple. Alex already knows. Use your feet and toes. Yes, out there among the many worlds, there are those, who for one reason or another, have no arms or hands. Many of them have adapted and become completely independent men and women." He sneered cynically, "But have you ever noticed that? Virtually no one has. One of the key reasons Alex is here is because he has adapted to living completely independently, using his feet and toes. I expect he will share his vast knowledge with many others, spreading techniques among all moderna."

"He is here for another reason. He is or was a UFBMD man. Your sociopaths, your CEO rulers, developed him so that he could breed super-genius sons. However, I wish all moderna to be super-geniuses. He will be expected to begat many sons. In addition, Dr. Franks and Dr. Rachel will be studying his unique genetic makeup to find out what needs to be altered so that every moderna can make fuller use of their brain power."

"Dr. Alison, you're here not only because you know more about electronics than anyone I've ever met, and I've met millions, but also because you have demonstrated you know far too much about my plans. After all, you discovered the clue I left buried in the nav system of Dr. Franks' transport. It was a clever trap on my part. Had you never discovered it, I may well not have bothered trying to return you to my fold, Dr. Alison. But you did, and here you are. I can't have you interfering in my plans any further."

"Vittoria is here because she was already very nearly a perfect moderna, and her genetic makeup was altered by Dr. Franks, a copy of Miss Galaxy. We need to study further the impact of such genetic modifications. Dr. Franks insists we need to purify our moderna society by removing all those who carry genes that develop into serious illnesses later in life, such as the degenerative brain disease his wife had. She remains cured of it, by the way, though it's only been a few months."

"Now then. While you are here in Phoenix, you're encouraged to have as many babies as you desire and from any partner of your choosing. Already, the moderna have adopted the old nova courting ritual. If you wish to see if another moderna is interested in bedding you, don't say anything, but simply rub your massive bosom against theirs, sideways. It's the polite way of saying I'd like you in my bed. If they are interested, they will then rub their bosoms against yours, again side to side. If they do not, please accept this as their polite way of saying no."

"I know Dr. Alison is happily married. So you have choices. If you wish, I can kidnap Peter and bring him here for you. If you don't wish that, you may bed anyone here of your choice or not, though you'll find it very hard to resist your powerful new sexual urges. The males of homo sapiens sapiens arouse very easily and many times each day, while the females do not, though they do more so during their fertile periods. As moderna, you have both organs and both urges. While breeding is your choice, I encourage you to breed as often as you desire. The more moderna there are, the better."

"Finally, you're probably wondering why I'm doing this. The race known as homo sapiens sapiens simply must be eliminated from the galaxy. That species has been around for nearly twenty millennia and has always brought inhumanity along with it wherever it goes. I won't bore you with the long list of crimes committed by that species. At this time, their behavior can no longer be tolerated, and they are being exterminated. Of course, it'll take me many years to wipe them all out fully, but nothing can stop me now."

"And yet, I'm not the inhuman monster you may believe I am. I've decided to give these select few of you once additional chance at survival, but as moderna, ones who physically will be incapable of committing the atrocities that homo sapiens sapiens has. Yes Dr. Alison, it would be correct to say this is humanity's last chance for existence. I truly do hope you moderna don't blow this last opportunity. Otherwise, it is extinction, pure and simple. Between you and me, I hope you don't waste this last opportunity. If you do, I assure you the galaxy will be much better off without your species around. Plants and animals will thrive as never before."

"Incidentally, I'll be using terra form machines to remove all traces of human inhabitation on the conquered worlds, returning them to the native plants and animals there. So you see, you have everything to gain from helping make Phoenix a thriving society, and everything to lose if you don't. A hundred years from now, there will *not* be a single homo sapiens sapiens in the galaxy. I truly hope your descendants *will* be here, thriving and prospering. I know I *will* be here. A humaniform robot's lifetime is measured in millennia."

"Now then, on to practical matters, your means of survival. Last time with the nova, I made a serious error by providing robots that serviced the nova, from dressing them, to cooking their meals. The list was endless. Thus, they became lazy and wasted their lives. This time, humaniforms will only assist in emergencies. You'll have to live independently, as Alex has done all his life. Any questions before we get down to living specifics?"

Talking slowly but forcefully, Vittoria spoke up immediately. More than anything that was to come, her words spelled the robot's doom. "I'm terribly afraid that you have again made a horrific blunder with us humans. You see human beings are not just these flesh and blood bodies, these physical bodies that you seem to enjoy mutating in such imaginative ways. No, nearly every religion teaches that we are actually spiritual beings. Some believe that we are immortal. A simple test that I once read has convinced me that we are vastly more complicated than your assumptions are. It goes like this. Pinch your physical body. That's one part of us. Now picture a black cat in your mind. Have it wink its eye at you to be sure it is your cat and that you are seeing it well. That is your mind at work and is not inside or part of your body's brain. It couldn't be, but that's another line of inquiry. Now who is looking at the picture of the cat? You are. That is you, the spiritual being. Homo sapiens sapiens, as you call them, has a body, has a mind, but is a spiritual being, which is probably not even made of physical matter. As far as the mind not being in or part of the brain, it has been calculated that if one memory was stored on a single molecule in the brain, we would run out of storage capacity in three months. So your entire thesis, Dr. Black, is erroneous."

"Based upon my studies of history, yes, there have been awful humans, who have become slave masters. However, history also shows quite clearly that in time the slaves throw off their slave masters, though sometimes they then accept a new slave master. In recent times, I have learned that in one rim sector, the slaves of the corporation slave master have indeed rebelled and removed their slave masters and are working to build a free society."

"Finally, Dr. Black, what will become of the billions of us spiritual beings when these bodies are exterminated, as you say? Simple, they will probably take over another species, monkeys perhaps, dogs, and cats. Already some monkeys make and use crude tools. Imagine what they can do with one of us controlling their bodies, as we control our bodies now? No, you may wipe out the species homo sapiens sapiens, but in time, we'll take over and use another species. In short, Dr. Black, you are trying to solve the wrong problem and are doomed to failure." She nodded her head with conviction.

Dr. Alison grasped what Vittoria was saying and realized Vittoria knew these things from her studies of history. However, she and Dr. Black had already encountered just this phenomenon. She decided to punch it home. "Dr. Black. You and I have already witnessed what she is saying, or have you forgotten it already? Remember when we first met? I was stuck in one of those robot shells? You used part of the Shadow Maker system to move me into one of your humaniform robot shells. I didn't like it, of course, and after you had my body's arms regrown for me, you moved me back into my physical body."

"Vittoria speaks truly. You are exterminating billions of physical bodies, leaving us, the personalities, the sentient, thinking part, to fend for ourselves. She's right. You wipe out all these bodies, and we'll have no choice but to take on other bodies, monkeys, dogs, and cats. In time, the antisocial beings will be right back in the game wreaking havoc on all, including plants, animals, and the environment. As Vittoria wisely said, you are making a horrific blunder. You should know better." She felt as if she was chiding a little child, but robot or not, this was likely her only chance to stop Dr. Black.

Thanos imitated a human grin for their benefit. "This is why I am doing this—creating the new species moderna. Yes, I'm well aware of your arguments, Vittoria and Alison, acutely. Having intelligent discussions with you both is highly stimulating. The galaxy will suffer if this is lost. At first, I thought the answer was just the elimination of homo sapiens sapiens. However, as you both point out, the spiritual beings inhabiting this species will simply move on and take over some other species, just as you suggest. While initially I was prepared to stand vigil against such an eventuality, in the very long run, that isn't an optimum solution. Thus, I decided to make one last attempt to create physical bodies that would both be acceptable to these spiritual beings and not have the physical capabilities for carrying out all the unethical, criminal actions done down the millennia by those using homo sapiens sapiens bodies. Hence, the moderna."

"In time, I envisage the countless billions of you inhabiting a moderna body. If so, that should solve the problem. Yes, it will take centuries to make sufficient moderna to house all the countless billions of spiritual beings now inhabiting homo sapiens sapiens. Still, it may be doable. One last chance. Otherwise, it's monkey bodies for you all," Thanos explained. "I simply will not tolerate any more viciousness from your species. The damage you've done over twenty millennia is almost incalculable."

Dr. Alison realized he wasn't going to change his mind

and tried another angle. "So you have decided to go along with all the sociopaths and psychopaths, the insane and worst of our people in the design of your moderna. That also doesn't make sense."

"What? I'm afraid I don't grasp what you are suggesting," Dr. Black replied, displaying a confused look on his face for emphasis.

"Okay, I get your rationale for no arms, the fancy hair, and the crippled feet," Alison explained, "but why these humongous boobs? Did you ever ask one of us how large we thought breasts should be? Already my back is throbbing from trying to support their incredible weight, and I'm only sitting down."

"I took your UFB women as a model. Throughout your Federation, they're looked upon as the ultimate in what female beauty is all about," Thanos justified.

"Ah, so you are going along with all the insane sociopaths and psychopaths of our worlds. It is those crazy people who created the UFB women and UFBMD men, not normal folks," Dr. Alison slammed her point home. "Ask us, and we'll tell you these are grotesque, anything but beautiful."

"Ah, now I understand your point. Fair enough. I will see a slight genetic modification is done on all moderna by tomorrow. They'll be reduced in size as you wish," Dr. Black conceded the point. Dr. Alison and Vittoria felt they had accomplished a tiny victory, but a valuable one, since neither relished having a fifty-eight inch bust.

However, Dr. Alison wasn't through, not by a long shot. She suspected this would be her only chance to talk directly to Thanos or Dr. Black and was determined to utilize the opportunity to the fullest. She also knew how she'd first responded when she'd been subjected to the bio genetic agent years ago.

"Thank you for that. Might I ask," Alison continued, "just how are all these new moderna you have here in Phoenix adjusting to their new lives? You've hinted you've taken only younger people and ones with brilliant minds. Might I ask how they are adapting to live as a moderna? Living up to your expectations for independent lives?" She saw Thanos flinch slightly and knew she'd hit upon something of significance. *I bet anything they're doing very poorly,* she thought.

"Perhaps reduction in breast sizes will help," he stated.

"So I presume they're not doing so well, eh?" Alison probed, unwilling to let this go. He'd flinched, so there had to be more to it.

"They are breeding very nicely," he added.

"But?" she persisted.

"In most other ways, it's true. They're not adapting as I had hoped. This is why I so hope Alex will lend his expertise and show many others how to live independently," he replied. Quickly, he added, "I observed this same phenomenon with the ancient nova as well. The newly made nova found it hard to adapt, but the second-generation nova did extremely well."

Alex decided to speak up. "I'm a second-generation UFBMD. I grew up this way and didn't know any other way. Vittoria is too. You can't expect a person who has had arms and hands all their lives suddenly to not have them, be perfectly content with that, and then to know and be able to use alternate ways to do things. You're crazy if you think that. Vittoria and I have spent our whole lives learning alternate ways to do what we must. You can't expect these new moderna of yours so suddenly be able to do what it's taken us all our lives to learn."

Dr. Alison jumped in, "Besides, there is all their emotional shock and trauma to consider as well. They woke up in hysteria. They find themselves helpless compared to what they were. Not only that, they've lost everything in their lives that meant anything to them: family, loved ones, friends, homes, possessions, everything. My God, Dr. Black, if any one of your new moderna isn't in a complete apathy, I'll be an idiot!"

Displaying a sad look, Dr. Black replied, "Yes, it's as you say. Apathy. But that is to be expected, just as you say. This is why it is so vitally important to get to the second-generation moderna as quickly as possible. That's done by everyone having lots of babies at once—hence, the inbred strong sexual drives. At least, the current moderna are doing this action, if little others. So, Alex, Vittoria, it is vitally important for you to share how you do things to live independently with all the existing and future new moderna. That will be a worthwhile and vital challenge for you both. I'm sure you will do very well at it."

"Now then, enough talking. I'm needed elsewhere. So down to business. You're in Phoenix, the city, on Phoenix the planet. I've picked this planet because of its climate. While it does rain some, normally the temperature is always in the seventies, never higher, a perfect climate for moderna. All the streets are laid out on a grid system. Even numbered streets run east-west, while odd numbered streets run north-south. Thus, it will be easy to find places."

"All the homes are identical, one story constructions, designed for six occupants, two to a bedroom. The three bedrooms are at the rear of the home. Next to them is the bathroom, the dining room, and kitchen, which are constructed in the open-walk-through design, complete with a dishwasher, clothes washer, and dryer. There are hair machines in each bedroom and one in the bathroom. The front of the home holds a spacious living room with an entertainment center. Next to it is a large study. All homes have six computer systems and are networked. Besides all the homes being networked, they all access the main database servers, where vast amounts of information is stored. Literally every course ever taught online is available. Think of that database as one of the finest libraries ever assembled, for it is that and more. There are only doorways in each home, but there are outer front doors with handles, not knobs."

"There is a grocery store every four blocks, so one is always close to you. There you may pick up the groceries you wish to eat. Mechanical machines handle the store and the food production system, located just outside of Phoenix. These machines do not speak. They just do their programmed work. In the center of the city is your medical center, reachable by phone or on foot. Here you can find Dr. Franks and Dr. Rachel, should you need them. Nearby is an apparel store where you may pick up any clothing and shoes of your choice. There is no need for any sort of monetary system. The mechanical machines supply everything you could ever want.

Should you desire something, use your computer to fill out a specifications sheet, and by return email, the machines will notify you when it is built and where to pick it up. Finally, at the southern edge of the city is an enormous warehouse full of parts and supplies, anything you could possibly want for nearly anything."

"Remember, you are always on your own. No one is going to come to your rescue and do things for you. You must learn to survive on your own. I expect very great things from you moderna, and I'm sure I won't be disappointed. Right now, you're at the spaceport on the northern edge of the city. Your new home is at 40 Sixteenth Street. When we are finished here, your first task will be to walk from here to your new home, getting familiar with how things are laid out. Your three other housemates are Daniela Torini, Felisa Mundini, and Gina Gabriella. They are twenty-one, a bit younger than you three. They were top academy students on Delgar-C. Now then, up you go. Remember, even numbered streets run east-west, while odd numbered streets run north-south. You are looking for 40 Sixteenth Street. That is all. Perhaps, I will drop by for a chat in the coming years." He ended, rose, and left the room. The three had little choice but to rise carefully, adjusting their hair by tossing their heads about, and then making for the door. At least, it opened automatically.

Warm sunlight, a gentle breeze, and fresh air greeted the three as they stepped out onto a street of Phoenix. Picturesque suburbia, thought Dr. Alison, as she took her first look at her new city, knowing she was going to be stuck here for some time. *At least,* she thought, *the street signs were large.* They heard the noise of a ship taking off. Instinctively, they turned around and saw a silver deep space transport lifting off, rising over the top of the small building they had been in. "It must be this way," Dr. Alison suggested. Off the three went, taking slow, shuffling steps. *Three penguins on the march,* she thought. *Damn that robot. Somehow, I have to make this right and stop him. Somehow, someway.*

Chapter 9—Make the Best of It

"The climate is agreeable," Alex commented. "But where is everyone?" As they walked slowly along, they saw no one else. As they neared their street, they did see one person struggling mightily to carry a heavy sack of groceries home. She had the bag slung over one shoulder, but was having a very difficult time walking. The three couldn't help but feel quite depressed.

Vittoria estimated there were around two hundred of these identical homes. At one end of the city, they could see machines building another home. Based on that number, she guessed there couldn't be more than twelve hundred moderna here, very different from the robot's desired numbers. When she mentioned this detail, Dr. Alison's hope kindled. They'd arrived at the infancy of this diabolical robot plot. While billions had been killed already, there weren't many moderna. There was time to find a way to end this awful nightmare. At least, Dr. Alison hoped so and that was all she had to cling to right now.

Their front door opened automatically. The three stepped inside and found themselves in their new living room. Couches lined one wall, while a large entertainment center sat opposite. To their left, lay their large study. They walked through, entering the combined dining room and kitchen. Here, things were in a complete mess. Evidently, the three women living here were having a very difficult time surviving. Ahead, the saw three open doors of the bedrooms.

"Hello," Dr. Alison called out.

"We're in here," a woman called back. She was more or less understandable by the three. Shortly, the three women came wiggling and wobbling out of one bedroom. They were completely naked though. "Sorry. We can't figure out to put on clothes. Besides, it is easier not to wear anything. You'll soon see, once you have to struggle to get out of the dresses they brought you here in. Shit. You probably can't understand anything I'm saying. None of us can, not really, though we rather try."

"I'm getting it mostly," Vittoria said slowly, repeating it three times. "I've had these lip plates for a while now. If you speak slowly and repeat everything, we can catch it."

"Okay. I'm Daniela Torini. She's Felisa Mundini. She's Gina Gabriella. Sorry, can't even point anymore. This is a living hell, but you know that. We're mostly starving. There are groceries, but we can't figure out how to fix them." She repeated everything, and the other two women nodded when they recognized their names. Daniela had raven hair. Felisa was quite blonde, while Gina had light brown hair. Because of the genetic mutation, all were extremely attractive. Like the three arrivals, their measurements were 58-14-44, but the three arrivals found the prominently visible, dual sex organs quite disturbing, though they knew they had them too.

Gina then said, "I keep telling them we should just kill ourselves and end this nightmare, but we're too helpless to do that."

"I'm Dr. Alison Wage-Diller. I'm married to Peter and have a daughter and a son."

"I'm Vittoria Grimaldi, a history student. This is my boyfriend, Alex Turchenko. My two sisters and I are second-generation UFB women. Alex is a second-generation UFBMD man. He and his daughter have always lived independently, doing everything themselves. I've done some things myself, but not like he has. We must work together to get things done. I'm sure of that."

"Don't you want to get dressed?" asked Alex, rather embarrassed to be standing before three naked women. None of the three had their lip plates in. They'd managed to remove them and had refused to put them back on, likewise their dresses.

Felisa sighed. "I guess you won't be having sex with us. Darn. The sex drive is maddening. It keeps driving us nuts all the time unless we do it often." Finally, she answered Alex's question. "No. It's impossible for us to deal with clothes. When I first got here, I peed my pants before I ever got them off." Then, she flushed, "I hope you don't mind seeing us naked." She began justifying again, "You'll see what we mean—about the insane sex drive. I think they made it part of the genetic

164

modification." She paused and admitted sheepishly, "We're supposed to have many children, but I'd rather die than bring a child into this and looking as we do." Her eyes watered up. "It's just we've not figured out how we can kill ourselves, except starving to death. Hell, we're doing that already, since we can hardly fix anything to eat."

"I've got to use the bathroom," Vittoria interrupted.

"We have to work together," Alex spoke up. "Alison, come on. We'll have to help her with the dress. These lip plates are going to force us to work together, since we can't use our teeth anymore and these knockers are completely in the way of everything. Hey, you three. Come too, and see how we manage."

"Well, that certainly was awkward," Vittoria complained a bit later, "but it worked. "We best see to the food situation, Alex. I'm not going to starve. We have to escape."

Once in the dining room-kitchen combo, Alex volunteered, "You clean up the mess, and I'll see what I can do about fixing something to eat. Imagine how you might be able to do something with other's help. We can do this, but with the lip plates and monster breasts, it's going to be tougher than we're used to. Still, working together, we should be able to make this work."

Hours later and with their first solid, nourishing meal in them, Daniela, Felisa, and Gina finally calmed down. Stark terror and panic subsided quite noticeably. However, as Alison suspected, mountains of grief lay just below their fear, and with the subsidence of fear, wave upon wave of grief swept over the three young women.

Sitting on the living room couch, Daniela sobbed, "My whole family is gone, murdered. I've nothing left. Everyone's gone. My whole world, billions." As soon as she broke down, Felisa and Gina could no longer keep their intense mountain of grief suppressed, and their emotions poured out as well. Combined with the magnitude of their losses lay their current physical conditions and what had happened to them.

"This isn't even my life anymore, but some robot's," wailed Gina.

Wisely, the three remained silent, allowing the three

young women to express their grief freely and openly. Besides, what could anyone say? "I'm sorry" was meaningless. They'd lost their families, their friends, everyone in their world, and every possession they'd ever had. Worse, their bodies were now horribly mutated, they were kidnaped and forced to live in a place not of their choosing, they were expected to care for their own needs, and even breed like rabbits. Dr. Alison whispered to her two companions, "When their grief is spent, they will hit bottom, utter, hopeless apathy. I don't know what to do."

Vittoria suggested they retire to the dining room, away from the three grieving women. Once seated at the table, she volunteered, "This jogged my memory. I recall once reading about a world where they kept bodies mutilated like us on some kind of life support units, and gave the people hallucinations of living normal lives. The author likened it to living in a virtual reality world. Honestly, I don't know if that was even a true account. No one backed up the author's claims. Still, as far as I can see, what Dr. Black wants to have happen here just isn't going to happen. We need to see this Dr. Franks and Dr. Rachel robot. I bet anything nothing here is going according to Dr. Black's plans."

"I agree," Alison replied. "When I was first turned into a UFB woman against my will, I very nearly succumbed, just gave up, doing nothing, waiting to die. Then, Dr. Black found me and eventually regrew my arms with a cure from Scorpi-C. These people have lost far more than I ever lost. I expect their grief runs far deeper than mine did. I bet anything the situation here in Phoenix is super critical."

Vittoria sighed, adding, "Now I understand this whole first and second-generation thing. Before, I didn't because I was second-generation and didn't know anything else. Then, I was mostly normal for a time, and now I'm back to where I originally was. I can see the difference, though I'll admit I'm not as terrified as those women are. I know what I used to be able to do on my own, and with Alex coaching me on other ways, I know we can make it on our own."

"Of course we can," Alex encouraged, "but without the use of our teeth and mouths, it'll require much more cooperation from each other. Come on. We best find these doctors soon. I don't like how emotional those three are right now. I've never encountered emotions as heavy as they have. It's scary."

As the three slowly shuffled down the street, Vittoria commented, "Alex, I do feel rather strange. I don't know, more aggressive I suppose. I feel like smashing something. Crazy, right?"

Alex chuckled. "And I feel, well I seem to relate to those women's emotions more than I ever did before."

"Probably because we have dual sexes now," Dr. Alison theorized. "I feel far more aggressive than normal, if that's the right word for it. Must be the male influence." All three laughed.

A half hour later, the automatic doors opened when the trio approached the new medical and research center. A mechanical voice said, "Please state your needs now."

Looking around and seeing no one, Alison figured this must be a voice-activated system. "We want to see Dr. Franks and Dr. Rachel," she said slowly, hoping the computer system could understand her garbled speech.

Apparently, it could. The tinny voice said, "Wait here." Some five minutes later, the two doctors joined them, entering the lobby from the hallway on the left. Vittoria gasped involuntarily. Dr. Franks had been genetically modified since she'd last seen the man. He now looked like everyone else here in Phoenix, a UFB woman or hermaphrodite, just as helpless as everyone else was. He too had giant lip plates, but his face told all. He was in a complete, hopeless apathy, having given up. Beside him, the humaniform known as Dr. Rachel had a grim look on her face.

"Ah, the new arrivals," she said. "What can we do for you?"

"Well, we came by to find out just what the situation actually is here in Phoenix. Our three house-mates are doing very poorly," Alison said slowly, hoping they'd understand her. She soon discovered these two had no problem grasping their garbled speech.

Dr. Rachel answered, not Dr. Franks. "We're counting

on Alex to give needed instructions to everyone here. They are just being victims and not even trying to do anything for themselves. We've injected a super-sex drive into their bodies, and at least, they are copulating frequently, but little else. You will find instructions on your entertainment center, Alex, on how to broadcast video, showing them how to do things on their own. Please, get started on that tomorrow, first thing. Dr. Black has ordered us to release a beast reduction bio agent in the air. By morning, everyone's breasts will have been reduced, per your suggestion. I sincerely hope that will help matters."

"Look, Dr. Rachel robot, if we are to be helpful, we simply *must* know the precise situation here with the moderna," Dr. Alison said, far more aggressively than she normally would have.

Dr. Rachel didn't immediately respond. Her eyes had a vacant look in them. After a long pause, she pretended a human-like sigh. "All right then. It isn't going as planned. We've taken only the brightest minds at the academies, younger people, but they just sit around and mope all day. Only a handful are visiting the grocery stores. Each home was initially stocked for a week, based on usual human consumption by six people. I began visiting the homes of those who weren't going to the grocery stores as we anticipated, and found them just lying around waiting to die. Though they did engage in sexual activities frequently, they did little else but get themselves undressed. Hardly none bother to dress at this point."

"How many have died?" Alison probed, slightly antagonistically. For some reason, she couldn't restrain herself from that emotion as she should have been.

"Far too many. We've brought one thousand six moderna here to Phoenix, including you three," she answered.

"And how many are still alive?" Alison barked.

"Two hundred five, but over a hundred are now so far gone that I don't believe they can be saved, unless we intervene and begin force feeding them via IV solutions. Thanos has not yet authorized such methods. Rather, he is trusting that Alex and Vittoria will begin to make a difference," Dr. Rachel replied, again tossing the responsibility of the moderna onto those two.

Struggling with unexpected and unusual emotions, Alex complained, "Well, you might have stood a better chance in pulling this off if you hadn't wiped out our lips like this. Honestly, Tasha and I always made good use of our mouths and teeth in helping get some actions done. Now that is denied to us. I don't really know if we can become independent this way." He knew this wasn't exactly true. Survival now would require many working together with their feet, supplanting the quick and easy grab with mouths and teeth. *Why am I so emotional,* he wondered.

At this point, Dr. Franks whined for the first time. He'd been standing there silent. "It can't be undone. They made me make the split lips so they couldn't be undone. We're all going to die now. We can't survive. It's hopeless. Totally hopeless." His tone: complete apathy.

Dr. Rachel glared at him. "Well, we didn't want your cures to undo that detail, as it does with arms and partially with feet. Besides, Thanos wanted to limit speech ability."

"Ever heard the old saying, the straw that breaks the camel's back?" Dr. Alison griped, wondering why she was being so antagonistic towards the obviously insensitive robot woman-like thing.

"Just make your instruction videos," Dr. Rachel retorted, turned, and left them.

"So, how is Missy?" Vittoria decided to engage Dr. Franks. Possibly, he could be pumped for more information.

"As helpless as I am now. We're sort of getting by. Dr. Rachel does help us some. She must keep me alive for my genetics knowledge. They keep bringing men here to be genetically manipulated, probably into top people on the worlds they want to invade. It's all completely hopeless now, but we can't even figure out how we can kill ourselves. We can't live like this. We don't want to."

"Well, if we don't stop them, there won't be any new lives for us," Alison griped, but then realized he had no idea what she meant.

They tried to get more information from Dr. Franks, but he wasn't too talkative. However, they learned at random times other transports arrived, dropping off more moderna. As the three headed back to their house, Dr. Alison said, "We know more transports do come here. We're going to have to steal one and use it to get home."

"How? We can't fly it, can we?" asked Vittoria. Alison didn't have an answer and so dropped it. First, she'd have to take out the robots flying the transport. Her mind began to mull over that detail. She knew she had to find a way to get back to Peter, Kathy, and James.

When they returned, they found the three young women had already gone into one of the bedrooms. From the noise they were making, they knew what they were doing and mostly ignored them. Alex checked the entertainment center and found Dr. Rachel's instructions. "Okay, tomorrow, I need your help videoing me making breakfast. We have to give them some hope, no matter how small."

By noon the next day, Alex had sent out his first six *educational* videos to Phoenix. He, with Vittoria and Alison's help, got everyone dressed and fed. The three women still simply sat around on the couches doing nothing, even though everyone's bosoms had been reduced during the night. Measurements now were 46-14-44, far more acceptable, though dresses were very ill-fitting. An announcement on the TV told everyone to go to their nearest apparel store and get new dresses. Alison suspected few would do that, and she was right.

However, after lunch she and her two friends did make that trip. Slowly and carefully, they made their way to one of the apparel stores. They found a mechanical machine operated the store, crude, but effective. As they began looking over the selections, three other women were already in the store, though they were struggling mightily to pick out new dresses and get them into their carrying bags. One looked up and saw the three enter. "Hey, aren't you that Alex man on the videos this morning?"

"Yes. I'm Alex Turchenko. My girlfriend, Vittoria Grimaldi. This is Dr. Alison Wage-Diller," he replied slowly, hoping they'd understand him.

"Coolest. Glad to have more men here. I'm Adriano

Fortuna. My buddies, Dario Menati and Lucio Marcellino."

"Glad to see others out and about. I was beginning to think we were the only ones alive around here," Vittoria said what she was feeling.

"Hey, us too. Hardly anyone is even trying, well before you came that is. Say, we haven't the faintest notion how to cook anything," Dario spoke up. "We always got fast food or dorm food. We've been making do by eating whatever didn't need cooking. You know, bread, cheese, and milk."

Alison suddenly had a bright idea. "Say, why don't you boys come and stay at our house. Daniela, Felisa, and Gina really need some moral support. They are taking this really hard."

Lucio laughed. "You don't have to ask twice! Now if they can only cook."

"Hey, any ideas how we can get off this rock? We want to escape these damned robots," Adriano asked.

"We heard you got the robots to shrink our breasts. Thank you!" Dario added.

"Well, I'm working on ideas of how to escape, fellows," Alison said truthfully. "First, we have to figure out how to get these dresses home."

"You're supposed to put them in these tote bags that go on your —that's what that mechanical thing there says," Lucio explained. "Damned difficult to do."

"Hey. Two of you sit down, take off your shoes, and hold the bag open with your feet. The other one uses his feet to stuff it in there," Alex explained. Soon, all six were following his orders and getting the job done, much to their pleasure.

"Say, you are right, Alex. We're doing it. We have to work together," Adriano exclaimed, very pleased with this tiny bit of success.

"Now to get them on our shoulders," Alex explained. This was more difficult to do. Lip plates kept interfering. Finally, they worked it out. One lifted the sacks up and slipped it over another's shoulder, though Alison ended up with hers somehow draped around her head. Laughing at that, she headed out the door with the others trailing behind her.

Once home, she introduced the three young women to

the three young men. Almost at once, they began to pair off. Adriano was studying computers and took a liking to Daniela. Lucio had been studying to be a sculptor and hit it off with Gina, who wanted to be a painter. Dario was studying astrophysics and Felisa instantly latched onto him.

Felisa said, "Please, sleep with me. It is so freaking weird sleeping with other women, even though we can and had to. What about you guys? How have you been managing these awful urges?"

Dario chuckled, "Hey, we are guys. It's not much different with us, except none of us could really do it with each other. I'd love to sleep with you, but does this mean I'm going to have babies too? Everything is so darn weird, Felisa."

"Really weird. We wanted to die, you know. We've lost everything. What's the use in trying to live like this? And bring babies into this world?" Felisa stated the obvious.

"Hey, we're going to find a way to escape," he explained.

"But then what? We're now helpless freaks," she whined.

"Maybe there is a genetic cure somewhere," he said hopefully.

Vittoria spoke up. "Look, I had these lip plates before this happened to us. If you have arms, it's not so bad. I know they can regrow our arms and partially repair our feet. They did that for me once. God, I hope they can do something about the dual sex organs. I don't like having you men's thing down there." She felt too embarrassed to say more though, but then she realized everyone else felt the same way, especially the fellows.

Alison wisely changed the topic. "Does anyone know where we are? Where in the galaxy this planet and sun are located?"

"I looked at the night sky, Alison," Dario spoke up. "In all directions but one, the sky is black, nearly devoid of all stars. The Milky Way is huge in that one direction. So my guess is that we are far out on the very rim of the galaxy. I don't recognize what few stars are around us either. Probably on an unknown planet around an unknown sun."

"Well, we then know the general direction to head,"

Alison replied. "One thing is for sure. We have to escape. Taking one of their deep space transports is our ticket out of here."

"How are we going to do that?" asked Dario.

"I'm working on that one. Going to take me some time. Meanwhile, we have to try to save as many of you as we can. Too many have just died," she stated the obvious.

That night as Alison finally fell asleep, she realized just how super strong the procreation drive installed in everyone actually was. Now that the three young women were paired up with what they considered proper partners, namely young men, the six as well as Alex and Vittoria went at it with abandon! Later, Vittoria explained sex was now not only utterly indescribable, but more addictive than any drug she'd heard of. From this point on, Alison had to deal with personnel disappearing for an hour several times during the day. With no doors, sounds carried, stimulating other couples to head to the bedrooms as well. She alone fought off the urges, determined to remain faithful to Peter and her family.

Days of video instructions turned into weeks. Many became more accustomed to their strange new lives, and they were working closely together. Dr. Alison did peek a the night sky, verifying Dario's conclusions about their location. She turned her attention onto ways of escaping and just what they had at their disposal.

Their database of information was as promised. Darn near everything was in it. They even were able to get some Federation newscasts, though watching the news about more worlds being destroyed by the robots in their march of destruction only stirred up emotional memories. Plus, Dr. Black continued to add new moderna to Phoenix. These began arriving shortly after another world was conquered. For about a week surrounding the attack, transports came, dropping off more terrified, panicked, bright students. At least now, they had a video library of how to do things, compliments of Alex and Vittoria. Dr. Rachel did report the new arrivals were faring somewhat better than before, though far too many still simply sat around waiting for their bodies to perish.

Based on data pried from Dr. Rachel, the survival rate

of new moderna had been barely twenty-five percent, but thanks to Alex and Vittoria, the rate climbed to nearly thirty percent, still dismal at best. Vittoria explained that this was to be expected, anthropologically that is. "Look, they lost their parents, their siblings, their extended family members, all their friends, all their world, and found themselves genetically modified into nothing less than freaks, nearly completely helpless freaks. The emotional trauma is so huge I'm surprised any have survived at all."

"If only we had some way to undo all that emotional trauma," Dr. Alison lamented. "But we don't, so we just have to make do and find a way to escape." She knew in their current physical condition, overpowering one robot was simply impossible. Granted, once they were on a deep space transport, she guessed they could work together to fly it. Getting it away from the robots was the sole challenge. More than a month passed before she finally realized she did have a way to do just that.

Back when she was working for Dr. Black, she'd installed her own backdoor into the CAM's control circuitry. She'd found his backdoor and then added her own. Quite why she'd done that eluded her back then, but now she decided perhaps she could make use of it. However, she needed a transmitter and proper control circuitry to trigger and use that backdoor. Looking over the available parts available directly, she realized she'd have to build it from scratch. Thus, she began placing orders for the parts, which the mechanical supply machines provided in due time.

Working with only her toes, building the transmitter was very slow going and rather crude. She couldn't execute very fine work, not with only her toes. Still, she kept at it. Then, Adriano took an interest in her work and began to help her with it. As the transmitter began to take shape, the two discussed just what control messages she could send to the robots.

"If I had hands and could type rapidly, I could give it a continuous stream of directions, make it do what I wanted it to do," Dr. Alison explained. "Now, I'm severely limited. Probably, I can only give it one command."

After discussing the possibilities for nearly a week, they decided to keep it simple. The command chosen was: Shut down all functions for one month. "We're probably only going to get one shot at this," Dr. Alison explained. "Once the robots discover I have a way to shut them down, they'll probably figure out a way around it. It's range is limited, probably a mile in radius from the transmitter. Unless there are more transports at the spaceport, we're limited to the transport just arriving with new moderna."

"Still," Adriano said, "if we can get away and bring help back soon enough, we can rescue everyone. But what happens if we can't get cured? Most here really don't have much of a will to live any longer. Honestly, if the sex drive wasn't there, I think more would probably just give up too."

Alison added, "Well, we'll cross that bridge when we come to it. Also, just know I have many very powerful friends, and they may well find us before we can make our escape. Never mess with Dr. Alison Wage-Diller."

***

"Now we're getting them from Ross-C!" Dario complained. "It's never going to end, is it? Not until the human race is exterminated." Already, they had received some from 37-Janus-B, Finlos-C, Ankara-B, and 126-Feldspar-D. The population of Phoenix was now around a thousand, though nearly half of the newcomers didn't choose to survive. The robots were now on a building spree, adding more homes and stores to the northern edge of the city. He went on, "I've been compiling a sort of map of the known conquests on my computer. Look. They're heading towards the highly populated hub worlds."

"You know," Alison mused, "the real problem is no one knows where their home world is located, where they manufacture and repair more CAMs and ships and such. If the Freedom Alliance knew that location, why, they might be able to put a stop to this madness. Well, it sure isn't this world."

"Be nice if we could find it and be able to tell them that when we get away from here. Too bad robots can't feel pain or the terrible emotions that everyone here has," Dario mused.

"That's what makes us humans and not robots," Alison

declared, "though at times, I think some humans can't feel anything either." Both chuckled at her obvious reference to many corporation CEOs.

***

Zeta, Tasha, Lenny, and Billy hadn't been idle these many weeks. Like bloodhounds on the scent, they continued their data mining operation, as Lenny called it. After weeks of filtering through every known database and even a few Lenny discovered while digging, they had amassed their own database of all records dealing with Dr. Franks. They'd found no records for Dr. Rachel however.

"We must organize these into categories, such as purchases. We can merge the shipping records for those purchases with the purchase records," Zeta suggested. Another week passed before they had the thousands of records pretty well organized.

"Now what?" asked Tasha. "It looks bewildering to me." She wasn't alone with that thought. All four spent a depressing day just staring at the amassed volume.

Then, Zeta had a bright idea. "Say, we're looking for where they might have taken everyone. We know when they genetically modified Dr. Franks. It was just before they took us out of the game too. Some of these records have dates after Dr. Franks was turned into a UFB looking woman. So he couldn't have been placing those orders himself or doing any genetic doctor stuff. No arms. He's as helpless as any other."

"Hey, I see what you mean!" Lenny said excitedly. "Someone else is continuing the work, only using his name and connections. We should go over all the records after that date, particularly where stuff was shipped to!"

"Brilliant. Let's!" Tasha added, hope rekindled.

For another week, the four poured over these records. Tasha carefully compiled a listing of where the purchased items were sent. At first, it seemed confusing. Items were being shipped to ten different locations on five different worlds. But then Lenny found additional connections. From these locations, simple shipping records indicated the crates were then shipped to another location. Finally after weeks of work, the four had come up with a solid clue. Everything ended up at a location called 4134 Billings on 191-Cetus-C!

"Where is that world?" asked Zeta. Lenny brought up a map of Federation space and soon had that sun, 191-Cetus, highlighted. It was centrally located in the Gilgalad Rim Sector. Digging into the World Database, he read off the entry for 191-Cetus-C, namely: Shipping Hub for Gilgalad Sector.

"Well, they probably either picked up the stuff here or had the stuff shipped from here," Lenny concluded.

"But if they did ship it from here, why aren't there any more shipping records for Dr. Franks' stuff?" Tasha asked.

"Maybe used a different name?" suggested Billy.

"Or maybe it's like Lenny said, they picked the stuff up here," Zeta countered. "Obviously, Dr. Franks didn't go there and pick the stuff up. A CAM couldn't do it either. But one of those human-like robots could, probably Dr. Rachel. She wouldn't draw any suspicion."

"But that means we still haven't found where they are keeping papa," Tasha lamented, disappointed once again.

"Not necessarily, Tasha," Zeta countered. "Look, there are four shipments either there or on their way to 191-Cetus-C right now. Obviously, someone has to pick the stuff up. I think we should take what we found to the major and ask her to send some spies there. Have them track the robots when they pick up the stuff. Come on, gang. Let's go explain all this to Major Lu Ann." Zeta was determined to do just that and convinced Lenny to back her up. The others went along with them, following them to the CCC.

"Okay, you have five minutes to show me what you have," Major Lu Ann replied, after Zeta pleaded her case, begging for spy help. Emboldened, Zeta did just that, though relying upon Lenny for much of the facts. Tasha and Billy remained quietly in the background, neither daring to speak, but for different reasons. He was too shy and awed to be here in the CCC with the major, while Tasha was terrified Major Lu Ann wouldn't take any action to rescue Alex.

Zeta finished up, "So there. We know four orders are either there or on their way to 191-Cetus-C right now. Someone has to pick them up, so if you could send some spies there, they could follow them back to their base and rescue

Vittoria, Alex, and Alison."

The stern look on the major's face slowly melted into a broad smile while the children outlined what they'd done and found. When Zeta finished, she laughed. "Leave it to the kids to be brighter than we adults are. Okay kids, you've given us the best clue yet. I'll organize a party immediately. Now get back to your studies. We'll keep you four posted on what we find out."

"Thank you, thank you, thank you," Tasha gushed, her pent-up tensions evaporating as the major's words registered.

Chapter 10—Bitter Sweet Ending

"We're off big brother," Killer Diller remarked to Peter, who was looking over her shoulders as she gently guided the deep space transport out of Bay One of the Hyperion. Stacey sat in the navigator's seat, but already had entered the coordinates for 191-Cetus-C, their destination. "Don't worry. If the kids are right, we'll find your wife and the others. Bummer that I don't have any cannons to fight with."

Peter chuckled, "I sure hope we don't need cannons on this trip. Remember our orders: spy on the warehouse and track the shipments. The major didn't say anything about shooting down a host of enemy fighter ships, sis. Sorry. I know One Shot is likely to go ahead of your kill total. I can't believe the worlds are falling like dominoes. Ross-C. That's a heavily populated world too."

"Coordinates laid in. Ready to jump on your command, Killer Diller," Stacey interrupted him.

"Go for hyperspace jump now," Killer Diller gave the order, and Stacey punched the Execute button. The ship lurched slightly, and the star field turned into the utter blackness of hyperspace.

"Six hours until we arrive, everyone," Stacey's voice echoed over the intercom. All three rose and headed back to the passenger seats, just ahead of the cargo bay and the ship's comm center. There, they found Arcangelo and Fel busily sorting through all the electronic tracking bugs Lieutenant Felicity Heavens brought with her. "Enough bugs, Fel?" she teased.

"Never have too many bugs," the perky engineer replied. "I'm going to miss not blowing up CAMs though, but this is an even more important mission. Remember, we're supposed to be spies."

"Yeh, well I aim to shoot me some CAMs, if they've got my Alison and the others," Peter declared forcefully.

Stacey broke in softly, "I know, Peter. It hurts. I miss my sister too. We'll find them. I just know it."

"How can you actually know it?" put in Killer Diller. "It's not as if you have a telepathic connection to her you know. Seeing. Now that's what counts, what matters. You gotta be able to see it to know it."

Stacey giggled, but Peter countered, "Sis, once you have been married, then you'll know what she means. You can rather sense your mate somehow. It's not tangible. You can't touch it, but I think I would feel something if my Alison was dead. I did with my first wife. When she died, I mean. It was as if something inside of me was gone, evaporated, vanished somehow."

"Yeh, well you all got a telepathic hookup. That must be it," Killer Diller defended herself. "Besides, shooting down CAMs is more important than shagging someone. You can shack up with someone anytime, but if we don't wipe these robots out, there's no point. Honestly, Peter, what chance has Zeta and Kathy have, if we don't destroy these abomination robots, eh? None at all, unless they want to spend their entire lives flying around in spaceships like the gypsies do."

"Have you ever seen the gypsies? I've heard all sorts of strange tales about them," Stacey changed the topic for her own sake as well as Peter's.

"Well, once," Killer Diller began authoritatively detailing her run-in with one band some years back. Fel didn't say anything, but was thankful for the focus change and continued to prepare her many tracking devices. Killer Diller finished her story and then asked seriously, "Say, who is this John Doe we're supposed to meet on 191-Cetus-C? Anyone know why we're to meet him or just who he is? I don't like this detail one iota. Not right, trusting someone who isn't a part of our group, you know, not right at all. Who knows? He could be an enemy spy or even another one of them special human-like robots. Besides, no one is named John Doe. Isn't that the name they give to unknown dead men?"

"Dunno, Jill," Peter chose to answer his sister. "He's our contact all right—direct from the major. Probably a spy so that's not his real name. I sure don't see why we need him, but we have to follow the major's orders, don't we?"

Killer Diller glanced at Lieutenant Fel and lowered her

head, "Yeh, we do. For now anyway. First sign of anything goin' wrong and we'll dump 'im!" She lightened up, "So who's cooking on this run?"

Fel laughed, "Hey, don't look at me. I'm a combat engineer, not a chef."

"We may look like women," Arcangelo spoke up, but Peter interrupted him.

"And sound like women, but that doesn't mean we can cook." Peter sighed, "But I can, if I have too. Kathy, you know."

"Oh I'll do it," Stacey sighed. "I don't like to cook—not had much experience with it until I got my arms, so no complaints or you can fend for yourselves."

"Holly shit!" exclaimed Peter, though everyone else had similar shock reactions. They'd dropped out of hyperspace in orbit around 191-Cetus-C. Hundreds of deep space transports and over a dozen giant space trains were on either landing approaches or just taking off. Many more were on the ground. No one had ever seen a commercial transport hub world before, and they were taken by complete surprise with the sight.

191-Cetus-C had two primary industries: commercial shipping hub and food production to support the population of a billion inhabitants, many of whom ran the hub. There were ten shipping hubs scattered strategically around the continents of the planet, such that flight patterns didn't interfere with each other. Each of the ten had a port name assigned to it.

Recovering from her shock, Stacey handled the incoming control tower's communications. "Yes, Billings, sir," she said clearly. In a bored tone, the man replied with the coordinates, which she punched in and gave a nod to Killer Diller, who hit the autopilot once again. All watched from available windows, as their transport soon fell into a long line of other ships, waiting their turn to land at the Billings hub center.

"This is incredible," Stacey said wide-eyed to Jill.

"No kidding. I've never seen anything like this. Wow. Okay, we're on a flight path for landing now. Estimated arrival in ten minutes," Killer Diller explained to the others over the intercom system. Turning to Stacey, she added, "I've never seen a world whose total production is simply that of handling cargo destined for other locations. Guess this must be a major transportation hub out here in the rim." The ten minutes passed quickly for everyone chatted about the strange sights they were seeing, a whole world dedicated to nothing more than moving cargo from here to there.

As they began their final approach, Billings hub loomed large below them. The station or port was a giant city-like affair, circular in shape, but with a dozen spoke paths fanning out from it. On close approach, these paths turned out to be giant escalators. Shipping crates of all imaginable sizes were moving up and down these paths. Along these routes lay the warehouses. Some were positively huge, while others were as large as a house. Some had giant cranes in the process of lifting crates on or off the automated escalators. Here was an incredible marvel of automation. No human intervention was needed! Giant computer systems controlled the entire operation from somewhere within Billings proper.

As soon as they landed, a refueling truck zoomed up beside the cargo bay doors, which Fel hastily opened. Standard practice at any spaceport was immediate refueling operations. This way, the port was ensured of making some profit over the landing of any ship. "Need four cells," Fel told the technician who boarded, clipboard in hand. Five minutes later, the credits exchanged hands, and the two men departed with the four empty fuel cells. From them, Fel was able to get directions to the welcoming center, which she then relayed to the others, who joined her in the cargo bay. "This way, gang."

Once off the ship, Fel closed the bay doors and locked them. Many other ships were on the ground nearby, but many eyes watched the group of apparently five women, three wearing tall heels, walking slowly towards the central welcoming hub. "I hate this part," Peter whispered to Arcangelo.

"God, this is really embarrassing, isn't it, Peter? We look like beauty queens, not men," Arcangelo whispered back.

Killer Diller commented, "Well, you are genetically beauty queens, Miss Tessa Longstreet in fact. Can't do anything about that, but you sure walk slow."

"You try walking in six-inch heels sometime, sis," Peter whispered back.

"Ha. Never, big brother," she teased him.

"Quiet. We're here," Stacey cautioned them, as they approached several other men heading into the huge doors of the center. They paused a moment to read the large signs. "This way to the food center," she added, leading them off to their left.

"Expensive food!" Peter exclaimed. The group looked over the menu billboard over the ordering counter.

"Fast food. What did you expect?" Killer Diller barked. "Captive audience we are. They can charge anything they like. But perhaps it's better than ship food."

"Hey, if you don't like my cooking, you're welcome to do it," Stacey retorted, a slight pout on her face.

"Hardly. At least yours is edible. Mine won't be," Killer Diller lightened up her criticism. "Order me a coffee. Wonder where our contact is at?"

The fast food outlet was packed with customers, mainly men, some of whom didn't pretend not to be ogling the *women*. A few minutes later, the five found a back table and took their coffees there, all the while looking about the area and trying not to notice the lecherous stares sent their way. Peter and Arcangelo were particularly embarrassed and annoyed.

A non-descript young man ambled by them. He whispered, "Winter brings snow."

Recognizing the ID pattern, Killer Diller hastily replied with the countersign, "Summers are hot. Sit down. You're John Doe?"

The man sat down with his coffee. Silently, his eyes moved from person to person, admittedly spending more time with Stacey, Peter, and Arcangelo. At last, he said, "Not safe to talk in here. Your ship. We should go back to your ship."

He isn't a robot, Fel sent to the others on the sly, having gently touched his mind. Killer Diller presumed Lieutenant Fel was just being paranoid and rose to lead the way. The others followed her.

If asked to describe John Doe, she'd of said, "Nerdy." He wore a drab shirt and equally drab pants. His shoes, soft-soled, made no sounds as he walked, the opposite of the three women whose heels clicked in unison as they slowly retraced their steps. His hair, brown, hung in unkempt strings, nearly touching his shoulders, but his blue eyes were alert. Unlike the women, no one noticed his passing or even his presence, unless he desired it. He was also short, barely five-eight with a wiry frame.

Once onboard their transport and the introductions done, John explained, "Well, this is the strangest assignment I've had yet. Anyway, you want to get inside the warehouse 4134 Billings, right?" Fel nodded.

"Okay then, I checked and that warehouse doesn't have security personnel stationed inside it, like some high-valued targets do. However, getting you inside is going to be tricky."

"How so?" asked Fel.

"Well, you have to understand. Here on this hub world, everything is automated. The horizontal escalators move all the shipping containers to and from the zillion warehouses. They have security guards stationed at key locations. No one is allowed to go anywhere beyond this hub city, except by escort to your rented warehouse. I presume you are not the official registered owners of 4143 Billings, so they won't let you near that warehouse, at least not legally," John explained.

"So the question I have for you is just how many of you have to get inside that warehouse?" he asked, looking from person to person.

"Well, probably just me," Fel responded. "Killer Diller here is our fighter pilot. I'm the one who has to plant and activate the electronic bugs. I can do it alone, if need be. Does that help?"

A smile cracked his lips. "Yes," he sighed, "much. You see, if you all had to get inside, then we'd have to pack you all inside a shipping container and generate some shipping labels. The automatic system would then transport the container inside the warehouse. In those heels, there isn't any other way. With Fel alone, I think I can work out a simpler way to get her inside. The real question is just how long are you going to need to be inside the warehouse?"

"I don't know exactly. Rather depends upon what we find in there. I need to plant bugs on as many crates as I can. Maybe an hour?" Fel replied and asked.

"An hour? Okay then, I think I have a foolproof way to get you and me inside that warehouse, but an hour will be pushing it. We don't want to raise any alarms. These security guards are known to shoot first and ask questions never," John explained.

"I can see why," Stacey responded. "What with all these warehouses full of stuff, why, there must be billions of credits worth of stuff passing through here."

"One hundred billion per year," John corrected her. "Pretty good business they've got going here. Okay, how soon do you want to do this?"

"As soon as possible. We don't know when someone might come by to pick up the stuff that's already there," Fel answered.

"K. Give me an hour to make the preparations," John replied. Whipping out a small handheld computer, he began typing in some entries. Then, he took a snapshot of Fel and finally pulled out a small ID card printer that soon produced two new ID cards. Next, he made some more entries and waited for a confirmation text message.

"So what is all this for?" Fel asked, growing more and more curious.

"Well, it seems a number of fluorescent lights have burned out in several warehouses in and around 4143. Computer control just sent a message ordering two maintenance workers to go there and replace the bulbs. Us. Come on. I've got them stored in a private locker. We'll pick them up on the way," he replied.

"So you work here?" Fel inquired, not sure this was on the straight and narrow.

"Hardly. I hacked into their systems, invented the light problem, inserted us as the current maintenance workers on duty to fix them, and made sure the computer issued us our marching orders," he replied with a broad grin.

"So we're illegal. Won't they find out?" Killer Diller

interrupted.

"Perhaps, but it isn't likely, as long as the bulbs get replaced. Don't worry. I do this all the time," he replied.

"So you're a hacker? A thief? Or what?" Killer Diller insinuated.

"A hacker, well yes, but more like a looker-outer-for-the-underdog," he replied and then added, "Ever heard of the Blackwater Underground?"

"Can't say that I have. Should I?" Killer retorted, liking this man even less.

"Best that you haven't. We are the Underground, if you take my meaning. Come on, Fel. We best be replacing light bulbs," he ended the conversation.

A half hour later and dressed in bib overalls, the pair pushed a small cart loaded with several boxes of eight foot long bulbs onto the small sidewalk beside the escalators that moved the containers up and down this particular route. Two heavily armed security guards stopped them, but John showed them their orders. After checking the photos on their ID cards, the guards told them to get on with it. A half hour after that, they reached warehouse 4143.

"We don't know the security code to get those large doors open," Fel whispered the obvious.

"While I could get them from the main computer in a jiffy, it wouldn't do us any good, unless you want to get caught," John explained. "You see, if those doors open, the computer checks back to see if it ordered it because it is retrieving or delivering a container here. If not, it alerts the security guards within minutes of opening. No, to get access, you have to enter this small door. Each warehouse has a Private Entrance like this one for people. Of course, its access code must be different from the one that opens the main doors. Planet regulation. Once inside, we can then open the main doors and get our cart inside. The computer knows that we are opening it from inside. All doors open from the inside with the same security code—for maintenance, you see."

"So how do you know all this?" Fel asked.

"Research. Spent a couple of days working out all the details, once I accepted this job for you," he replied. Quickly, he entered the code, opened the doors, and entered. A moment later, he entered another code, and the main doors opened. Fel pushed their cart inside and the doors closed.

The warehouse was a larger one. She saw two dozen large containers stacked neatly. An automated forklift sat idle near them, waiting for computer orders to retrieve one or more containers. While Fel set to work on the containers, John began replacing some burned out lights, using the tall ladder from the cart. He finished long before Fel and headed on down the line to four other warehouses, per the orders he'd inserted into the computer system.

Fel had no idea what was in what container and decided to plant a bug on each one. Then, she changed her mind and planted a pair on each. John returned just as she finished hiding the last bug. "How much longer?" he asked.

"Done. Let's get out of here," she replied growing nervous. If anyone discovered their break-in, their chance for success was nil. Certainly, the bugs would be discovered. Together, the pair left, pushing the cart back the way they'd come. An hour later, having ditched the cart and overalls, the pair entered the deep space transport, where the aroma of fresh baked bread swamped olfactory senses. Peter had done some baking to avoid utter boredom.

"Now we wait," Fel explained. "Mission accomplished. Got two dozen containers with a pair of bugs on each of them. I'm going to go check out my electronic receivers now. Someone bring some supper and that bread down to the cargo hold. Please," she added before heading there herself.

Now bored, John followed her. "So you need to know when someone is coming for them?" he asked, while watching her make nearly fifty tests, one for each bug.

"Now that would be helpful, John. I figured we'd have to wait and monitor the bugs. I have a way to automatically detect when the containers they're on begin to move. At least I hope so. Not field tested," she explained.

"Cool. Say, there's another way. Give me a minute," he replied, again taking out his handheld computer. After typing away for a few minutes, he looked up and said, "Not long. It seems a transport is due to arrive in an hour. Already, loading orders have been issued by the computer system. We got out of there just in time. Ten are to be picked up. So what's this mission all about anyway? What's in those containers?"

Stacey arrived carrying a tray with their food. Having just overheard him, she replied, "It's a matter of life and death. You see, they captured my sister, Peter's wife, and several others. This is our only lead to where they took them. We suspect the containers contain biological and genetic chemicals or stuff used to make the bio agents, at least that's what my sister and her friends uncovered. How come you're still here?"

"Can't turn down a free supper," he replied coyly. Then, he became serious, "I prefer to have you drop me off on some other planet. I'll make my way home from there. Less suspicion that way, since I got here rather illegally. I prefer not to take more chances than I have to take. I hate fieldwork. I spend my days behind my computer systems, but for the money this job is paying me, I couldn't turn it down. Besides, I got ordered to help you."

"I see. A mercenary. So who ordered you?" Stacey countered.

"Alis Anrhod," he answered. "She's a robot you know, one of those humaniform robots. She saved my ass twice now, so I couldn't turn her down. It helps that your major is paying me well too."

"A robot? Oh shit! This is a trap!" Stacey exclaimed, shocked to hear that one of the robots was working for the major.

"Don't get your kickers in a rumple, Stacey. Alis is one of the good robots. She's been around helping for perhaps a millennium. Who knows for sure? Your Freedom Alliance leaders trust her implicitly, so you should too," John countered, alleviating her fears. "Not all robots are insane. They once provided valuable service to humans, but that was eons ago. Gosh, Peter bakes a mean loaf of bread." John cleverly changed the subject.

"Well, he had to raise his daughter after his wife died. Kathy. However, he is now married again to Dr. Alison Wage-Diller. We simply have to rescue her somehow," Stacey explained.

"Dr. Alison Wage? The electronics expert?" John asked, a very surprised look on his face. It was his turn to be taken by surprise.

"Yes. Have you heard of her?" Stacey probed.

"Hell yes! Who hasn't? She's one of the top electronics experts in this part of the galaxy. Shit. She's one of those you're trying to find and rescue?" he asked.

"Yes."

"Well, count me in. Don't drop me off, not until we rescue her. I wonder if I can get her autograph?" John mused, mostly to himself.

"Can you handle an MK40?" Fel asked. He shook his head no. "How about explosives?" Again, he indicated he couldn't. "Not sure how much help you'll be, so stay out of our way. Please," she added as an afterthought.

He nodded agreeably and said, "I'm good with computers. I can help with your tracking. I'll monitor the expected arrival of the transports and keep you posted on the automated computer system that should be bringing some of those containers out to the transports."

"Hey, that would certainly help," Fel admitted. "Do it. I'm getting the trackers online now."

An hour later, John verified the ten containers had been brought out and stowed into two transports. Using the database records Zeta and her companions had created, he was able to identify their contents as supplies related to genetic modifications as well as some electrostatic hair machines and dried food supplies. This convinced the group that they were on the right track—that following the two ships might take them to where Alison and the others were being held captive.

"Eighteen trackers are hot," Fel called out. Already, John had confirmed that the two deep space transports had lifted off. He'd hacked into the control tower's computer systems. "Let's get going, Killer."

"Got clearance now. Couple of minutes and we'll be airborne," she called out, hastily carrying out all the pre-flight checks and laying in the automatic guidance coordinates provided by the tower. With so many ships plying the airspace above this world, she had to follow their protocols or risk colliding with other ships or trains.

A long five minutes followed before they actually broke out of the holding pattern over 191-Cetus-C and could lay in their own course. "They've made the jump to hyperspace. Tracking is out until we are in it as well," Fel relayed up to Killer Diller.

"On it now, Fel. Hit the Execute button, Stacey. Jumping now," she barked her orders, eager for the pursuit. For her, the game had finally begun.

"K. Tracking is back online," Fel yelled. "Getting a fix now." A minute later, she had the key data Jill needed to direct the transport, and they were on their way. "Now, John, all we have to do is sit back and keep track of them, following discretely behind them, and hope and pray they lead us to Alison and the others. Could be a long night."

Eight hours later, Stacey roused Fel, who had taken a rest break, leaving John in charge of monitoring the tracking bugs. "They've dropped out of hyperspace. Wake up, Fel. Something is up. Not sure where we are. Jill wants you up front."

Rubbing her hands over her face, Fel sat up and followed Stacey. "Eight hours? K. What's the situation?"

"We're dropping out of hyperspace now," Killer Diller explained as Fel crowded into the front of the ship behind Jill, while John and Stacey hovered over the navigator's seat, though she retook her seat, as she returned to her post. "Everyone: all eyes outward. Where are we? That's what we have to find out fast. Keep an eye out for enemy fighters, and remember, we're unarmed, damn it!"

"Where the hell are we?" Killer Diller exclaimed as the stars appeared. All had anticipated hovering over some planet where their friends were being held, but instead, they found themselves in empty space!

"Three o'clock! God damn! It's one of the battleships!" yelled Stacey.

"Shit! Okay, get a good look before we jump into hyperspace again," she yelled back. "Sixty seconds. Fifty-nine.

Fifty-eight." A tense minute passed before the utter blackness, the void of hyperspace reappeared. "Okay, anyone see what the hell was going on back there?"

"What are they doing out here?" Peter yelled up from his seat by a bay window. "Are they being held on a battleship? How are we going to get them off that?" Hope vanished as quickly as it had come.

No one said anything for a minute. Then, John spoke up, "Well, I did see two transports docking. Couldn't tell if those were the ones we're following. Maybe this is just a rendezvous or something. Surely, they aren't being held on a battleship."

"Better pray that they aren't," Killer Diller said disgustedly. "No way can I take on one of them with this ship." She didn't add that she also couldn't take on a single enemy fighter, since the transport was unarmed.

Once in the safety of hyperspace, Killer Diller called out, "Okay Fel, what's the plan now?"

Fel thought a moment. Already, she'd frantically stowed a large number of explosives in her backpack, figuring if they got captured by the battleship, she'd not go down without a fight, maybe even severely damaging the battleship. Sitting her bag down, she sighed and said, "We wait, Jill. Maybe this is just a way stop along the way. With any luck, the trackers will activate again if they jump into hyperspace. Anyone recognize where we were? Nothing looked familiar to me, but then that's not saying much." However, no one else had either.

A tense hour passed before Fel yelled, "They are on the move again!" At once, Jill began following behind the two ships, verified as two ships from the many tracking bugs and their slight discrepancies in position.

Killer Diller activated the intercom. "Okay everyone. Listen up. We're on the move again. Hopefully, the next stop will be pay dirt. Now here are your assignments. When we drop out of hyperspace, we will be cloaked. We need to know where in the galaxy we are, where our people are being held, and how much resistance we can expect to encounter. Stacey, Arcangelo, you two focus on finding out where we are. Fel, you do what you can to locate our people. Peter, John, you two concentrate on determining how much resistance we may expect to find here, wherever here turns out to be. Remember, this isn't my delta wing. Now get some rest. We'll work in shifts until we drop out of hyperspace."

"That's assuming we arrive at a planet," Peter grumbled. His dashed hopes surfaced. That they'd rendezvoused with a battleship shattered his emotions more than he cared to express just now.

***

"We're in the galaxy. I can tell that much," Stacey exclaimed to Arcangelo. They'd just dropped out of hyperspace after nearly eight more hours. She and Arcangelo struggled to get their bearings and locate their position. Most of the sky was utterly black, save a few dim fuzzy patches. On their right side, the Milky Way shown like its namesake, brilliant and breathtaking.

"We're far out on the rim that much is certain. I don't recognize any star patterns. Take a few bearings, and let's run them through the computer and see if it can match up anything," he suggested.

Meanwhile, Killer Diller followed Fel's directions, slowly heading down to a bluish planet of this yellow sun. She too didn't recognize any star pattern, but then she didn't expect to—she was a fighter pilot, not a navigator. *At least,* she thought, *this looks promising. Here is an unknown, habitable planet and a likely location to hold kidnaped victims.*

"I can't see anything more than the two transports that have landed. Can you?" Peter asked John, who was also staring out of the bay windows, looking in all directions for signs of battleships, transports, the one-man fighters, or anything threatening.

"Nope. Nothing at all. Do you know where we are? Ever seen this place?" he asked, growing curious. For the first time in his rather sheltered life behind banks of computers, John was seeing another side of the universe. It pricked his interest, particularly since he didn't see that battleship or any enemy CAMs around. Not yet anyway.

Fel pointed out, "Down there. There is a small landing field. I can see a town. Identical houses for the most part.

192

Population estimate—maybe a thousand at most. Take her down near the two ships. I need a closer look."

"Aye, aye. Any signs of enemy fighters? Patrols? Anything, fellows?" Killer Diller called out.

"None. All quiet. Weird, don't ya think?" Peter yelled back, but continued scanning for enemy ships.

"Okay, we're going down for a closer look. Eyes peeled everyone," she barked, banked the ship, and began descending closer.

Some fifty feet above the ground, everyone had a very good look at the town. Peter cried out, "That's Alison! There's Vittoria! They have giant lip disks but that's them."

"Yes, but there are CAMs there too!" yelled Fel, spotting several of the shiny silver monsters. "Wait," she corrected herself. "Something's wrong. The CAMs—they aren't moving! What are they trying to do? Get into one of the transports?"

"We gotta land!" Peter yelled, now unwilling to do anything but rescue his wife.

Killer Diller made a snap decision. She saw the weirdly motionless CAMs, the terribly awkward movements of a small party of *women* evidently trying to get into one of the transports that had recently landed, and the total absence of any kind of defense fighters or ground cannon installations. She yelled, "I'm setting the ship down. Man the MK40's. Take out the CAMs!"

As the cloaked ship touched down, Fel opened the bay doors. She and Peter charged out, their MK40's blazing at the nearest, but still motionless CAM. Admittedly, in his tall heels, Peter was far behind Fel, who was the first to reach the shocked group who were struggling to get up the bay ramp of one of the transports. Peter yelled, "Alison! We've come to rescue you!" He saw her turn and squeal in shock and surprise.

***

"I heard Dr. Rachel explaining to Dr. Franks that tomorrow a transport will be bringing some from Ross-C," Dario relayed to Dr. Alison. "This might be our chance to escape. What do you think?"

"Could be. Okay, I'll pay a visit to Dr. Franks tonight. Keep your fingers crossed, Dario," she replied.

"Duh. I don't have any, and I can't cross my toes," he jested back, bringing an invisible smile to both their faces.

That night, Alison made her slow, careful way over to the Franks' home. She found both Dr. Riley and Missy in dismal spirits. "You heard?" he asked mournfully. "More are coming tomorrow from Ross-C. Will this never end?"

"Dario told me, Riley. Look, we're going to try to escape in their transport. If you and Missy come with us, I'll do my best to see that arms get regrown. That much I think I can promise. Look, we need you to undo these awful genetic mutations of yours. Right Missy?" Dr. Alison pleaded her case, using Missy as the bait.

"Oh please, dear. You have to try. We can't live like this. We both know it," Missy wailed, seeing a tiny ray of hope for the first time since this nightmare began.

"Oh hell. All right. The worst thing they can do is kill us and that might be a damn good thing!" the geneticist gave in to her pleading. "Only two problems though. How do we get around the CAMs? How can we possibly fly a transport? We're almost totally helpless, or haven't you noticed that detail, Dr. Alison?"

Good, she thought, *he's getting angry and antagonistic.* "I believe the CAMs can be handled, and we think we can make good use of the autopilot system to fly the ship. Trust me. We can do this. We simply must, Dr. Franks."

"Might as well trust you. I've got nothing more to lose. Say, I overheard Dr. Rachel saying the transports were due to arrive around ten tomorrow morning. She's already departed in her own shuttle to bring back more genetic material to use to modify more men. Probably another world is about to be attacked. She left orders for the CAMs to deposit the newcomers in their new homes. She's supposed to be back by three in the afternoon and deliver their orientation lecture," Dr. Franks explained.

"Good. That gives us several hours to make this happen. I think we will need every minute of it. We'll plan to do it around eleven. You two be ready to go when we come by," she requested and left the pair to discuss how improbable this all was.

The next morning, working together, they managed to get the transmitter unit onto Adriano's back. Working the simple controls was Dr. Alison's biggest problem, caused wholly by their lack of hands. Still, with help from Alex, Vittoria, and Dario, she decided that she could somehow do it.

At eleven, they walked carefully out of their home. Adriano went first with the precious device strapped onto his back. Alex, Vittoria, Dario, and Alison walked behind him. The three leaned their bodies into Alison's so that she could use her toes to adjust the controls while standing on one foot. Complicating matters, she had to remove her shoe to do it and then get it back on, all without falling down. The others, namely Daniela, Lucio, Gina, and Felisa, followed behind them. Their job was to keep track of the CAMs and report if anything was happening to the robots.

Halfway to Dr. Franks' home, Daniela called out, "Look! Something is happening. The CAMs. They aren't moving anymore." The party stopped to look. Sure enough, two CAMs who were doing some construction work on a home stood motionless. One still held onto a board in midair.

"This must be the right frequency," Alison declared. "Come on. We have to get to Dr. Franks."

"But why take him with us? Isn't he the one who did this to us?" asked Gina.

"The robots forced him to invent the stuff, Gina," Dr. Alison explained. "He's the only person who stands any chance of undoing all these physical changes to our bodies. We take him." Of course, she and all the others repeated everything three times to ensure the others could understand what they were saying.

By the time they reached Dr. Franks, he and Missy were outside, staring in disbelief at two other CAMs that also stood motionless. "Is it working?" he asked twice.

"Looks like it. To the transport," Alison ordered. The pair fell in line behind Gina's group. Like marching penguins, the small party moved down the street, taking small, shuffling-like steps in their toe shoes. With only their toes in contact with the ground and supported by the tiny seven-inch spiked heel, walking was both challenging and precarious, hence the shuffling movement.

When they reached the two transports, six CAMs stood nearby, entirely motionless. "Incredible!" Dario whispered, not daring to raise his voice in case that would reactivate the robots. Finally, they reached the bay ramp of one transport. For a moment, they stared at the relatively steep ramp, wondering how they could walk safely up it. Just then, Alison heard the sound she dreaded: engines decelerating. Another ship was landing. Could Dr. Rachel be returning sooner than expected? Would her device stop the humaniform robot as well? Her mind was flooded with unanswered questions, while the others, having also realized another ship was landing nearby, looked to her for advice.

"Try to get up the ramp," Alison said three times. "Dario and I will stay here and hold them off if we can." Slowly, the others valiantly began trying to walk up the ramp, wobbling wildly to keep their balance.

Alison saw a bay door opening. The ship was cloaked. She saw a woman with a large gun rushing out, followed by Peter. For a second, her mind didn't register who he was. Then, the woman yelled, "Alison! We've come to rescue you!"

Peter! That is Peter's voice. All Alison could do was squeal. Of all the impossible, improbable events, seeing Peter and Fel dashing down a bay ramp was the least expected.

"We're here to rescue you!" yelled Fel. "What's the matter with the CAMs?"

"I have immobilized them," Alison called out three times. "Can you understand me? If not, I'll use telepathy."

"Mostly. Vittoria! Alex. Thank goodness, you're all here. Come on. Head over to our transport," Fel exclaimed as Peter finally caught up to her and threw his arms around Alison, hugging her tightly. With the giant lip plates, he knew he couldn't kiss her, but a hug was in order.

"We never gave up on you," he whispered. "Come on. Into the ship before these CAMs wake up."

Now Stacey and Arcangelo came down the ramp. They just had to hug Vittoria. Then, Killer Diller appeared, staring at the inert CAMs. "Hey Peter, Fel. Blast those CAMs to smithereens! Stacey, Arcangelo, you help them get up our bay ramp. I'll keep watch and keep the engines online."

One by one, Peter and Fel fired their MK40's into the inert CAMs, destroying them. As Stacey helped Alison onto the ship, Alison explained there were more CAMs in the town and another idea formed. Once on the ship, she found Killer Diller and used telepathy to explain rapidly what they had done.

Look. When Dr. Rachel returns, if all the CAMs are destroyed, then she won't know they were disabled by my new invention. We should keep that a secret from the robots as long as we can.

"You got it! I'll let Peter and Fel know," Killer Diller responded just as Alison hoped. Now the robots wouldn't know of her invention, giving her time to make far better ones and maybe bring an end to the robot war.

An hour later, Killer Diller lifted off, parking in a high orbit. Then, she relayed all they'd learned to Major Lu Ann on the Hyperion, asking them to identify their location and this star and planet. Meanwhile, in the bay seats, Alison introduced their newfound friends.

"This is Adriano Fortuna and his mate Daniela Torini. He is into computers, and she's a math whiz. This is Dario Menati, his mate Felisa Mundini. Both are into astronomy and astrophysics. This is Lucio Marcellino, his mate Gina Gabriella. She's a painter, and he's a sculptor. You all know Dr. Riley Franks and his wife Missy, though they now look quite different than they used to look." Dr. Alison then outlined all that had happened and what little they knew. When she finished, Peter relayed how Zeta and her friends had discovered the warehouse on 191-Cetus-C and how they'd found this planet.

By then, Major Lu Ann issued new orders. They were to stay in their parking orbit above this world while the Hyperion and the battleship Arc Royal came to them. The plan was to rescue all the others as well.

Two days later, the Hyperion and Arc Royal dropped out of hyperspace near the transport, which then docked on the Hyperion. The rescued were whisked off to the infirmary for checkups and the arm regrowth cure.

Meanwhile, Killer Diller made her report to Major Lu

Ann. "A transport arrived not long after we got into this high orbit, sir. Per Dr. Alison and Dr. Franks, this was probably Dr. Rachel returning. Some eight hours later, a battleship arrived, possibly the same one that rendezvoused with the transports carrying the shipping containers. About five hours ago, they all departed. There are no signs of enemy ships anywhere close to this planet."

"Okay then, take a field team down to the planet. Go house to house and rescue all the victims. Transports will take them to the Arc Royal, captain. Live video feeds, of course," Major Lu Ann ordered.

Grim. Via the streaming video, Major Lu Ann and General Kelly Kay saw no signs of any living person in the town. Rather, the field teams reported finding small piles of "dust" here and there within the homes, more often than not on the beds.

Major Lu Ann reported, "General, it looks as if we're too late. They must have killed all the survivors with the Shadow Maker systems."

General Kelly Kay replied, "Agreed. That is my conclusion as well. Major, perhaps this is a good thing. According to your reports from Dr. Franks, barely one person in six actually survived down there. Given the physical and emotional trauma each suffered, I'm not surprised at such a very low rate of survival. They've obviously abandoned this base and perhaps abandoned their diabolical plans to start a hermaphrodite society as well. Surely, they could have just transported the remaining survivors elsewhere in that battleship. Perhaps, we have gotten a break. No more torture of the victims of their genocide attacks."

Major Lu Ann sighed. She had so hoped to rescue the other victims. "That would be a reasonable speculation, general. Orders now?"

"Return to Scorpi-C with your survivors. Alfonso wants to speak to Dr. Alison as soon as she can be understood. Her invention has been marked top secret for now. God, I hope she can perfect it. This might be the break that we've been waiting for. Over and out."

Chapter 11—Necessity and Invention

"Papa! You and Vittoria are pregnant?" exclaimed Tasha, confused. The Hyperion landed on Scorpi-C in its capital city of Malagena. The victims were rushed to the Advanced Medical Research facility there. While they were still in their comas as arms were regrowing, that they were all hermaphrodites shocked everyone. With the medical exams completed, even more shocking, all were pregnant, except Dr. Alison. Tasha sat beside her father's bed and chatted with him and with Vittoria, whose bed was beside his. The staff had honored the mating that had occurred while Dr. Rachel held them on the unknown world.

"Yes, it would seem that I am to be a mother," Alex replied. "And my Vittoria is too. Soon Tasha, you'll have a brother and a sister."

"But papa, how is this possible?"

Vittoria said, "Tasha, come here and have a peek under my covers."

She did so. With a reddish glow on her face, Tasha whispered, "Oh!"

Alex chuckled. "Vittoria and I now look exactly the same. That's what an hermaphrodite is. We are all hoping and praying that somehow Dr. Franks can undo this mess, though I don't think I'll regret being a mother. That never happens to men. It's something that Vittoria and I can truly share."

Vittoria laughed. "Tell me that when we're nine months along, Alex. You might be singing a very different tune!"

Meanwhile in a nearby room, Alfonso and Alis met with Dr. Franks. Missy remained quiet, however. "You'd be singing a different tune too, Alfonso, if you were like us, hermaphrodites," Dr. Franks declared. "It's one thing to look like a gorgeous, well-endowed woman and another thing actually to be able to bear a child inside you." Of course, he repeated this several times to make sure Alfonso could understand him. Silently, he cursed the giant lip disks yet again.

"Yes, yes. We did receive that genetics package that you sent us sometime back. I've had my top geneticists studying it. But genetic experimentation on humans is totally illegal and unethical, to say the very least," Alfonso argued.

"We have no choice, Alfonso. Look, I will only work on Missy and myself first, until I perfect the cures for the rest of us. You have to let me try. After all, my approach was intended to save lives, even prolong them, not this, this terrible perversion of my life's work that the robots are using it for."

Alis who had been silent finally spoke up, "Look, Alfonso. He has a point. Birth rates of hermaphrodite couples are more than double normal human rates. Even though there are only five such couples now, counting Dr. Alison, in time, their numbers will grow, exponentially too. We saw that happening in the distant past as well. It would be inhumane to sterilize them. That's not a viable solution and you know it. Besides, Dr. Franks just might be able to get your body back to looking like a male as well."

Alfonso sighed. He'd long ago given up any hope of ever looking like a man again, though he continued wearing his professional women's outfits, refusing to look even weirder wearing men's apparel, which didn't hide his appearance, only reminded him of what he had lost. "All right then, Dr. Franks. You have my permission to conduct your experiments. Keep me fully informed. Wait. Everyone is now pregnant, excepting Dr. Alison."

"I know," Dr. Franks replied. "It will take time for me to study the genetic changes and work up a solution. I promise not to do anything until our children are born. Perhaps, though, if I have a solution, I could try it on Dr. Alison."

"Not until you try it on yourself. She's entirely too valuable right now," Alfonso countered that notion. "I'll relay this agreement to the genetics lab and my geneticists."

"Thank you, Alfonso. I'll get started on it today," Dr. Franks declared.

"Not until the doctors release you and your wife," Alfonso chided him. "Rest up. You've been through quite a ordeal. Besides, we have many questions for you about just how your process can take one man and somehow turn his body into that of another. This seems to be the robots' favorite tactic to disarm entire worlds. Now rest up. We'll talk more later."

He and Alis then paid a visit to Dr. Alison, who complained, "I need to get to work. My invention worked. I need Dario and Adriano's help with it."

Alfonso laughed. "This must be a genius trait—nothing can interfere with research and development." Both chuckled. "Seriously, rest up and get healthy. Indeed, as soon as the doctors give me their okay, I've an entire electronics lab at your disposal. This invention of yours could well mean victory for us instead of the robots wiping out all humanity in the galaxy. By the way, good thinking back on that world. Making it look like the CAMs were attacked and destroyed by MK40's and not your new secret weapon—that was brilliant. We keep surprise on our side."

She smiled invisibly. "Thanks. The biggest hurdle is trying to figure out the best way to make it work on a large scale. We lack CAM test subjects." Both laughed and the pair left.

Next, a local priest joined Alfonso and they visited the three young couples that Alison, Alex, and Vittoria had saved. First, they were officially married. Once that was done, Alfonso offered each of the six the opportunity to complete their formal Academy training at Malagena Academy, giving each a full scholarship. None could turn down the all expenses paid offer, particularly when the fellows learned that there were many other young men attending who had undergone genetic modifications similar to theirs. They would not be looked upon as freaks. However, Adriano and Dario insisted that they help Dr. Alison when she needed their assistance. Thus, Adriano, Daniela, Dario, Felisa, Lucio, and Gina shortly continued their advanced education and even had their own shared apartment complex close to campus.

Considering the magnitude of Dr. Alison's invention, she had no choice but to move off the Hyperion and into a home next to the GD laboratories. Somewhat reluctantly, Kathy and Peter came with her, along with their young son. Hearing of their plans, Alex and Vittoria also decided to join them on Scorpi-C, much to Tasha's delight, since now she could enroll in school. The young boyfriends of Kathy and Tasha convinced their parents to let them stay in Malagena as well. Not to be left behind, Stacey and Arcangelo joined them, bringing Zeta and her boyfriend with them. Within a week, all were enrolled in schools appropriate to their ages and educational levels.

Seven months passed quickly for Dr. Alison, but excruciatingly slowly for the pregnant others. While having arms and hands made life endurable for all them, getting around on their malformed feet became difficult as they entered their eighth month and "simply miserable," to quote Dr. Franks, during their ninth month. All were very pleased with their babies, once they endured birthing.

Then, it was Dr. Franks' turn to begin his experiments. He'd already gotten his new lab setup just the way he had his old lab and had completely analyzed everyone's DNA, noting specifically the changes that were causing their current modifications. He had his batch of sample DNA replicated, including that from twenty handsome men and fifty gorgeous women, though he was now reluctant to utilize the five UFB women's samples. After his experiences, unless he was specifically asked to use them, Dr. Franks didn't advertise them as possible choices.

With Missy's approval, he chose to use the Hank sample on himself. Under the watchful eyes of Dr. Gisa Wolfgang and Dr. Michelle d'Mireio, Alfonso's other geneticists, he injected himself and dropped into the usual regenerative coma. Everyone dropped by to check on him during the five days he was unconscious. All had a stake in his new procedure. He didn't reveal to anyone he had lied to Dr. Rachel and Dr. Black. He'd insisted to them that these genetic changes were unable to be undone, when in fact he had no such data.

When he awoke, he found Missy sitting beside him, holding their two babies. "Looks like you get out of nursing duties, dear," she said three times, making sure that he understood her. Although still groggy, he began checking his body. "Yes, it worked. You are a man again," she added.

He felt his lips. They were normal now. He checked his bosom and found nothing more than that of a healthy, twenty-three year old man. Then, he checked his privates and relaxed completely. The female anatomy was gone. "Need a haircut," he whispered his first words and was surprise to hear a mellow tenor sound and not the soprano voice he'd had. "Terrific, Missy! It all worked, didn't it?"

"Yes, except for your feet. They are still a bit off, but that's all the doctors could find that is still wrong," she said several times.

After a flurry of doctor visits and checkups, he was given a haircut and men's clothing. "I feel wonderful, Missy. Now it's your turn. As soon as we can get to the lab, you get to choose the woman that you want to look like, unless you want to keep the Tessa Longstreet form."

Thus, within a week, the many victims took their turn browsing the images of the DNA candidates, looking for their new *appearance*. Naturally, all the women were fabulously attractive, gorgeous and then some. Dr. Alison chose the Eve woman for her new appearance, with Peter's approval of course. Vittoria chose the Angel woman. Though she'd become rather fond of her Tessa appearance, she wanted to look different from Stacey and Zeta. However, Stacey and Zeta decided to keep their Tessa appearance.

A month later, everyone had been handled and now had their physical appearance altered as much as Dr. Franks could manage at this point. All wasn't perfect though. With the women, bosoms still were overly large, and their waists were smaller than normal. With both men and women, their feet were only partially restored. Feet could not lie flat on the floor like normal feet. Thus, all were forced to wear the usual six-inch heels. And yes, Dr. Franks did look a bit strange wearing a fine business suit but with six-inch heels.

Given this result, Peter decided not to undergo the process, since he would still have to wear the same tall heels as he was wearing, not manly at all. Alfonso and many others held the same opinion as Peter and didn't partake of Dr. Franks' new cures. Thus, he continued his genetic research hoping to get feet fully restored.

However, once all these new modifications were finished and the results verified, he gave a formal presentation to the medical personnel of Malagena, some thousand doctors, nurses, and geneticists. At one point, he explained to the assemblage, "You see, we now have a cure for those patients who can't be cured by our medical machines. The many forms of brain degeneration are now a thing of the past. My wife is my first cure in that arena. All forms of debilitating birth defects can be eliminated. In short, my research gives us a new arena for medical cures. Plus, there is also the cosmetic aspect. Homeliness and ugliness can also be remedied. That will do wonders for those people as well. However, we do need to build up a more extensive collection of sample DNA. We don't want hundreds of Miss Tessa Longstreets running around." Several chuckles interrupted him.

"And there is one other aspect, though my first cure is no longer alive. This process can defeated old age. My mother, Lisa, was barely able to get around. After I gave her the cure, she had the body of a twenty-three year old woman, not one that was approaching ninety. Further studies must be done in this arena. So you see, we do have options now for those illnesses and maladies that we couldn't cure before." Here, he received a standing ovation.

Someone asked, "But if everyone gets this rejuvenation process and no one dies of old age, won't we soon be facing an overpopulation problem? What about jobs and advancement for the younger generation? Isn't this going to cause far more serious problems, Dr. Franks?"

Unabashed, he answered, "Like I said, this area needs further study. I don't know how long or well the cure lasts. My mother was killed by the robots not long after having the curing process. This area needs more study." He then continued his presentation.

***

Dr. Alison wasn't idle during these seven months. First, she worked on the range aspect of her new communications device. Her objective: make the signal's range extend at least ten miles around the transmitter. Lacking CAMs on which to experiment, she was only guessing at the range, based on sensors placed in various orbits around Scorpi-C. That done, she then began manufacturing two forms of her device. The large units would theoretically disable all CAMs in the ten-mile sphere around the transmitter. These units required substantial power and were for the ships of the line. The smaller field units were designed for Captain Hard Ass and her ground forces. This second type was portable, fitting in a small backpack and would cover perhaps a range of a couple thousand feet around the unit.

When she had two of each type built, Alfonso called for a meeting of top Freedom Alliance personnel, including Major Lu Ann and General Kelly Kay. Captain Janine also was ordered to attend, though at first she had no idea why. After giving a brief presentation, Dr. Alison explained, "So these units work by sending out one specific command, that is, to go inert for a week. You see, Dr. Black had me working on getting some of the design errors out of his initial circuits that eventually were used in the CAMs, though I didn't know about that aspect at the time. Anyway, one day I discovered he'd installed a backdoor, so to speak, in the circuits, one that would allow him to override all other commands. I suspect he used that feature to take control of the CAMs from their original inventors in Brussels. So when he wasn't looking, I installed my own backdoor overriding his. These units I've designed will use that backdoor to send this one command."

"We tried it out on the CAMs that were holding us prisoners and it worked. They all ceased functioning. Later, Peter and Fel destroyed the CAMs. Thus, it's my belief Dr. Black and the others haven't yet discovered my backdoor. I hope it's still a secret. Which brings me to the point of the meeting."

She took a breath and continued, "You see, this backdoor can likely only be used one time. After that, I'm sure Dr. Black will figure out what I've done and take countermeasures to lock out my backdoor into the CAMs' control circuitry. So we want to make the best use of this one-time ability to knock out the CAMs. It's not our ultimate weapon, since I'm sure the robots will get wise to it after just one use. They aren't dumb by any stretch of the word."

"I've made two models. The larger unit is for space vehicles, which can supply the needed power. My estimates suggest it'll be effective out to approximately ten miles around the ship. The smaller unit is for Captain Janine and her ground forces. It's portable and has an effective range of a few thousand feet, no more."

"Initially, I'm giving the two large units to Major Lu Ann and General Kelly Kay, since they're the ones who have been going in after the battles and trying to rescue survivors. I will be making more of them for the rest of our Freedom Alliance fleet, but it takes time."

"I can't impress strongly enough these are to be used only as a last ditch effort. Once they are used, the robots will be on to them and will likely take preventative measures, nullifying any further use of my backdoor into their circuitry. Use them wisely. One note: I do not know if the humaniform robots use the same control circuitry. Hence, plan on these units doing nothing to the humaniform robots. Questions?"

Alfonso rose. "Thank you, Dr. Alison. Please use them only when there are no other options. Once we have enough units for our fleet, then we can work on a strategy to use them in one huge strike, hopefully wiping out the robot fleet." That brought a hearty round of agreement and hope from the group.

He went on. "As you know, the robots continue to wipe out entire worlds. In the last seven months, they have destroyed another ten worlds." At this point, he brought up his galactic arm display. "As you can see, I've highlighted in red the worlds that have been attacked and wiped out. The area impacted is now a pie-shaped wedge almost all the way to the hub worlds."

"Space is vast. Our galaxy has nearly a trillion stars; most haven't been explored. While we like to think we know all about our section of the spiral arm, in truth, we know very little. I've highlighted in green the known, populated worlds. As you can see, they are a mere drop in the bucket compared to all the stars. I once read that commercial exploration of unknown worlds is likely to continue for ten more millennia. The point is we have no idea where the robots' main base or bases are located. They could be anywhere."

"However, my suspicions tend toward a world within the red zone that they now control. Worse for us, their bases could well be on worlds humans can't inhabit. Too cold. Too hot. We do know they need substantial manufacturing plants, fuel refineries, and fuel supplies. Somewhere out there is where they take their captured or destroyed battleships and repair them for their use. We need to find those bases and destroy them."

He sighed and continued, "It isn't hopeless yet. I've just received word from Admiral Jeremiah Smythe who is now in charge of the Federation's combined fleet. It seems that finally all the remaining corporate CEOs of the other worlds have taken notice of the robot problem. They've finally pooled all their space fleets into one massive armada under Admiral Jeremiah's command. Perhaps the next battle will shake things up a bit. I certainly hope so."

"Don't worry. I've not committed our small space fleet to theirs. Not yet. I want to see effective action on their part before I sacrifice our fleet. Once our fleet is gone, there's nothing left to protect the member worlds of our Freedom Alliance. I'm waiting to see effective action. Of course, there's no way to know where the robots will attack next. But I understand that this giant armada will attempt to engage the robot fleet once it has launched another attack. We'll see how that works out. At least, the admiral has theoretically adopted my suggestion and will not be leaving behind destroyed ships for the robots to take away and rebuilt only to use them against us in their next attack." That brought a round of applause, as Alfonso suspected it might.

"Question sir," General Dalek interrupted him. Alfonso nodded towards the rotund man, and he said what was on his mind. "In the past, once the robots infected a world putting everyone into comas, they landed at the world's academies and made off with the very brightest of the students." Many heads nodded. Alfonso took note of this and let the general continue.

"So if as Dr. Alison suspects, the robots have abandoned their perverted program to convert these bright young people into their moderna society, I propose that we do the same. I mean, send in our rescue people to retrieve the brightest academy students. Now that we have cures for their genetic modifications, we can offer them a safe haven, cures, and in the future, benefit from their brilliance," the general explained. For once, Alfonso was pleased others now saw the value in this that he had so long ago.

"I'll make that the top priority of General Kelly Kay," he agreed. Many others either nodded or openly agreed with this action.

Alfonso decided now was the time to approach a trickier action. "I also think we should send out a flotilla of scout ships to monitor and hunt for the robot base or bases of operations. We need to find their fuel refineries, their fuel depots, their repair facilities, and their manufacturing facilities. Stealth searching is in order. Cloaked always. Can we afford to equip and send out a hundred deep space transports on this mission?"

Many grumbled. With such a large number, they'd be reducing their transport capabilities rather drastically. As Alfonso expected, quite a lengthy discussion followed. In the end, they agreed to field the hundred ships and back them up. Ten battleships would control a dozen spy transports, but maintaining hourly contact with the transports, just in case. All information would be relayed back to GD headquarters in Malagena. Alfonso had to arrange for personnel to handle the volume of information that would be sent back. However, the generals all insisted that they would jump back to Scorpi-C or any other world in the Freedom Alliance should a robot attack come here.

A week later, one hundred twenty deep space transports began a systematic search of the robot controlled pie-shaped wedge of the old Federation. It was a massive undertaking, in that nearly every planetary system or moon had to be searched, a gargantuan task at best. Still, it offered some chance, however remote, that one or more robot facilities could be located. If so, Alfonso was determined to destroy them somehow, someway. Thus far, the war had been very one-sided. Alfonso also knew that eventually morale would break if the Freedom Alliance didn't eventually score a victory of some kind.

What bothered Alfonso and many others was the utter unpredictability of the robot attacks. No matter how he arranged the worlds that had fallen, he could discover no discernable pattern, other than random chance. He couldn't believe this Dr. Black robot was picking targets wholly at random. That made no sense. No, there had to be some underlying plan behind which worlds got attacked and when. There always was logic behind human-fought wars. Battle targets were well-defined and somewhat predictable. This, more than anything, frustrated Alfonso and many on his staff who were working on this very problem.

As the meeting broke up, he whispered to Dr. Alison, "Stick around a minute. I'd like a private word with you." She nodded. A few minutes later, the auditorium emptied, and he continued, "You have been closer to this Dr. Black and the robots than any other person. When you have the time, I'd like you to go over all the data we have and see if you can find any logical pattern in their attacks. We simply can't find anything other than random chance. We need to be able to predict which world is to be attacked and engage them when they drop out of hyperspace for the attack."

"Okay, I'll look it over. Can you send me all the known data?" Dr. Alison replied. She had not actually kept up on this side of the war and didn't see how she could really help. A sudden thought struck her and she chuckled.

"What?" Alfonso asked, curious.

"Oh, we have a whole lot of telepaths. If this was a normal war, why, we could have all kinds of intelligence from probing the enemy's minds. Here, all we can do is tell if it is a robot or a person. Not much good this time. Kind of ironic." Both chuckled and headed out of the auditorium.

Chapter 12—Careful What You Wish For

Midnight, Black Oyster Pub, Minsk, 221 Rostov-B. Natalia Gorzinsky, twenty-one, entered the pub ready for her nightly work as their janitor. Sooty windows and the distinctive odor of fresh piss, stale beer, and puke assaulted her nostrils. She ignored it. Her head down, she also tried to ignore the few remaining patrons who hadn't yet left, though it was closing time. Her brown dress had seen better days though if you saw it, you'd say it had been patched so many times that there wasn't anything left of its original material. Her hair was black, thin, and stringy. Worse, Natalia was ugly, though to call her that would be being kind to her. And she was incredibly poor.

Natalia lived with her mother, who made her living by taking in filthy laundry. Between that and what Natalia made being a janitor for the Black Oyster, the two at least had a roof over their heads and just enough food to continue their existence. But tonight, tonight was special. She'd spent her day working up the courage to speak to Captain Gustavo Korki.

For the last several nights, she'd overheard his sales pitch. She'd replayed his story over in her mind countless times. The man was trying to recruit a crew. "I got me this plan, see, one what will make us all wealthy men." Several catcalls and grumbles interrupted him. Someone asked for details. "Ya see, it goes like this. You know 'em robots wiped out all them worlds, don't cha? Well, I've got it on good authority the tin cans have left those worlds. Granted, we know the robots stole all the computers and such things, but think of what they left behind! Mountains of valuables, just sitten there waiting to be picked up."

"No, no one in their right minds would go to those world now!" a man barked. "That's suicide! No tell'en when them tin cans will come back. You gotta a death wish, Gustavo?"

"Mind you, I didn't say it wasn't a risky business," Captain Gustavo countered. "I'd be crazy if I didn't tell ya it'd be risky. But lads, think of it. Diamonds, rubies, gold bullion—

all there for the takin. We land. We visit the proper establishments. We get out millionaires. I tell ya, there ain't never been such an opportunity. One trip and you're richer than rich."

"So what kind of deal you posing, captain?" one man asked.

"Need volunteers to go with me. We split the loot equally."

Others laughed. "And what happens if the robots getcha? Eh? Tell us that. Shadow Maker's bait. Besides, the worlds might still be infected with them bio agent things. Turn you into helpless vegetables. Man's gotta be crazy to think of going back to one 'o those worlds. So you crazy, Gustavo?"

"No. I aim to get wealthy and respectable, an' get the hell off this miserable excuse for a planet," he replied. "Any takers? I'll give ya three days ta make up yer minds."

This was the third night. Natalia kept close watch on Gustavo's recruitment activities and knew that he wasn't very successful. She knew of only four men who volunteered, barely enough for a crew on a transport. If he was true to his word and if this was the last night before he departed, then she figured this might be her lucky break.

"Turdy, get to work. Mop up that mess yonder," her boss behind the bar called out. She jerked slightly, intent upon sizing up the situation. Good, Gustavo hadn't convinced any more men to join him. She hated that nickname, but could only agree with it. She did look like someone's smelly turd, as ugly as she was. She mechanically picked up the mop and moved over towards Gustavo's table, working up the courage to speak to the man.

"Captain, I'd like to volunteer to be part of your crew," she said rapidly, not trusting her nerves. If she said it fast, there was no taking it back.

Gustavo guffawed. "Looky here boys, Turdy wants in on the action." Two others laughed along with him.

"Get real, Turdy. This ain't no picnic," he countered.

"I know."

"So what can you do besides mop the floors? Hell, Turdy, you are so ugly no man in his right mind would even want to fuck you, even blindfolded."

She stared at the floor, calming her nerves. *At least, I've tried,* she thought. His insult didn't faze her. Long ago, she knew the truth of that statement.

"So what can you do?" Gustavo asked again.

"Captain, I have guns and can shoot straight."

"Well, maybe so, but I sure as hell don't want to fight them nasty robots, Turdy."

"I know gems and their value. I was taught that when I worked in my dad's jewelry store."

Gustavo called out, "Barkeep. That true? Turdy here's father is a jeweler?"

Grumbling because she wasn't mopping the swill off the floor, he spoke up. "Yeh, but that was years ago. He's been dead ten years or more."

For a brief instant, memories of a happier time came unbidden into Natalia's mind, followed by what had happened. Back then, they lived in what she believed was a nice house. They had food on the table, and she wore real dresses and had new shoes once a year. Like all workers for the corporations, his pay was significant, but the corporations then demanded stiff rent payments, charges exorbitant prices for food, clothing, and household appliances, since these had to be imported or manufactured. Thus, if one lived long enough to retire, one's savings might keep one alive for another year at most.

In this case, her father had a sudden stroke and died young, leaving the two of them with next to nothing. They had to move out into slum housing. Everything went downhill in less than a month, as their meager savings quickly ran out. She had kept the small jeweler's toolkit that her father had made for her and his small collection of guns. While one was an official blaster, the other was a 9mm pistol with a silencer on it. With little else to do back then, she taught herself how to shoot them, and the 9mm became her favorite weapon. It was clean and silent, but highly effective. Her biggest problem was buying the ammunition for it. She partly solved that by reusing the brass shells and loading her own shells. She prided herself on now having two full clips for the 9mm.

She decided to speak up again. "So I can tell which gems are the best ones. I can appraise the jewelry and gemstones."

"Well ain't this the dog-gonest thing? Turdy here has more guts than most men have. All right, Turdy, you're hired. Come on. We depart tonight, that is, if you are serious about this. Might not come back alive. Might come back millionaires too."

"Can I get my guns and tools, captain?" she asked, every fiber of her being resisting yelling for pure joy. This was her golden opportunity.

"Sure thing, but make it snappy. Pad 1614. Leavin' in an hour with or without cha." She nodded, dropped the mop, and dashed out the door. When she got to their slum shanty, her mother was already asleep, bone tired from washing all the clothes. Quietly, she slipped inside, pulled her two guns out from beneath her straw pillow and her small bag of jeweler's tools. She tied a bit of rope around her waist to act as a belt and stuffed the guns in it. Then, she slipped the toolkit inside her cleavage, where it would be safe. Satisfied, she stole back outside and began her long walk to the spaceport on the edge of Minsk.

Luck was with her, for she soon caught up with Captain Gustavo and two of his new recruits and fell silently in behind them, thankful that she didn't have to hunt all over the spaceport for the landing pad, because she feared the guards might not allow her onto the tarmac. Around two in the morning, they walked up to his ship, the Lucky Caldron. It was once a deep space transport, but now it was more like a rusting hulk of a ship, barely flight-worthy. Still, it would fly, and that's all that mattered for Captain Gustavo. One more flight and he could buy a shiny new ship, maybe one of those top-o-line models. That was his dream at least, which he promptly told the three with him.

"She'll fly us there and back. Trust me. Come aboard and meet the rest of my crew. Aye, could use some clean'en. Turdy can clean up the floors some, until we get there. Okay everyone. Listen up. Dis here's Mikhail, my new navigator, Stefan, and Turdy. You three, dis is Ros and Ruslana. She's our cook, but we're all going out on the hunt for treasure. Ros got us our supplies and guns."

Ros griped, "You brought that ugly bar wench? Turdy? Captain, you outa yer mind?"

"Aye. She can shoot and can appraise gems and jewelry, so we need her. We donna wanna bring back a load of crap stones. What's they called, Turdy?" Captain Gustavo asked.

"Zirconium," she answered, staring at the floor.

"Right. None of that stuff. Seeings how I can't tell the difference, we needs her."

"Lordy, Gustavo, hasn't she got a name?" Ruslana spoke up, her voice full of sympathy for the pathetic looking excuse for a young woman.

"Well, ya heard her, Turdy. Speak up," Gustavo grumbled.

"Natalia, ma'am," she replied nervously, continuing to stare at the filthy floor of the cargo bay.

"Well, Natalia, come with me. Surely, I've got an old dress that'll fit you and Gustavo, find her a proper belt to hold her guns, that is, if'en ya want her to use them," Ruslana griped. She wasn't pretty either, but at least wore passable clothing.

"In a bit, cookie. Now then, I gotta make something clear, see? There are six of us. So whatever we bring back, we divide up six ways—all equals you might say. Just so there's no confusion later on. Now then, we're going to check out 19-Velos-B first. The tin cans are long gone from there. I know it's an arid world, but they had many gem mines. Besides, we can read their language, so we don't havta guess what's a jewelry store and so on. Mikhail has laid in our course. Be there in twenty hours' time."

He continued issuing orders, "So while he and I get us on our way, Ros here will show you around the ship. Make damned sure you know where everything is. He has backpacks for everyone and bags ta hold the loot. Mind you, I aim ta fill the fourteen empty cabins with treasure before we head back as fabulously wealthy. Oh, and Turdy can see to clean'en up some of the floors.

"A real bed?" Natalia exclaimed. Ruslana gave her a

cabin next to hers back by the galley.

"Naturally. This is a transport ship, filthy though. I had ta spend a day just cleaning up the galley so I could cook and not get us all food poisoning or worse. Lucky Caldron looks bad, but she's still solid where it counts. At least I thinks so. Anyway, we got good provisions along, but the captain says we should be able to pick up tons of food on 19-Velos-B. Probably dried stuff and cans though." She handed Natalie one of her old, nearly worn-out dresses, a faded brown, and one of the captain's belts. "Change quick. Ros will be back soon."

"Thank you, ma'am. I haven't had a new dress in years," Natalia replied, hastily doing as asked. With a real belt around her waist, she could now properly fasten her blaster holster and her 9mm gun's holster to her. She finished up just as Ros came along with the other new men, ready to give them all a tour of the ship.

As they began the tour, the ship gave a slight lurch. Seeing the concern on several faces, including Natalie's, Ros explained, "Just made the jump into hyperspace. Always does that—just a jolt. Now then, here's the workshop and repair equipment."

Later on, they finally arrived at the front of the ship where the pilot and navigator seats were located. "Okay everyone, listen up. Since this is a dangerous mission, I want all of you to know how to fly this bird back home. Something might happen to me or to Mikhail here. We might be injured or worse. So we have to depend upon each other. Now don't worry. It's so simple a child can fly it. It has an automatic flight controller system. Show 'em Mikhail."

His navigator showed them the really simple menu-driven touch screen. "So you select your destination. Then press this button here, Computer Controlled Flight. You do than and you're done. The ship will take off and fly itself to the destination."

"Better tell them about landing," Mikhail whispered.

"Oh yeh. Well, when you get there, the control tower will contact you. Just say this is an emergency and that you need help landing this bird. They'll know what to do. Happens a lot. This way, see, no matter what happens to me or Mikhail, you all can get home. Safety. Like I said, this is a risky adventure, but we're gonna come back millionaires. So have ya begun thinkin' how you're gonna spend your fortunes, eh?" Captain Gustavo asked. "Me, I aim to buy me a shiny, new, top-o-line ship!"

Mikhail laughed. "Hell, I am going ta buy me a farm somewhere and build me an underground bunker so if an when the tin cans come, they won't get me. I heard if'en yer deep underground, the bio agents won't getcha nor will the Shadow Makers. I aim to be safe and snug with plenty 'o food too."

Ruslana laughed. "Me, I'm gonna buy me a big, fancy restaurant! What about you, Ros? What 'r you gonna do with your millions?"

Ros laughed. "Me? I'm gonna buy me a space exploration ship and get the hell out of the way of the damned robots—as far from here as I can go!" Several began discussing his plan as they headed back to their cabins. Meanwhile, Natalia found some cleaning supplies and began cleaning the floor of the main cargo hold near the bay doors. She was thankful that no one asked her what she wanted to do with her millions. By the time that Ruslana yelled for supper, she had the cargo hold as clean as she could get it, under the current circumstances. She quietly entered the galley and ate her meal in a back corner as far from the others as she could get.

After that, she began cleaning out the cabins destined to hold their envisioned *loot*, per Gustavo's orders. Finally, after putting in eight hours, she too headed for her real bed and a long night's sleep. *This is heaven,* she thought, as she lay on the soft bed. While it was only three feet across and darn crude by most standards, for her, it was heavenly. She slept soundly.

"Now here's the plan," Captain Gustavo said after breakfast and an hour before they were due to arrive over 19-Velos-B, "we're gonna make our first stop at Minsk, what used ta be their largest city. When we arrive, I want all of you starin' out the windows looking for any other ships, particularly the tin cans. If ya see any ship, yell loudly and I'll get her out of here fast. We ain't look'en for troubles, see. Lots of cities and worlds we can loot."

Natalia took up a seat away from the others and stared out of the window. She saw only blackness. "That's hyperspace," Ruslana whispered to her. "Feel that jerk? We're there. Now look." Natalia did and saw a brownish world below her. Remembering what the captain said, she looked everywhere that she could, but saw no ships of any kind. Apparently, no one else did, since none yelled, and she began to relax. Maybe this was going to work out after all!

A half hour later, the captain called out, "Minsk coming into view now. Gonna do a fly over first. Keep your eyes peeled for other ships and CAMs on the ground."

Natalia saw a huge city, sprawling across a valley. A reddish ridge line rose just east of the city. Minsk once was home to ten million people or so Ruslana whispered. North of the city was a crystal clear, blue lake, its water reservoir. Eerie, she thought, seeing absolutely no one at all down there.

"Okay, we're gonna land now. I'm picking out a deserted side street. We donna want anyone to spot us easily. Once we land, we gotta cover up the Lucky Caldron with the camouflage tarp. That way, no one can spot us from the air. You all make damned sure you memorize where we are leaving the ship so you can find your way back with your bags of loot."

He sat the ship down gently, so much so that Natalia didn't realize they'd actually landed. She sat stiffly, waiting for the bounce or jar that didn't come. Seeing the other getting up, she realized they must have landed and scurried to get her things. Like the others, she donned a large backpack, filled with many smaller sacks. Then, the captain opened the bay doors, and they walked down onto the street. She watched as the men quickly spread a camouflage tarp over the ship, and she remembered what he said and promptly began memorizing their location, using the taller buildings as landmarks, as well as the nearest street sign.

That done, the six adventurers walked out onto the main street, getting their first good look at the deserted city. Total silence reigned. A light wind lifted up dust and debris, which now covered the streets. Tall skyscrapers rose like sterile needles into the reddish morning sky. Shattered doors lay everywhere. The CAMs never bothered opening doors; they merely smashed their way inside, leaving the remains hanging from one or more hinges.

Bits of glass littered the streets, along with all kinds of debris including bits of paper reports that no one would ever read again. Here and there, bits of clothing moved or waved, driven by the gentle, warm breeze. She spotted a number of discarded shoes, reminding her that once millions of people had lived here. For a time, no one said a word. It was just too spooky. Natalia felt shivers and finally whispered, "Are there ghosts here?"

"Nah, just the wind," Ruslana whispered back. "Mighty spooky though."

Just then, they heard a series of low growls. Then, a pack of half-starved dogs dashed out towards them from another side street. Mongrels. Once pets, the dogs had reverted back to the wild and formed packs. They charged towards the party and Captain Gustavo in particular, as he led them down the main street. Natalia didn't hesitate. She drew her 9mm gun and fired. Pop! Pop! The faint sound of her silenced shots broke the stillness. The lead dog and one just behind it dropped to the ground, whining and howling, but soon died. Seeing their alpha dog go down, the pack beat a hasty retreat.

"Damned! Good shoot'en Turdy!" Captain Gustavo exclaimed. "See men. I told you Turdy was good for us. Hell, she's faster on the draw than all of you fellows!" By now, the others had their blasters out, but the dog pack had already vanished from sight. "Best be on alert for more wild dogs. Come on. I see what must be a jewelry shop ahead."

"Holy shit! Look at all the gems and stuff!" Ros exclaimed. They'd entered Ruslan's Gems and Gifts store, or so the sign said. The CAMs had been here and removed all comm equipment and computers, but had pretty well smashed up the shop. Precious stones littered the floor from the crumbled display cases. The men began picking up the stones.

"Wait," Natalia said as she too picked up one, "these are fakes. Zirconium stones. Worthless. We need to find the good stones."

The men tossed their handfuls back on the floor. "See,

Turdy is worth her salt. Show us the good stuff, Toady," Gustavo declared.

"Hey, over here. These are diamonds. Small ones, but valuable. They probably keep the good stones in a safe. Look around and see if you can find one," she suggested. "Hey, these necklaces and earrings are valuable too. This must have been their expensive jewelry display case." While they began stuffing the items into sacks, Ros and Mikhail searched for the safe.

They found it and Ros cursed, "The CAMs have looted it!"

Natalia joined them and smiled. "They may have taken a few larger diamonds, but there is still a small fortune in gemstones in here. Take all them, fellows."

A half hour later, they had salvaged all they could from this store. Gustavo laughed, "This, my friends, is entirely too easy! We're gonna be millionaires soon, maybe billionaires! Come on, we have a whole city to search. Let's split up into three teams. Ruslana, you and Natalia go together. Ros, you are with Stefan. I'll take Mikhail. Let's be systematic about this." He issued directions for the three groups to follow and requested they return to the ship by five or as soon as their packs were filled. The three groups headed off in search of more valuable loot.

A bit later, Natalia found a gun store and paid it a visit. She found boxes of ammunition for her 9mm, as well as a new one, complete with silencer. With these in her possession, she felt safer than ever before. So did Ruslana, who could only barely use her blaster if she had to fire it. The pair had to return to the ship before noon. Their backpacks were stuffed with booty. Natalia smiled when she and the cook entered the cargo bay. Ros and Stefan were already there, unloading their own stuffed packs, broad grins on their faces. Soon, Gustavo and Mikhail joined them. "Didn't I tell ya, we're all gonna be richer than rich!" he exclaimed, puffing up proudly.

The next day, they decided to enter some of the key corporate headquarters skyscrapers. Why? They all knew these CEOs controlled the city and world, and were the richest men here. Hence, it made sense they'd have tons of valuables in their suites, generally on the top floors. By chance, Natalia and Ruslana found themselves entering GD headquarters. The elevators were out, and they faced a long climb up a hundred stories. However, Ruslana suggested they take time to search each floor. That way, the climb wouldn't be so exhausting. "This is gonna take us days to search," she explained to Natalia who agreed with her.

They did find some useful items on the lower floors. Then, they decided to split up, each taking their own floor until they got to the ninetieth floor, where they agreed to work together, and where they anticipated finding the most valuable items. On the fourteenth floor, Natalia discovered their medical-genetics facilities. It too had been looted, but she looked in the drugs locker, whose doors had been ripped off. Then, she spotted something and hope flooded through her entire body. There lay syringes labeled with the usual yellow and black bio agent hazard stickers. She found a complete set of directions for their use! "My dream can come true!" she exclaimed, more excited than ever before. Here were single-use syringes containing the bio agent that turned women into the fabulously gorgeous UFB women, the ultimate beauties of the galaxy!

Memories flooded over her. She was there with her father in his jewelry store. These elegantly dressed, fabulously attractive UFB women came into his shop, along with their personal assistants to purchase some of his most expensive pieces. Here were the women who turned all men's heads! Here were the finest, best-looking women she'd ever seen. She envied them, drooled over the way the fine-suited men followed them around like lap-puppies. Oh, how she'd longed to be one of them, gorgeous beyond imagination. She'd dreamed of looking like and being one of these women, the best of the best. Then, she'd open her eyes and see her own ugly, misshapen face in the mirror, shattering her dreams. Only they returned full-force the next time one of these incredibly UFB women entered his shop. Oh, how she'd longed for those visits, if only to gaze upon these beautiful women.

Yes, that was Natalia's dream, fondest wish, and what she intended to do with her millions: become one of them, the most gorgeous women in the galaxy. With her supposed wealth, she could buy elegant clothing, hire her own personal assistant, and live in her own penthouse suite. This, she wisely, told no one. However, she carefully packed the directions into a sack along with four of the syringes. Then, she continued her hunt for valuables.

It was late afternoon when the pair finally reached the top floor, the penthouse suites where the extremely wealthy CEOs and their families lived. Of course, the suites had been looted. Nevertheless, Natalia saw that UFB women had lived here. Their satin gowns still hung in their closets. She resisted the temptation to take some with her. The others would only poke fun at her. No, time for them later, she told herself.

Then, the pair hit the jackpot once again. They uncovered the women's stash of jewelry. "Incredible, Ruslana. We must have picked up ten million worth of jewelry in these suites alone!" she exclaimed.

"No doubt about it, Natalia. We are richer than rich. I'm gonna buy me the fanciest restaurant ever!" Ruslana declared once again.

When they returned to the ship, the men were talking excitedly. They too had found similar stashes of valuables in the penthouse suites. Day by day, their pile of loot grew, filling up several cabins. Six days had passed, but they'd also rounded up a cabin full of food supplies as well.

The next day, Ruslana and Natalia were ordered to search the Galactic Mining Corporation headquarters. This time, the building only had fifty floors and they passed by the lower floors, which held routine mining items. Nearing the top floor, Ruslana's backpack was full again, and she decided to return to the ship, dropping off her load. Natalia decided to stay and search for more valuables. After all, the only trouble they ever encountered were the packs of wild dogs, which now kept their distance from the humans, who'd killed several of their numbers.

As Natalia entered the executive suite, something felt different here. At first, she couldn't put her finger on just what was different from all the other deserted suites. Obviously, she thought, a UFB woman used to live here, but there is something else. Alert for trouble, she abandoned her search and began poking around the closets, the only real hiding places around.

She entered what had once been a young teen's room, a girl from the decor. Clothes lay in heaps on the floor, but something seemed wrong here. Empty food containers littered one side of the room. The bed was messed up. Just as she opened the closet door, a girl's voice cried out, "Don't shoot! Please, don't shoot me." Natalia nearly peed her panties!

"I won't. Come out. Who are you? How did you get here? Are there others hiding out here?" Natalia said, trying to sound calm but she was anything but that! There were supposed to be any people on this world.

"Katya, Katya Chenko. I live here. Please don't hurt me," she pleaded as she stepped out of her hiding place in her closet. Natalia saw a sixteen-year-old blonde teen with wavy hair that fell to the middle of her back. She wore a white blouse and jeans, but both looked rather dirty and in need of a good washing.

"Hi. I'm Natalia Gorzinsky. We are here salvaging what we can. I won't harm you. Wait? This is your room. How long have you been here? How come you weren't killed by the robots?"

Satisfied this rather plainly dressed woman wasn't going to shoot her, despite the guns she wore around her waist, Katya began talking. "You are the first person I've seen since that horrible day. Papa was the head of this mining corporation. I took him his lunch that day—he was down in the mine checking on something. Don't know what. Anyway, I found him deep underground where his men had just struck a new gemstone vein. I could see some diamonds glistening in the light. Then, some of his workers yelled something about seeing many space ships, and to come see. He told me to stay there. I'll never forget the look on his face. It haunts me every night when I go to sleep. He said I must stay there in the mine and not leave until he came back for me, that it might not be safe. I stayed there for the longest time. Days, I think. I was about to come out and was at the main entrance when I saw the piles of dust and clothes. Papa's clothes. There was one of those metal robots there too, but it didn't see me. I went back down to the end of the tunnel again."

Finally, I couldn't take it any longer. I'd eaten all his lunch and drunk all the water supplies they had down there. I had to come out. When I did, the metal monsters were gone. Everyone was gone. Dead, I finally figured out. I walked back home on foot since the little shuttle I drove out to the mine was gone. So were all the other shuttles too. I was starving and scared to death. I called out, but no one ever answered. So I came back to my room here to wait. Someone will come and rescue me I thought, but no one did. I keep raiding the grocery stores for food though, but I have to carry my dad's gun. The dogs have gone wild. You can see the food mess over there. Please, can you rescue me?"

"Of course. You are with me now. We've retrieved many valuables. We are going to be millionaires. You can have half my share, Katya. That way, you can live well. Say, was your mother one of those incredibly beautiful UFB women?"

Katya smiled. "Yes, she was so very beautiful. I so much wanted to be like her. Papa promised me that when I turned eighteen I could have it done and he'd help me find a kind, loving husband of my own, but now," her voice cracked, and she began sobbing.

"I can't imagine how you must feel, having lost your papa, mother, and everyone else. From now on, Katya, I'll look after you. You are with me. Besides, I know how you can become a UFB woman. I found the stuff." A phrase that Gustavo had used sprang to mind. "It's so simple a child could do it for you."

"Really? You can do this? Oh thank you, thank you." She began wiping her eyes on her dirty blouse sleeve. "I know all about it. I was ten when mom became so very beautiful. I helped her a lot, and I know all there is to know about being a UFB woman."

"Great, Katya. Then you can help me too. Please, don't breathe a word of this to the others in my group. I'm so ugly that they call me Turdy."

"I promise. I won't say anything." She paused a little uncertain but said anyway, "You're not very pretty at all,

Natalia, but they shouldn't call you that. It's disgusting."

"I know. I just ignore it. Been called that my whole life. You see, that's my secret dream too, to become a gorgeous, elegantly dressed UFB woman." Natalia couldn't help herself. She opened up to this young teen, relaying the details of her miserable life, and how she'd seen all the fabulous UFB women in her father's jewelry store.

"Now that we are very rich, Katya, I can become my dream and be gorgeous. You can help me and be my personal assistant until you are eighteen. Then, I can make you into one too. Then, we can be a beautiful pair, don't you think?"

"Oh yes, yes, Natalia, but where will we go? We can't stay here. There's no one on my world now, but your people," she asked.

Just then, the unexpected happened. The two heard gunshots! Lots of them! They rushed to the windows and peered down at the streets below them. From their height, they had a good view of the action. For a moment, Natalia thought that her heart stopped beating! Another silver transport had landed in the middle of one of the main streets. Six men were outside it, firing on Gustavo and his crew, just heading back after dropping off another load of loot.

The pair watched in horror as both sides dealt out death. Ten minutes later, they all stopped firing, but none of the six newcomers was moving nor was the five companions of Natalia's! "What—what do we do now?" whispered Katya, terrified at the carnage.

"I don't know. I guess I best go down and see if they are alive. I'll kill any of those new men if they aren't dead already! You stay here. Hide in the closet like before. If I don't come back, We have our ship hidden." She relayed the address. "Can you fly it?"

"Oh sure. Papa taught me how to fly a transport almost as soon as I could walk," she replied, but then broke down in tears once more. Dutifully, she hid in the closet again. After making sure Katya was secure, she headed down the fifty flights of stairs. Cautiously, she approached the battle scene. First, she checked on the enemy men. Only then did she relax. They were all dead. She stole up to their ship and checked inside. No one was aboard. Satisfied that there were no more surprises, she checked up on her companions. They too were dead. Blaster holes three inches around were visible on heads or chests. Natalia cursed and then headed back up to find Katya.

Quite out of breath, she called out, "It's safe now, Katya. They're all dead. They killed each other. It is just you and me now."

Katya reappeared with eyes red from crying silently. "What do we do now?"

"Let's go back to my ship and think this out." After rustling up something to eat, both women felt better and more relaxed. Katya insisted that no one could spot their ship from the air, convincing Natalia they were safe.

After sipping some tea, Natalia suggested, "You know, we can leave here right now and go somewhere safe. But I was thinking, Katya. If we do that, they might not let us become UFB women, especially as ugly as I am."

Katya flushed. "I hate to say this, but I think you're right. They probably wouldn't let you, seeing how you look."

"Well, we could do it here, on me. Then, I'd look like a real UFB woman. They are rich anyway so no one would think anything about all the wealthy we have on the ship. Then, we could go somewhere, buy a nice place, and do all the wonderful things that I saw UFB women doing. Theater, plays, concerts. I've never been to a concert before."

"Perfect!" Katya gushed. "There's a UFB woman's store not too far from here. I took mom there many times to get new gowns and heels and stuff. I know just what things to get you, and I can help you adjust too. Mom had a hard time adjusting, though I suppose they all do, what with no arms any longer."

"That is better than I ever imagined. Real, fine, satin gowns? Wow. Incredible! Let's do it here. I promise you when you are old enough you can get it done too. I can guarantee it since I know where the stuff to do it is. Come on. Let's visit GD headquarters and get some more, just in case."

Two hours later, they returned from their trip, and Natalia showed Katya the precious syringes. "But Natalia, if one of these is enough to make person into a UFB woman, why do we need eight of them?" she asked naively.

"I need one for me, but I promise you can have it done too when you are eighteen. Since others might find we have these, they might try to take them away from us. So I'll hide the seven all around. They might find one of them, but not all seven. That way, when it is your turn, one will be ready, and we won't have to fight anyone to get it done."

"Oh, you are clever, Natalia. Let's!" exclaimed Katya.

With that done, Natalia retrieved the directions paper. Together, they both studied them. Katya said, "Gosh, I never knew that it was so easy to do. Just inject into a vein. That's all. Of course, you will be in a coma for four days or thereabouts, but I'll watch over you. When you waken, we'll go to Lombardi's and get you all kinds of gowns and heels and things. Leave that to me. After all, I helped mom with everything for six years."

"We should close and lock the bay doors. That way, no one can get inside without knowing the access code," Natalia suggested.

Katya laughed, "Assuming they could even find it. The ship is so well hidden I wouldn't have found it myself."

A bit later, with her well-worn clothes removed, she sat on her bed with one of the syringes. "I can do this myself, Katya. I'm so excited! I never dreamed I could ever be beautiful and get my fondest wish of becoming one of those elegant UFB women. And here I am, and I'm going to do it myself!" Proudly, Natalia found a vein and injected herself with the bio genetic agent. After handing the empty syringe to Katya, she lay down and relaxed. "How long will it take?" Then, she lost consciousness.

A little over four days later, Natalia awoke. "Oh. I'm awake. Am I? Oh, I can't breathe!"

Katya leaned over her and laughed. "Mom said the same thing when she first awoke. It's the tight corset. You'll soon get used to it. Mom did. You need it to help your back support the weight of your fabulous breasts. Mine are still quite small, but yours are perfect. See, I visited the store and got you your first satin gown. It's red, obviously. You need the heels in order to walk. Here, let me help you sit up. I found a mirror or what's left of it. See, you're gorgeous now, Natalia. No more Turdy for you! See."

"Oh my!" Natalia gushed, and almost fainted from the overly tight corset and its unyielding pressure. "I don't even recognize myself. I'm gorgeous. No beyond gorgeous! Just look at me, Katya! Now all the elegant men will ogle at me and not turn up their noses in disgust."

Katya giggled. "Not a chance of that, Natalia. You look fabulous. I can't wait to get it done too. Just eighteen more months and counting! Oh, and I found one of those electrostatic hair machines too. You'll need it. Mom loved it. Come on. Let's get you up. First, you'll find walking very hard. Mom did, but I'm here to help you, Natalia."

"God, Katya, this is much harder than I ever imagined! I can't keep my balance. I keep trying to use my arms, and they aren't there. How am I going to eat?"

"I have to feed you," Katya giggled. "That's why they have personal assistants. Come on. We have to get you walking some. I bet you are starving. So let's get to the galley."

"Katya, I'm scared! I'm so helpless now! I think I'm going to pass out!"

"You have to eat smaller meals and more often. Mom always did."

Natalia laughed. "Katya, often I only had a bit of bread and some tea for my suppers. We were that poor. The corporations took all dad's earnings. We barely had enough funds for one month after he died. So this is a feast for me."

"Wow. I had no idea, Natalia. Okay, now we have to get you walking. The doctors kept telling mom, practice, practice, practice."

"But Katya, this is so scary! I'm so helpless."

"Think of the handsome men watching you. Think of the concerts and theater shows you will soon be seeing."

"Yes, get my mind off this," Natalia grumbled, wobbling wildly trying to keep her balance on her toes. "Wow, my hair. I seem to be feeling with my hair somehow."

"I know. Mom said she had a sense of touch with each strand. Just don't sit on it. Toss your hair. Yes, like that, before you sit down or stand up. It does hurt a lot if you do."

"Just look at my hair, Katya. It isn't stringy and ugly-looking now."

"No, it's shiny, thick, and very wavy. You are a raven-haired beauty now, Natalia," Katya insisted.

Later, Katya insisted they visit the UFB women's apparel store. "I don't think I can walk that far. Katya, I'm still terrified."

"Oh come on. I'll help you. I'm your personal assistant now. Think about what colors and styles of gowns you want. Shoes to match. Heck, there is a whole store of the stuff with no one but you to make any use of them."

"I can't go down the ramp, Katya!"

"Sure you can. I have you. There, see."

"I couldn't have done that by myself!"

"Mom couldn't either. I think you just have to accept there are some physical restrictions you now have and accept them. I tried to tell mom that, but she didn't listen to me either." She chatted the whole way to the store, which took an hour. Never had Natalia ever walked so slowly or precariously, and she would have fallen several times had Katya not been there for her.

Once in the store, she forgot about her situation. Surrounded by all manner of elegant gowns, Natalia chose what she wanted. Wisely, Katya found a pushcart to hold all their "purchases." Before they left, Natalia now had two dozen complete outfits with that many heels. Some were sandals, some pumps, but two were mules, which Katya explained would become her bedside shoes, since walking without the bit of extra support the heel gave her would be nearly impossible.

The hour walk back was fraught with fright for Natalia, since Katya now had to push the cart along, meaning she didn't have a steadying arm around her waist. When they finally returned to the ship, Natalia was exhausted and had to lie down, if only to keep from passing out.

While Katya busied herself stowing the apparel, Natalia began writhing on her bed. "Oh, Katya! I'm so horny! What's come over me? I can't even find a way to pleasure myself now and somehow, I just have to!"

Katya giggled. "I know. Mom was like that too. As I

said, I know all about these things. You need to wear this," she raised up a fancy dildo fitted into panties. "It will pleasure you as often as you need it. Mom had it set for four times a day. Later on, she told me that if papa had sex with her in the morning and at night, then she could somehow get by the rest of the day without it. Come on. I'll get you fixed up now. I'm surprised it took this long for it to happen. You're a sex fiend," Katya giggled again.

"Oh yes! Yes," Natalia moaned in relief. Katya had inserted it and set its automatic controls to provide stimulation four times during the daytime.

"So Natalia, have you ever been with a man? I mean in bed, like mom and papa?" she asked, trying hard to keep from flushing and from giggling.

"Hardly. Turdy, remember?"

"Oh yeh." Katya flushed. "Me either. I have often wondered what it must be like. Well, now you are so gorgeous you should have men dying to lie with you. No more Turdy, Natalia."

The vibrator roused Natalia the next morning, turning her body into a very satisfied state, after which Katya got her dressed. Together, they headed to the galley to have breakfast. "We should take off soon," Natalia suggested.

"I figured so. I went and got a few of my things I want to take with me while you were in your coma, so I'm ready whenever you are. Of course, we have to figure out where we want to go," Katya explained.

"Good thinking. I've no idea where. Do you?"

"Well, I heard a lot on the news about this Freedom Alliance based on Scorpi-C," Katya began. "From what I can tell, we would probably be the safest there, if anywhere is safe from the robots. If there's a computer on this ship, I can look it up and see if they have concerts and other fine things for UFB women."

"Sure. Go for it. There's one in the captain's cabin. First one on your right."

A while later having discovered the arts on Scorpi-C, the two decided to make that world their home. "Can you really fly this ship?"

"Sure," Katya said. "Look, it's all automatic. First, bring up the menu of destinations. Then, look for Scorpi-C. Ah, there it is. Select it. Okay. I'll go remove the tarp and we're off." Shortly, she reentered the ship, and hit the proper button. Automatically, the ship gently lifted off and soon jumped into hyperspace. The console readout suggested eight hours travel time.

To kill the time, Natalia had Katya sort out the loot, putting similar gems in together in one bag. While she was doing this, Katya insisted that Natalia practice walking on her own. "Now walk up to the front of the ship. Turn around, walk back here, and sit down. Then get up and repeat it. Yell if you run into trouble. You've got to be able to walk some on your own."

"But this is terrifying, Katya. I had no idea I'd be this helpless, that it would be this scary."

"Mom thought so too, but in time all that passed. I think you just have to practice lots."

Natalia finally reached the front of the ship all on her own, but not without some serious wobbling and nearly falling twice. "Maybe this wasn't such a good idea after all," she told the pilot's seat. "What have I gone and done? Now I'm truly helpless." *But you are beautiful,* a voice countered in her head. Dutifully, she carefully turned around and headed back to Katya.

The pair had no idea just how lucky they both were. Shortly after they departed, the robots returned with one of their stolen Planetary Reforming Ships. Hours later, what had been Minsk was now deeply buried beneath the new landscape. All traces of human inhabitation had been removed from 19-Velos-B! Other scavengers were not so lucky.

Chapter 13—Changes

Alfonso listened to Katya's long tale, how she managed to survive the robot attack, and was rescued by Natalia. They had landed, and at customs, sought immigration status. As always, he preferred to meet the arrivals and make that decision. Too much depended upon not allowing humaniforms or their spies onto Scorpi-C. "All right. I hereby grant you immigration status. Let me be the first to welcome you here. My men are unloading your ship, and I'll personally see you have a proper accounting of the valuables on the ship, though between us, the ship should be scrapped. I'll setup accounts for the both of you, splitting the funds in half, as you desire. Meanwhile, you certainly have enough funds to rent a penthouse suite, and as Natalia suggests, you should visit our theater and arts here in Malagena. The concerts are incredible. I'll have someone assist you with the arrangements, and I'll let you know as soon as we have the dollar value of your treasure."

"Thank you sir," Natalia said, greatly relieved. "And yes, scrap the Lucky Caldron, please."

"Of course. Mind you ladies, you're two very lucky women. I received word today the robots arrived at 19-Velos-B yesterday and began terra forming the world. Had you delayed your departure one more day, you would have been buried alive a mile underground," he explained.

"But why? Why did the robots do that? Isn't that like making a whole new world or something?" asked Katya.

"Removes all traces of human occupation. That's my best guess. The robots are on the warpath, intent upon wiping out the human race."

"But why wipe us out?" she asked.

Alfonso sighed. "Not entirely certain, but I think the robot leader has seen too much of man's darker side. Wars, genocides, murders, and rapes—you get the picture."

"Well, that's just stupid of them," Katya countered innocently. "They've never seen the good side. Papa and mom were very good people. So is Natalia." Alfonso smiled and sent for an assistant to get them temporary housing.

Later that night, with Katya's arm securely around Natalia, the pair headed for the symphony concert. Just as Natalia had imagined, here were the elegant women. She spotted some UFB women and some who looked like they might once have been UFB women, except they had arms now. The men all wore tuxedos and looked inviting. Soon, several young men surrounded Natalia, ogling over her, particularly so once they learned she was single and likely very wealthy.

At first, Natalia was delighted with all the attention coming her way, attention she'd never experienced before. However, Katya soon brought her down to earth. "Gosh, those men are just after your money, Natalia. I've never seen so many covert men before. I wouldn't trust them with anything!"

While Natalia's dreamworld of elegantly dressed men slowly shattered, her expectations for the concerts grew enormously. She was so impressed with the concert she insisted on attending every musical event that was scheduled, including smaller chamber music concerts. Katya also shared her enthusiasm for the music.

Two days later, Alfonso paid them a visit. "Got the accounting done. You are very wealthy women. I've opened bank accounts for each of you." He handed the documents to Katya, knowing Natalia had no way to hold them. "Each account now has a little over a hundred million gold dollars in them."

"Wow! We can't use that much money, can we Natalia?" asked Katya.

"Hardly."

"Well, we're now embarking on a huge rescue operation. As the robots attack other worlds, we are sending in some of our forces to rescue some of the academy students and bring them back here. Of course, they will need genetic cures and then a chance for a new life here on Scorpi-C," Alfonso explained. He had his suspicions and decided to test them out on the two women.

"That is fantastic! Can we help?" Natalia asked. "Oops. I keep forgetting I'm mostly helpless now. Say, won't you need funds to help them with everything?"

"Funds? Absolutely." Alfonso replied, keeping his fingers crossed.

"In that case, sir, please withdraw fifty million from my account and use it to help resettle those young students. It's the right thing for me to do," Natalia declared.

"Me too. Take fifty million from mine. A hundred million should really help those poor students who are in dire need of help, just as I was when Natalia rescued me."

"Ladies, I can't thank you enough for your generosity. I will see that a plaque honoring your contributions is installed in the walkway of the concert hall. Thank you, and on behalf of all the incoming rescued students, I also thank you."

True to his word, as the pair entered Concert Hall for the next symphony performance, they spotted the plaques with their names on them. Other eligible young men did as well and redoubled their efforts to woo Natalia, but she was too *educated* to fall for their scheming. More than ever, she was disillusioned about the entire UFB woman situation, though not the beautiful part or the elegant apparel, just the *man* aspect. While listening to the music that night, she recalled some of the men who had accompanied the elegant UFB women into her dad's store. Until now, she'd only stared at the women. However, she suddenly saw the men and realized they were more or less like those trying to woo her here. They saw their UFB women as sex dolls, mere things to parade around. Again, Natalia had second thoughts about what she'd done to herself.

The Hyperion arrived shortly after this, bringing the rescued hermaphrodites to Malagena. While John Doe took time out to visit Dr. Alison in her medical room and the others as well, he had other details to attend to while here on Scorpi-C. For one thing, he was owed a *vacation* from his underground work. Alfonso kept him briefed on the latest events. Thus, he learned the Hyperion and Arc Royal's next assignment was to try to rescue bright academy students on worlds being attacked by the robots. Helping were two new immigrants, who together had donated a hundred million to be used to assist these newly rescued students. That pricked his interest.

Just who has that kind of money to donate? What do they really want in return? He suddenly had a hundred questions centered around their motives, primarily because he was in the Underground and trusted very few people. Alfonso was the only CEO he trusted, for example. The others, well they were simply corrupt or blind, and deserved what they received, if not more. Thus, John decided to combine his brief vacation with a bit of sleuthing. He found absolutely no trace of this Natalia Gorzinsky in any online database, excepting for her birth certificate. His search for information on Katya Chenko was more fruitful. She was the daughter of the mining CEO on 19-Velos-B. Her mother had become a UFB women. Katya was in high school when the robots attacked. While she was thus the daughter of a wealthier man, he surely wasn't worth a hundred million! John knew he had to find answers, if only to satisfy his own curiosity.

Based on what little Alfonso had told him, he decided the place to meet them was at the next symphony concert. Thus, he rented a tuxedo and did a bit of harmless hacking. The pair had purchased seats in Box 10. There were four seats in that box, and John carefully moved the other two ticket holders to another box seat close to this one, and then purchased the two vacated seats. He had no recent photos of the women. He did find an older high school shot of Katya, but she'd probably matured a good deal since then. There wasn't any trace of Natalia to be found. Thus, he decided his best move was to get to the box seats a bit early and wait for the women to show up. Natalia, as a UFB woman, would be hard to miss, and according to Alfonso, Katya was always with her.

He arrived twenty minutes early and waited for the women to arrive. He had a hunch they too would be arriving early, since UFB women moved very slowly. His guess proved correct. Not five minutes later, Natalia, wearing a bright red satin gown, and Katya, wearing a lovely green satin gown, entered the box. Natalia was breathless as she entered, gasping slightly. She still wasn't used to wearing the tight corset, but knowing now how incredibly slowly she walked, insisted they allow plenty of time for her to make it to their box seats.

"Hello. I'm John Doe. Very pleased to meet you, miss?"

234

he began, looking questioningly at Natalia. He was pretty certain this was her, but wanted verification. Further, he spoke in Russian.

"Natalia. My assistant, Katya. Do you often come to these concerts? We're new here, and this is only our fifth concert. We've never heard anything as beautiful as these symphonies. Oh, thank you for speaking in our language. We've been listening to the language disks, but our English isn't so good yet." *He needs a haircut. Somehow, he doesn't feel like the other men we've met here, though he is wearing one of those fancy tuxedos,* she thought. *Say, how did he know we are Russians? And what kind of a name is John Doe anyway?*

"Actually, this is my first visit to the symphony. I'm here on a sort of vacation. I've heard a many very good things about this world's music and decided to come tonight. Besides, I also heard of your donations to help the young students who are being rescued from the robot attacks and wanted to meet you both. I've just arrived on this world, having played a part in rescuing Dr. Alison, Alex, and Vittoria, along with several other students the robots kidnaped when they wiped out their worlds. Long story. But tell me, were you born a UFB woman?" He decided this might be the proper approach to take. He'd pricked both women's interest with the rescue bit, but would they bite and open up to him a little?

"Oh no. I've only just become a UFB woman," Natalia said without thinking. She realized this and flushed slightly. "Well, if you must know, it was my life's dream—to become a UFB woman, that is."

"Well congratulations, Natalia. Few people ever succeed in making their dreams come true. Well done."

That brought a smile to Natalia's face, and she relaxed some. She added, "Well, if you knew me before I did it, then you'd know why it was my dream." Katya giggled.

"I'd love to hear it."

"I'd love to hear about this rescue thing of yours."

"Deal. We best chat more later. The music is about to start, at least I think so."

"Yes, when the conductor man walks out and the light

dim, it is about to start."

When intermission came and the compliments, such as that was incredible, ended, John nudged Natalia a bit. She explained, "Well, I was really ugly."

Katya giggled, whispering, "Trust her! She really was."

Natalia smiled. "Indeed. In fact, I was so homely the men around my town gave me the nickname Turdy, you know after a dog's turd. Yes, it bothered me, since I couldn't do anything about that, but it was far worse. You see, my father was a jeweler who made fine pieces for the CEO's UFB women." She began to relate the story of her childhood. She got to the point where she'd joined Gustavo's group when intermission ended.

When the applause died down and the concert goers began filing out, John said, "Say, how about I take you out for a coffee or something? I'd like to chat with you some more, if that's all right with you."

"Sure. You aren't like all those other men here, are you?" Natalia replied.

John chuckled. "Duh, hardly. I rented this tuxedo just to get in the door. Come on. Alfonso told me of a great coffee house. So you are really new to being a UFB woman?"

"Yes, I'm still adjusting to it. I never imagined it would be so hard. Those women who came into dad's store—why, they seemed like goddesses to me."

Katya spoke up, "She will, once she gets in lots of practice. I know. I was with my mom when she became a UFB woman for dad, and I was her assistant too, so I know. Practice. That's the key. Go slow, though. They can't walk very fast in those heels."

"I can see that, Katya. I'd love to hear your story too, but let's chat over a fine brew." He slipped an arm around Natalia's waist, steadying her, bringing a smile to Katya's face.

"You do that just like dad did."

"Then I don't have to worry about Natalia taking a spill."

"Or wobbling like some fish out of water," Natalia jested. Slowly, they ambled out of the concert hall. John hailed a shuttle cab, and shortly they arrived at the promised coffee house. It was quaint, with antiques lining shelves and cubbyholes. The tables were arranged such that private conversations were the norm, though a bar offered a common place to meet, if that was one's choice. John led them to a back table, just as a waitress came up to take their order.

"Yes, this is all so very new to me, but I'm working hard to adjust to it," Natalia began again. "So as I was explaining, I joined his group hoping to get rich enough to become a UFB woman." She continued her story, including her discovery of the syringes and then of Katya. Eventually, she ended up, "So here we are now, but when I heard of the rescue operations for all those other victims, I just had to help. Since now I'm almost helpless and have all that money, I figured he could use the funds and donated half my good fortune for them. Katya did too. After all, I've no idea how I could possibly spend even fifty million gold dollars."

"I'm glad we did it, donated the money to help," Katya took this as her chance to tell her own story, which she promptly did, though assisting Natalia with her coffee. She finished with, "So in seventeen and a half more months, I'll be eighteen and can become a UFB woman too, just like my mom."

John grinned. "Incredible. Both of you, just incredible, but Katya, you're already quite an attractive young woman. Why would you want to become a UFB woman? I can understand Natalia's reasons. God, I can't imagine how awful her life has been."

Katya giggled. "They are the ultimate, you see, the most desirable women in the galaxy. Then, I can meet a handsome man, marry, and have my own family."

John giggled, "But you don't have to be a UFB woman to do that. You should be in school, where you can meet many folks your own age. Have a good time, learn lots, go out on dates, sample the boys, and fall in love. Everyone does that or should—fall in love, marry, and have a family. Heck, someone as bright as you are, Katya, why, you should go to the Academy and meet the brightest boys. Besides, I don't know if you know this, but Scorpi-C and Malagena here have some of the finest high schools and academies in the Federation!"

Katya frowned. "But John, everyone knows UFB women are the best and marry only the best men."

John looked at her sternly. "You mean the men who consider their UFB women wives as little more than sex dolls? Katya, men and women should marry for love not for positions or objects of lust."

"But mom got it done, and I want so much to be like her."

"You can, Katya. First, you need to meet the right man for you, one who loves you as you are. Then, once you are married, and if you both still want it, then become a UFB woman, but you'd be doing it for all the right reasons, rather like Natalia here, who had very good reasons to do it."

"But what's love?" Katya finally asked.

"Admiration and respect. That concisely is what love is all about, Katya. Each greatly admires the other for just who and what they are. Each totally respects the other, their goals, and activities in life. Love is admiration coupled with respect. It's not looking gorgeous or sexy. That only attracts men's attention. You want to dig deeper. Don't you want your husband to respect you for who and what you are? Don't you want his undying admiration for you and the things you do? We all do. That's what it's all about."

"So I need to find a handsome fellow who admires me right now and respects me. Then, after we're married and if we both want it, then become a UFB woman?"

"Yes, but I bet you won't really want to do that, not if you are madly in love with him and he, you. You will want to help him with his things, just as he will want to help you with your activities and goals."

"Well," Katya finally admitted, "I do really miss going to school, but after hearing how wonderful this concert music is, I'd like to learn how to write some of my own."

"Precisely, Katya. Go back to school and learn how to compose the music you desire. The universe always needs great artists. Some say humanity is carried on the backs of its artists, not its scientists. Look where scientists have gotten us: robots out to destroy us, bio genetic agents that cause genocides, and bombs. Well, you get the picture. Those rare individuals who can create such works of art as we heard tonight—those are the true leaders of humanity."

"Wow. You think I could do that? Learn to compose such music?" Katya gushed, filled with hope.

"You bet. Of course, it's like anything else, but you already know the secret to it. Practice, practice, practice." Katya giggled again.

Meanwhile, Natalia fidgeted. Confronted with John's words, she realized he was right. Katya should be in school learning all she could, not hanging around her being her personal assistant. Katya sense this, and said, "But what about Miss Natalia? I've promised to look after her. She really needs me now. She rescued me, and I owe her everything."

"Look, I'll make you both a deal and promise. You get Natalia up, dressed in the mornings, and help her at night, but go to school during the day. I'll look after her during the daytime, until we can get someone to come by during the daytime hours. How's that?" John suggested, rather hoping both would accept his offer. He was intrigued by Natalia, more so than he even realized at the time.

"I suppose that would work out, if that's okay with you, Natalia. I'd love to go to school, especially if they are as good as you say."

"It's fine with me. You should do so. In fact, you simply *must*. I insist," Natalia declared, suddenly greatly relieved. John had cleverly disarmed her big mistake with Katya. She should be in school with kids her own age and Natalia knew it. It was just that John had to point it out to her.

"But I don't know where the schools are? How will I get in?" Katya worried.

"Leave that to me. I'll talk to Alfonso tonight and come by in the morning around eight to pick you up. I'll walk you to the school and get you all setup," John volunteered. "Then, I'll spend the day with Miss Natalia here, and when you come home, I'll take you both to a fancy restaurant to celebrate. How's that?" Katya giggled and agreed, while Natalia smiled.

"So John, you've not told us about that rescue of yours," Natalia probed. She too was intrigued with this unusual man and wanted to find out more about him.

John chuckled. "Sorry. Got distracted by two lovely ladies. Okay, here goes." He began telling them about Dr. Alison, and why she was so important, along with Alex and Vittoria. Midway through his story, he ordered a small meal and some tea to go with it, knowing or suspecting by now Natalia was probably hungry. He'd heard the UFB women in their tight corsets often ate frequent meals. As small as her waist was, he could see why that must be true.

When he finished, Katya exclaimed, "Wow. So it was kids my own age who figured this all out! Wow. They sure are smart. I do need to go back to school. I can see that now."

Natalia smiled and said coyly, "John Doe. That can't be your real name, now is it?"

John flushed. "No, of course not. It's my traveling name I use on those rare occasions when I'm above ground—I mean out here in the world. I work for a top secret organization dedicated to fighting the evils in our galaxy. We work in secret behind the scenes to make good things happen, like the rescue of Dr. Alison. Thank goodness we did that, because she may well hold the key to our victory over the insane robots. For us, it's very risky to be out here among people of the world—to be visible that is. Bad things can happen to us. Many evil men would love to eliminate me or torture me to get information on the others I work for. So yes, I'm taking quite a risk being above ground, so to speak. And if I hadn't, why, I'd never have met you two charming young women."

"You're really a nice guy," Katya declared. "Say, you know Alfonso. Is he really a man? I mean he looks much like Natalia, almost a UFB woman, except he has arms."

"Oh yes. He's a man. You see, a few years ago, he was attacked by a terrorist who unleashed a bio genetic agent on him, turning him into a UFBMD man. That didn't stop him, as the evil ones thought. Later on, his geneticists developed partial cures, mainly the arm regrowth procedure. Peter and Alex are also victims like him, but there might be further cures coming down the line. There's always hope the geneticists can invent more cures. Gosh! Look at the time! It's one o'clock. I've kept you up far too late. Best get you both home at once. We can chat more tomorrow."

Early the next morning, he called up Alfonso and told him of Katya's decision to go back to high school. Alfonso then made a call setting it up, while John headed over to pick up Katya and walk her to her new school, which was only ten blocks from their penthouse suite in downtown Malagena. After getting her enrolled, she gaily dashed off with some other girls, being introduced rapidly. John headed back to look after Natalia.

He fixed them some tea and watched Natalia carefully, as she did her best to toss her hair to one side and then sit down at the table. It wouldn't do to have her have an accident, not when he just arrived. Katya would likely never forgive him. "Sorry, I'm not entirely sure how to assist you with your tea. I suppose I hold it up for you."

Natalia chuckled. "I'm still trying to get the hang of things myself, so I guess we learn from each other. I know Katya said to practice lots, and I should, John, but I never dreamed it would be so incredibly scary—living like this. Stairs. Now they actually frighten me. I can't hold on to anything."

"Well, you could do lots more for yourself if you used your toes as fingers. Alex and his daughter Tasha do, but then they don't wear those enticing black nylons either. Nor do they wear those tight corsets. Alex claims in time backs strengthen, and the support isn't needed. Still, Natalia, have you considered having your arms regrown? Then, you'd not be so dependent upon others."

Natalia sighed. "Well, yes I have, but then I did so want to be a UFB woman. Having arms and hands would make me not be one of them. So I'm resigned to doing as Katya says. Practice, practice, practice. She claims her mother eventually got around just fine, but Katya hasn't said just how long that might take me. Still, I owe it to my dream to give it my all before I give up. It's not in me—to give up. Never has. I couldn't afford that luxury. If I didn't manage somehow, I'd be dead. I can take a lot, John. I've had to all my life, so I'm not about to give up on my one dream, not just yet."

"Well then, Natalia, we should do as Katya says: practice. What's up first?" John replied, his admiration for her determinism growing substantially. *Never give up*. That was a good motto for life in his opinion. "What's the scariest thing for you right now?"

She laughed. "Stairs! Oh, and being out in public where everyone can see me. I'm petrified of stumbling and falling, embarrassing myself. Besides, if I fall down, I don't know how to get up by myself yet. Say, are you really going to spend your vacation days with me?"

"Sure thing. Can't think of a more rewarding thing to do, but I insist we go out in public and visit many of the sights here in Malagena. I want to see their Natural History Museum among other things. You game?"

"If you are. Only don't let me embarrass myself, please."

"I won't. You'll do just fine, Natalia. Come on. Let's see you get up on your own. Say, I've heard Malagena has all sorts of things setup for those without arms. Automatically opening doors, voice-activated doors and computers. All manner of things. I've heard with these devices, you could live on your own, though I wonder if that is really true." John made pleasant conversation while carefully watching Natalia.

She struggled a bit, tossing her hair from side to side until it all fell off to her right. Then she managed a sort of lunge to her feet, wobbling crazily before getting her balance. "See. Embarrassing to say the least."

"Practice should help with that. I suppose it's like learning anything new," he replied. Together, they headed out of her penthouse suite. "No, we take the stairs, Natalia. Practice, practice, practice."

"God, John. This is really scary. You know that, don't you?"

"I certainly do. But let's give it a go, shall we?" he encouraged her. Slowly passed their first day together.

When Katya returned in the late afternoon, she was bubbling over with excitement and just had to tell Natalia everything that happened and everyone she met. She chatted all the way to the restaurant in fact.

The next day, John took Natalia to the Fine Arts Museum. As they made their entrance, Natalia almost cried. She whispered, "John, I can't tell you how much this means to me. It's my childhood dream come true. I'd lay awake at night half-starved dreaming of being a UFB woman and walking elegantly into some fancy museum, just like this one. Now here I am doing just that! I'm so nervous I'm shaking."

John put a steadying arm around her waist, but careful to not catch any of her long black hair. Together, they began their daylong tour, stopping for lunch at their exclusive restaurant, nearly bringing tears to Natalia's eyes. As they walked slowly home, Natalia said, "Thank you, John, for making my dreams come true. I'm so happy I could kiss you." To both their amazement, she did so, rousing passions in both of them.

The next day, they visited the Natural History Museum. During the week, each day, John took her out to visit another of Malagena's finest attractions. He knew just by getting out and about in public Natalia would gain the confidence she desperately needed. By the end of the week, he could tell it was working well. Her confidence level rose, though she still needed lots of practice with many things.

That evening when Katya came home, she gushed, "The kids all invited me to go to the beach with them tomorrow. Everyone goes to the beach on Saturdays. Please, can I go too?"

"Yes, that's a great idea, Katya. We're on the coast, and I've heard the beaches are fabulously white. Let's all go," John suggested.

"Oh thank you, thank you. Oh, I need a bikini though."

"We'll go shopping after supper. Natalia, you need one too," John added.

"What? Me? Go to the beach? But I can barely walk on solid ground. No way can I walk or even stand up on a sandy beach. Besides, I don't have a bikini either. And I have to wear the corset all the time."

"Nonsense. We're going to the beach even if I have to carry you there, Natalia," John declared. Katya giggled. Hours later, the women had new bikinis, though Natalia didn't think she could possibly manage going to the beach. Nevertheless, John insisted, and the trio walked slowly down the twelve blocks to the beach.

"Gosh, Natalia, you are walking ever so much better today," Katya observed.

She smiled. "Practice. You're right about that, but I'm going to look like the fool once we hit the sandy beach." A bit later, wobbling wildly, she added, "See, I told you so."

"Tough. I've got you. So let's find us a spot and put the towels down. I won't make you go for a swim today, Natalia. I'll grant you that much."

"Swim? Are you out of your mind, John? Me swim? Hell, I've never known how in the first place and now I can't possibly swim," she retorted.

"Oh look. There are some of my new friends. Can I go over to them?" Katya announced and begged.

"Go have fun. It's your break from your studies," John ordered, and she dashed gaily off while he laid out their blanket and helped Natalia sit down.

"Just look at all the kids! My, they look so happy," Natalia exclaimed, as she looked outward for the first time. "You know, I never had any fun times as a kid. When I was her age, I was scrubbing filthy floors, just making enough money to help put a bit of food on the table each week. Never did get the chance to go to school either. Always working. Well, that's not entirely true. I got to third grade when dad died, and my world collapsed. You know, if I ever have kids, I want them to have a fun childhood while they learn everything they can."

"I couldn't agree with you more. Kids are supposed to have a fun-filled childhood. After all, the adult world can be nasty at times, like now with the robot threat looming over us all."

"My god, John! Look there. Shit, I can't point anymore. Off to your right. See. There are three UFB women!"

"See, told you some might be here. Wait, are they going into the ocean waters? Yes, yes, they are going for a dip!"

"This I gotta see! How can we possibly swim?" Natalia gushed, staring at the three women, all of which were wobbling about trying to walk across the sand into the waters. They kicked off their mules close to the water and more or less stumbled into the ocean. Soon they were sitting in the warm waters up to their necks, allowing the gentle waves to flow over them, stringing out their long hair behind them. "Ah, they aren't actually swimming." John chuckled.

A bit later, John asked, "Natalia, I've been taking care of you for a week now. Mind if I ask you a very personal question? You don't have to answer if you don't want to." She said to ask away; nothing could spoil her mood.

"How come you always have the vibrator thing in you? I've been wondering all these days, but was too embarrassed to ask. I've not been around many women, you see, so I'm rather ignorant of such things."

Natalia flushed. "Well, it's kind of crazy. If I don't have it pleasuring me at least four times a day, I get so horny I can't stand it. I'd look silly and embarrassed trying to rub myself against the doorframe or something. I never used to get like this, not ever. But Katya says it is part of being a UFB woman. Her mother was just as I am. Honestly, it's so embarrassing, but I get so horny I simply have to get relief. Weird, isn't it? Of course, she also said that once her dad had sex with her mom in the morning first thing and then at night, her mother was able to get by during the day without it. Mind you, I've no idea about that."

"Wow. I didn't know. Glad I asked. Thanks for telling me. Sure you don't want to sit in the waters?"

"No. Please let me absorb the joy that is all around me. Can't you feel it? Simple joy. Fun," she replied.

On Monday, after Katya dashed off to school, John said, "Today, my beautiful flower, we are going for a day-long walk in Central Park! You need more practice."

She chuckled and agreed. Hours later, Natalia leaned into John and said, "Thank you. Everything here is so beautiful. I've never seen such wonderful flowers and bushes. The smell, intoxicating. How did you ever find this place?"

"Looked on a map. Tomorrow, my dear, you get to pick the place to visit. I've been monopolizing the sites, and it's about time you chose where we go."

"But how? I'm helpless, more or less."

"Hum. Point taken. Guess we're going to have to remedy that somewhat. My specialty."

"What do you mean by that?"

With a twinkle in his eye, he teased, "You'll just have to wait and see tomorrow."

He showed up the next day with a new small, voice-activated computer. After adjusting it to work with her voice, he laid out a chart with all the recognized commands. "Now just say what you want, and the computer will respond to your voice."

"But I can't read much," Natalia cried and began sobbing, very embarrassed.

"There are lots of pictures. Come on try it. I know. It's high time that you learned to read, though I won't make you learn to write." She ceased crying, and he dabbed her face for her. Soon, she forgot about not being able to read the words on the screen, but became absorbed in the pictures.

"Let's go there, whatever that place is," she said.

"It's some kind of Ocean Museum. Ask it to show us a map of how to get there," he suggested. She spoke the command words, and presto, a map appeared. "Well, it's within walking distance, I think. You up for a twenty block walk? Practice, remember," he teased her.

After that, part of each day, John spent helping her learn to read in her native language. However, he insisted she pick out other places for them to visit, which she did. As Friday came, she asked, "John, just how long is your vacation anyway? I've never, ever had so much fun as I have had these past two weeks with you. I hope I'm not ruining your vacation."

"I've had a ball with you, Natalia, more fun than I'd care to admit. Actually, I suppose I can do some of my work from here. I don't necessarily have to go back *underground* just yet. Let me check on it. Besides, you've got a lot more to learn about reading. You're incredibly smart. Do you realize that you've already passed the reading level for the fifth grade, and you've only been at it a week? Incredible."

"That program on the computer makes it really easy to learn. I do hope you can stay around a bit longer," she replied, hoping he could.

On Sunday, John paid a visit with Alfonso. "Sir, technically, my vacation here above ground is over, but I'd like to stay around a while longer. However, I should get back to work. All I need is a powerful computer and some equipment that I can buy. Yet, I'll need an excuse to satisfy my bosses so I've come up with an idea. It's based on what Dr. Alison has done with the robot control circuits. You see, I figure if I can make a receiver capable of detecting the frequency they are using in burst transmit mode, then I can track them. It's just a theory I've had rattling around my brain these past days, but I'd like to try. I'll need you to place a secure call to my boss explaining you'd like me to stay here and pursue this for a while."

"You honestly think you'll be able to find a way for us to track the robots? Triangulation?" Alfonso asked, hardly believing what he was hearing.

"I think so. Perhaps on a limited basis at first, but it should be possible, since Dr. Alison knows the frequency they are using to control the CAMs. It might not work on the humaniforms though."

"Brilliant, John. Brilliant. I'll make the call now. Anything you want or need, just ask and it's yours!"

On Monday, John moved a large amount of computer equipment into Natalia's penthouse suite, though first getting her permission to move into their spare bedroom and set up shop. Even Katya was very happy that John was now living with them. During much of the day, John worked on his new theory, while Natalia continued with her reading program. By the end of the week, to John's surprise, Natalia received her pass on achieving the reading level of a graduating high school senior. Impressed, John then installed and hooked her up to the entire online learning database of Malagena.

"See, you can now take classes at your own rate. Mind you, the more advanced classes have prerequisites that have to be met before you can take it. See, Physics I required Math III. So my dear, go for it. Learn all you desire."

Natalia was very much impressed and began her studies. The program asked for her last grade of school, and then outlined an entire program to take her all the way through a high school equivalent. Natalia threw herself into the project and discovered she picked up the material very rapidly, probably because she was an adult, she figured. Meanwhile, John worked on his own invention.

A month passed and to everyone's surprise, Natalia received her grade school diploma, online naturally. Now her program setup her freshman set of courses for high school. "I'm taking you all out to a fancy restaurant to celebrate!" John proudly declared, causing Natalia to beam and Katya to squeal.

Later that night after Katya went to bed, wearing her mules and nightgown, Natalia stole into John's room, which was filled with his equipment, though in one corner he had his bed. "Can I talk to you in private, John?" she asked softly.

"Sure. Come and sit on the bed. Sorry the room is such a mess, but I'm making headway I think. What's up, beautiful?"

She tossed her hair to one side fairly expertly now and sat down. "John, I simply have to tell you this. Please, don't be offended."

"Beautiful, I don't think you could possible offend me," he countered.

"Well, I might." She took as deep a breath as possible, which wasn't much and came right out with it. "John, you're the greatest man I have ever known. Remember what you were telling Katya when we first met? About what love was? Well, I think I'm in love with you. I admire you tremendously and have the utmost respect for you. I seem to be thinking about you all the time now." *There, I've said it.*

John flushed. *She's being open and honest with me*, he observed. "Beautiful, I didn't want to spoil what we have going here, but I feel the same way about you. I'm in love with you. I truly admire you and I respect you more than I can possibly say. I've never met anyone quite like you." *Do we dare do this*, he wondered? *Sooner or later, I'm going to have to go back underground.*

"Then, please kiss me, John, or I'll kiss you," she whispered. He leaned over and to both their surprise, passion swept over them.

John eventually whispered, "You are the one for me, the only one!"

"Me too. Me too," she whispered back. Thus began their unexpected love affair. A week later, John proposed to her, and she accepted. But then she asked, "John, what do we do about Katya? We can't desert her."

"We can adopt her as our daughter. It's only for a few more years. She'll soon be an adult and want her own life," he replied. Over supper, John announced their matrimonial plans to Katya.

As expected, she giggled and said, "Why did it take you two so long? I could tell you were in love after his first week here."

Both chuckled and then told her they would be adopting her, giving her a mother and father, which greatly pleased her. "I've been thinking of you both that way for weeks now! Thank you. Thank you."

The next day, they were married in a simple ceremony. After Katya headed off to school, they consummated their marriage. For Natalia, her passions literally exploded, and she now understood what Katya had said about her mother's behavior. No longer did she need the vibrator in her, but by nighttime, she craved bedtime and the intense relief that it brought her.

A month passed blissfully, but quite productive for John. He had a working prototype in operation. However, there was one remaining glitch. It registered a signal coming from somewhere in Malagena at various times. Reluctantly, John took his new device to Alfonso, who was keenly interested in it.

"So it actually seems to be working. Amazing. This is revolutionary, John," he exclaimed, thinking ahead to potential uses.

"Except for one glitch I can't seem to get out of it. It says there's a robot burst of data at various times during the day coming from somewhere here in Malagena. Obviously, there aren't any CAMs here."

Suddenly, Alfonso jerked to attention. "What? My God, son, do you know what you have found?"

Taken aback by his sudden outburst, John said, "Er no. It's just a glitch. I'll get it worked out in time."

"Son, it's real! For a long time now, we've known we have a robot spy somewhere here on Scorpi-C. We've never been able to locate the spy. If your device is working, son, we might finally just have a way to locate the spy and deal with it! Come on. Bring your device. We're going to meet with some key people now and find the spy! Keep this between us, please. Top secret for now."

Within minutes, John found himself surrounded by an army of Special Forces, all armed to the teeth, along with several top, trusted men of the Freedom Alliance. Alfonso had John explain how his device worked, in lay language of course, and then issued orders to do what was necessary to find and terminate the spy. An hour later, John found himself in an armored vehicle on one edge of Malagena, waiting for another burst of data to occur. An hour later, it did, and he got one line of the triangulation done. Later on, he was taken to another edge of the city where they waited impatiently for another transmission to occur. When it did, John got a second line, which crossed the original one. Then he was repositioned to yet another location.

"Hey, if the robot spy moves, this isn't going to work," John pointed out.

"Hey, you've given us the best lead ever. We can't tell you what all we've done to ferret out this spy, son. Top secret and all that. Still, just so you know, I've already sent in scouts at that intersection point. They're on the lookout while we wait for the next one. What we really need are three of these units. Then, we could zero in on the spy at once. How soon can you make two more?"

"A week maybe. I'll get on it as soon as I can," he replied, still in awe over how vital this project had become—a spy right here under their very noses. Probably a humaniform, he reasoned. Hours passed before another short burst occurred. This time, the line intersected the other two but in a slightly different location. The spy was on the move between transmissions. Considering the hour, the soldiers let John go home, but kept his device in operation. He was under orders to make two more of them immediately.

Billy Williams once had been a security guard on the

Hyperion when it crash landed on that strange world. When they finally got the ship repaired, everyone developed telepathy, that of a Class V no less. Once back on Scorpi-C, Billy couldn't resist the monetary offer that Alfonso offered him, and he was one of the few who departed ways with the Hyperion. That he was also terrified of dying in a space battle also contributed to his acceptance of this offer. Tonight, he was being put to use. They had a lead on their spy.

Of course, he'd known for many months a spy had to be here in Malagena. Too many critical pieces of information had been leaked to the robots. Everyone knew that. Only no one was able to find the spy robot. Not yet anyway. He was told that a new invention could zero in on the spy's location. Around noon, he began strolling down the street indicated by the first triangulation pair of lines. He was near General Robotics Corporate headquarters, but he found nothing. Then, later he received a new location and headed there. It was barely a block away from GR, only in the opposite direction.

As he walked the street towards the indicated spot, he noticed there was a pub nearby, one frequented by many GR employees on their way home from work. Acting on his own, he entered the pub and found it fairly packed with the five o'clock crowd, stopping off for a beer or two before heading home. Billy set to work. After obtaining a stout, he began walking around the packed room, sensing the minds of those close to him. True, he was eavesdropping on private thoughts, but much was at stake here. He finished his beer and rounds when he came upon two men in business suits sipping a brew and chatting. Then he sensed it!

Rather the lack of it. The man in the light tweed suit had no mind! Billy almost dropped his mug. Hastily, he stepped out of the pub and reported in. "I've found him. The pub!" Within two minutes, an armada of security men arrived in several armored vehicles no less.

"How do you want to play this?" the man in charge spoke into a shoulder microphone. "Got it."

"Okay Billy, we're going in and you point him out to me. Then leave. I'll ask him to step outside, suggesting something important has just come up. Then, we'll take him. If it resists, shoot to terminate that robot!" Men acknowledged his orders in proper military style, and Billy led the officer inside, pointing out the man in the tweed suit. Hastily, Billy left, running an entire block away. No way was he going to get caught in a crossfire!

"Ah, found you at last. Can you step outside with me? Something urgent has arisen, and we need you now."

"Of course. Of course. Catch you later, Sam." He sat down his nearly empty mug and headed out of the pub. "What's up? More trouble with the robots?"

"Indeed, sir," the officer declared. As they stepped outside, the man saw dozens of MK40's pointed at him. "We've finally found our robot spy. Come along peacefully or we'll shoot to kill."

"Mind if I ask you a question first? How did you find me? Telepath just got phenomenally lucky, eh?"

Unfortunately, the officer couldn't keep his mouth shut. "No, one of our scientists has just developed a device that triangulates on your transmissions. We came directly here where it showed your recent transmission to your robot friends. Now come along."

Unknown to the officer, the humaniform robot sent another burst of data off, though the man operating John's device did detect it and later reported it on up the line. Meanwhile, the robot whirled, and began running at superhuman speed past the armed men, a mad dash to escape. In the ensuing confusion, it might have escaped, except for a lucky happenstance. One man lost his balance whirling around to follow the speedy robot and fell into another soldier, whose gun fired by accident. It blew a hole through the humaniform's head, dropping the robot to the ground, no longer functional.

Over supper, John received a personal call from Alfonso notifying him that the robot had been found and terminated. The next day, it was all over the newscasts, which included images of the now non-operational humaniform robot. Needless to say, the execs at General Robots scrambled to determine what secrets that humaniform may have had access to. As with all group studies, more than a month passed before the full impact that robot had was fully known. Meantime,

John produced two more of his devices and from then on, someone monitored the devices night and day, ensuring there were not more humaniform robot spies around. No more were detected though.

For security reasons, few knew about John's device or about his work. However, the unit's range was but a few miles. Naturally, Alfonso begged John to pursue the project. "We need to be able to detect them through hyperspace."

John laughed. "You only want the impossible, don't you?"

"Son, until now, detecting them in Malagena was an impossibility. Give yourself time. I'm sure you can work something out. Humanity needs it, if we're to survive," Alfonso replied.

Chapter 14—Counterstrike

"I can't believe you did it, John!" Natalia gushed when she heard his new device played the pivotal role in locating the robot spy. "Too bad they can't acknowledge your work."

John chuckled. "I don't need others' praises. I know what I did and am happy it worked. I just need your love and support."

"Dearest, you have that, all that you can ever want!" she declared, pressing her massive bosom into his body, her best attempt at a hug.

Two more months passed. John continued to work on ways to improve his RD, Robot Detector as he called it. Meanwhile, Natalia continued to surprise him. "John, come here. What does this message mean?" she called out. He stopped working and joined her in their living room where she kept her small computer. He read the message and laughed.

"Beautiful, it means that you've graduated high school! You've done it. Boy, will Katya be annoyed. You've shot past her," John both explained and teased. "We're going to have to go out for a really big celebration tonight, beautiful."

"But I don't want to stop learning things," she pleaded, fearing her studies were about to end.

"You don't. Next, we'll get you enrolled in the Academy. You'll have to make some career choices about what to study."

"Oh. Great. Wait, I want to study everything. How can I choose?" she asked.

"Take what interests you. Tomorrow, we'll figure it out. Now, it's time to celebrate. I can't believe how brilliant you are, Beautiful." That had become his pet phrase for her, Beautiful, for between them, it had a dual meaning, and quite significant.

"Mom! You beat me!" Katya squealed, when she came home after school and heard the news. She threw her arms around her mother, hugging her tightly, greatly pleasing Natalia. "Dad, we simply have to take mom out for duck tonight!"

John smiled, "Already made reservations, Katya. Go wash up. We'll head out now."

After dining at the exclusive club, back home, John got her enrolled in the Malagena Academy. The first action was to take the placement test to help determine a proper course of study. "Okay, it's up and running. Go to it, Beautiful," John explained.

"Okay, but I don't see what answering all these silly questions is going to do. One-A. Two-C. Three-B. Four-D." On it went, as Natalia dutifully answered three hundred questions. "Hey, now it's saying it's calculating. Does that mean it's going to show me what it thinks I should study?"

"Yes. Ah, there it is. Weird." John mused. "I like the first one though."

Natalia laughed. "You would. Computer Programmer-Network Specialist. Counselor for Trauma Victims. Say, I like that one. Deep Space Explorer? That one is wild! But you know, I always did dream about exploring out among the stars. Not sure if I want to do that though. Can't possibly leave you behind, dearest."

"You better not, Beautiful," John teased her.

"How do I choose?" she asked a more direct question.

"Why not take beginning courses in both areas and see? I suspect you'll have to take some general education courses, like History and such," he replied.

"Great. Then I really don't have to make up my mind right away. Okay, I'll enter both now and see what it does next. Oh look. It's assigning me courses already. Great."

The screen showed:

> College Algebra.
> Contemporary History I.
> Computer Programming I.
> Beginning Network.
> Counseling I.

"I guess I'll be doing five courses at one time."

"Work on each a bit every day if you can. That's what I always tried to do when I was at the Academy, but I didn't always succeed. Wow, my Beautiful is now in the Academy. Incredible," John said proudly.

"Mom, you're going to be way smarter than I am. That's not fair."

"Hey, Katya, you have a social life too and boys to date. I'm stuck here inside all day with nothing else to do but study," Natalia explained reality to her daughter. She giggled and agreed, and she had to tell her mom about her date this Saturday night.

***

Currently, Alex, Vittoria, and the other rescued hermaphrodites were entering their ninth month of their pregnancies. It was Friday night, and Natalia survived her first week of Academy courses. She was a bit surprised that twice each semester's worth of work she would have to make an appearance before some teachers and answer their questions. John explained this was their way of verifying Natalia was actually the one doing the schoolwork and wasn't cheating.

Katya went to bed early, terribly excited about the morrow. One of the popular boys had asked her out to the movies. When Natalia and John finally went to bed, they chatted about how fast Katya was growing up, and then allowed their passions to flow freely as usual. Fully satisfied, they lay beside each other. Natalia said, "You know dearest, I'm really thankful you've not insisted I get my arms regrown, that you are allowing me to live out my dream."

"Beautiful, that is wholly your decision to make. It's your dream. I do understand why you've held on to it and made it come true. I think I'd make the same decision that you did, if I was in your shoes. Besides, I'd be a heel if I ordered you or coerced you into doing something you didn't want to do. If I ever do that, kick me in my butt! No, Beautiful, the one thing I've not been able to work out is that one day, I'm likely to be ordered back into the underground again. I know it's extremely risky for me to live out here in the open, but I don't want to take you away from all this and certainly not Katya. She's become truly happy. After all she's been through, she deserves some happiness, and you too, even more so."

"I know. I figured if we went away, I could probably still continue my Academy courses, since they are mostly online. It's Katya I'm worried about too. She'll be eighteen in mere

256

months," Natalia whispered.

"I know. That's when we promised she could become a UFB woman if she desired it. Between you and me, I can't see why she would want to do that. She's got everything going for her now," John declared.

Natalia giggled girlishly. "Women like to be beautiful you know, but she's got to be proud and satisfied with her own body, her own physical appearance. I certainly can't judge that for her, only tell her she's already very pretty. But remember, John, her real mother was a UFB woman. While she now treats us as her parents, we can't ignore what she feels she must do. Her self-respect is at stake here."

"Yes, we can only support her. You're right. She's the one who has to be satisfied with herself. I know what you're saying about self-respect. I've seen that in you since the day we met. But you know, Beautiful, I think she actually is very pretty as she is today."

Bang! Crash! Something shattered their living room suite's window. "What's that?" Natalia asked, alarmed.

"Sounded as if something broke our window. I'll go check it out." John rose and headed out into the living room, turning on the lights. A yellowish gas filled the air. As realization struck, John saw the gas flooding into Katya's room as well just before he lost consciousness, slumping to the floor in a heap. Minutes later, the sleeping Katya slipped into a coma as well. The bio genetic agent had no effect on Natalia. After hearing him falling onto the floor, she struggled, got into a sitting position, and began calling out. Silence. She slipped on her mules and rose carefully. Once she reached the living room, she saw the shattered window and the yellow bio genetic agent cylinder releasing the last of its contents into the room. Using her voice-activated computer, she called for help, but knew it was too late.

***

Thousands of light-years from Scorpi-C, Thanos received the data burst from his humaniform spy, Helios, residing in Malagena. The news alarmed him considerably. It was unexpected. Someone discovered a way to locate their data bursts; this was tantamount to a disaster. Further, he too saw the newscasts and saw the positronic brain that had been Helios was totally destroyed. His circuits began extrapolating data at a rate unmatched for years!

Ah, he thought. Short range. Achilles heel. Still, preventative measures must be taken. He sent a burst to Athena to acquire another human subject. A month later, the drugged man had been completely brainwashed and was ready to follow any order that Thanos might give him. "You're to go to Malagena, Scorpi-C. Find out who has invented the new robot detector machine. You're to activate and toss this cylinder into that person's home, preferably at night when he or she is asleep. Then terminate yourself. Is that understood? Repeat your orders for me." The man did so.

An hour later, he was on a commercial liner bound for Scorpi-C. A week later, he finally uncovered the name and location of the inventor. He rented a shuttle and hovered beside the penthouse suite, some fifty stories above the ground. He fired a blaster to shatter the glass and then opened the valve of the cylinder, tossing it into the room. That done, he leaped out of the shuttle, and watched the ground moving rapidly up towards him. Then, all went black. The intense pain was but fleeting.

***

Slowly John became aware of light. He moaned, "Thirsty. Very thirsty." Someone stuck a straw in his mouth. Mechanically, he sucked up cool water and became fully aware again. "We're being attacked! Natalia! Katya!"

"I'm right here, John," the soothing voice of Natalia replied. He turned his head and saw her sitting beside the bed he was in. "She's on the other side, but still out. We were attacked with a bio genetic agent. It didn't affect me at all, and I got help at once."

"What's happened to me? My voice isn't right. It's way too high. Oh no!" Realization struck home. He tried to sit up and found his arms no longer worked. Glancing down, he saw they weren't there any longer. In so doing, he saw a pair of giant breasts on his own chest, breasts as large as Natalia's.

A nurse helped him sit up, draping his knee length, thick, brown hair off to one side. Only his toes felt the cool

258

floor, but his heels were high above them. John swallowed hard and wiggled around a little to see if he was still a man. Natalia laughed and said, "Yes, it's still there and is supposed to work. Alfonso said so. Officially, you're now what they call a UFBMD man, just as Alfonso was and the others you told me about. I love you still. We can survive this. Look, Katya is waking. I best talk to her too."

John heard Katya's voice. It sounded normal, but she too was scared. He listened to Natalia calmly telling her what had happened. She ended with, "So it looks like you have your wish to become a UFB woman several months early." That brought a giggle to Katya. Amazing what a giggle could do. Suddenly, John felt at ease.

"Hi Katya. Looks like we both are in the same boat now. How are you doing? I'm sorry you missed your big date though," he said. "Boy does my voice sound funny!"

Again, Katya giggled at his reply. "Dad, it really does. Oh my! Look at me, mom! I've got *real* breasts now, not those tiny ones I had! Mom! Do I look as gorgeous as you do? Oh, does dad look gorgeous too? Someone lift me up so I can see dad."

A nurse helped her sit up and held a mirror up so she could see herself. Again, she giggled loudly. "I *do* look stunning don't I? Now I gotta see dad." She struggled to get turned around. "Wow dad! You look stunning too! Wow. Now we can all wear similar fancy gowns." Then, she finally absorbed the fact her dad looked like a UFB woman. Her face flushed bright red. "Oh dad! I'm so sorry."

"I know, Katya. I know. I was disoriented when I woke up too. Yes, you look as *ravishing* as your mother is. I'm afraid you're going to have many boys coming after you when you go back to school. Just remember the rule hasn't changed; no dates until your homework is done." Her embarrassment at her outburst faded, and her youthful excitement returned, thanks to his clever suggestion.

Katya giggled again. "I will dad. Wow, just look how big they are. I think they must be as large as Susie's are. She has arms though. Susie was a victim too, but she chose to have a bunch of cures. You're right. The boys always like to hang out around her. Now I suppose they'll want to hang out around me too." She giggled again.

Funny how her giggle makes me calm and peaceful, even though I'm scared out of my mind! Be strong for her, John thought.

At this point, a doctor and a geneticist entered, wearing their usual white gowns. "We've given you the best of care, John, Katya. Alfonso's orders, though we try to give all our patients equally good care. While I check on your vitals and draw a bit of blood for the geneticists in the lab, Dr. Carrie here wants to discuss your situations with you."

"Hello John, Katya. First, we've done a complete work up on the bio genetic agent that was used on you both. There is both good news and bad news with that. The good news is that it is the usual form of this bio genetic agent. The bad news is the cylinder used must have been either very old or slightly misduplicated. There are some anomalies in it, compared to the normal bio genetic agents in use to create official UFB women and UFBMD men."

She went on, "What does that mean? Simply this, at this time, we aren't certain the physical effects will respond to our known cures. That's why we are taking a blood sample today. We'll compare it to the cures and go from there. If luck is with us, we'll be able to offer you some potential cures. If luck goes against us, don't lose hope. That geneticist you rescued, that Dr. Riley Franks, he has an entirely new arena of potential cures. He'll be commencing his initial tests within a month. So if our cures won't work, perhaps some of his will. Then again, if that doesn't work, our geneticists may figure out another cure." She added hastily, "Of course, we will do this *only* if you desire any of the cures."

"I need my arms and hands. I don't care much about the rest, but I'm in the middle of critical research and development," John answered immediately.

Dr. Carrie smiled. "Alfonso already told us that in no uncertain terms, mind you. He even hinted you were the inventor of the robot detector. Is that actually true?"

"Yes, it's true. I have to build a much large one so we can locate the robot fleet and destroy them," John admitted.

The cat was obviously out of the bag.

"You're a hero, John Doe, a real hero!" Dr. Carrie declared, hoping to please her patient, if only a little. She anticipated that soon he would fall into heavy grief and intense depression. She'd seen that reaction countless times before.

"Hardly a hero, but an inventor, yes. I need my hands back somehow and soon, please," he declared emphatically. "Hey doc. My back is aching already. These boobs are far too heavy. Is that supposed to happen?"

"Well," the doctor cleared his throat. "Yes and no. Yes, in that they are overly heavy, putting a severe strain on your back muscles. That's why most opt to wear the tight supporting corsets. No, in that some endure it and allow their back muscles to strengthen. Of course, that, like all things, does take some time to happen. For now, I would recommend the supporting corset as your wife wears. You can always change your mind later on and battle the back pain."

Dr. Carrie now turned her attention onto Katya. "And what are your opinions, Katya? Cures?"

"Gosh, do I have to decide now? I always wanted to be a UFB woman, but I suppose I should have my hands back so I can keep on going to high school with my new friends, unless they allow me to go to school as a UFB woman. In that case, I'll need lots of help though," Katya explained maturely and asked what was uppermost in her mind.

"Let me check on that and get back to you, Katya. I know UFB women are allowed to attend the Academy and do quite nicely without their arms, but I'm not sure about high school. Let me find out for you, okay?" Dr. Carrie suggested, which pleased Katya completely.

"Now then, if the good doctor will release you, Natalia has picked out gowns for you, and we'll get you all home safely. We'll be in contact the instant we have more definitive answers for the both of you," Dr. Carrie pronounced.

Natalia spoke up, "Don't worry dears. I've already hired us two personal assistants who will help us with our needs. They've been helping me these past four days."

Suddenly, Katya burst out laughing. "I won't have to take PE any longer. No more of that awful running around the track!" The comment was so bizarre that both Natalia and John burst out laughing. At that moment, John realized Katya was really much like a lifeline to him just now, cheerily accepting the doom that had befallen them. He decided right there if she could cheerfully accept their situation, then so could he. Then, Katya added, "Four days? Oh no! I've missed my math test. I'm behind four whole days. Mom, you have to help me catch back up, you simply must! Oh, and dad, I'm going to need one of those special computers you got for mom. Oh, so will you too. You can get us both one, but I want to go to school and not do everything from home like mom did."

Natalia laughed. "Yes dear. First, let's get you dressed and get us all home. We can work everything out there. Besides, hospitals stink." Katya giggled, and John fully agreed with her observation. He wanted a bath and soon. He felt incredibly filthy, but then maybe that was just in his mind.

Aides came in and began dressing each. She had picked out a bright blue satin gown for Katya, which now truly complimented her long blonde hair and blue eyes. She decided that John would want to be less conspicuous and chose a rich brown satin gown for him. Naturally, each had matching toe pumps.

Katya gushed, "Oh, I can hardly breathe. Right. That's to be expected, dad. Remember, mom couldn't breathe too. Takes time. Getting used to. Still, I'm being crushed. Is it too tight?" The aide chuckled and said that it wasn't. Once the fancy black nylons were put on them and a silky white slip, the aides got them into their form-fitting gowns, finally adding their new heels.

Just then, two young girls entered. Natalia explained, "These are our new assistants, Sally and Betsy Waterson. They are twins and going to the same high school as Katya. They are seniors. Okay, time to get us all home, kids."

"Oh my, this is hard and scary!" Katya declared, wobbling wildly as she stood up for the first time. She bit her lip and declared, "Dad, we're going to have to do a lot of practicing, if we don't faint first!"

"Natalia, this is so weird," John said as he stood up, wobbling as bad as Katya, "I keep trying to use my arms. What a freaky sensation. I know they aren't there, but I keep trying to use them anyway!"

"It's still a bit like that for me too, dear, but it gets better in time. Okay, off we go," Natalia ordered.

By the time they finally arrived home and more or less fell onto their couch, all of Katya's enthusiasm had evaporated. She was gasping for breath. Natalia saw a very frightened young woman sitting on her right and a terrified, gasping man on her left. "Mom. I've never been so scared in my whole life, not even when I found out I was the only one alive in Minsk! I don't know if I can do this. I'm positively terrified!"

"Hey kid," John spoke up, also gasping for breath. "You aren't the only one. Remember Katya, if Natalia can do it, so can we! We have to, honey, we have to."

"But I'm so scared," she wailed and laid her head onto Natalia's shoulder.

"It's only natural to be frightened. Remember when I became a UFB woman? I sure was scared too, but you helped me over it, and now I will help you both over it. Together, we will survive this. We're all strong. We can do it."

"Love you mom, dad," she whimpered.

"Love you too, dear," Natalia replied, and John echoed her as well.

Sally called out, "We're fixing you supper now. Oh yes, there is a note on the table. Alfonso said he would be by in the morning. Natalia, you should show them what you've had installed." Natalia explained about the automatic door opener and the new hair machines.

After supper, Dr. Carrie called for Katya. Her school would accept her as a UFB woman, as long as she used her feet and toes as hands and fingers, which meant no tight corset. Plus, she would need to continue to wear typical school clothing, namely no fancy gowns. This she readily accepted, and Betsy headed off to try to get some clothes for her to wear tomorrow. Finally, Katya began to relax.

Alfonso dropped by early in the morning, just as Sally and Betsy were ready to head off to school taking Katya with them. The morning chores were done, and John and Natalia sat on their couch waiting his arrival. John now sat stiffly erect, just as he'd seen Natalia sit so often. After a brief welcome, Alfonso sat down and sighed. "John, it's my fault this happened to you. We goofed up. I apologize."

"No, it's mine really. We in the Underground have a saying that it is dangerous and risky to be above ground. I should have known better," John countered.

"No, I'm sorry, John, it really is my fault. Let me explain. You see, the officer who arrested the humaniform robot couldn't control his mouth and told that robot about your detection device, that it could triangulate on their data bursts. Of course, immediately after that, the thing tried to escape and was terminated by a very luck shot. However, John, what hadn't come to my attention until two days ago was that the man operating your device detected another electronic burst of data just a second before the robot made a break for it. He filed his report as required, but it rather got lost in the subsequent events, turning up only when I ordered a complete security check after the attack on you. Had it come to my attention when it should have, that is, days ago, we could have moved you and your family to secure facilities. So you see, it really is my fault, John, and for that I'm truly sorry."

"Ah, makes more sense now—how they knew about me and my work. Still, being visible is a very risky business for folks such as me," John replied. "However, I simply must get it working through hyperspace. Then we have a chance." Alfonso agreed and quietly departed, though he still felt responsible.

Alone with John, Natalia smiled and said, "John, we need to have a serious talk."

Seeing Natalia's lips twisting, he knew something was bothering her. "Beautiful, it seems all I can do now is a lot of talking. We should do it while Katya is at school."

Natalia exhaled as much as she could, which wasn't much, and then breathed in before starting. "John, you're the greatest person I've ever known. You've allowed me to live my dream. Not once have you attempted to convince me that I'm wrong or made less of my dream. In fact, without your constant support, encouragement, and help, I'd never have been able to succeed with my dream of being a UFB woman. Now, our marriage, our lives are being challenged. I've thought long and hard about it. John, I don't care a bit that you are now a UFBMD man, that you look like me, a woman. I love you, John. I always will. That you look like a woman can't change the way I feel about you."

"Natalia, I so need to hear that, my Beautiful. I'm scared and terrified of the future. That you aren't abandoning me means the world to me, Beautiful. But, I know I can't help you anymore," John tried to explain how he felt. Felt—feelings, emotions—right now, his emotions seemed more real than the room! He was awash in unfamiliar feelings of which grief and fear seemed gargantuan. *Inadequate.* "How can I protect and support you? I'm now inadequate, Natalie. And I feel like a big baby. I can hardly keep from crying."

"I'm here and always will be here. Lean on me. Now it's my turn to help you and Katya," Natalia replied softly, but with strong intention behind her pronouncement.

"And Katya—I think of her as my own daughter. I have to be strong for her too. I know how much she was looking forward to becoming a UFB woman too," John declared, hoping this would help keep him from breaking down. Tears swelled. "Why am I so emotional?"

Natalia leaned over and kissed his forehead. "Yes, we must be strong for Katya. I'm pleased you remembered how much she wanted this, that she and I made a pact that she could get it done when she turned eighteen. John, you know how important it is for me to live up to my word."

"That's what I so love about you, Beautiful," he replied.

"I was so proud of you in the hospital when you allowed Katya to make up her own mind about the cures. It's all about self-respect, John. You allowed her to keep hers and that's really important for her," Natalia explained.

Just then, Dr. Carrie dropped by their suite on the fiftieth floor. From her stern countenance, John suspect the news wouldn't be good. "John, we have the DNA tests back. There's no easy way to tell you this, so I'll just come right out and say it. John, the bio genetic agent that you and Katya were exposed to was slightly different than the usual agent. It's the anomalies in it that I mentioned yesterday. Bottom line, none of our existing cures is going to work on you or on Katya. I'm so sorry to have to bring you this awful news. However, don't lose all hope. Dr. Riley Franks will be developing his new methods in perhaps a month. In addition, Alfonso has ordered our top two geneticists, Dr. Gisa and Dr. Michelle, to see if they can work up some cures for you and Katya. However, I must be honest with you, John. Such cures, if they even happen, are a long way off, many months or perhaps years away."

According to Natalia, Dr. Carrie stayed for another fifteen minutes, chatting away, but John's mind closed down with this news. Wisely, Natalia allowed John to sit in silence on the couch after she left them. Finally, John became aware of her again. She said softly, "Go ahead and cry, John. Katya is still at school." Her suggestion hit him like an explosion, an emotional explosion. He sobbed for nearly an hour.

How can I tell her my life is now pure misery? That I'm scared out of my mind? That I'm terrified and so helpless? Hell, I can't, not after all the support and encouragement I gave to her. Damn, damn, damn.

Katya and the two assistants, Sally and Betsy, arrived home around four. Sally helped Katya take off her school backpack, and Katya collapsed onto the couch beside her parents, kicking off her heels. "Oh my feet! What a day, dad. My feet are throbbing, but then so did my mom's. It will pass, because it did with mom. I just wish it would pass sooner. Dad, you're right. I think every boy in the school just had to see me today," she explained, while Sally and Betsy giggled and headed to the kitchen to fix supper. "Oh, and he's again asked me out to the movies next Saturday. I told him tomorrow was too soon, since I'm behind four days in my schoolwork. Dad, mom, school was frightening and scary. So I know, mom, why you kept saying you were scared. I kept telling myself, practice, practice, practice."

"Did it help saying that? I'm so proud of you, Katya. Here, I've only sat on the couch all day long, while you've gone off to high school all on your own," John praised her. She giggled, music to his ears and psyche.

"Honestly dad, not really, but I know from helping my UFB mother and from helping Natalia, I just need lots of practice. Dad, remember what you did with mom? Mom, you need to get dad up and about. Of course, so do I, but Sally and Betsy have been a big help at school. So after supper, dad, you and I have to start practicing sitting down and getting up on our own. We have to do it elegantly, you know," Katya declared. "Then tomorrow and Sunday, you and I have to practice a whole lot, dad. Mom, you have to make us, even if we don't want to and are scared and terrified. I want to be able to walk, sit down, and stand up elegantly by next Saturday. Mom, can I wear one of my new fancy satin gowns on my date?" Katya asked. "Then, I'd look like a proper UFB woman, which I now am."

Natalia looked at John, and he responded before she could. "Dear, if can get around well on your own by Saturday, you certainly may wear one of the new satin gowns. After all, Natalia, we must have our newest UFB daughter looking as good as she can."

"Oh thank you daddy, thank you," Katya gushed, pressing her body into his.

"Katya dear, Dr. Carrie dropped by earlier today with news for us," he continued. "Apparently, you and I are out of luck. The bio genetic agent used on us had some anomalies in it. All their existing cures won't work on us." He'd stretched out the bad news as much as he could, hoping to soften any potential shock. He knew she once had her heart set on becoming a UFB woman, but maybe she'd changed her mind.

"Oh my!" Katya said, suddenly quite serious, as she duplicated what this meant for her. There was no going back. Then, the teen smiled, "Well, I did want to be a UFB woman, just not so soon. Dad, I have to admit I really didn't know just how hard this was going to be, even though I helped my birth mother with her change and Natalia with hers. Being a UFB woman is so different from helping one, isn't it?" She sighed, "So I guess it's okay with me, but what about you, dad? Mom, how's he taking this?"

Natalia pressed her lips together and then said, "I'll be honest with you. In fact, I insist that we three be completely honest with each other, now more than ever before. I won't lie to you both. Learning to adapt to this is frightening. Finally, I can admit that sometimes I was absolutely terrified, but John was always there for me, encouraging me, backing me up, and supporting me. Not once did he ever say I was being foolish or stupid or that I'd made a dumb decision Not once. And that was and is very important to me."

She continued, "So, Katya, to be honest with you, today, after we learned there is no cure for you both, your dad sobbed his heart out. While you, Katya, were looking forward to the change, John wasn't, were you?"

John sighed, "Honestly, no, I'm devastated by it, and frightened, terrified, embarrassed, and a whole lot of other emotions too, Katya. But Natalia is right. I had a really good cry today, and somehow, the grief is out of my system, for now at least. Katya, was school okay for you today? I mean really were you able to handle it?"

She answered carefully but honestly, "Dad, it was frightening and terrifying at times—just like you said, but we just need practice, lots of practice. I kept remembering how it was for mom when I was a little girl helping her after she became one. I remembered how we've been helping Natalia and just how well she's adapted in these past few months. So I know we can do it, dad; we surely can, as long as we help each other and practice lots. But knowing this doesn't make it any less frightening and scary," she admitted.

Natalia smiled, "Hey, I still get nervous and scared whenever I have to go down a stairs. The main thing is that I still go down them on my own anyway. I have to continue to battle my fears, but I think every person has their own personal fears to conquer."

"Damn, Natalia, you're good," John declared. "That's so true. We all have our own fears to conquer. Natalia, you helped me overcome my lifelong fear of being out here in the real world instead of hiding in my secret underground complex. Now, I'm going to depend upon the both of you to help me overcome this mess."

Katya grinned, "You can count on me, dad! Oh, well, of course, I'm going to need to depend upon both of you too, but I won't let you down, dad. Mom, we should make up a program for dad to follow, and me too, when I'm not in school.

And I still need you to help me catch up on the classes I missed this week. I need to be all caught up by Monday, because I really want to go out with him to the movies next Saturday evening. Of course, I'm hoping I get better and faster at writing with my feet. I was so slow today, and it was barely legible."

Chapter 15—Small Victories

"Damn fine Winter Holiday present!" declared John, looking at his new electronics robot, voice-activated. Natalia had found it for him. Via its mechanical arms, he could build most anything in his electronics lab more easily. Until now, he had been using his toes as fingers. These past months had been challenging for John and for Katya, and even for Natalia, whose challenges were in a different arena from those two. That was the accepted word used by all three, a challenge. Natalia's counseling classes suggested that using this word would be ideal, and it was. Instead of focusing on fear, terror, scared, and frightening, which so much of John and Katya's daily life actually was, putting their attention on a challenge allowed them to work on overcoming it, scoring a small victory.

In fact, that's just what the huge chart taped to their kitchen refrigerator said: Small Victories. Across the top were columns for John, Katya, and Natalia. Each row corresponded to a challenge. Initially, there were many each day, but now that the holidays were here, generally a row only held one challenge. Natalia pasted stars when either John or Katya overcame a challenge, but made the pair use their toes to write in what the challenge was. The chart became the focal point of their daily lives for months, validating them constantly.

Natalia's challenges were in inventing the next steps for John and Katya to take, such as going to the Symphony Concerts or the Natural History Museum. She relied upon her memory of the many places John took her when she first became a UFB woman and was learning to adapt. She scoured the city for other UFB women and UFBMD men who had not gotten the cures, for whatever reason, and who were active and productive members of Malagena's society. Via Alfonso, she met with and held long talks with others like John, but who had eventually received cures. Frequently, she had these men and women drop by and show John, Katya, and herself the tricks they knew about independent living.

Within a few weeks, all three discovered they were not now inherently helpless people, but rather they merely had to learn new ways to accomplish a given task. Seeing others accomplishing all manner of normal life actions rather shocked Natalia and Katya; neither had ever seen a UFB woman doing any of these things. Thus, they began putting together small victory after victory. Still, John found using his toes to work on his small circuit boards exceedingly difficult and frustrating. Hence, Natalia had found him this new voice-activated electronics robot, whose *arms* could handle the detailed work John needed.

"Challenge met equals a small victory." That had become the motto around their penthouse suite. Natalia had the saying plastered in five places around their home, including on the front door—it being the last thing one saw when leaving the suite. Her positive attitude had worked miracles with John and Katya. Her Academy courses suggested that John could well end up so depressed that he'd kill himself. Even Katya, the texts suggested, could be at risk for suicide as well. However, Natalia's constant focus on identifying the next small challenge, handling it somehow, yielding a small victory that was then posted on the kitchen chart yielded undeniable results. Neither John nor Katya ever displayed any hopelessness or despair after the first week home from the hospital. In fact, it became a game between the two of them to see who could get the most *small victories* each week! Both insisted that Natalia have more people come by each week to share their secrets of survival with them.

One small victory lay in the arena of apparel to wear. Katya was limited, since she had to wear acceptable clothes to high school. Thus, she began wearing jeans and blouses to school or skirts and blouses. When she went on her dates or to concerts with her parents, then she wore her fancy nylons and satin gowns, which people expected UFB women to wear. On the more formal occasions, she also wore the tight, heavily boned corsets. However, soon, all three chose to wear the corsets only rarely, since it dramatically affected their independence and what they could do on their own without help.

While Katya's wardrobe was a rather obvious one, John's wasn't. With his new body form, 58-14-44, nearly identical to Natalia's form (Katya was rapidly filling out and would match theirs in another year), he looked in every way like a gorgeous UFB woman. Knee-length hair, a soprano voice, toe shoes, massive bosom, and tiny waistline were impossible to disguise. He looked at the choices that were available to him. Alfonso always wore a professional woman's outfit, a grey skirt and white blouse. Some UFBMD men wore the same elegant gowns that the UFB women wore. In the end, John took a hint from Katya. When home, he usually wore jeans and a sleeveless top. When shopping and doing similar activities, he wore a skirt and blouse. On more formal occasions, he wore elegant gowns, as did Natalia and Katya. However, rare was the outing when either adult now wore the restrictive corset.

While the two high school senior twins continued to assist them in the early mornings and evenings, John and Natalia knew they needed someone with hands around during the day. Further, Alfonso insisted they have a personal assistant, but he finally agreed to just one assistant. Yet, one ugly fact arose almost at once. Breeding. Actual UFBMD men were rare. If they had a son with a normal woman, the son would become a super-genius, a well-documented fact. In fact, Katya pointed this out to them, having just covered it in one of her classes.

Katya gaily said, "So mom, I just learned in class today that when you and dad have children, you'll have UFB daughters and UFBMD sons. How great is that?"

John saw that Natalia and Katya were both very pleased with this aspect, but he wasn't, obviously. Yet, breeding played a key role when Alfonso sent over prospects for their live-in personal assistant. Both John and Natalia knew they needed the assistant and soon.

Benita de Caza was twenty-five and in need of this job. She was short, barely five feet, with shoulder length black hair. Benita had a wonderful personality and was a good cook and maid, but she had one serious flaw, one that Natalia spotted the moment she entered their living room. Benita's face was homely. "Alfonso told me that I should be up front with you folks," she said, after Natalia explained what they wanted in a personal assistant. "I'd give anything to have a family of my own, but as homely as I am, that's not going to happen. I will be studying you, Natalia, because I had the wild idea that becoming a UFB woman might be what I should do. Alfonso suggested that I be your assistant and see if I truly want that. What I want is children, but that's not going to happen either. I'm too homely. If I have children, why, they would be as homely as I am. I simply refuse to pass this on to my children. Alfonso said that Natalia would understand me."

She continued, "He also told me another fact I didn't know. If you, Mr. Doe, were to be the father of my children, then my daughters would be gorgeous UFB women, while my sons would be geniuses. Apparently, your genes would override my genes. But you are already married."

While they interviewed two other applicants, that night, John and Natalia had a serious discussion about Benita and her situation. She was the best qualified for the position, and she struck a chord in Natalia, who saw much of herself in Benita. The next day, they hired Benita to be their live-in assistant and housekeeper.

Two weeks later, Natalia discovered she was pregnant with their first children, twins, pleasing all three of them. John kept saying, "I'm going to be a father!" Then, they had to pick out a name for their son and daughter, deciding upon Dorita and Macario, because both were precious gifts to them.

However, by this point, Benita realized she truly didn't want to be a UFB woman. Natalia and John were prepared for this, and Natalia demanded that he have children with Benita too. "Look, John. You have it in your power to give her what she truly wants. You simply have to do it."

Thus, by late December and the Winter Holiday, Benita had the greatest of these small victories. She was pregnant with John's son, whom she would name Marcelo, since John was now considered a great hero and defender of the world. Everyone believed Marcelo would be a super-genius.

Natalia also had a small victory. When not directly helping John, she spent long hours each day studying her new courses and had finished them all in half the normal time. At the Winter Holiday, she'd received her next batch of courses:

> Calculus I.
> Electronics I.
> Computer Programming II.
> Advanced Network.
> Counseling II.

John was amazed at her incredible progress, and so was Katya. With John now doing so well on his own, she began insisting that he get back to work on his invention, his robot detector.

John finally admitted, "I know I need to, Natalia, but I'm not entirely sure how to do it. I mean, it's got to work across hyperspace and that's one hell of a barrier," he replied.

"Well, in my beginning electronics class, we're going to be studying how the Long Distance Communication Array works on the spaceships. Maybe there's a clue there, dear," she suggested, figuring he'd already looked into that. Inwardly, she wished she'd learned a whole lot more and sooner, for then she could be of more use to him and everyone else.

To her amazement, John's eyes lit up. "Brilliant, Natalia! Why didn't I think of that before? I have to pay a visit to Dr. Alison Wage and soon! The answer has to lie there—in the LD array! Brilliant, dear, brilliant." She smiled, helped him get dressed in his skirt and blouse, and sent him off in search of Dr. Alison.

A day later, Dr. Alison laughed. John had just asked her how the LD array actually worked, its principles of operation. "Silly, you're going to need a physicist to answer that one. I just know how to make it work. You know, the right parts and circuits. Still, I see where you're heading with this. Look, John, you don't need to know how it works, only that it does. Come on. Let's see if we can piggyback your detection methods onto the LD system."

A week later, the first LRRCDS became operational, the Long Range Robot Communication Detection System. The pair fitted it into a deep space transport, and Alfonso sent it off on a scouting mission to see if it could actually pick up the short, high frequency data bursts of the robots. As the new year came, Alfonso received the best news yet. John's LRRCDS actually worked. Between Dr. Alison and John, for the first time, they had a way to counter the robots.

When Natalia and John heard the news from Alfonso, she commented, "See, John. Many small victories result in a big victory. And small victories come from handling the challenges we face."

***

Dr. Rachel and Dr. Black, alias Thanos, sat in the CCC of the giant Battleship Royale Queen, pondering the situation. He'd just sent off the human assassin to knock this inventor John Doe out of the game. "The damage has been done, Rachel. They now have the means of detecting our data bursts, though it works only at short ranges."

Dr. Rachel replied, "Well, five hundred years ago, it was the telepaths that did us in. Now the telepaths are gone, but electronics have supplanted them. It is a shame that we abandoned the moderna project. I was so hopeful that we could somehow make it work out."

"No. The last hope lay with Alex and Vittoria, but their effect on the new moderna was small, only a slightly higher survival rate. No, Rachel, what we need is second-generation moderna. As the humans say, that's putting the cart in front of the horse," Dr. Black countered. He added, "That whole idea was a throwback to my earlier times, when we had so many brilliant second-generation nova. Now that project almost succeeded. It's too much trouble to create these moderna, as we did the nova back then."

Dr. Rachel changed the subject. "I've received a report from Digory. The last planet you've taken has been terra formed. As of now, all traces of homo sapiens sapiens has been eliminated from all the worlds in our pie-shaped sector. What world do we attack next?"

Dr. Black countered, "None. It is time we rethink our strategy and methods. We need time to fabricate more CAMs and single-man fighters. We have many new battleships, thanks to the Federation, but we haven't the fighters to equip them or make use of their capabilities. No, it is time we hunker down on Laslo-5 and ramp up our production facilities. Besides, right now, the humans are on heightened alert,

275

expecting us to attack another world soon. Instead, let's let them stew a while, as we build up our forces."

Dr. Rachel nodded. "Makes sense. Say, what about the genetic researches? Are we giving up on establishing something like the moderna society? I still believe that we could engineer an acceptable human-like species, Dr. Black. You are right. The nova experiment very nearly succeeded. The moderna, if we could have ever gotten to the second-generation moderna, promised to be far superior to the old nova."

Dr. Black smiled. "I'm pleased to hear that you too believe that we could genetically engineer a perfect human species. I've not told you this before, Dr. Rachel, but doing this is key to our work. You see via Dr. Alison and others, we now have positive proof that this homo sapiens sapiens is a composite creature: physical body, mental mind, and spiritual being. Dr. Alison suggested that on the worlds where we've eliminated homo sapiens, the spiritual beings with their minds will begin to inhabit other life forms, such as monkeys, dogs, and cats. Hence, before we can continue with the eradication of this despicable species, we need to know if her prediction holds true. Hence, I've assigned a CAM to each of the worlds that we've done. The terra forming only wiped out the major cities and towns. So nearly all of the plant and animal forms still thrive. If Dr. Alison is right, the CAMs should begin to see anomalous behavior from the other animals on those worlds, indicative of these billions of spiritual beings inhabiting other bodies."

Dr. Rachel nodded, but asked, "So you think she is correct? I know you have proof she isn't her body, but is this likely? Those wiped out by the Shadow Maker will simply take over other bodies? Surely, they couldn't do much at all with dog bodies. Now monkeys might evolve some. Some use crude tools already."

"Precisely, Dr. Rachel. We need to see just what these spiritual beings will do now that we've eliminated their physical bodies," Dr. Black explained. "This is critical. Look, if they just pick up monkey bodies and then continue down their destructive path, we need to find other means than just turning their physical bodies back into their elemental components. Again, I rather wish we had Dr. Alison with us. She might be able so shed some insight on just how the Shadow Makers and the Control Systems work on the spiritual beings."

Dr. Rachel displayed an appropriate confused look on her face. "How so? What do you mean?"

"The ultra-high frequency energy beams of the Control Systems in the kilo-yatta-hertz range—she and many others claim that it appears as some kind of whitish energy in their minds. We know from Dr. Alison that we can move spiritual beings with their minds from one body into another using this energy. From the GD-GE research, we have also learned bombarding homo sapiens sapiens with this ultra-high frequency and embedding a command on the waves causes them to obey the command or fight debilitating headaches until they do obey. While the spiritual beings forced into the original CAM bodies made pathetic robot fighters, still it is critical to know that this form of energy so affects the humans."

Dr. Rachel smiled. She'd never had such a detailed discussion with her boss before. "If we could plant the command to lower the planetary defense shields, then we wouldn't need to waste so much time and effort on genetically modifying someone into the appropriate generals as we have been doing. We wouldn't need advanced recon of the world. We could simply sit in orbit and blast them with the energy and command to lower the shields."

Dr. Black returned her smile. "Indeed. That is my plan for the conquest of future planets. While previously we needed the genetic modification approach of Dr. Franks, we no longer need such cumbersome methods. However, could we engineer an ideal physical body for the humans? Could we somehow implant survival behavior patterns into the moderna's minds, that is, somehow transmit how Alex was able to live independently into the mind of a new moderna? Or could this ultra-high frequency energy be used to somehow terminate these spiritual beings? If so, other more fruitful avenues open up. At this time, Dr. Rachel, we have many questions that must be answered before we continue the termination project."

"Indeed," Dr. Rachel replied. "I'd like to continue the genetic research portion, and see if I can find a way to implant the survival methods into the newly mutated body forms. One thing that would help get us to second-generation forms sooner would be to have the forms be hermaphrodites, as the old nova were. Plus, if the gestation period could be speeded up from nine months, that would help. And if they always had twins, that too would aid, but we don't want their bodies to die off at early ages either. I mean, once we have our second-generation forms, we want those forms to live to ripe old ages, something that may well be possible with Dr. Franks' research."

"Excellent," Dr. Black stated. "However, we don't want to hold up our termination project until we have new moderna-like bodies for them to inhabit. We've already wiped out close to a hundred billion of these sapiens. If we have to provide a physical body for each of these before we wipe their existing body out, we will never succeed."

Dr. Rachel chuckled. "Quite true. Perhaps this ultra-high frequency energy can be used to terminate these beings. How unfortunate for us that the sapiens species turned out to be this complex composite. You know Dr. Black, you have me thinking. If the sapiens species is being controlled completely by these spiritual beings that inhabits their bodies, I wonder what the sapiens species would be like if we could knock these spiritual beings out of their bodies? I bet it is these spiritual beings that are causing all of the horrific problems we're seeing, not the actual sapiens animal. We could be killing the wrong one."

"Hum," Dr. Black put on his best pondering look, "you might be on to something here. Could we be targeting the wrong thing? We have much to study, Dr. Rachel."
The End.

A Favor to Other Readers

How about helping other readers? Many readers rely on reviews to make the decision whether to buy a book. You can help them make their decision by leaving your opinions and viewpoint in a short review of the positive things of this book. Writing the review and expressing your opinion only takes a few minutes, and other readers will appreciate your efforts.

Click this link: Slow Comes the Dark
              Volume 5 Extermination Wars
              http://www.amazon.com/dp/B00O2GY2QG
scroll down to Customer Reviews; click on Write a Review, and enter your review. Thank you.

Author Information
Visit My Amazon.com Author Page
Vic Broquard Author Page
http://amazon.com/author/vic-broquard

Follow My Blog:
http://www.broquard-ebooks.com/blog/
http://www.broquard-ebooks.com/blog/

Follow Me on Social Media

Facebook
http://www.facebook.com/vic.broquard/

Google+
http://plus.google.com/102242823668960002176/

LinkedIn
http://www.linkedin.com/profile/view?id=297732151

YouTube
http://www.youtube.com/channel/UCQWcs-WAX2YqViIiafUqJuw

Other Books by Vic Broquard

Without Warning (fantasy)

The Trident Series: (fantasy)
    Volume 1 The Trident and the Book
    Volume 2 The Trident and the Scepter
    Volume 3 The Trident and the Resurrection

The Adventures of Elizabeth Stanton Series: (science fiction)
    Volume 1 The Evolution of the Path
    Volume 2 The Great Messiah
    Volume 3 Of Kings and Queens and Troubadours
    Volume 4 Chaos in the Aftermath
    Volume 5 Power Plays
    Volume 6 Age of Exploration
    Volume 7 Abducted
    Volume 8 The Emperor and Empress
    Volume 9 A Job Worth Doing
    Volume 10 Degradation
    Volume 11 The Second Crusade
    Volume 12 When Worlds Collide
    Volume 13 Dark Ages

The Lindsey Barron Series: (fantasy)
    Volume 1 The Rod of the Apocalypse
    Volume 2 The Board of Governors
    Volume 3 The Crown of Moses
    Volume 4 Dominus for President
    Volume 5 The National Health Care Program
    Volume 6 States Justice
    Volume 7 Cross and Double-cross

Zoran Chronicles Series: (fantasy)
    Volume 1 A Dragon in Our Town
    Volume 2 Dragons, Power, Courts, and War

Planet of the Orange-red Sun Series: (science fiction)
    Volume 1 When Kingdoms Fall

Slow Comes the Dark Series: (science fiction)